The Brother Kiss

Before I fall into that black pit of wanting him, I pound on my physician's chest. "Carew, get up. Our prostitutes will be back to rescue us."

"No prostitute. You should not consummate, the joining of flesh . . . You need to hold dat till yuh married. Not here, little girl. Not this. Not you."

Little? Not now, not his old way of teasing me returning. Not hating Stephen Adam Carew is impossible. I hate him.

And when he topples, I let him fall. I want him to spill onto the wet floor. But on the way down, he grabs me and bumps his lips into mine. And I want to kiss him. I want to kiss him hard to shut his stupid mouth. I want to kiss him big, like I'm bad and bold . . .

But he's not in his right mind.

I am. So I push him away. "Let's finish getting you dressed."

"W-a-i-t." His breath is pepperminty. Our hands tangle and I'm not sure if we're trying to escape or undo the good work I've done buttoning his breeches.

The knock on the door makes him release me, and I drop to the sopping floor. Now I'm wetter and more in love with this fool than ever. "Sir, our prostitutes have returned."

Yawning, groaning, Carew slaps the mattress. "I've ruined you."

Yes, you have, for others, for any other man, for a long time. I hate him, but I hate me the most. Because of him, I'll continue putting my heart on a shelf out of everyone's reach. "Be quiet, Carew the elder, and we may get out of this."

His eyes are shut. His breaths ease, but his smile makes my insides mushy, like warm butter on toast. "Missed you too, Scarlett."

Also by Vanessa Riley:

Betting Against the Duke
A Gamble at Sunset
A Wager at Midnight

The Lady Worthing Mysteries
Murder in Westminster
Murder in Drury Lane
Murder in Berkeley Square

The Rogues and Remarkable Women Romances
A Duke, the Lady, and a Baby
An Earl, the Girl, and a Toddler
A Duke, the Spy, an Artist, and a Lie

Historical Fiction
Island Queen
Sister Mother Warrior
Queen of Exiles

A
WAGER
at
MIDNIGHT
VANESSA RILEY

ZEBRA BOOKS

Kensington Publishing Corp.

kensingtonbooks.com

For Tia, Toni, Kara Saun, and Kim, my Sense & Sensibilities Girls

For Alfonso Thornton, Thomas White, Ruben Riley, Jr., Linda Riley,
Brenda Riley, and David Riley—miss your smiles.
For Nicole Perkins, keep fighting.
For Glenn at Planet fitness, George Sinkfield, Asa Worth and Unoma,
blessings upon blessings.

For everyone who forgets to live in every moment,
Find your joy.
I'm betting on you.

List of All Characters

Character	Other Names or Distinctions
Benny	Benjamin; Carew's man-of-all-work and driver
Carew, Stephen Adam	physician
Charles, Anya	Jahleel's sister
Charles, Jahleel	Duke of Torrance
Chrysanthemum	Courtesan
Daisy	Courtesan
Princess Elizaveta	Jahleel's mother
Eveline Gray	Baroness of Derand
Maryanne Halland	Mrs. Smith's daughter, Stephen's cousin
Hampton, Lady	see Wilcox, Katherine
Livingston, Earl of	see Melton, Alexander
Lord Flanders	Man of Science
Lord Lange	Man of Science
Madame Rosebud	Brothel Owner
Melton, Alexander	Earl of Livingston
Mrs. Cantor	Lydia's Nurse/Governess
Mrs. Ellis	A maid to Mrs. Smith
Palmers, Tavis	Viscount Hampton, Katherine's deceased husband
Prahmn, Marchioness of	Mark Sebastian's mother
Prahmn, Marquess	Mark Sebastian's father
Samuel Pepys Cockerell	The duke's architect
Sebastian, Mark	Jahleel's friend, Georgina Wilcox's husband, Son of the Marquis and Marioness of Prahm
Steele, Jonathan	Jahleel's butler
Telma Smith	Part of the Aunties - Community Leaders; Carew's blood aunt

Theodora Randolph	Part of the Aunties - Community Leaders
Thom, Mister	man-of-all-work for the Wilcoxes
Torrance, Duke of	see Charles, Jahleel
Wilcox, Cesar P.	late father of Katherine, Georgina, Scarlett, and Lydia
Wilcox, Georgina "Georgie"	Katherine's sister, Lady Mark Sebastian, Lord Mark's wife
Wilcox, Katherine "Kitty"	Lady Hampton, married to Tavis Palmer, Viscount Hampton
Wilcox, Lydia	Katherine's little sister
Wilcox, Scarlett	The youngest marriable aged Wilcox

Character	Other Names or Distinctions	Mentions in Other Books Series
Lord Ashbrook	Daniel Thackery, The Earl of Ashbrook, Barrister	*An Earl, the Girl, and a Toddler*
Mr. Croome	Neighbor to Mr. Carew	*The Bashful Bride & The Bewildered Bride*

Chapter 1

PHYSICIAN STEPHEN CAREW— LISTENING TO FOOLS

June 3, 1816
Anya House
London, England

If someone had bet me a fiver that I'd be sitting in one of the finest dining rooms of Mayfair, drinking champagne and conversing with peers of the realm, I, Stephen Adam Carew, would've offered to examine their cranium for a head wound or sign their admission into Bedlam.

"Let me tell you about Madame Rosebud's bosom. Big and bouncy, strewn with pink blossoms and the fragrances . . ." Alexander Melton, the buffoon Earl of Livingston, again used the lull in the conversation to talk about women. The whoremonger was a brilliant man of science. How, I did not know. But research papers didn't lie.

Even after getting to know him during my visits here, I still couldn't reconcile his scholarly aptitude for eye anatomy with his abnormal appetite for courtesans.

Ignoring him, as I often did, I reveled in the surroundings. The warmth of the gold-and-silver-threaded Russian tapestries hung along the freshly painted light blue walls. I sat back in my elegant walnut chair and allowed the finely turned spindles to support my back . . . or more so my spine.

Why was I letting a lusty fool sabotage me? No more hesitation. "Your Grace, I think we were discussing my proposal for the hospital building project."

Our host, Jahleel Charles, the Duke of Torrance, seemed distracted. He rubbed his chin. His pallor was restored from his last episode of sickness. No one could tell that this strong-looking gentleman had come close to succumbing after his triumphant ball. The diet of beetroot for anemia seemed to help. He made a soup of the vegetable and called it borscht. "One moment," he said as he whispered something to his manservant, the wise Mr. Steele.

The ash-blond Scottish man's secret reply made the duke laugh. "Carry on, Mr. Steele. Make sure Miss Wilcox and Miss Lydia Wilcox have dessert brought to them in the library."

So, Scarlett Wilcox is here. Wonder what trouble that one will get into today?

Alas, whatever it took to get a patient to heed, including borrowing the Wilcoxes as his adopted family, I wholeheartedly encouraged it. The duke, at thirty-three, needed to focus on joy and listen more intently to what his body was trying to tell him. Chronic illness could be both painful and deadly.

With my own thirty-first birthday coming by year's end, I needed to be more settled, more deliberate. Before the new year, I hoped to have a new hospital commissioned, and a wife—in that order.

With hazel-colored eyes darting between me and the earl, Torrance asked, "Before we discuss the project, I want your opinions on why attendance has dwindled at my science meetings."

The earl wiggled and hemmed and hawed in his seat. "Well, the peers and gentlemen with courtesans as mistresses probably do not want to attend. They don't wish to risk exposure."

The statements made the duke chuckle. "Then they should know better than to be my enemy. There were four men who voted to invalidate my parents' marriage. Prahmn was the lead."

The way Torrance said this, without emotion, almost stiff, was more frightening than when his voice held anger. I tried to ignore it. I had a tendency to worry and, as Miss Wilcox said, think a thing to death.

But I couldn't. Like nosy Miss Wilcox, I needed to know. "What does that mean, Your Grace?"

"Nothing. Or everything, for the three left who helped delay my hearing and cost me all that mattered, including my sister's life." His chuckles were bitter, menacing. "See? Almost nothing."

Livingston tapped the table. "That's the attitude which makes people wish to avoid Anya House."

The duke looked away for a second. "It's a flaw, sir. I'll deal harshly with anyone who threatens me or those I care for. And when it comes to family . . . I can have the temper of a d'yavol."

It was obvious from the ball Torrance held at Anya House he'd do everything in his power to expose and destroy his detractors. It took great fortitude to set up a scheme that caused a guilty person to confess publicly to their hypocrisy.

The duke's skill was grand. He involved the papers to protect Georgina Wilcox and, to some degree, her new husband, Lord Mark Sebastian.

"It's sad," I said, "that these consequences of the Prahmn scandal have affected Anya House. Your science meetings were surpassing the efforts of the Royal Society."

I set down my knife and stopped eating for this next bit. "But the impasse will not last. I mean the Marchioness of Prahmn has probably forgiven her husband, that is after he's confirmed to not have picked up warts or syphilis or gonorrhea from his affair."

"Can you please contain your language, Carew? There's food present." Livingston responded. "And no, the marquess remains unforgiven. His well-deserved embarrassment is legendary. It will be the talk until there's a new scandal."

My words were deliberate. Though the earl claimed he was careful in his dealings with courtesans and brothels, those dangers existed. He needed to be reminded. As a physician, I'd seen far too often the damage those afflicted suffer.

Picking up his coupe, turning it so the candlelight flickered on the pale champagne, the earl said, "I hear Prahmn's close friends are very concerned. They'd love to know how to make peace with you. It's a conversation I have at White's."

Torrance smirked. The short smile quickly disappeared. I'd have missed it if I looked away. "White's, the club for gentlemen, landed gentlemen, that excludes our friend Carew. No White's for you."

The duke had a sense of humor. He straddled all communities—the ton, immigrant sections, and the parts of populous London where one found men and women with more color in their skin. Oh, the aunties of Cheapside, the women who bring together people foreign to London, would love to get a hold of him. My immigrant stronghold would have him married to a *nice* girl in no time at all. "Hypocrites need to be wary," he said softly. "Kingdoms and heavens are shut to those who practice and teach hypocrisy."

That sounded cryptic and threatening . . . and he'd shown London he could bring thunder and brimstone. Goodness, I was mixing up my metaphors like . . . Miss Wilcox. Well, her humor and criticisms were infectious.

Livingston gawked at the duke as if he'd spoken in Russian. "According to Lord Mark, the ton is also uneasy with his bride's elevation."

The earl eyed us as if he'd said too much, like he suddenly realized he was dining with men with tanned or darkened skin, men of color—Blackamoors, as we were known in London.

"Don't get me wrong," he continued. "Georgina Wilcox is perfect for Lord Mark Sebastian. The man is deliriously happy. But with three Wilcox sisters left, peers might not be willing to risk their sons to Lady Hampton or Scarlett, or even Lydia Wilcox in due time."

"Lady Hampton is still grieving. She's not again on the marriage mart." I glared at the earl. "The other two are children."

The earl looked down into his glass like it would reveal a fortune in the rising bubbles. "One is a child, Carew. However, the other—"

"Careful, Livingston." The duke had his cane raised like he'd strike the fool.

I would, too. Scarlett Wilcox was a handful, but she was a good . . . well, mostly good girl. "Settle, Your Grace."

The duke cut his gaze at me. "When Scarlett and Lydia are ready, they will have substantial dowries." He set down his cane. "I'll ensure it. Nothing but their happiness matters. Carew, you'll have to keep me fit to do so."

Now that I had his attention, I returned Torrance to my initiative. "Your Grace, I want to know your opinion on building a new hospital."

"Carew, are there not enough hospitals in London?" The duke flicked a finger to one of his servants. Instantly animated, the fellow in the silver livery changed from a statue positioned at the side of the room to a madman whipping from the chestnut sideboard to the table, refilling our crystal goblets.

Torrance's thick brows came together as he savored the Veuve Clicquot, the best champagne I'd ever tasted—lemony with the sweetness of apples.

"A wealthy city like London," he said. "It seems quite prideful of its efforts in the sciences and medicine. Why are there not enough hospitals?"

The earl smirked, then drained his glass. "Your Grace, our friend Carew is ambitious, very much wanting to change London. But there are many hospitals. St. Bartholomew's was founded in 1123. Then there's St. Thomas, which has served almost as long. I could go on."

"There are many hospitals for those with connections," a loud, Scarlett-like voice from the hall said. "Most of the operating hospitals need letters of admission from a benefactor. How are the poor to gain those?"

"How indeed, Miss Wilcox? Please come from the shadows." The duke's invitation sounded humorous. "I thought you were studying in the library."

The pretty girl, with her light olive complexion and dark, dark eyes, stuck her head into the room. Her lithe body followed, and she centered herself under the curved entry of the threshold. A high chignon with tendrils falling sculpted her face. She was soft but bold.

And I prepared for her to say something outrageous.

"I was studying, Your Grace. But as I suspected, the gentleman's argument for more care lacks a proper defense."

The earl snickered. "That's our Carew. Always garnering support from the ladies. And planning grand gestures to win them."

Never tell a fool you read for relaxation. And if said fool was told about the powerful women in my life, the aunties, of course he'd get everything twisted. Sigh. Being considered a man of the world wasn't awful.

As if he were conducting an orchestra, the duke put one finger up to silence any potential response from me, then curled the others requesting Scarlett to enter. "The physician cannot help but be charming. I think a Caribbean accent does better than Russian. But Livingston, you could learn much from him. And Miss Wilcox is learning not to hide her opinions. I hope, in some small way, I'm encouraging her."

Yes, but to what end? Scarlett possessed a sharp intellect. She was learned, a gentleman's daughter. Mr. Wilcox, by owning property, was one of the first Blackamoors to vote for parliament. Nonetheless, she, like all women, would have to conform to the way life was. I merely prayed she found a tolerant husband, one who could recognize her brilliance and had the patience to withstand her tongue.

Donning men's boots as some sort of conceited sign of independence, she glided into the room, then curtsied. Head up, poised and balanced, she said, "Your Grace, I didn't mean to interrupt . . ."

"Sure," I said in a cough.

"But I was merely walking by, and I felt Mr. Carew's reservedness. The need for more hospitals is great."

Though she omitted eavesdropping, her excuse sounded innocent. Make no mistake on that one. Scarlett Wilcox was a minx, a vexing viper in training.

Attempting to take back control of the discussion, I cleared my throat. "Miss Wilcox is correct about the need. The requirement of a reference reduces access for sick people, particularly among immigrant populations. A new hospital such as what I propose would provide care for those communities."

"Immigrants?" Livingston hiccupped. "You mean the Jamaicans? Or is it Trinidad . . . Trini . . ."

"Trinidadians." My annoyance rose. "Livingston—"

"And the Dominicans, even Russians." Scarlett folded her arms and glanced at the buffoonish earl as if he were refuse—old, spilled milk, or God forbid, cassava pone cake that spoiled. "London is a port city, known to trade with all regions of the world. Who else do you expect to come when British appetites are global?"

It would be rude to clap, so I sat still, admiring her fury while it was turned on someone other than me.

Older and wiser, this one would be stunning, setting the world on fire. Well, that would be if she could learn to navigate the world as a proper young woman, not a tomboy or an easily excitable miss.

"Mr. Carew is right, Your Grace." Her tone sounded so arched, her chin lifted. "People need a place to feel secure when they seek medical attention."

The gaze she offered the duke made me think the two had secrets. That was an unsettling notion. I wouldn't want to imply that the young woman was sneaky or conniving but she possessed the same fearlessness that made her father, the late Cesar

P. Wilcox, a coal millionaire. In a woman, that streak was admirable and frightening.

Though Miss Wilcox advocated for me now, in the next breath, she'd cut me direct. Her words will be sharp, slashing through my innards better than a scalpel. Heaven help the man who loved her. And please, let him be worthy of the Wilcox family and their duke.

"There's a great deal to consider," Torrance said. "When do you need an answer about investing and championing the project, Mr. Carew?"

His Grace hadn't refused. His answer wasn't a no or a yes.

"I'm still gathering investors," I said.

The worlds barely left my mouth when the mostly angelic vixen turned on me. "Why delay? The need is now. The duke could fund the entire project."

"Now, Miss Wilcox . . ." The room felt ten degrees hotter. All eyes were on me. "It's not polite to count what's in a man's pocket."

The silver fork in my grasp spoke to the duke's great wealth. Though he could be over the top in his gifts and parties, Torrance remained levelheaded and—most of the time—without airs. He hadn't changed from the person I knew when we were both struggling students in Inverness.

"Is that a Trinidadian saying that means to delay forever?" Her sharp tone stabbed. "Or is this just another idea you'll start and not finish?"

Scarlett's verbal scalpel went through my rectus abdominis muscle, slashed the oblique, and twisted.

"Carew is smart to delay, young lady." The earl tapped his glass for more champagne. "He wants a wide base of support so that everyone will partake of the hospital. It won't be a Russian thing—"

"Or a Blackamoor thing, or a people-with-natural-tans thing. That is your actual concern, isn't it, Lord Livingston?" She put her hand on her hip. That meant Scarlett was seconds away from another lethal wordy attack. "Mr. Carew is not frightened by backlash, not when he sees the need. He's a man of great principle and doesn't require expensive liquors or brothels to give him false bravery or silly opinions of his self-worth."

The earl shrank back into his chair.

The grinning duke signaled for more champagne to be poured.

Livingston finished one glass and waited for a second pour. "A mouth on that one. Almost as bad as the venomous viscountess. Lady Hampton still ripping into you, Torrance?"

"Da," the duke said, confirming the intense relationship he had with Scarlett's oldest sister. "Some habits are hard to kill."

"Well, Mr. Carew." One boot tapped on the polished mahogany floor. She stared at me, and I felt inflamed and shamed.

"Tell him that it doesn't matter who invests."

It did matter.

It mattered when the hospital hired staff.

It mattered which physicians would want to be associated with it.

There were even those in my own area of Cheapside who would be wary of a hospital that exclusively focused on immigrants and people with different backgrounds and skin color. Sometimes Blackamoors only wanted what the ton had.

Knowing I'd let her down, I sighed. "I want everyone to support the hospital. Beginnings are important, Scarlett."

Her mirror-black eyes turned on me, then rolled up. I doubted she admired the ornately molded ceilings, but rather wished for the plaster filigree to fall on my head. "So, more delay. Can you be considered a champion if you never fight?"

"I fight, little girl. It's just typically you. You and I bicker as I answer your medical questions while indulging your lack of decorum and manners."

Her cheeks reddened. "I tried to defend you. Worthless."

The earl scoffed and drank half his glass. "Torrance, please send the little lady back to the library so we can talk about more important things—Seasoned Women."

Shaking his head, Torrance said, "My dear, go check on Lydia.

Though the angel is with her personal maid, I like to continually make sure she is happy and well."

"My little sister is very healthy, Your Grace. She's drawing pictures for her official sixth birthday in a month. I know she can't wait to see what you will do."

The duke's countenance brightened. "Elephants. It will be amazing. That is as long as Lady Hampton allows us all to have fun."

For a moment, those fearless dark eyes grew small. Scarlett's chin lowered. "I'll go check, Your Grace."

With poise, she curtsied and left.

"She floats from the room like a descended angel." The duke raised his goblet to her.

"Then, would that make her Lucifer?"

The duke glanced at me. He looked confused, but I thought the metaphor was fitting. Scarlett Wilcox, the young woman I begrudgingly admired, was beautiful . . . a beautiful devil.

Chapter 2

SCARLETT WILCOX—MEN ARE STUPID

When a person, no matter how brilliant or handsome, called you out of your rightful name to be Lucifer, the fallen angel, the fool deserved hell. And with my boots, I'd gladly kick Carew into the flames.

I couldn't believe he said that after I tried to defend him.

Sighing and hissing like a steam kettle, I walked away from the dining room. My boots echoed in the grand hall of Anya House.

Stephen Adam Carew probably knew I was listening, probably said it on purpose. Probably thought I'd do something undignified when I heard his retort.

Halfway down the hall, I still fumed.

Devil? Mr. Carew was the d'yavol, as the duke would say.

Fury roiling inside, I trudged forward and stopped at a gilded framed mirror. Did I look like a devil?

I wore one of my old shapeless gray gowns, something Katherine bought me when we mourned old Tavis, her late husband. It was one of the few dresses that fit without showing off my hips.

This was nothing like the ballgown of aurora red satin that I wore to the duke's ball a month ago. That dress fitted to my waist and captured the curve of my bosom for all to see. The men at the duke's ball, including that obnoxious physician, did not look at me as a child. I pushed at my cheeks. They were lean. No baby fat at all. They'd never mistake me for Lydia.

What had changed? Was I always to wear such extravagant things to keep a man's attention? Well, then it wasn't worth it. I didn't sing. I didn't exhibit. I'd burn a kitchen down before I baked anything. And never would I ever dress provocatively to gain any man.

If I returned to the dining room, I'd catch the smug physician either being waylaid by the Earl of Livingston or engaged with the duke about nonsense that did nothing to push the hospital campaign forward.

Ten years was the difference between me and the physician, but I'd never wait for calling. Would reaching his age make me timid? How terrible.

I pitied him. I hated Stephen Adam Carew. I hated his charismatic smile, the way he bit down on his lip when he was in thought. I hated when those lips were dry because he forgot to take care of himself. I even hated when he caught me being less mature.

And above all, I hated that he hesitated before acting. His current delay would cause the physician to lose funding for a new hospital. This dream of Carew's was old. It was one of the litanies of things he and my father discussed whenever he visited our house on the other side of the Thames. Then Papa made him promise to be a protector and mentor for my curious mind.

I guess that meant Mr. Carew was to be a brother . . . not a lover or anything else. I hate myself for wanting more.

Shaking my head, I trudged up the carpeted stairs and went into the crisp whitewashed library. This room, lined with ivory bookshelves, was the happiest place in Anya House.

Lydia had her head down, drawing what looked to be a map, while the gray-haired matron napped in the corner. Mrs. Cantor was a nice woman, typically very attentive, but my little sister had a lot of zeal.

When I got to the table, I bent and kissed her brow. It was

good to see her happy, fever and pain free. Lydia was so much healthier since the Duke of Torrance came into our lives. My sister Katherine, who acted at times like Lydia's mother, had to start seeing him as a benefit.

To find a cure to keep Lydia illness free was my life's goal. I'd do anything to learn about the sciences which govern the body. I'd be the best physician the world had ever seen, if given the chance.

"You look mad, Scarlett." Lydia kept drawing. She didn't look at me.

"I'm not, not anymore. The men are meeting in the dining room."

She giggled. "You wanna be there. Don't you?"

I moved to a bookshelf and fingered the leather spines. The duke surely possessed a fourth . . . no, a third of all the books in the world. "Well, if I'm there, I can't be up here with you."

The little girl shook her head. "Scarlett, I know you are mad. Mr. Carew probably teased you, sort of the way the duke teases Katherine."

"You mean how they both tease each other?"

She tilted her face toward me. Freckles on her nose. Big eyes with flecks of gold. "Katherine's not kidding. She don't like our duke."

The little face looked so sad, I kissed her brow again. "They'll make nice because of you, dear heart. You have the great power of bringing everyone together."

She held my arm and leaned her soft cheek against me. "But I know Mr. Carew is teasing you. Just tell him you love him. I told the duke I loved him, and he gave me a pony."

The high-pitched, squeaky voice echoed, and I glanced to see if Mrs. Cantor roused.

She didn't.

That was good, because I didn't know what I felt for the physician who believed he was always right, and I wouldn't want the kindly nurse to offer opinions. And I couldn't tell Lydia any more about Carew. How could one love a man who doesn't leave room for anyone else's opinion? What good was he?

Before I could sit beside Lydia, the child was up and dancing on the furry rya in her bare feet. The thick rug swallowed her toes with each step. The summer was warmer, but I didn't believe in taking such chances. "Lydia, where are your stockings and slippers?"

She pointed under the table. "I can be without them for a little bit. Katherine says if I don't air my toes, they'll get stinky."

Such a gentle soul with genteel soles. Why was I complaining?

Any day Lydia hopped around out of bed without a fever meant another day of her being healthy. I rushed to her and scooped her up. Then I swung her around and around. Her pink dress with frills at the hem flapped with the rush of air. I set her down and she descended like a hot air balloon. She bounced until her little legs steadied her along the floor like ballasts.

Her sweet arms surrounded my neck. "So are you going to tell him? That will make everything good. Mama used to say only love mattered."

I remembered those words. I could hear our mother in Lydia's voice. The little girl was so precious . . . and misguided. Being wrong about how problems were solved was a gift of childhood. She missed the arguments of our parents. Surely, she heard Tavis and Katherine's. Love wasn't enough.

"Let's put on your stockings and slippers and go see what the men are doing. The duke will want to see you, Lydia. No shoes will disappoint him."

Her big eyes, tawny and gold, were damp, like she thought she'd never see the Duke of Torrance again. Lydia panicked and shot under the table. One cream slipper flew out. Then I caught the other. "Help me, Scarlett. I must see my duke. Never let anyone take him from me."

Mentioning His Grace in any circumstance solicited the best behavior from the child. "Of course." I sat on the rya and the little girl flopped onto my lap.

"I'll be extra good. Katherine's been hinting at having my birthday without the duke." She swiped at her wet face. "Tell her no. He's a part of us now."

Those eyes struck me like a fist. My chest caved from the punch. Our beloved patriarch, Cesar Wilcox, never had time for her. Papa was too busy building a fortune, the one my late brother-in-law made disappear. I was so glad Lydia had her duke. I wished Katherine could see this, too.

On my knees, I hugged Lydia again. That feeling of failing her filled my insides. I hadn't found a cure to give her the longest of lives. The duke made her happy and made every moment she breathed joyous. He was becoming the father she never had. "I'll try. You know Katherine can be stubborn."

"My duke. Duke." She sang this little chant until I had the final slipper in place.

Today, I couldn't fight the feeling of dread from swallowing me. As long as the duke held up his end of our agreement, to find a husband for me, one who'd publish my scientific papers, the duke would win his bet with Katherine. Her having to spend time with him would mean Lydia would get to live with them, too. If my oldest sister could release the venom she had for the man who saved us from ruin, I knew she'd do the right thing and marry him. Lydia deserved to have a father and mother figure who adored her. Unless I found a cure, we truly didn't know how many years the sweet girl had. Or how long the duke would be in good health and remain our protector.

Why was Katherine so afraid of a union with a man who claimed to love her and Lydia?

Swiping at my own eyes, I stood and went back to the table. My newspaper remained in place, not a mark of pencil or charcoal on it. I loved that Lydia respected my orders. The newsprint looked the same as when I left to go snooping. I checked it again and made sure I'd found a plausible reason for the low attendance at Anya House that didn't have to do with scandal or color.

The girl nudged my arm. "Let's go to the duke."

"Wait, I have to bring them some new information. Just a moment." I scanned the elopements, the acts signed into law by the Regent. There had to be another reason. "I know I saw something earlier."

Flipping through the papers, I scoured the column inch by inch and found a noteworthy event, the Annual Exhibition at Somerset House. This had to be it. "Let's go take this paper to the men. It will help in their conversation."

Lydia clasped my hand. "I get to see the duke."

Her warm fingers curled in mine, and I remembered another moment when my palm was about this small and I held a fevered hand. The world failed us . . . failed me, then. No doctor could be found. My other half, my twin brother, died at age six because of a fever. A hateful, evil fever. That was the d'yavol's work.

If a hospital was available for people on the other side of the Thames, that would make physicians more accessible for people like us. More children like my brother, Scotland, could get their miracles.

"Scarlett, you alright? You look weepy."

"Yes." I forced the word out and caught my breath. Taking my time, I rolled the newsprint and stuck it under my arm. "Let's go."

Hand in hand again, the two of us tiptoed. The thick rya muffled the sounds of our shoes. We left Mrs. Cantor and headed out of the library sauntering toward the stairs.

As we approached the dining room, Lydia tugged my gown. "Mr. Carew is nice. Georgie and Katherine said he does well. Tell him you love him, and I'm sure he'll get you a pony."

There was something lovely and innocent about little-girl logic. But I liked a take-charge attitude. I appreciated the way the duke made things happen. That was not the physician.

Nonetheless, none of these tactics, truth or power, applied to a foolish man who'd let the opportunity to build a hospital die because he was too concerned about manners or the ton's expectations to do what was right. Stephen Adam Carew, no matter how nice he was, didn't have the guts it took to win.

Chapter 3

STEPHEN—WHY DO FOOLS FALL IN LOVE?

The duke's chef wheeled out a silver cart with desserts. A plate of strawberry tarts looked tempting, as did the sugar-powdered kartoshka.

As I glanced at the cart coming closer, the duke leaned on one elbow. "Couldn't find cassava, Carew."

"Cassava, Your Grace? Why?"

"Miss Wilcox said that cassava pone is your favorite. I would like to reward you for the care you've given myself and Lydia Wilcox."

"No bribe is necessary." It was touching that the duke went to such trouble and that Scarlett remembered this small detail. Asking again for his support and funding for the hospital project seemed a natural thing to do. Yet, I hesitated. I would wait until it was just the duke and myself. No Livingston. And no eavesdropping Wilcox.

From the cart, the earl selected a tart. That seemed fitting. The man began again to ramble about some new courtesan or brothel or wrestling match. I realized I'd lost count and interest. I found myself looking again to the entrance. Was Scarlett Wilcox done having her say?

"Livingston, this Madame Rosebud is interesting," the duke

said. "But do you still conduct science, or are brothel women your experiments?"

The earl wiped fluffy cream from his face. "Yes. I'm working on a lecture on eye anatomy. I did some work before the war in Paris. I'll do so again now that Napoleon is gone. It will be conducted after the Annual Exhibition."

"What exhibition?" The duke lifted a second kartoshka onto his plate. The cream oozed from the crumbly texture. "What is that?"

"That actually might be the reason attendance to lectures at Anya House is down. The wild art exhibits at Somerset House are always a draw. Most love art over science."

I made my voice loud to see if Scarlett would again interrupt, but she didn't. Oddly enough, I felt as if she were listening.

"Torrance," Livingston said, "the physician is right. The exhibition is drawing huge crowds. It's hard to compete against."

The earl swirled his champagne. The translucent liquid reflected the glow of fire from the gilded sconces rimming the room. For a moment, I waited for the surface of the champagne to burst into flames, maybe offer a specter's voice to tell us what to do for Anya House's meetings to regain public favor.

Then I chided myself, remembering the old tales and wonderment I grew up with in Port of Spain, Trinidad. Specters weren't a thing the ton considered. Nor did they agree with natural medicines or foods to improve health like beetroot.

"Oh, Somerset House will be crowded for weeks." Livingston smirked. "Torrance, you'll have to wait until summer is over to draw people. But we can help you apply that zeal to something more substantial." I began the countdown. Three. Two. One . . . "Let me take you two to Madame Rosebud's. She has the cleanest courtesans."

How on earth was this foolish man a leading scientist? Did he stand in some line? Maybe it was a heredity title or something.

"You need to have a mistress, Torrance." The earl raised his

arms, spreading them wide as if to welcome the duke to hedo-
nism. "Men need someone to cater to our whims."

"I have a staff and a French chef. These whims are fine for
now." Torrance sat back, his ring finger wiping up leftover cream
from his kartoshka. "I'm working on the mistress part. I have a
bet to collect."

I'd heard snippets of the theatrics between the duke and Lady
Hampton from Scarlett. Give the girl a bowl of pineapple ice and
she'd confess to a crime. "Your Grace, here's a thought. Find a
woman that actually likes you. You're a good man. It can't be that
hard. Come with me one Sunday to Cheapside. The aunties,
Telma Smith and Theodora Randolph, will have you married in
no time."

Torrance offered a patient smile. "Time is something no one
can count on." He sighed, and I felt a small sense of his hopelessness. Of course, I didn't know how he could've fallen so
deeply in love with a woman he'd only known for less than two
years.

I'd become acquainted with my special lady four years ago.
This year, after the start of my hospital, I would propose.

"So tell us how, Mr. Carew. What makes these Cheapside
women so good to you?" The duke tapped his lips. "I recall, though
you are popular, that you are still very much a single man."

"For now. But the aunties have introduced me to the perfect
woman."

"Auuugh!" Scarlett moaned as if she'd fallen in the hall.

I started to rise to see if she was hurt.

"No, Carew, sit," Livingston said. "You can't drop such a statement onto the duke's beautiful table and run. Tell us about your
perfect woman."

Easing back into the chair, I fluffed the charcoal-colored tails
of my coat. "This is why I don't bet. I try never to lie and typically keep discussions of my romantic life to a minimum. If I talk
too much, something will go wrong. A perfect woman is a figure
of speech."

"English is my second language." Torrance frowned. He seemed genuinely lost. "I don't know this expression. What is the perfect woman?"

Livingston shook his head. "You don't know because there are none. All women are terribly flawed. It's not their fault. They are built to be cruel."

"And men are picnics." An unhurt Scarlett stood again under the curved threshold. With a newspaper in one hand and little Lydia's hand in the other, this young lady was prepared for battle. "Is this all you gentlemen do when alone? Drink and disparage the fairer sex?"

Before he could answer, the youngest Wilcox, Lydia, danced away and came closer to the table. "Duke, I have on my shoes and stockings. See?"

She hiked up her dress and showed off her knees. Scarlett ran and lowered the hem. "Lydia, we don't do that."

"Well, if I show the duke I'm good, he'll come up to me at bedtime for stories. You will come, right?"

"What kind of question is that? Of course I'll be there. I'll hire actors to perform a whole ballet for you."

"Torrance." I lifted my glass to him. "You put a man who loves grand gestures to shame."

"No gest . . . gestus, just Duke, just you, my duke." The child's smile made Torrance sit up taller.

That little Lydia—his affectionate Lidochka, as he often called her—had His Grace wrapped around her finger. One little pout or sniffle and the duke stepped into action, making her laugh. He would solve anything, do anything for her.

Come to think of it, Scarlett pretty much had him doing her bidding as well.

The duke flexed a finger and servants stood at the ready to pull two chairs to the table. "Ladies, sit. There are plenty of desserts."

Lydia ran and flung herself onto his lap. "Good. I think we can hear much better here than in the hall."

"We weren't listening. Well, not a lot." Scarlett's cheeks reddened.

Taking my eyes from her, I put my gaze on the earl. Livingston seemed more focused on Scarlett. Even sotted, you could see he approved of her. He, and a few others, had noticed her at the duke's ball.

Truthfully, there wasn't much to disapprove of—tall, but not too tall. Graceful in her movements but not flamboyant. Light olive skin and midnight eyes that appeared smoky, or like jet-colored glass that sparkled when her mood changed. No, there wasn't much anyone could disapprove of, except the boots. She loved to wear men's boots.

"That is my point." Livingston wobbled and waved his arms like he tried to swim in place. "Now the two of you are distracted. The child and willful young woman will rule your world."

"Woman?" I felt my hackles and brow rise. "This little lady is fresh out of leading strings and pinafores." That sounded condescending but it was our joke. Scarlett and I traded barbs like this all the time.

But this time she didn't say a word. She remained silent staring at the floor.

"She's twenty," the duke said. "That's old enough to be presented at court. I think Queen Charlotte would enjoy meeting Scarlett Wilcox."

Twenty. Truly?

Had that much time passed?

Eight years of being the Wilcoxes' family physician had allowed me to see her mature and always asking the smartest questions, but I'd never admit to that. It was too much fun teasing her. "I find Miss Wilcox too opinionated for her young age."

Snatched from her spectral trance, Scarlett lifted her chin. Her eyes targeted me, and I prepared to battle.

"Mr. Carew, opinions are the one thing I possess that are totally owned by me. Something you men should learn to admire, for I'll never change." Scarlett went to the table but waved away the servant waiting to pull out a seat for her. "I'd rather stand."

"Look at this, my princess," the duke said to Lydia. "You will see your British sister outwit a man from across the sea."

"What of me, Torrance?" The earl hiccupped. "Can she outwit me, too? I'm from Hertfordshire."

The duke offered a proud gaze toward Scarlett. "I'm afraid, Livingston, you wouldn't last a minute."

The earl frowned, but the good-natured drunk always had a little fight in him. "Well then, Miss Wilcox, what are your opinions on the perfect woman? The duke and, I daresay, Carew, think you are intelligent, so you must have a good answer."

Drawing the newsprint to her chest like a shield, she folded her hands about it. Scarlett had long pretty fingers, which she kept very clean. Tomboys usually didn't. "Before I give my say, I'd like to hear what each of you think. Do start, Lord Livingston."

Caught in his own trap, he sipped from his goblet. It took a full two minutes for him to say, "Beautiful, wealthy, loyal. See, I have simple but necessary criteria. Though it will never come to fruition, I will never marry again."

Scarlett turned her perfectly smoky eyes toward the duke. "And you, Your Grace?"

"Well, I don't require a fortune, but I do hope the woman would be wise about money. A pretty face is a delight." He rubbed his chin. "But Livingston is right about loyalty. It's a very important characteristic. The perfect woman must be someone with whom I can have no doubts in her character. Long or short, I shall trust her with my life."

Lydia grabbed his neck, pulled his face forward, then kissed his cheek. "Then you think I'm perfect, for I'll protect you. I think you perfect, too."

His arm wound about her. For a moment, I saw a man who would slay dragons for this child, for as long as he could. I smiled back, knowing how rare it was to witness such devotion.

Unfortunately, as a physician, I'd found many husbands who had no interest in their children or stepchildren until they were ready to arrange a marriage to advance their family's stature.

"Carew," the duke said, "let's hear your answer. Let it be less jaded than mine or Livingston's."

Taking my time, I tried to find a fitting jest for the wonderful Miss Scarlett. I finished my champagne but lifted the crystal goblet into the air. "A toast to Livingston who has described his perfect woman, a reformed courtesan with looks and a well-earned fortune. And to the duke, a loyal beauty. I do hope that you find her, and I pray she be less cantankerous than the current object of your affection."

Livingston took my gesture as a request for more drink. He beat a footman and lifted the champagne's small cask, refilling our glasses. "Continue, Carew. Tell him one of those things Shakespeare would write."

I ignored the fool and watched the Miss of Science.

"Bubbles?" Scarlett's nose wrinkled.

Not sure how I felt about the bubbles either. I read . . . or I thought Scarlett told me the monks tried to remove them, before a vintner determined the bubbles helped with fermentation.

Did I argue with her? Probably. Did I admit she may be right? Never. I set down the glass, wondering why that memory of our fiery exchange popped up in my cranium.

"Don't keep us in suspense, Mr. Carew." Scarlett's tone warmed as she tried to draw me closer to her verbal guillotine. "Well, sir? The perfect woman can't be such a hard concept for a decisive man like you. I'm sure you will add some anatomy to your description . . . and pauses, oh great hesitater."

Torrance chuckled and so did Livingston.

"Well, let me see," I said, stalling. A quip for my friend had to be, well, perfect. "The duke's ideal woman is more dignified than the earl's. Yet they both demand some level of beauty and loyalty. I don't think these ideas are enough."

Scarlett offered a yawn. "I think Mr. Carew has not an answer.

I've valued his abilities too highly. Hello, indecisive physician. I have a penny for your thoughts."

Reaching out, I tweaked her flared nose. "Better ask Torrance for a loan. My opinion is worth a pound."

"Pro . . . procrast . . . delaying." Lydia said.

I chuckled, then grew serious. "The perfect woman is demure, quiet, born of pedigree, an impeccable dresser, and beautiful. She's all of these things, and she's loyal and wonderful."

Scarlett tilted her head a little and stared. Her expression soured. "Quiet? Demure? She sounds as if she's made of marble. Did you sculpt her to have such attributes?"

"Well, if a chisel will work to smooth a few edges, what's a little dust?" I chortled and glanced at the stunned faces.

"So you wish to create the perfect woman? I knew you had a God complex."

I waggled my finger at the girl. "You . . . are impossible. I have given you a reasonable definition."

Livingston tapped the table. "Sounds like this is a real woman. What is her name?"

They all would know soon enough, since I planned to tell her my feelings this weekend. I wanted a long engagement, but I couldn't let the jewel slip away. I'd even use the dreaded L word to secure her agreement. The L word was the riskiest spiritual word. In the past, saying it aloud made those I loved go away. "Eveline Gray. Eveline Gray of Cheapside. I . . . I love her. She loves and understands me too."

My chortles stopped when Scarlett offered me a stunned, sad look. She bit her lip.

I lifted my hands. "Miss Wilcox. Don't be upset. We tease each other all the time. You will like Miss Gray. I've told her of you. Miss Gray and I have slowly courted these past four years. She's agreed to a long engagement. At the end of the year, I intend—"

"I'm so sorry, Mr. Carew." Scarlett looked troubled.

"What's the matter? You know I like to tease you. We always tease each other."

"But, Eveline Gray." Scarlett's tone was low. "That's a familiar name. Are you sure of the name?"

I sat back and folded my arms. "Of course. I intend to . . . She's . . . Scarlett Wilcox, what is it?"

The agitation in her cheeks disappeared. Her expression changed from sadness to something that felt like pity. "I'm so sorry."

"Scarlett?" My heart raced. "What?"

She bit her lip, then set the newspaper in front of me. "I read—"

"Oh good, this one reads, too." Livingston poured more champagne. "You know that's dangerous in a woman."

Mimicking the duke, I waved at him to silence, then turned my gaze back to Scarlett. "Please go on."

"Well, I borrowed His Grace's *Sun* paper to find out more about the Royal Society meetings and saw the Annual Exhibition at Somerset House. It's happening now."

"See, Torrance. I told you." Livingston turned the champagne cask up to his face. "Why are the Royal Society schedules important, Miss Wilcox? Women aren't allowed."

This time the duke stuck a big kartoshka roll onto the earl's plate. "Stuff that into your mouth and let Scarlett finish about Miss Gray."

The girl pointed to an item in the paper.

Shock and shame filled me when I read the name. "Eveline Gray of Cheapside has eloped with Baron David Derand." Eveline was now another man's wife.

Silence.

The flicker and dripping of the candles drowned my slowing pulse. "Miss Gray never said a word about there being anyone else."

But there was someone else. A peer . . . a man outside of our community.

"Sorry, Mr. Carew." The brave lass was the first to speak. No sass, no spite, just comfort—that was what Scarlett offered me.

Still, I couldn't understand this. Feeling discombobulated, I shook my head. "I just saw Miss Gray at Wesley's Chapel last week. We sat together in front of the aunties." Why did I say that L word? Why did I doom myself to hope? "She said nothing of an impending offer from Derand."

"Guess you were right about the quiet part. She was so silent you didn't notice you were losing her."

Livingston's words added an extra sharp kick to my gut. I slumped in the chair.

I didn't know what to say. I kept staring at Eveline's name in the newspaper. Then I felt an understanding hand on my shoulder.

Scarlett offered me a sympathetic smile. It eased my pain a little.

But I had to figure out how to survive the rest of the night and my aunties at church this weekend. They could be insufferable. Their pity would be awful.

"Saves me making a fool of myself, quoting Shakespeare in front of her parents to prove my love." I lifted my goblet. "I wish her well. To Eveline Gray, the new Baroness of Derand. May she be happy."

Everyone drank.

I sipped and found myself holding on to Scarlett's hand a little longer. She kindly sensed the ache in me and didn't cause more damage.

"Thanks, Miss Wilcox." I whispered my praise and saw tears in her eyes. Like a patient being tended to, I held on to her fingers, clinging to her empathy and wishing everyone else could ignore the embarrassed fool I'd become.

Chapter 4

SCARLETT—SAME OLD, SAME OLD

June 2, 1817
One year later . . .

Lying in bed, waiting for the acceptable time to rise, I see the sun brighten the drab curtains shrouding my window. My room is utilitarian except for the exquisite clock in the corner. My father's longcase clock. It's one of his possessions that gladly fell to me. I had it moved from his office at Wilcox Coal the week after he passed, when my sister began considering giving her husband control of the business.

A slow but bitter chuckle falls. That's probably why the clock is still in our possession, not sold off to pay Tavis's bets.

The clock's hand says six forty-five.

Footsteps. They are light with a clacking sound. Those are Katherine's heels. She's typically up by five doing the books for Wilcox Coal.

Sighing, I think of her spending all her energy to resolve a debt that doesn't need to be repaid, but my sister wants nothing from the duke—no kindness, no friendship, nothing. I love my sister. I admire her determination as much as I love Katherine's unruly nature. She lets people know what she feels, and she doesn't care if they are offended by her words. Not everyone is as secure as Katherine.

She works too hard. The poor dear is trying to double the company's profits so that she can prove we don't need the Duke of Torrance or his money. Her pride blinds her to all the reasons he should be in our lives.

Katherine's footfalls stop outside my door. That's different.

"Scarlett, are you up?"

Oh dear. Has she found out about my secret visits? Did she hear I spent time caring for the women at Bridewell prison? Did she discover one of the disguises that I use to attend lectures? I try to slow my rising pulse. I cough to make sure my voice works and doesn't sound guilty. "Yes, you can come in."

My door opens and my sister comes inside. She's in an indigo dress, which one might say indicates half-mourning. It's been well over two years since she became a widow. No one needs to be that devoted to foolish Tavis. "You are staying over at Anya House tonight?"

She knows this. "Yes, Katherine." I don't light a candle. I'd rather she not see the difficulty I have hiding my annoyance. "Monday through Wednesday, we're supposed to stay with the Duke of Torrance. We meet with members of society. Playwrights or musicians come. It's delightful culture."

"Yes, and you've made yourself at home there. Your room there has color. Here, it's dull, the same—"

"The same as when I was six? I shared a room then. Hadn't thought about much except my clock."

"The longcase is nice." She comes a little more into the room. "I know Anya House seems wonderful, and the duke is introducing you to gentlemen. Do not be fooled. Those are potential candidates. He's trying to pick a husband for you. You don't want that. You want your freedom, Scarlett."

Freedom is a wonderful thing. But what do you call someone caught in a war between two people who should have more common sense? "Katherine, if the duke finds someone who fits my criteria, I will marry. Then I'll be free from you trying to manipulate me."

"You don't think the duke is trying to manipulate you? I know he's turning each of you against me."

Katherine does a fair job of that all by herself. She pushes me to exasperation, acting as if her judgment is better. "I'll act in a manner for my own happiness."

"Don't go quoting that novel to me. Who feeds you such frivolity? I'm serious, Scarlett. I only need a little more time, and I can pay him back. Then, as wealthy women, we can have our pick of society."

Wilcox Coal will never earn enough to put us in a respectable sphere. We'll only attract more fortune chasing men like Tavis, the late Lord Hampton. It's been a year since I gave the duke the power to choose my husband. It was my bargain to have freedom to do research and go to men's lectures. Through his science meetings at Anya House, I've met some of the brightest minds in England, but the duke hasn't made any picks. He doesn't feel I'm ready. In a way, the Duke of Torrance acts more noble than Katherine. "Sister, why are you so desperate when it comes to the duke? Are you still trying to kid yourself that you're not attracted to him?"

She leans against the threshold. Her silhouette looks proud. "Torrance is not ugly."

"Katherine, women throw themselves at him. Mr. Steele has had to chase away two widows, three young ladies in their first season, and one mama and daughter combination. I don't think either cared who trapped him."

"Women?" She sighs loudly. "Fine, he's handsome."

I light the candle and sit up. I'm too agitated to pretend anymore. "He has one friend trying to get him a courtesan. You keep pushing him away, and he'll be caught in the arms of someone who won't let him be kind to us."

She shakes her head. "They can have him. I don't want his kindness."

"You don't have to marry him. Be his friend. Let him honor whatever promise he made to Tavis on your husband's deathbed."

Katherine fumes. I see her hands fist. She punches my clock. "When someone shows you who they truly are, when they hurt you, you can never trust them again."

"When did that happen, Katherine?" I pull out my pencil and trusty notebook. "When? I need dates and facts. For nothing makes sense."

The longcase chimes. My cuckoo comes out and does his broken dance. Seven o'clock on the dot.

A frozen expression forms on her countenance. She looks like she's about to burst into tears. How can she look so hurt?

"Sister, what has he done?"

She pulls her hands to her mouth. The palms are clasped together as if she's praying. "He's too extravagant. Lydia's birthday will be here soon. He brought elephants to her party last year. Live elephants. How do I compete with that?"

"Can't you both love her? He is far too invested in Lydia to abandon her. And how would she feel if he just left? Do you want to hurt her?"

Katherine seems to be shaking. "No, I'd never hurt that little girl, not on purpose. Talk to the duke, let me have this one birthday. Then I'll be easier."

"Why can't you share the one day so important to Lydia?"

My sister's lips tremble. When she finally glances at me she says, "Watch after Lydia when you are at Anya House. I need to leave for Wilcox Coal before I'm late."

"Of course, Katherine. You're entitled to your secrets. You can continue to act illogically and harass a man who wants nothing more than Lydia's well-being and the Wilcox name restored. But I'll not be swayed by what seems to be an irrational response to a friend to whom we are indebted."

"Scarlett, he's not good. It's all a trick to humble me." She swipes at her eyes. The motion is fast like I'm not supposed to see how emotional any mention of Lydia and the duke makes her.

"What are you hiding, Katherine? Tell me. Trust me."

She shakes her head. "Nothing. You need to trust me. Jahleel

Charles, the Duke of Torrance, is not the good person he's pretending to be."

"You're wrong. And you're being unreasonable. And, sister, I'm old enough to form my own opinions."

Katherine leaves, closing my door. Whatever the problem, it's big. I pray she can handle the consequences, but I have a feeling it will be exposed and the Wilcoxes will again be left destitute. The sooner I'm married, the more I'll be able to help my family when our world collapses.

In the interim, I have a friend to save. I push out of my bedclothes to engage in my secret life. By the time Katherine or anyone other than the duke finds out, I'll have accomplished my mission. Yet, I wonder if my being exposed will be worse than the secret Katherine's trying tó hide.

With a sigh, I part the curtains, and let the light inside. My window, its position on the wall, isn't large enough for me to see my small herb garden. Last year, the year without a summer, made me believe I'd lost the plantings. Mama and I had kept that garden alive for so long. I took it on completely when she could no longer leave the house. From her bedchamber, she saw the greenery and flowers. I like to think they gave her comfort when her health failed.

Making the divide in the curtains a little wider offers the needed brightness to apply the theater cosmetics. I have a transformation to begin. Errors cannot be tolerated. Trudging to my closet, my bare feet grace the rya, the Russian rug, gifted by the duke. He's thoughtful. The kind of man I wish Tavis had been.

Feeling sentimental, I square my shoulders. Tossing off my pink robe with silky ribbons, I pick up the basket of linen bandages. They are wide with very little stretch. I suppose a broken limb could be isolated with them, but these will be used to wrap and flatten my bosom. Round and round, I sweep the cloth about my chest. I keep going until all seems smooth and flat. A year ago, this took less time. I suppose I've grown. One might say my charms afford me a curvy figure, but that's the last thing I need for this disguise.

My white shirt slips over my head and covers the bandages. A glance in the mirror shows me to be flat and stocky. I have Lord Mark's build, somewhat, but my sister Georgie's husband is taller. Rooting in my closet, I pull out a pair of black breeches. I slide them up my thighs and carefully stuff my shirt inside. Then I button the flapping fall of the pants.

I steal another glance in the mirror once I don a burgundy waistcoat. Button after button, I close it, then pull on an onyx woolen tailcoat. Every curve is concealed, swaddled in fabric. My body's a manly rectangle in need of a cravat. Heading to my drawers, I dig underneath stays and corsets and find a nice ivory strip. Slipping it about my neck, I make a barrel knot.

A peek at the longcase shows seven thirty. I'm behind and quickly drag on stockings and my father's boots. More buttons close the pants to my shins. Tying a garnet-colored ribbon in my hair, I pull back a long dark braid. It isn't until I dab the dark black cosmetic on my chin to offer a hint of a beard's shadow and a little more along my brows to make them thick, and glue long sideburns along my ears, that I no longer look like Scarlett Wilcox.

Hanging a silver pocket watch from my burgundy waistcoat, I think I've done it. It's fetching. I'm fetching. I feel like Father. I've become the picture of a debonair young man.

When I put on a masculine hat, a slick jet beaver dome, my ruse is complete. "Father," I whisper, "don't roll over in your grave. Pretend I'm the son that should've lived." Scotland Wilcox, my twin, would've gone to defeat the horrid Napoleon. My brother would've distinguished the Wilcox name in battle. He would've inherited the coal business and never have let lousy Tavis run it into the ground. "Pretend, Papa, that I hadn't let Scotland down. And it's him here with me fighting for change."

I cover my mouth, making sure my hands do not smear the cosmetic, but I said his name aloud. None of my sisters say anything about my brother. They act like he never existed, like a stillborn who never had a name.

I swallow the rocks in my throat.

"You were supposed to have a life, Scotland. You mattered, and you'd still be here if I were smarter or if there had been a doctor available on this side of the Thames." I fan my face, then scoop up leather gloves.

Men don't cry, not over a long-lost memory. If I don't pull myself together, I'll be exposed. Never.

When I'm sure I'm not going to fall to pieces, I go into the hall. Stepping over to Lydia's room, I put my ear to her door. Little snores sound. She sounds good, her lungs clear. Every time I hear her sleep with ease, I feel it's a miracle.

The longcase chimes. It's eight o'clock. Time to go.

When I head downstairs, I hear a smattering of off-key notes. Then what sounds like kissing. *Groan.* The newlyweds are at it.

My sister Georgina's voice is light and flighty as she tells her husband how to speed up the crescendo.

Hmmm. I think they are talking about music. I hope they are.

It's illogical that two people pretending to court should fall so deeply in love. I'm convinced it's some sort of reaction to sudden embarrassment or coal fumes or maybe baking powder. Lord Mark did love my sister's biscuits, even before loving her.

Can love make anyone happy? I wish it were so. I pray those two are always in love.

I cover my eyes and walk into the parlor. "Lord Mark, Georgie. I'm leaving."

"You can open your eyes, sister. I've not ravaged my wife . . . yet."

Georgie blushes and taps his arm. His elbow lands with a plunk onto the pianoforte keys, striking a chord. They look at each other and say at the same time, "A minor. That's it."

He works the high notes, while she plays the low ones. Together, the two have finished composition after composition. It's a beautiful thing. It's also a financial thing, for these works sell.

"Scarlett, must you be in a disguise today?" Lord Mark keeps playing. "I know I'm new to the family, but isn't this dangerous? Shouldn't I be more insistent that you not do this?"

"It's only dangerous if I get caught, sir. I don't intend to be caught. Do not be concerned."

Lord Mark plays a few more bars. "I am. But the disguise is good. My sister-in-law is leaving the house looking like my brother-in-law. Oh, this feels wrong."

Georgie kisses him on the cheek. "We must trust that she knows what she's doing and that she knows we only speak up because we care."

He nods and begins to play more earnestly. "I care. Scarlett, I don't want you hurt. I don't want scandal to be a part of your world."

I dip my head the way the men bow. "Yes, Lord Mark. I understand. This is something I must do. I'm glad I can trust you."

"You can, Scarlett," he says, "but call me Mark, and please try harder to trust."

They want me to believe that they are ridiculously happy and that I should become a trusting fool again. Over the merry, heart-racing tune, I say, "Lydia is still asleep, but she's to go to Anya House. I'll meet her there. And Lord . . . Mark, I'm taking your shift with Mr. Thom today."

He stops playing and turns around. "Scarlett, he's not . . . Mr. Thom is having problems seeing. I'm not sure how long he can continue to drive for Wilcox Coal." My brother-in-law looks sad and concerned. "Sorry to stare, brother. But be careful."

I offer him a smile, a small one so my sideburns don't move. "I know about Mr. Thom. I'm working on a plan to help him."

Mark seems about as convinced about that as I am about love. He spins around and starts playing the pianoforte again. "Dearest wife, escort our brother to the door. Perhaps she'll listen to *your* caution."

She shrugs and leaves the pianoforte's bench. Tying up her peach-colored robe, she moves to me. Yet, as she gets closer, she gapes—and then starts bawling.

Mark leaps up, gathers her in his arms. "Hey, she looks quite good. If I didn't know Scarlett, I'd be fooled."

"No, dearest," she says. "She's dressed as a man before to get into science lectures. But with this makeup . . . you're Scotland. Oh my goodness. You look how I imagine he'd look."

Mark holds her a little tighter. "Who's Scotland?"

"Her twin. Our late brother. The makeup and the hat." She wipes at her cheek. "That's Scotland."

"At least you said his name, sis. And Mark should know his name."

I'm not sure who reaches for me first, Mark or Georgie, but I am sure my jet-black cosmetic and tears are all over his white shirt and her robe.

The strength in Mark's arms, for a moment, feels sent from the brother who isn't here. I hug him back, and I mean it.

"We need to say his name," Georgie says. "We stopped for Papa's sake. He was devastated at the loss of his only son."

"Mama was, too. But she had to keep it all inside to be strong for him. It made her weaker." I step away and swipe at my eyes with the handkerchief Mark hands me. "But we all let Scotland disappear. I, most of all, let it happen."

"No, you didn't," she says, "But Scarlett, you're right. We need to say Scotland. That's how we honor his life."

I give her another hug, then check my reflection in the small mirror outside the parlor. "Sideburns in place."

Mark runs past, vaults up the stairs, and comes back. "A gentleman needs a fragrance."

He hands me a small bottle of eau de toilette that smells of sandalwood and citrus. I dab a little on my cravat. I hand back the fragrance and offer him a true grin. Starting to leave, I pivot to them. "Katherine is trying to have Lydia's birthday without the duke. That will produce nothing but another fight."

Georgie drops her hand into her palm. "I'll talk to her. She should treat him better."

Why does it sound as if Georgie knows that the duke is the injured party?

"You'll be late," she says.

I want to ask what she knows of the duke and Katherine's history, but I can't miss the anatomy lesson on the eye. Fix one problem before becoming embroiled in another. However, I can't resist. "Please, sis, tell me what's going on. I can't stand not knowing."

She shakes her head. "It's Katherine's truth, her problem. She has to fix this. But I'll see what I can do. And I'll take Lydia to Anya House later."

Georgina Wilcox Sebastian, the Lady Mark Sebastian, is very good at keeping secrets. Patting my top hat down, I head out the back door. Trudging fast, I walk to Ground Street, then to a spot at the corner of the house.

The noises of barges sound like an invading army waiting to come ashore. The sulfur smell of the Thames further reminds me of how close we are to the river. I flip up the lid of my pocket watch. It's a little past eight thirty. I'm five minutes late. I may not finish the coal route and get to the Royal Society lecture.

Panic ensues.

Katherine is down the street at the Wilcox office. She could see me. Her fury would be on me and, of course, find its way to the duke.

The noise, the smells, the heat of all these clothes, my beating heart—I might faint before Mr. Thom gets here.

Finally, I see his dray. It's moving at a leisurely pace. An infinity passes, and then he stops in front of me. "You there, Wilcox."

"Yes, Scotland Wilcox, here."

He shakes his head. "So, another day risking everything to watch a group of men cut up an animal. Will it be another rabbit? Maybe a pig?"

"It was a pig." The last lecture on circulation used the dissection for illustration. Poor wrinkly fellow gave his all.

I walked to the other side of the dray. "I'm not sure what it will be. Seeing a pig cut up for research hasn't dampened my appetite for bacon. All in all, it will be good."

"Might not be anything. I hear the Mayfair set talking about some art thing. I think it's the Annual Exhibition again."

I climb in and almost want to fall out. Last year, the exhibition disrupted the meetings of the Royal Society, since both meet at Somerset House.

"Lord Livingston's going to lead a discussion on eye anatomy. It can't be canceled."

Blinking wildly, Mr. Thom holds the reins out to me, almost shoving them at me when I climb beside him in the driver's seat. "You drive. Sc—"

"S. Wilcox, or Mr. Scotland Wilcox."

"Fine. But drive," he says. "I need the break. My eyes are tired today."

The man never tires.

Waving my hand to his left doesn't make him flinch or move at all. "Your eyesight seems worse."

He nods. Both brown eyes have silver scales, and Mr. Thom looks pale. His rich brown skin seems dull. And when sick, the fellow wouldn't say a word until he was ready to drop to the ground. "I'm going to tell Lady Hampton I need to retire."

No. Someone healthy can't retire because he can't see. Science should be able to fix this. The duke is helping to get me tools. I need to learn everything and be able to practice medicine on this side of the Thames.

I will save his sight and life. I'm just the man—the woman—to do it.

Chapter 5

STEPHEN—SUMMONED TO SOMERSET HOUSE

Yawning, I sit back in my carriage—or, should I say, my traveling office. Beneath the onyx cloth tufted seats are compartments for the tools of my profession. There's even a freshly laundered shirt and cravat. Practicing medicine in London is often one part wisdom and two parts acting like a wise, fancy gentleman.

This existence is a far cry from my humble beginnings as a bone sawer, tooth puller, and elixir fixer. So many hands-on tasks that ordinary doctors around the world do daily. In London, a doctor is not respected, not like a physician. The distinction of book learning is supposed to be preferred to getting one's hands dirty. I shake my head at the foolishness. I'd rather save lives.

In Britain, a decent wage and prospects center around being part of the genteel, slightly useless class. I follow the rules to get ahead. Knowing I help is what helps me sleep, when I get the rare opportunity to rest in my own bed.

My carriage slows as we come closer to the river.

This part of the Thames is tame. Nothing like the chaos and hubbub on the other side. If I weren't so tired, I would go over to Ground Street. I need to see why Scarlett Wilcox has stopped speaking to me.

My carriage stops before I fully nod off. Out the window is the beautiful courtyard of Somerset House, one of the loveliest places in London. The architecture is perfect, with marble and limestone facades. The grass that surrounds the pavement squares seems lush and green. My aunties would have a glorious time making a communal picnic here.

Benjamin, casually known as Benny, my man-of-all-work, opens my door. "Weh here, sir."

The fellow is laughing, and I'm aching. "What's so funny?"

"At de mews, Mr. Carew, I heard a bit of gossip. It seems Lord Clapper has resigned from leading de Court of Chancery. The Lord Mayor walked in on him wit comp'ny."

I yawn and try to focus on Benny's dark bronze face. "Why did that make the man resign?"

"Sir, seems de company was de Lord Mayor's wife."

Benny's laughter grows, but my foggy brainbox thinks that's the second or third resignation from the court in the past year. And every time over scandal. *Hmmm.*

Chalking this up to rich people doing stupid things, I force my limbs to move, all while Benny giggles and shakes his head. I've known him eight years. He started out as my hackney driver taking me about town, even waiting for me during patient visits. I'm pretty sure Benny was enslaved at some point and made his way onto ships from there to here. We never talk about the hows and whys of his freedom; he's a London resident now, part of the immigrant community. He's free, and I'll fight anyone to keep him that way.

Stepping out, I reach into a compartment under my seat and tug out the fresh shirt and the special rinse of peppermint that will make my mouth feel alive.

Changing quickly and letting Benny fix my cravat, I notice maybe for the first time that Benny is about Scarlett Wilcox's height.

When he's finished, I yawn loudly, then say, "The crowds are coming. The Annual Exhibition will draw many."

"Mr. Carew, yuh don't look so good. Perhaps yuh go home."

"We just got here."

Benny has his hand on the carriage door. He hasn't closed it. Then he says in a loud, proud voice, "It's good to see yuh doing somet'ing other than work, but yuh visited with patients all 'cross London, two days straight. I know yuh have no slept."

This is true. "Sick people need a physician." Admission into the existing hospitals is still lacking. Regretfully, I've been so busy that I've not gotten much further finding funding to build a new hospital. "I have lying-ins to check on and hands to hold to bring comfort."

"Yuh do too much, sir. Yuh know how yuh get."

I tug on my jacket and am surprised at how it and my jet striped waistcoat lack wrinkles. "Last night, I stayed with an old woman who passed away waiting for her son to come home from the military. I read her *Sense and Sensibility*. She went in peace. If not for me, who'd provide this care and, upon occasion, hope?"

"Can't do all those t'ings if yuh fall over. I don't think yuh eaten."

"Benny, I nibbled here or there."

His eyes are small and call me on my exaggerations. "Make it a short meeting. Meh do stay close, sir?"

"Park in the usual place." It should be a short meeting with the Duke of Torrance, but then it could go long. "Once this is done, I promise I'll do nothing else but go home and sleep."

He shrugs, shuts the door, and levels his black hat. "Yuh know, if the aunties ask if yuh working too hard, meh won't lie."

Who can get a word in with them? "That reminds me, I need to check on my cousin." Maryanne is very pregnant and almost due, but that baby hasn't turned. I believe Maryanne's mother, my blood aunt, wants to retain another physician, one with more gray hair on top and perhaps less of a tan.

Some days, I think I'll never be more than a bone doctor to everyone, even to those in my own community. Maybe that's why, on a day that I should be resting, I insist upon answering the duke's request to meet.

Benny catches my arm when I start to turn. "Mr. Carew, yuh get lightheaded when yuh miss eating, especially wit no sleep. Yuh fainted at de last aunties' picnic. Meh carrying yuh home. Actually carrying yuh."

That was highly embarrassing. I wonder if that's why my own aunt wants to get another physician. "I've diagnosed myself to be fine. I won't miss meeting with Torrance."

"He hasn't been sick again, has he? He's a good one."

I glance at my driver, my friend, and realize I talk to Benny too much. Yet, what else can be done? My profession is a lonely one and being able to express what I've seen—the shock and violence and worry of it all—helps. "No. He's been fine as of late, but let's keep our voices low and not mention His Grace's welfare to anyone. It's not something he wishes to be known."

"That's right," Benny says. "Sure, Mr. Carew. Yuh keeper of the ton's secrets."

Wouldn't necessarily say what I'm the keeper of such, but I know many things. "Discretion is good. I need you to be discreet too. You are loyal, but your friendly demeanor can sometimes get us into trouble."

More crowds filter past, heading for the stone steps and neoclassical columns. "I'll find enough here to keep myself occupied. Go to the regular mews. Hopefully, I'll be done around two."

"Very good, sir. Yuh rarely take time off. Seems yuh will win de argument with Miss Wilcox after all."

"Argument, Benny?" Does he know what I've done to make her so mad that she now avoids me? "What are you talking about? Start slowly."

Benny raises a brow. I see skepticism radiating in his attempt to keep a serious face. "Well, yuh two are always arguing. I believe the last time, a month ago, she said that yuh weren't a serious physician. Or was it yuh too serious of a physician? Yuh coming here to prove something to her?"

"That couldn't have been our last words. But you are right. She hasn't talked to me in a month. Or is it two months?"

"Truly?" He rubs his jaw. "Can't have been that long."

My hands fall to my coat, the pocket with my blade, my best scalpel. You can take a kid from the streets of Port of Spain, but the streets will always be a part of me. A thief doesn't care if you are in the wrong part of town on a mission of mercy.

Easing my palms to my sides, I look again at Benny as he makes himself comfortable in the driver's seat. "You don't remember, either?"

He shakes his head. "But yuh will, and yuh always tell me. Yuh always do."

Watching my carriage drive away makes my head feel even lighter. Since when does Benny track my disagreements with Scarlett? And why doesn't he do a better job at it, so I know why she's no longer speaking to me?

Puzzling over this, I decide to get out of the sun and go into Somerset House. I see a woman in a bonnet, a soft blue one. I saw Scarlett wear one like it months ago. I speed up to catch her, but then I see it's another miss.

Disappointment rocks me. It's difficult to breathe. This lack of sleep is getting to me.

Yet, I know this ache is Scarlett. She's my friend. Well, we've been friendlier, less argumentative. Now, there's nothing. I've been so busy that I hadn't noticed how I miss her barbs. The loss of not speaking with her has finally struck. And it's horrible.

I walk a little faster up the gray pavement. Then, I charge up the stone steps to get to Torrance. The duke is close to her. Sometimes, they look as thick as thieves. He'll know what I've done to offend her. Then I can fix things. A grand gesture, perhaps?

At the top of the steps, I can see the banks of the Thames. The sun beams down on the river and makes it like a mirror. The reflection floods light onto Somerset House. May it guide me to enlightenment, or to an enlightened miss.

Even I groan at my terrible humor. Scarlett . . .

Shaking my head, I tip my hat, this way then that way, and walk into the south entrance. A statue of the River God sits there, stretched out with cornucopias. I've passed this statue tens of times to partake in a Royal Society meeting. Yet this time the marble face looks ominous. It feels like a warning.

My hand goes to my pocket. My fingers trace the outline of my surgical tool. Then I shake myself. My exhaustion and lack of eating has vexed me. The River God is not sending me a warning. My stomach is.

The air is stale inside Somerset House. Beginning to perspire, I whip off my gloves and head through the maze of opulent marble statues and crowds before passing the smattering of apartments or offices of state that have permanent residence here.

My steps slow.

My stomach churns as I see art and tapestries welcomed to these shores by British colonial aspirations. Many of these pieces bear the label tribal art, but these stolen pieces are conquests of the East India and West Indies Companies.

With a queasy stomach, feeling even more tired, I slow. Will London always look at its immigrants as tribal, less than? As an old woman and her husband take extra paces around me, I realize the sacrifice to assimilate seems less and less worth it.

"That is special. In St. Petersburg, we have many." The light Russian accent of the Duke of Torrance echoes in the corridor. I see him a little way down with a gaggle of geese surrounding him. The birds—very pretty women and their equally feather-adorned mamas—have him cornered.

I've never seen him hold court in public.

Of course it's rare to find him outside of Anya House. The closer I get, the more I notice a rainbow of women. It seems ambitious mothers from my Cheapside community, as well as some from Mayfair, are out at the Annual Exhibition in fine pinks, greens, and yellows, making eyes at Torrance.

The ladies are trying to catch his attention. Who can fault

them? Torrance is amiable, well-traveled, rich, and based on the sighs and fan waving, the ladies find him handsome.

The duke seems amused, but not enough to pay closer attention. I notice his gaze move from the ladies to surveil the hall. He's looking for someone. Could it be me? I'm early.

I almost wave, but that instinct in me for trouble rears. It's near, and Torrance is on alert, looking for something to manifest.

I wonder if the duke has called me here to provide medical support for the wounded, or to help in an attack.

Chapter 6

STEPHEN—HOLD UP, WAIT A MINUTE

My heart begins to tick a little faster.

Torrance sees me, but then motions for me to stand back. Oh goodness. It's about to commence, his latest act of retribution. Who's the peer he intends to wreak havoc upon?

With Prahmn's downfall last year, the embezzling viscount in January, the fellow with the Lord Mayor's wife, that would leave . . . the rest of London.

Oh no. The women? They can't be here to witness a loved one's fall from grace. The duke may have axes to grind, but he's not cruel enough to upset women. Is he?

Casually, I search for the impending threat. Readying for a fight, I ball my fists. *Words are wind, blows are unkind.* That's what my father said as he taught me to punch.

I forgo the scalpel in my coat; it's too obvious and would escalate the situation.

Moments pass. Women laugh. Torrance remains affable. Furthermore, I don't see any angry peers. Everyone is laughing and pointing at the art in Somerset House.

A minute or so goes by. Nothing happens. I've let my tired mind conjure up villains and shadowy figures. Even in my sleep-deprived delirium, I know Torrance is a man to keep as an ally.

Nonetheless, I gape at him, and then my own reflection, in an art piece made of mirrors.

The duke and the gentleman physician—two of us here in Somerset House, men of education, refined taste, with natural tints to our skin. I wonder if the Duke of Somerset, the hallowed Edward Seymour, the protector of England and the young king, had Torrance and myself in mind to grace these halls.

Probably not.

"Excuse me, ladies." Torrance bows, and like the Red Sea, the ladies part allowing the duke and his crystal-looking cane come to me. "On time, Mr. Carew. Excellent."

I take his extended palm. The grip is firm. In it there's power and strength and control. His health must continue to improve.

"Your Grace," I say, and dip my chin. "I wonder why I've been summoned. So naturally, I'll be on time."

"That is one of the things I like about you, Carew, your natural sense of curiosity."

I take the compliment, but deep down, I suppose I enjoy that no one is shouting that they're ruined, racist, or scandalized.

"Torrance, what do you want? You had your man duly summon me. And how exactly did you find me in Westminster? 'Twas a busy night. I was comforting a dying woman, after another visit where I set a minister's broken arm."

"Yes. The poor fellow at St. Margaret's. He broke it in a most peculiar manner."

Livingston said there were rumors that Torrance had spies all about the city, but that was just talk, right? Still, the duke knew where to send his henchmen, otherwise known as his footmen. Maybe he was more tsar than duke.

"I can't comment on any of my patients, Your Grace. It's my oath to each to maintain their privacy. I think it's a good thing."

"Punctuality is a good thing, too." He looks over me and to the side. "It's definitely something to count on."

His Grace offers a nod to someone in the corner but stays with me. Well, he needn't go after a thing. The duke doesn't chase anyone but the alleged woman he loves.

Yet, the way the ladies flock to him, the way he seems to enjoy the small talk, I wonder how much longer the duke will wait for Lady Hampton to change her opinion of him.

"The Annual Exhibition has again brought out everyone," he says, his gaze floating away. "I must say, if science must lose to another topic, I'd rather it be art."

"Do you paint?"

"My mother. The Princess Elizaveta Abramovna Gannibal is a great portraiture artist. She's making me something special for Anya House."

I feel my brow rise. The duke rarely mentions his mother by her full name without adding her married one—Charles.

Does that mean something, or is this my overly tired brain looking for conspiracies? "Is it something you will show off at your next ball?"

He gapes at me over his flared nose. "If I give another ball, it will be for a special reason. Perhaps to celebrate an engagement."

"Torrance, you sly one. You've moved forward. I saw you entertaining. Will you choose a new duchess soon? Is that why I'm here?"

His mouth opens, then snaps shut. "I wasn't thinking of myself." His gaze again floats away. "But surely you have, as you say, moved forward. The loss of that special someone last year seemed to affect you greatly. I've heard of no replacement."

Why was he trying to remind me of Eveline? And *replacement*? Is a woman like a shirt or a pair of shoes? "My practice has been busy, and I'm still having meetings about the hospital project."

"Yes, the endless fundraising meetings."

His tone sounds a little like Scarlett's, a smidgeon too condescending. I know Torrance can fund the entire project. I know if I ask, he'll do so without hesitation. That is the level of his gratitude for my care of his illness, but my vision of the hospital I want can't be without patients because the future patrons fear the funder or think him mad.

It can't be risked. "Soon, Your Grace. By next year—"

His attention has drifted to a conversation nearby. "That person mouthed something about rabbits," he says. "How odd."

"Probably rabbit dissection. That is what's promised for today's Royal Society meeting. Our friend, the Earl of Livingston, will be the man with the scalpel."

"Carew, that sounds like a waste of a rabbit. The creature should be handled by a chef and made into a rabbit pie, a kouneli stifado, or a lapin à la crème. Each savory dish is delicious."

My stomach rumbles. It's loud like a French horn and too noisy to ignore.

The duke's hazel eyes are on me. "Are you well, Carew? Perhaps you've spent too many nights on saintly pursuits."

"Just suddenly peckish. The rabbit talk and the stew makes me think of my aunt's cooking. The aunties usually cook a big feast once a month on a weekend. Missed the last three."

"The women in Cheapside?"

"Well, I wasn't speaking of the ones in Port of Spain, several seas away."

He smiles. "Ah. The rapier wit, has it returned? No more sulking over missed and delayed opportunities?"

Sulking? Does this notion have anything to do with Scarlett and why she isn't talking to me?

My head begins to ache. A cryptic duke isn't going to make my temples throb less. "Your Grace, let's get to the matter at hand. You summoned me, and I have cleared my schedule of all appointments as requested. What is it you desire, sir?"

I give him a little bow.

When I straighten, he's staring at a group of men heading into the exhibition room. One looks familiar. I can't place him.

"Follow me, Carew."

I do, and we go to a room that feels two stories high. Like Torrance's dining room, the ceiling is ornate and dovetailed corner to corner in rich molding. Nonetheless, there's an oddness to it, as it sports an elongated dome of a church or some old building from Italy. I do like how the long oval windows at the top allow the sun to highlight the art—the walls and walls of hanging paintings. One on top of the other, framed landscapes and portraits sit for inspection. There's no rhyme or reason in the placement. It would be confusing, if it wasn't so beautiful.

"So this is the Great Room for the exhibition." The duke walks deeper inside. "It's grand, but cluttered."

I eye a painted horse, then a landscape. "Where else would Somerset House hide its treasures, but in plain sight?"

"Where indeed?" The duke glances at the title card. "*The Archangel leaving Adam and Eve.*" He leans lightly on his cane, which I'm sure is mostly for show. "Must be when the couple was turned away from the garden."

Torrance dips his chin but glances at the group of men who've now entered the Great Room. "Was it an apt punishment for their crime, Carew?"

Adam and Eve ate the forbidden apple. A solitary apple. It wasn't even a slice of my Tantie Telma's tart. I shake my head. "No, Your Grace. I think the travail women experience in childbirth is particularly cruel punishment for a delicious apple. Pregnancy is often deadly for mother and child."

"And you would know. I hear you've delivered many babies. You even helped the late Mrs. Wilcox."

His tone sounds like a question. If he's searching for something, I am bound by my loyalty to my patients to never admit specifics. I stick to the barest of facts. "I've been of service to the Wilcoxes for a long time. You would've enjoyed meeting Mrs. Wilcox. And Mr. Wilcox."

"I did meet Mr. Wilcox. I showed up an hour too late to stop a wedding. He was a very gentlemanly man."

What wedding? He can't mean Lady Hampton's to the duke's former best friend, Tavis Palmers, the late Lord Hampton. I'm stunned at the possibility, but this is not a conversation for here. It's too public. London is ever hunting for gossip.

Instead, I lift my hands and try to reframe the image, but all I see is naked folks and an angel. "I'm a book man. I prefer words to pictures. A novel or a play is my delight. Do you like the painting, Torrance?"

The sigh he releases is harsh. "Not particularly, but the artist paints the angel with no wings. What angel has none?" The duke seems to glance a little longer, maybe more deeply, at the painting. "But the interpretation is excellent. A spirit battling for the truth shouldn't need them. A common man can be used for judgment."

"With judgment, there is a need for punishment. That is the next step, is it not?"

He shifts a little and then offers a small smile. "We all must pay. I suppose that is true most of all."

Why is the duke toying with me? He should just state my offense and be done with it. "Your Grace, I know I've upset Miss Scarlett Wilcox. You don't have to be cryptic. Just tell me what I did, and I'll fix it. She's charming but sharp witted. Perhaps we throw too many barbs. Perhaps what I meant as a jest has hurt her. That is the last thing I want."

He cranes his neck up to the ceiling. "If I knew something, not saying that I do, it wouldn't be my place to say. I mean if you knew something that I've gotten wrong, you'd tell me, Carew. Wouldn't you?"

Why has my question turn into an opportunity for one of Torrance's cryptic inquiries? I'm ready to go. I can get a nap and a luncheon before having to make my evening rounds. "I'm your friend. I'll always try my best to advise you. I do the same with all my patients. Now, please, tell me what this summons is about. Please say it has nothing to do with a bet. Lord Mark Sebastian disclosed the details of the last one when you tried to make me a match for Sebastian's bride."

Torrance starts to laugh and picks up his cane, the silver handle shaped like a rook from a gleaming chess set. An odd choice for anyone but the duke. I've seen his decor in his office—some of the rarest chessboards I've ever seen.

"How was I to know that you love Shakespeare? Mr. Carew, you bested all the clowns who came to Anya House to compete for the former Georgina Wilcox. Doesn't matter. She's happily married to the man she loves."

Guess that's some sort of compliment, to be able to read and like plays. I look directly in the duke's eyes. "If not for you, I'd not be here."

My friend offers a few chuckles. "Carew, we must make an art lover of you. That's something the future Mrs. Carew will appreciate."

"What?" I think I blink twice. "Have you been to Cheapside to visit with my aunts? All they talk of is marriage. They want me to find a nice girl, and when I do, they constantly measure everyone against Eveline Gray."

Torrance puts both hands on his cane. He sways for a moment as he holds in his glee. "No. I haven't sent my henchman, as you've called him, to spy on you. Mr. Steele has been very busy."

Does that mean if Steele were free, I'd be followed? Oh, the many conspiracies that come to mind when dealing with a conspiratorial duke. "Torrance, what's going on? I hate being late or feeling as if I've missed important news. That's a habit I'd like to break."

"Mr. Carew. There is someone for you to meet." He points to the group of young men.

The one who seemed familiar glances at us. His beautifully polished boots, in a sea of leather slippers, are something I've seen. Taking a closer look, I note that the young man is smartly tailored with a great barrel-knotted cravat.

He's shorter than I, the height of Scarlett Wilcox, the young woman who has stopped . . .

Cold sweat drips down my spine as I realize I'm witnessing a greater scandal than any I've ever known. Scarlett Wilcox is dressed as a man, and she's mingling in this crowd like nothing is amiss.

Chapter 7

SCARLETT—THE LAST PERSON ON EARTH

My heart begins to tick a little faster. My face feels hot. These pasted-on sideburns may slip or fall off.

The duke saw me earlier, but he carried on like nothing unusual had occurred. He knows I sneak into these lectures at Royal Society all the time, but I don't think he's ever seen me in my full disguise—sideburns, boots, and breeches.

Yet the duke's glance isn't what's dumped hot coals on me. That blasted Carew has seen me. He's here, and I've been pointed out. Why did the Royal Society lecture have to be delayed, today of all days?

I know he's crafting barbs to condemn me or tell me why I'm wrong. Maybe I'm too bold, but I have a debt to pay and I'll follow through. I'll save my friend's sight no matter what Stephen Adam Carew says.

The duke waves for me. The imaginary steam I see coming from the physician's head is surely enough to burn me alive.

I steel my courage. Plodding like an indignant man of science, I head to them. "Your Grace, a pleasure to see you and your company." I dip my chin, resisting everything that's been ingrained in me to curtsy. "Will you introduce me to your friend?"

"Why don't you start with your name?" Stephen Adam Carew

grouses at me. His tone is tight and grating. "Tell it to me with that horrid fake accent."

I have no accent. Carew's the one with the accent, one he tries to suppress. His quips are said to provoke me, to make me do something rash or stupid. He thinks I'm impulsive.

"Your Grace, it seems your belligerent friend has not learned manners. Good day."

When I bow to walk away, I see the anger in Carew's face turn to panic.

"Torrance, stop her—"

"Wilcox, do not be in a rush to leave." The duke seems calm, not rattled in the least by my appearance. "Come, tell us what you've learned. I've watched you enjoying the exhibition."

"The canvasses are everywhere, as are the newspapermen. They snidely stand side by side making notes of visitors as well as writing down observations of us as much as the art. I was just chatting with one who works for the *Sun*."

Carew's rich skin turns pale. He mumbles about columns and scandals. His words may have even become French, or is that Spanish? Maybe a mix, a special Trini dialect.

Then I clearly hear him call me a d'yavol. That's Russian—and rude.

The duke gawks at him. "Carew, you clearly owe Wilcox an apology. It's obvious that he knows what he's doing. Haranguing him about methods would be counterproductive, and perhaps too revealing for the Great Room."

My cough hides my laughter. My enjoyment of the physician's agony exposes my youthful zeal. That's our thing: antagonism. "Let me show you two my favorite." I lead them a little to the left, point them to a painting of two boys, standing in front of an angelic-looking lady. The boys tie the sad-looking woman to a bull. "According to the card, it's the *Punishment of Dirce*."

The duke leans a little closer. "By Howard. I saw a bronze of this in Glasgow. It's quite powerful. I want to say poor Dirce, but she probably deserves the punishment."

"Your Grace, Mr. Wilcox, are we to pretend nothing has occurred?" Carew looks as if he's going to rip up the hat in his hand. "This is wrong."

"No, you are wrong." I love saying that aloud. "The painting is exquisite. Look at the curve of the muscles, the tense stance of two wanting justice, even the rope around the bull's head, tightening, tightening . . . is so lifelike. That's power."

The duke opens then closes his mouth. "Such a way with words, Wilcox."

"I see curves, sir." Carew grinds his teeth. "Ones I shouldn't. Your breeches are too formfitting. Everyone can see everything."

Taking the hat from his hand, I reblock it, shaping the felt with my hands. "I could say the same of your attire, but you're the one complaining."

He colors more.

But his legs—very muscled, very toned—seem solid. My throat tightens a little. I hadn't noticed what good shape my physician stays in.

"That's enough looking, both of you." The duke snaps his fingers to raise our gazes. "Any more of this and one might think you've compromised each other. Perhaps that is why you two have had a falling-out."

"No. No. No." Carew and I say this together. We even sound alike.

"Well, at least you can agree on something." The duke turns back to the painting. "While reporters circle, let's talk of the technique the painter demonstrates. Such bold strokes, Carew. See the woman in the background, Wilcox? She looks so innocent, but it's she who's causing her twins to exact revenge."

"Twins? Tw . . ." My voice falters and I sound like old Scarlett, the one waiting for men with vision to fix things. No more waiting for the world to make a place for women in science, to pay attention to the plight of the sick. As my mama used to say with her bold Jamaican accent, *"If yuh waan good, yuh nose haffi run."*

She'd run her nose, celebrating the good I do, because Mama

believed that if you want something done right, you do it your-self. I look Carew in the eye. "If yuh waan good, yuh nose haffi run." My voice is bolder. I'm honoring Mama and I'm making change any way I can. "Guess the two sons are fixing things."

"You're sure that it's two sons?" Carew asks. "One can never be too careful."

"They're in tunics, sir. Not breeches. I feel confident you'll make minimal errors assessing their sex. Well, no more than usual."

Carew's brownish-black eyes shrink, becoming more pitiful. "What are you implying, Wilcox?"

"Not enough, if you don't understand."

"Monkey doh see he own tail." His accent sounds thick as he recites this adage from Trinidad. He collects himself. "It means you're quick to criticize and can't see your own flaws."

"Did you just call me a monkey?" Oh, if I had a banana or plantain, I'd smash it in his pretty face.

The duke steps between us. "Gentlemen, the painting. I see you're taking sides. Who's for the innocent mother, Antiope? She's maligned and tricked by Dirce, the woman in the front. Antiope is forced to give up her twins. That's years of separation. So much wasted time."

"And the obvious solution for women is to go to extremes. Typical." Carew frowns more. "Made her poor sons tie Dirce to an angry bull."

The duke shifts his hands like they are a scale trying to mete out justice. "Don't think vengeance is exclusive to men. My friend, look at the power. We are moments away from Dirce being dragged to death for her crimes."

I'm a little stunned by the glee in his tone. "Your Grace, that's sinister. Must Dirce die? Can't there be another outcome?"

The patient man stares at the beautiful but horrendous painting. "I don't know, Wilcox. It's a crime to deprive a parent of a child or children." The duke sighs. "Dirce's lies caused great harm to Antiope. Time is the one thing you never get back."

The tension radiating from him feels like an inferno. It's in the air, in the room filled with newspapermen. It's as strong as I imagine the rope wrapping about Dirce. "Your Grace, you've told me art is personal. Who do you see yourself as in the painting? Are you the wronged mother, or the wicked but helpless Dirce?"

Carew shakes his head. "Torrance is not..." He closes his mouth, then perhaps thinks. "Torrance, are you creating a metaphor to explain your revenge?"

The duke shrugs. "My view shifts. It's very dependent upon how I feel. I suppose I'm fickle. And that's why I need both of your help. There are some things I must do."

I fold my arms across my bosom, then immediately drop them to my side. "I'm not helping you rope any bull."

The physician groans. "I hate to admit this, but I agree with Wilcox. I think it's best to forgive and forget and let sleeping dogs lie."

"Mixing metaphors?" The duke chuckles. "I told you you were funny, Carew."

The laughter is false. Anyone who's been around the duke and seen the newspaper articles reporting about the resignations from Court of Chancery knows Torrance is the bull. Unfortunately, he's not done trampling his enemies. "Your Grace, where do they hang the mercy paintings?"

Mr. Carew glances at me. I know he agrees. I hate that I know him so well.

The duke folds his arms and hangs his cane from the crook of his elbow. "I believe they are yet to be painted. And if this is to be personal, I shall not be Dirce. I'll not be the one begging. Weakness has never been profitable."

Carew steps in front of the duke. "What's with you, man? Are you not feeling well? Your tone is too sinister, even more so for you. I demand to know what has occurred, other than the present Wilcox foolishness."

The duke looks vulnerable for a moment, almost cornered. He leads us to a private alcove. "My mother is coming."

"The Princess Elizaveta Abramovna Gannibal Charles is coming from St. Petersburg." Carew seems shocked. He covers his mouth, those full ashy lips. "Your mother, the one who never leaves her city of rivers."

"Da. She'll leave her cozy dacha by the river and come to dreary old London in a few weeks."

"Torrance, I've known you a long time," Carew says, "even before your elevation, when were you just Jahleel Charles. Why would the Blackamoor Russian princess who vowed never to let her slippers touch such an evil city as London come now? Is she coming for revenge, too?"

"My health is good for now." He bites his lip. The duke does look a little thin. Though his light olive skin seems warm, I detect no signs of illness. "You both know I can't stop another episode of my sickness from returning. The battle back to health gets more difficult. I need to be prepared. I need someone to advocate for me and those I love. A caretaker to protect what I hold dear."

I suppose it would be terrible to mention my sister's plans to exclude the duke this year.

Carew puts a hand on the duke's shoulder. "The conversation about making provisions for illness is one I have too often with patients. Often, it's too late, when they're on their sickbeds. But, as stubborn as you are, I know you're not giving up."

"My instructions are being written. They will be carried out. But like you two when you talk, I fight every day. I fight to be strong for my little Lidochka. I fight for the Wilcoxes, even the one who hates me."

No. I definitely won't mention that Katherine's trying to exclude him from Lydia's birthday party. I try to lighten the duke's tense mood. "Remember you have a bet to win, which will force that one to be nice."

Carew frowns again. Such a shame his mouth has no lotion or coconut butter to smooth away dryness. The man is either forgetful or working too hard and showing signs of exhaustion. Either scenario is a crime against such beautiful lips.

"Your Grace? Please let there not be another bet."

The duke shakes his head. "There are things to look forward to, even if Lady Hampton wishes I crawl back to the rivers of St. Petersburg."

I want to tell him not to leave, but I need to be as good of a friend to the duke as he's been to me and my family. "You could spare yourself more heartache. Think of how everyone teases Carew to move on from perfect Eveline. I mean, Lady Derand."

The duke cuts his gaze to me as if I've betrayed him. "It's not that simple, Wilcox. I'm too invested in Lydia's care to walk away. I love her as if she were my daughter. Pity her own father is dead."

His tone sounds dramatic, and he looks at me as if I have something to confess. I have nothing. I know he loves Lydia, all of us.

For some reason, Carew looks to the ground like he's unsure of where to step, even though none of us have moved. When he finally looks up, he says, "It's good that you care for the little girl. I was there when she was born. It's been a struggle for her to live, but you've made a difference. I've never seen Lydia livelier."

The newspapermen begin to leave.

The duke puts the tip of his cane on the floor. "Carew, I'll get to the point. I have things to take care of. Wilcox here needs a chaperone, and Mr. Steele can't do it. He's on his way to St. Petersburg."

"Scarlett Wilcox needs no chaperone. She needs to go home." Carew blinks like his head has become light. He gets like that when he works too much.

With a firm handshake, I grasp his cold fingers. "S. Wilcox. Scotland Wilcox to be sure. Respect the name." I make my voice sound extra deep. "The physician can go. I need no supervision."

"It's trouble," Carew says. "It's a scandal. It's a Scarlett."

"Keep your voice down, sir." The duke leans closer to me. "I need you to keep Wilcox in your sights."

The physician waves his hand from my top hat to my boots. "Exactly how am I to miss this? When she's dressed—"

"By not pointing." The duke glares at him. "Wilcox needs a chaperone. I need this favor."

"Your Grace," I say, "I'll be fine on my own. I'll catch a hackney to Anya House when I'm done with the lecture, that is, if it ever begins. Lord Livingston is supposed to be teaching on eye dissection. The start is so late, that I fear it might be canceled. I should be gone by now. Mr. Thom—"

"I've sent him away to rest," the duke says. "He's over-worked. That can lead to problems."

Carew rubs his eyes. "I'm your friend too, Sca—Scotland. I believe you have forgotten this." He pauses trying to lower his voice. "And this disguise is terrible. Torrance, you're good with her dressing up like a man?"

There he goes again. Because he's a gentleman, Carew thinks I have no right to an opinion or breeches. I almost put a hand to my hip and call him *Mr. Stuffy*. "I can take care of myself."

"But that's not our bargain, Wilcox," the duke chides me. "We stick to the rules."

"Bargain? What bargain, Torrance?" Carew sounds wound up like a tight spring. "It's another crazy bet? I walked into the last one blind. I want to know what it is."

"Blind is correct," I say. "I think you're always in that state. When will you and others join Lord Livingston's work to fix these conditions?"

"Livingston's not solving anything except waiting times at brothels. Too much book smart, no street smart." Carew says, "You're supposed to be a young woman. You get caught and the Wilcoxes will face ruin again."

Can't back down, even if he has a point. So I laugh. "You act like this is my first time. Hardly."

"What do you mean, not your first time?" Carew's brownish-black eyes scatter.

"Not a virgin to troubles, I see."

The duke holds up a hand to him, almost like he wishes to punch the physician. "Is this how you two argue? And you complain about Lady Hampton and me." He shakes fingers at both of us. "This is unprofessional behavior. I need you both to calm."

"Carew should go. He's trying not to yawn, Your Grace. Perhaps if he weren't out trying to find the replacement for Miss Perfect, he'd get more rest."

"Don't be concerned about my sleep, Wilcox. I don't have a false beard or have to falsify my attendance anywhere. I'll take no advice from you."

"You should." I force my tone to lower. "Last week you could hardly stay awake for bunny dissection."

"Well, it's bunnies, Scarle . . . tt. You were here last week too?" He steps closer, and if I didn't know him like the back of my hand, I'd think he's about to throttle me.

"Scarlett, you're reckless." Anger lives in the tightening muscles of his jaw. So handsome and stupid, working—or carousing—too hard. Why are men stupid?

"Sirs, I'm going to find the room for the Royal Society meeting and just wait. Hopefully the delay won't be too much longer. Lord Livingston won't disappoint me. He never does. Good day, Your Grace. Mr. Carew."

The physician clasps my arm. "Wait. This isn't settled." He won't let go, and tells the duke, "Yes, I'll babysit. I'm one born to suffer fools. This one I suffer gladly." Carew fixes a smile on his lip, stretching the ashy corners of his mouth. "See, I live to serve Scotland Wilcox."

Torrance glances at me. "Please, S. Wilcox, indulge me."

When I nod, the duke turns to the physician. "It's agreed. Return Wilcox to Anya House when you're done."

Another wave of newspapermen fills the Great Room as we

leave. The duke disappears, leaving me with Mr. Carew, who refuses to let go.

"Listen, spoiled one. Do exactly what I say or I'll put you over my shoulder and take you out of here and drop you to your sisters at Ground Street."

"Isn't that just like you, Carew? Making promises you can't keep."

With my thumb, I smudge the ash from his mouth. The fresh polish of my leather gloves does the trick, making those lips smooth. "There, something nice to look at, if you must stay."

I turn, walk against the crowds to go to the lecture. My physician fusses and follows. I think he's rambling about being Antiope, and that he's the innocent one. Seeing more peers and newspapermen gather at Somerset House, I know I'm the one who'll get trampled by bulls in this male-dominated world.

Chapter 8

SCARLETT—SOMERSET HOUSE, CARIBBEAN ESCORT

Hurrying through the crowds, I turn down a corridor and hear my boot heels clacking against the bare marble floors. I'm again at the entrance. Before I turn back, I see the duke. Torrance stands by the marble River God meeting with a man—a nice-looking, tall one with warm brown skin.

In London, seeing dignified Blackamoors is not rare, but ones who are barristers with a nearly perfect record of wins for the Crown and often drawn in sketches for the newspapers is. "He's a lot better looking than in the cartoons."

"What? Who's better?" Carew is at my side, looking left and right.

"Keep your voice down." I point to the duke and the famed Earl of Ashbrook.

The physician snarls and glances at me, like he always does, with heated contempt. Carew will never see me as an equal or as someone with valid opinions or a mind for science. Just a silly little woman. Now a spoiled woman in men's clothes.

"No explanation, Wilcox? I'm waiting." He wants my words, but that doesn't mean he's ready to listen.

Ignoring him, I turn back to the River God, but the duke and Lord Ashbrook are still talking. Is it a meeting? Does the duke need legal advice?

Carew bumps into me. "Sorry."

"Go home and sleep. I'm quite fine navigating Somerset House. Probably better than you."

I turn and his long arm clasps my shoulder. "Not so fast."

The slight accent ramps again. When he's not self-conscious, he lets it be free. Then, his words, that of the Trinidadian medicine man, are as potent ever.

"Please, Scarlett. Be reasonable." There's a low begging quality to his voice that makes this tone irresistible. "Come away with me."

"Why?"

"You're heading the wrong direction."

"I know—" Before my response has fully left my mouth, I trip and fall into the physician. For a moment, his well-muscled arm wraps around my padded chest. Sadly, I feel nothing.

He keeps us both upright. I'm grateful for my padding and the hope that my heart has moved on from wanting the impossible Stephen Adam Carew.

I shake free. "Thank you."

His gaze falls to where my bosom would be. Frowning, he says, "I'm not sure why you've made a misstep, but you smell nice, Wilcox."

Mark's eau is the scent. "It's a gift from a real man."

"What, Wilcox?" he says. "I have difficulty hearing you. Your sideburns must be muffling things."

The physician yawns and follows me as I walk closer to Torrance and Ashbrook. Perhaps I can read lips.

"Why do you care about Ashbrook, Wilcox? He's married with two children. He's not someone the duke can foist on you to win his bet."

If I turn and slug Carew, I'll probably hurt my knuckles along the hard palatine bone of his nose, or the maxilla of his jaw. So, I settle for menacing bluster. "Must you talk? Can't you just follow me around like a lost puppy?"

The physician gets to my side and sighs so loudly I think the statue of the River God might awaken. "If you give this up now, I'll take you to get an ice."

A sweet dessert?

That's what he thinks will fix everything. "Stephen Adam Carew, you're stuck in the mud. I refuse to be stuck with you. I won't let you deter me from my mission. While you wait, the world still turns."

His brow furrows like he's heard me, but I know the stubborn man only hears his own thoughts.

"Nothing wrong with being deliberate, Wilcox."

"Deliberate or snail-like? Sir, you'll always be too slow in making up your mind. I'll act and live."

"Didn't hear anything about you being a thinker. You're quick to jump to conclusions but slow to apologize. Consider reversing these stances."

"No more advice." Like the duke, I flick my wrist at Carew. "I have no use for you. Be gone."

"I'm not your servant, but Torrance has appointed me your guardian today. Do your sisters know you have such a rude mouth?"

"Yes. They all do."

His handsome face of deep bronze, like roasted cocoa pods, shakes in laughter. "I missed you, Wilcox."

I . . . I'm stunned.

The man notices nothing but illness. The old me realizes that this singular moment of Stephen Adam Carew being kind or thoughtful will pull me back into a dark place—reading into words that mean nothing, sharing glances that leave me bereft and alone.

So, I can't be kind to him. Ever. "How does one miss the bane of her existence? If I seek anyone, it will be one who's daring, not a fool who refuses to give his opinion unless it is a barb."

"That's harsh, Wilcox. Don't pout, little one."

"You're a Neanderthal who'll continually make my age or station in life the butt of his jokes. You're not someone I'll ever miss. In fact, these moments with you make me ill."

While he gathers his face from the floor, I notice that the duke and Ashbrook have left. I turn and walk the other way.

The duke's dealings will be a mystery to figure out later.

Carew steps into my path. His height towers, but I'd feel his presence from across the room.

"You need to convince me why this costume is necessary. Women and children can come to the exhibition, Scarlett."

He's said my name.

He's the only one who lets it hang in the air for at least a second longer than it should. His voice sets my teeth on edge, and I feel like he wants to punish me for being naughty. For some reason the notion is exciting. The proper torture would be his ashy lips against mine.

"You're perspiring, Wilcox. Are you having a reaction to the paint on your face? It does give you a very good shadow of a beard, but the cosmetic or coal paint can't be healthy."

He bends down. His face is close. His breath smells of delicious medicinal peppermint. "Scarlett?"

Blast it. "I'm fine. Bye."

"Scarlett," his tone sweetens—all honey, peppermint, and accent. "You're the person I wanted to see. Not like this, though."

He blathers on, but I ignore everything but the word *person*. Not woman, or beloved being, and with the way I'm dressed, not even man. I'm forever a nobody in his eyes, forever unreachable or touchable.

I offer him what I hope is a manly smile. "Thank you for your concern. Now run along." Again, I give him the duke's dismissive wave again. "So long."

"Now, Wilcox, don't be like this."

I toss him a *whatever* look, turn and leave.

But his hand clasps mine.

Not sure what happens to my brainbox, or any one's brainbox when feelings, unequal or unrequited or unimaginable, rage.

My mind blanks.

My skin warms as his fingertips, gentle firm ones, skilled with a scalpel or suturing needle, find the slim unprotected spot on my wrist.

Skin to skin contact—not my leather gloves or dancing gloves—but person to person, man to woman.

We've held hands once or twice, if dancing counts. Sort of . . . maybe. I know I held his, once.

I took charge.

The man was having the worst day. The strumpet he thought of marrying got tired of waiting and married someone else. I offered the foolish hurting man comfort, hoping my touch would say all the things I couldn't. That he was worthy of honesty. That he deserved better.

When he got up from the duke's table, his eyes met mine and he offered me a pat on the head. I have hated him with the passion of a thousand suns ever since.

But he is still holding my fingers in his.

A noise draws his attention away. He lets go. I'm free.

His glance returns. And I know the brownish almost black eyes see me as nothing but a fool in a waistcoat. Is ten years' difference in age an insurmountable distance?

Then he says, all pepperminty and smooth, "Reporters are here. I won't let you get caught. I'll cause a distraction. I'll save you."

There's no saving me, not from danger or waiting on miracles. I have nothing but science. That's enough. "Walk away. Let the wayward soul suffer consequences alone."

I start to the lecture room. My notebook of sketches is in my satchel. I have paper and pencil to take notes.

A shadow soon overtakes me. I stop, and he keeps going for a moment. It's a lovely view—squared shoulders, thick twists of curls on top, low on the sides. Warm eyes turn to glower at me. He's furious. "I won't do that. I'm a gentleman. Though I'm not indebted to your minder, I do feel protective of the Wilcoxes. I'll help you and hope my name and aspirations won't burn to the ground for you."

Can I be simultaneously horrified and joyful at such a grand gesture? This is why I can't be around him. I'm supposed to be a logical woman of science. I refuse to let an accent infused with peppermint distract me.

"Thank you, Mr. Carew, but I shan't keep you. Lovely to see you again." There, that is said with the calm and the coldness of ice. Katherine would admire my hateful tone. "Good day."

I turn from his stunned expression, but his voice won't leave me. "Now, Sc . . . Scotland. I might've been too hasty. Don't go."

Stupid me. Stupid heart. I fight myself and spin back to him.

There's no need. He catches up to me and extends that sweet brotherly smile. We get to the lecture room and it's still empty. I can sense Carew's growing pleasure at my disappointment.

"Come, Wilcox," he says. "While we wait on Livingston, let's view more art together. And then I'll take you for an ice. You do like Gunter's pineapple. This I recall."

He nudges my shoulder, and I see people are looking. I've probably acted too much like a disappointed silly female, one who can't resist a pineapple ice. "Fine." I plod next to Mr. Carew, remembering to walk like an uptight male and to keep my hips stiff. As I've gotten older and wider, they love to sway and betray me.

Funny, Carew doesn't walk like the others. There's a bit of rhythm in his steps and, like the duke, there's a confident swagger. Most men don't have that. They are too busy observing others.

We duck into the Great Room. Among the hanging canvasses, I see one that seems out of place. A couple with hands entwined, one finger has a visible gold band. "Look at that, Mr. Carew. Such an odd and showy painting."

His brow furrows. "You think it wrong?"

"Wrong? No. But maybe I'm offended by its snobbery. It's bragging of domestic bliss."

He laughs a little, then holds in more. "Let's see what the card says. Hmm. *The Wedding Band.*" His chortle sounds sharp. "Speaking of wedding bands, you're not seriously going to let the duke or Lady Hampton choose a mate for you?"

A quick glance shows me no one is listening to us. "Never

Katherine. She made a wrong choice." A fun-loving, husband-that-burnt-up-all-your-money choice. "I'd never let her pick."

Carew's face sobers. "But you'd let the duke?"

"As far as I know, he's not had a bad marriage."

"That's not an answer." Carew's head tilts and he begins to flatten my collar. "Please tell me you've not agreed to this."

Agreed to what? That his fingers shouldn't be near my neck? Agree that he must oil his hands in lavender and cocoa butter, but not his lips?

He finally pulls away, and I breathe more deeply.

"Get your tailor, Wilcox, to . . . What am I saying? This charade needs to stop."

"What charade? I come to Somerset House for the lectures. That has nothing to with the duke or my sister."

"Good, then you'll not let Torrance—"

"The duke and I have an arrangement. I'm allowed under supervision to go about my research in any way I see fit. He's allowed to choose who I'll marry this year."

That mouth of his forms the biggest frown I've ever seen. "That's not right, Wilcox."

"I think it is. And he knows me well enough to choose wisely. Marriage after all is nothing but a name change. My want of a mate is the use of a name to publish."

Carew blinks so fast I think he's about to faint. "Torrance doesn't know you. I've known you longer, and I don't think—"

"Carew?" The Earl of Livingston comes over. "That is you. Now, here, I didn't think you were much of an art lover."

Stephen Adam Carew quotes Shakespeare beautifully. What would give the earl, or anyone else, the impression that the physician doesn't like art?

The earl gawks at me. My pulse panics. I fear he can see through my disguise. "Who is this? Wait, I've seen you in my lectures."

"Well, I enjoyed your past lectures. They're always so insightful. Today's lecture is late, I hope it's not canceled." I make my voice deep. "I came specifically to hear your lecture on eye anatomy."

"Because of the large crowds for the Annual Exhibition, the committee canceled my lecture. They sent word late last night. They had a time finding me." Lord Livingston grins, waggles his thin brows. Then his chest puffs up like a hot air balloon. "So, you've been to past lectures. Have we been introduced?" The earl taps his chin. "There is something familiar—"

"No, not possible," Carew says. "I mean, he's just returned to town recently."

This starts the earl looking at me more intently, but I'm greatly disappointed at the canceled lecture. Up early for nothing. Arguing with Carew is also worthless.

"Do we know each other, sir?" The earl taps his chin. "I'm good with faces."

Uh-oh. I must distract him. "Well, everyone knows the research of Alexander Melton, the fourth Earl of Livingston. Your knowledge of the eye is superior to everyone. You are renowned."

Smiling widely, the earl puts a hand to his buff coat. "Renowned? Well, I don't like to brag."

"Yes," Carew says, "don't."

"And so, Carew, who is this, and does he come with a large purse? Since you won't risk your money in card games, perhaps this gentleman can."

I lean forward. "I'm Scotland—"

"Scotland Carew," the physician says, "my cousin visiting for the summer."

What? Why the lie? Mr. Carew hates lies, but once a thing is said, there's no changing it. "Yes. Just taking a break from Inverness Academy. I wish to be a physician like my dear cousin."

"A student." Livingston frowns, looking much less impressed. "Well, that means low funds. Where are the visitors, the ones coming with the plantation or habitation money from their fathers? Or does that wealth only happen for the daughters?"

I cringe at his statement and begin to reconsider the notion of

Livingston being a great man. Nonetheless, he's one of the few who knows the intricacy of eye anatomy in London. Beggars can't be choosy.

Mr. Carew looks bothered. "Sir, I think you have to go to the coastal communities for that type of money. I hear from a friend of a friend that the author of *Sense and Sensibility* is working on a novel about a woman from the islands who bring deh kind of money." His accent becomes stronger. It's intentional, putting emphasis on his d's, adding rhythm to consonants. "Meh. I believe there's a boardinghouse there for women of color. Deh sez taking in women of large fortunes."

I don't believe Stephen Adam Carew just said that with a straight face—no laughter curling his lips. And I have to keep my humor to myself. It's another fun discovery about him. He's a reader of frivolous novels by A. Lady. Carew has the same taste as the Prince Regent.

"Bath, you say?" Livingston nods, then chortles. "You kidder. Carew, you get funnier the more we become acquainted."

I don't want to be more acquainted. I want the lecture. "But, sir, when will be the next time you present at Somerset? I must learn eye anatomy from the best."

"It will be some time, Scotland Carew."

I'm heartbroken. Mr. Thom doesn't have long. The cataracts will progress and destroy all of his sight. "Oh, I see."

The earl nods. "I see your cousin is disappointed. I have an idea. A few of us are going to White's on St. James. A card game will be afoot, and then a couple of blocks away is one of my favorite places for evening entertainment. I'll take the time to share my lecture and answer all the questions you have if you come."

"I have sketches, my lord. I'd love for you to annotate them."

"Like an autograph?" The earl's chin lifts.

He's a brilliant fool, but I'm desperate, so I say, "I'd love you to."

Carew shakes his head and sighs in peppermint. "We'd love

to, but not today. Cousin, we have to go to that thing. We can catch Livingston's lecture another time."

My alleged cousin tilts his head trying to motion for me to leave. He's looking over the crowd for a path to escape. "Come along, Scotland Carew. Since Livingston is not teaching today, he must be here for the art."

"Yes, but I'm bored. And when the Royal Society meets next week, they've invited anatomy models from Henry Fuseli. They will perform a study of muscular and skeletal concerns in the nude. I'm not sure why the special effort. One can just go to Madame Rosebud's."

The earl is giggling like a schoolboy, and they have the nerve to think women are silly.

"I'd rather talk about ocular health today. Lord Livingston, let's go to White's."

The earl claps. "Excellent. White's it is. Bring that island money."

"A little." I jingle my coin purse. "See you later, cousin." I dip my head and proceed to leave with Livingston.

Then I hear a cough and a grunt. "It would be rude to not go with my cousin on his first time at White's."

I turn and see an expression on Carew's face I've never seen. He looks in pain. The agony he feels, fretting about what I'll experience in Livingston's company, makes me . . . happy.

Stephen Adam Carew, my new cousin, may not see me as an equal, but he will learn that I can be a great terror to someone short on patience.

By the darkening of his cheeks and his eyes, I think the good physician is about halfway en route to an implosion.

Chapter 9

STEPHEN—WHITE'S GENTLEMEN'S CLUB

It takes an eternity to find Benny. He hasn't parked at the closest mews, but one further down the river. When I finally find him, I fall into the carriage mumbling about Scarlett and White's. *So tired . . .*

I think that is when I died. All I see is darkness, and something feels like it's shaking me.

"Mr. Carew! Mr. Carew!"

"Yes, Lord!"

"Sir, wake up."

I open my eyes, ready to see angels . . . hoping for angels. "Benny?"

The sun has begun to lower. There are pinks and reds in the darkening sky.

"Sir, yuh need to go home. Yuh been up too long. Yuh saying daft things about Scarlett Wilcox."

Oh goodness. "What did I say?"

"That she's a man and yuh wished she was a lady."

Well, that's true.

"And he smelled nice."

I sit up straight. I have nothing to correct. Scarlett as Scotland did smell nice. "Are we at White's?"

"Yes. But, sir, yuh need to eat, to sleep. Yuh don't need to be chasing Miss Wilcox."

"He . . . she is under my protection. If I tell the Duke of Torrance that I lost her to Livingston, he'll kill me."

Benny jerks me to my feet. "Yuh didn't say Torrance was involved. He's got people everywhere snooping, looking for scandal. Yuh lose the Wilcox girl, yuh lose him as a funder for yuh hospital project. Yuh lose him, yuh lose the two investors yuh've secured."

I don't mention that I've already lost the others because of my delays.

My man-of-all-work panics. Benny looks unhinged, talking of loss while he paces. He points at me. "Yuh always saying how smart Miss Wilcox is. Could she truly be in dat much danger? Are we in trouble?"

I grab his arm to stop him going back and forth. "She's in there with Livingston. I'll go get her."

"With the drunk earl? So she truly dressed as a man and went into White's? That wasn't tired babbling? Yuh know yuh say the craziest things when yuh're exhausted. And yuh faint. It's wild."

"Yes, Miss Wilcox is in disguise." I say. "It's a gentlemen's club. She's not a gentleman and none of us are white. Can you not see how many problems can arise?"

Benny howls with laughter. "It's White's. A gentlemen's club. A brown lady in breeches has infiltrated."

When he put it like that, it's even more terrifying.

"Boy, sir. She's bold. No wonder yuh always talking about her."

Well, at least he's not pacing anymore. "You finished? Please park at the close mews or stay here and be vigilant. I'm going to grab her, and we'll need a fast getaway."

"Be careful grabbing the gentlewoman, sir."

I shake my head. I leave my hat and gloves on the seat of my carriage and head into White's.

Could Livingston have picked up on Scarlett's disguise? The earl is a smart fellow. If he hadn't driven Scotland, I'd have taken that girl to Anya House. And I would have enjoyed every minute of telling her how foolish her actions are.

Scarlett has robbed me of the immediate opportunity to set her straight, but I will get to it before the night is over. "Yes. Stay close. I'm going to get her. Over my shoulder, dropped into the carriage, and then back, to the duke."

"Stay calm, sir. You can do anything." Benny yells this as he drives past me.

I stand on the pavement outside the oldest and most famous men's club in London. It's probably packed in there. Flexing my fingers, preparing to wrench her scrawny neck, I hope and pray she hasn't already been exposed.

I want to curse under my breath, but I need too much favor. At the door, about to go inside, I'm struck by the notion that something must be causing her to be reckless. Maybe whatever made her stop talking to me is related to this irrational behavior.

I rub at my eyes. I feel irrational. Maybe I should've told Benny to follow behind the magistrate's cart when they send me away for throttling the wild woman.

Trying to remain calm, I count my steps as I enter White's. A man at the vestibule asks, "Are you a member?"

"No, but I'm meeting Lord Livingston."

The man nods. "He said to expect you."

The greeter is dressed as a gentleman, but I feel as if he's truly a tall footman ready to toss out all who are unwelcome. He flips through papers, and I wait for him to tell me where to find the earl.

Every moment, every second of delay that keeps me from seeing Scarlett—ensuring she's fine, not exposed—tortures my soul. "Excuse me, where might I find Lord Livingston?"

The fellow clears his throat. "You don't have a hat or coat?"

"My carriage. I left them there. I don't intend to stay long."

He nods. "Next time, if you bring the hat, I'll give you a marker. If you bring the coat, I'll give you a second marker, Mr. . . . ?"

"Mr. Carew. Please tell—"

The attendant flips through a book on the table he stands behind. "Bring at least a hat next time."

Time is ticking away. "Yes. I'll bring one." I must've lost my mind. This delay is hell. "Yes, I've learned my lesson. Help."

The fellow killing me slowly leans a little over the table and points into the club. "The earl and his party are upstairs."

With a nod, I move deeper into White's. The pale walls are washed in candlelight. Tables and elegant sofas are all around. Men lounge and drink and make wagers over the silliest things. One just said something about hot-air ballooning.

This place is for the ton, the highest peerages. In the choice seats like next to the bay window sits the august Duke of Wellington, the man who defeated the nasty Napoleon.

I've been here in the company of Torrance and a few other members. I'm not a member, have never sought to be one, not that this place is looking for or hurting for new blood.

No one's looking at me until I reach the stairs. I like that I'm mostly invisible. That means I won't be asked awkward questions on how I've become a gentleman. No one will assume or pretend to assume that I'm part of the waitstaff.

The invisibility means I'm protected from the anger of those hating the changes that the world has thrust upon their doorsteps.

Livingston makes jokes of plantation money. Many here have no need to joke about it. The transactions and trades of the islands pay for their lifestyles—those Mayfair homes and expensive White's memberships.

My palm is tense as I grasp the baluster. This trembling feeling isn't invisible. It's tight, holding on to my gut, squeezing, wishing I wasn't becoming more and more embroiled in a scandal which will give everyone license to mock me and question everything about my existence.

Midstep, halfway up, I hear a loud raspy voice, *betting on which island will be the next rebellion to rebel.*

I bristle.

I know that noise is for me. Trinidad has only been under British rule for less than twenty years. It might as well be us, the latest to rebel. I stand a little straighter, hoping the fool takes no comfort in my invading their space.

At the top of the stairs, I see Scarlett. Carefree, drinking with the men. When did she begin drinking? Well, maybe not drinking. There's a goblet in front of her but she hasn't touched it.

The sight of her puts me at ease. Her masquerade hasn't been discovered. She sees me and waves at me like the infernal duke. I'm ready to deal with Scarlett, calmly and rationally. Though I detest falsehoods, I'll pretty much say anything to get her out of this gentlemen's club.

I proceed to their table and claim one of the empty high-back chairs. "I'm sorry to be late. I trust you carried on without me."

Livingston chuckles. "Hadn't even noticed. The conversation has flown."

"My cousin doesn't get out much." Scarlett's voice sounds heavy and strained. "Thank you for entertaining my questions, Lord Livingston."

My heart rejoices, seeing her unexposed. The breath I didn't realize I was holding releases. The scent of cedar and cigars fills my nostrils. "Finding a mews took a little longer than expected."

"Well, White's has plenty of distractions." Her head turns and the hair pulled back by a ribbon sweeps her lapels. She sort of looks the part of a young English soldier heading off to war on the Continent.

I didn't quite realize how long her locks were. They're usually pinned up.

"I've heard the game of faro described," she says, "but I hadn't actually seen it. Fascinating. Winning and losing differs by a few points."

"Well, don't waste a learning opportunity, young Carew." Livingston is preening like a true mentor. "Did you know this one was so talented?"

"Of course." I didn't know, but her feat of pretending to be a man and getting away with it shows a perverse sense of accomplishment. "What skill in particular are you admiring, Livingston?"

"These sketches." He points to pages in her notebook. "These are remarkable."

Scarlett's eyes are bright. "You should've seen earlier. We had a crowd of admirers."

"I must say we did. It was large. My peers in the science community, peers of the ton, all came to bow and pay homage to such brilliant sketches."

Livingston cuts short his praise. He looks dead at Scarlett, and I hold my breath again.

"Carew the younger, perhaps you can illustrate the next paper I wish to publish on eye health?"

What? I pry the notebook from his hand, and I'm shocked at the talent and the descriptions. Scarlett Wilcox has drawn the eye with such detail—showing the cornea, the white sclera, the thin conjunctiva and lens.

The image of the eye and all its parts seem lifelike, a true dissection. The window, also known as the cornea, bears a proper label. The colored diaphragm, or iris, has a different shade of charcoal, all done so that the differences are easily detectable.

The notations on the lens describe different types of cataracts. "These are masterful."

Scarlett smiles, a true one, like when I answer her questions about medicines and herbs. How many times have I seen her hovering in a corner with charcoals and that notebook?

I'm shamed; I didn't know her capable of this. "It seems you've drawn a patient with advanced cataracts. The rate of growth will have to be measured, but eventually, sight will diminish until it's gone."

Her face blanks. It's as if I questioned her abilities or kicked a dog or something.

Oh no. This renegade is trying to draw me in. I refuse to give in; I won't indulge another scheme.

"Don't look so upset, Carew," Livingston says to me. "Your cousin has been a delight to talk with."

"That's because every word has been about you," another man says as he joins us. This fellow, with gray hair and spectacles, sits at our table. "You must be energized to have your fame spread to the young."

The earl salutes the man with a raised glass. "Lord Flanders, you cannot be jealous because my research has admirers and yours does not." Livingston sounds very conceited. "I'm sure fungal species in the wild are very exciting."

Yes, an arrogant scientist the earl is, but this is normal behavior for him.

"You know Mr. Carew, whom we'll now call Carew the Elder, and you've met his cousin Scotland Carew, wisely to be known as Carew the Younger." Livingston looks at the sketches again.

Scarlett glances at me. "The advanced ca-tar-acts, as you say, cousin . . . have you ever found it treatable?"

She's mocking my accent. This is probably one of her wordy traps. Something to tease me. I must proceed with caution.

"Cousin," she says looking at me with those I'm-getting-away-with-this jet eyes, "what treatments can there be?"

"If it's soft and milky, there's not much that can be done but to wait," Livingston interjects.

"I agree," I say. "Not much but make the patient comfortable. Prepare them for loss of vision in that eye."

"But in the research I've seen from France," Scarlett says, "their men of science suggest a lenticular cataract can be treated. Lenticular meaning very hard. Hypothetically, it has made the lens clouded and crystalline. Some sight has been regained by pushing the lens deeper into the eye cavity."

The earl looks stumped. "That sounds painful."

Lord Flanders takes off his spectacles. "Any procedure involving jabbing the eye like what young Carew describes is risky."

"Every procedure has risks," I add. Realizing this is not a jest,

I decide to become more serious. "The pain of such a procedure must be high. Is the patient awake or asleep when this is done?"

"I don't know." Scarlett's voice is soft, almost ladylike again.

"It's important," I answer. "One may have to make modifications to the lens based on a patient's comfort."

Conversations on techniques continue, but Scarlett looks dejected.

"There may be other procedures." Livingston picks up another of her sketches.

"Your esteemed colleague has given his opinion on displacement of the crystalline lens. Carew, share yours," she says. "We all know my cousin's word is as God's."

Scarlett's tone wants to be dismissive, but her eyes beg for my opinion. That must be our problem. She needs a mentor. I wish to keep her a friend or friendly enemy. Yet, there are times like now, I question if I hunger for more. Do I want her soft voice to ask for more—more care, concern, maybe love?

"Carew?" Same tone, same wanton eyes. Same questions I've had since last year's ball about her and what I feel, what I've tried to ignore.

"I am not God, but I've not seen this condition in many patients." I lean over and examine those perfectly black smoky eyes. Seeing them sad, even aching, makes my heart unexpectedly race. I want to know whose eyes she has drawn. Who has this condition?

The earl taps the table. "I think the new research you have discussed earlier, young Carew, has merit. It might be worthy to try, given we find the patient."

"Do you, cousin, have someone in mind?" I glance directly into her eyes.

Scarlett takes up the papers. "It's immaterial. The earl has given me his opinion. He's the renowned expert on the eye at this table. Thank you, my lord, for listening. Now I have much to think about on ca-tar-acts."

"Cataracts." Livingston's tone is more forceful in pronunciation, but I seethe . . . well, I seethe a little more. The nerve of Scarlett trying to pretend she has an accent. And to value the earl's opinion over mine.

And then I scold myself. I'm jealous.

How many times has Scarlett wanted to show me something and I ignored her? Her not talking to me, avoiding me, tells me that I want her attention. And this need is different. I've known her forever. I swore to her father to be a protector and mentor. Now I swear to my awakened weary soul that I want more.

With a sigh, I sit back. They discuss more body parts while I observe the burgundy tapestry running the length of the room. I see body parts all the time. That's why I must escape to Shakespeare or a novel. With this one, will she want to discuss dissection when I'd rather compliment her complexion? Could she be my respite? Or will she drain me with questions and talk of procedures? Does having more with Scarlett Wilcox mean no escape from work?

The rooms goes black for a moment. When I open my eyes, I focus on the moldings. They are ridged and dental cut about the room. A glass chandelier sparkles over my head. This picturesque setting is a haven for rich men, ones of leisure who can describe fanciful operations they'll never perform.

I wake up a little and notice my cousin, the renegade, impresses me. She can hold her own with my colleagues. Part of me laughs on the inside. They've let Scarlett invade this world and hold court. The brown young lady pretending to be a gentleman has infiltrated White's.

Deep down, I must thank Scarlett for forcing me to be a rebel. I want to tell the rude man downstairs that the war is over. The invading forces have won a place in White's.

Blinking, I see Livingston lifting his hands into the air, tracing womanly curves, probably telling jokes no woman or man of decency should hear.

My anger rises again.

I'm not a renegade. I'm someone who's protective of a woman who shouldn't be here. A glance out the window shows the sun has set. Except for the reflection of a link boy's fire torch directing carriages out front of White's, darkness covers the panes.

The duke has entrusted Scarlett to my care. How have I bungled this? She should be at Anya House safe and sound in her bed, not giving me such sad eyes because I gave her the truth about cataracts.

Livingston's arm waves to a servant who begins to pour a new bottle of some Bordeaux. He says to Scarlett, "These are the best detailed sketches I've seen on the subject. You are masterful at illustration."

Illustration or illusion? Maybe both. Glancing down, I see again why all are amazed. How did she get so good at human anatomy?

Why must the fool Livingston discover this, instead of me?

I notice Scarlett looking at me. There's a shy quality, almost fearfulness in having me review her work. Alas, I'm a bad mentor to her. What type of friend have I been to her?

When she sips from the glass . . . the way her mouth touches the glass, seems . . . well, accomplished, playful.

I've never noticed that before, the fullness of her lips. It's disturbing to remark this now, when I've started to decide we shouldn't be more. This is like my new favorite, *Sense and Sensibility*. It's by A. Lady, and her character, Marianne Dashwood, starts to like Colonel Brandon after deciding they shouldn't be together. Except I'm not sure who's Dashwood and who's Brandon, me or Scarlett.

My thoughts are scattered. Sleep is coming for me. I blink my eyes, happy that Scarlett's unharmed and relatively in the same condition of rebellion as she was in Somerset House.

Her brazen eyes briefly meet mine, before they are again on Livingston. "Sir, repeat what you were saying. I think it profound."

Okay. Now I'm glad she's a man. Livingston would eat this attention up, if he knew it was coming from Scarlett.

"Thank you, Carew . . . the Younger." That brilliant fool is eating up the attention regardless.

I want to drag Scarlett out of here, but I'll stay if it means she won't be angry when I take her to Torrance. There's something going on between Scarlett and me, something beyond the costuming and lies. When I take her to Anya House, we'll hash things out.

I pop to my feet. "Cousin, we've taken up enough of the earl's time we should—"

"No, Carew the Elder." Livingston says, "Relax. I like this conversation."

"Perhaps you should have something to eat, cousin. I'm not sure you've had anything today. I do believe you often skip breakfast."

Why is Scarlett telling my personal habits to these men? How does she know so much about me? I fold my arms and sit back in the chair. "I'm fine, but as we each have full days tomorrow, we should consider leaving."

"You can go, cousin. I'll make my way home." Her eyes cut a defiant gaze. She's daring me to expose her. Instead, I'm forced to back down and brood. Watching Scarlett act like a sycophant to Livingston, I burn that she ignores my counsel.

Chapter 10

SCARLETT—PAPA, LOOK.
NO HANDS.

Oh, Papa, if only you could see what your little Scarlett has done. I peer up at the chandelier hanging in the center of the upstairs gaming room in White's.

The inside of the building is not as fancy as I imagined, definitely not as big or as ornate as any room in the Duke of Torrance's home. But what is? He's over the top with his decorations, all his actions.

My sister Katherine sees it as some way to make her envious or look bad to Lydia. It's not. It's him.

Speaking of looking bad, poor Mr. Stuffy looks withered. Stephen Adam Carew has droopy eyes. He's frowning and fussy and refuses to eat a thing. He's not himself, but that's probably because I'm not myself.

I try to catch his gaze to see how much more aggravation he'll take before he leaves. Then I'll catch a jarvey and head to Anya House. The man with perfect posture can't help but slouch. *Give up!*

He won't. He's as stubborn as me. If I wasn't certain this act is to make me concerned, I'd be fretful. His talkative driver Benny once told me how Carew fainted at some aunt's picnic after working three days straight with no sleep and nothing to eat.

I hope he's just pretending. I take note of his condition—his skin doesn't appear clammy. He's not perspiring like me under this makeup. Yet, he's nodding off.

Go home!

Men. They are no mind readers.

Leaving him to his oddities, I search the room. The glass sconces add a little brightness to the corners. The new ones the duke is having made for his study seem like suns.

I sit back and clutch my papers. Livingston, the renowned expert, has approved of my sketches. The couching procedure sounds like the approach for Mr. Thom. I'll have to learn more.

The earl's laughter draws my attention.

"And then she told me . . ."

Too late. I hear *buttock*s and *slippery* and more imagery than I care to have lodged in my brainbox.

Pitiful. It appears that with a bit of fermented grapes, Lord Livingston tosses away his brilliant mind and again becomes a caricature of a man with no morals. He's describing brothel women with Lord Flanders and the nodding off Carew. Flanders seems just as enthused at visiting a rosebud as the earl.

I refuse to laugh. I have principles. I've gained the knowledge I need. The insight I need for Mr. Thom is worth the itchy sideburns, the weight of the paint on my face, and the boorish change in the conversation.

As my physician yawns, I look toward the large window, arrayed in blue and gold velvet curtains, framing a now dark night sky.

How many times have I seen this particular room from the outside? The happy memories start. Scotland and I sit next to our father as he proudly drives his coal dray through Mayfair.

Through five-year-old eyes, I witness Papa scrambling to make deliveries, looking at his son holding the reins, his daughter tracking our route stops. We often drove past White's.

As in my best dreams, he motions to Scotland, saying *One day son, you'll be able to walk into places like this.* Guess my being here is a kind of victory. One for us, Scotland.

Another bottle of wine is brought. Luckily, the earl, or Flanders, doesn't notice I'm not actually drinking. Papa would never let his guard down, no matter how friendly his customer might be.

I do eat more of the cheese Mr. Carew refuses to try. It's delicious, light and creamy. He's missing a treat. But that's his natural stance, to be slow and deliberate and filled with regret.

"Cousin, I think you should eat something."

He doesn't say no or move. Maybe he's becoming more stubborn.

I can be a mule, too.

Lord Lange has finally returned to the table. He was here earlier but walked off when eye anatomy took over the discussion. He sits to my right drinking brandy. He's had some sort of recent heartache. The blond young man is not interested in science, but he's told his tale of woe, twice.

How can he not see the woman in question, the engaged future duchess of another man, was only using Lange to make her fiancé come up to scratch? Lange is not that smart. Or maybe, like me, he's trapped in seeing things as he wishes them to be, and not as they truly are.

Lord Flanders to Carew's left has participated more in the conversation but he keeps looking over his shoulder as if he's expecting someone.

Imitating him, I glance this way and that, making sure I'm not blind to what might be coming. There's a battle of cards happening two tables from the window. One man seems to wager about it raining next week. This feels sad, to invade this world and to find men at leisure are like women gathered doing needlepoint—gossiping, gambling, gaining pleasure from food. All are resting marionettes, waiting for an emergency to pull their strings and force them to move, then they forget how idle they've become.

"Blast it, Randolph. You won again. I miss my old mark, Tavis. He surely took stupid bets."

My throat goes dry, for there aren't too many with that name. I sip the sweet poison in front of me. I try to stretch to be a little more observant. I'm sure the person says Lord Hampton.

Tavis was admitted here? Of course he would be. What peer wouldn't be? And he kept betting and losing, betting and losing, until he drained the Wilcox coffers and took a wager that broke his back and killed him.

Though he gambled away all our money, I liked Tavis.

He made Katherine laugh. She'd stopped laughing. Thank goodness Mama's Lydia survived. Two stillborn babes would've been terrible. At least the mistake of marrying Tavis brought us the Duke of Torrance. Perhaps, if I tell the duke what happened and how it devastated Katherine, it will help him to have more patience with my sister. The duke must remind her of the past.

"Carew the Younger," Lange says. "The cabernet's not to your liking?"

"It's fine, but the fermentation may be off. My face itches." My chin and jaw really do. This black powder will probably cause bumps. I'll have to use the bottled salted water from Epsom Commons to get rid of them. The cosmetics should've been off hours ago. "Might just be my youth, to not appreciate the flavors."

I look at the dour Carew . . . the Elder. No witty remark? Nothing cutting? My statement is an opportunity for him to strike.

He does not look well. Now, I'm genuinely concerned. "Perhaps it's time—"

"Carew, have you gotten over Miss Perfect?" Livingston pokes the physician. "It's been a year, sir, since you discovered that the lady you held in such great esteem married Baron Derand."

Oh, dear. Livingston's going to tease him about the infamous Eveline Gray. Poor Carew never got over the one who got away.

"In consequ . . ." Carew slouches more. "It's inconsequential. We ready to go yet, cousin? Not feeling . . . much myself."

Before I can respond, Livingston becomes animated. "That's what's wrong with you. You're still grieving a woman who has moved on. You need to move on. Gentlemen, we should head to Madame Rosebud's."

"Madame Rosebud? Truly. That's your answer?" I know when I say it, I should've kept quiet. Now the earl's looking at me like I'm twelve.

He starts to grin. "A green one? What is it with you Carews? I thought the islands were where all the heady adventures happen. The physician is virtually a monk, and I guess Carew the Younger is a virgin."

What do you do when someone calls out your truth when you're supposed to be hiding in a lie? Eyes wide, I look at him and say, "Never kiss and tell, gentlemen."

That leads to a round of nods and laughs.

"So, you're a man of the world." Flanders's voice is loud. "You should think of trying a professional."

The snickers of these men goad. "Lord Livingston, how can you think of going to a brothel? Those women often become sick and go to Bridewell."

"Bridewell?" Flanders looks uncomfortable, decidedly more uncomfortable than my fake-cousin. "Perhaps young Carew has a point. The conditions at Bridewell Hospital are terrible. How many courtesans—"

"Prostitutes," I say, for there's no need to cater to fools by making the brothels sound exotic. "But do go on, my lord, enlighten our party to the troubles of Bridewell. You do know it."

Flanders looks down at his hands.

Lord Lange stops chuckling. "Flanders, does young Carew know something we don't?"

Lord Flanders sighs. "Bridewell is not quite a hospital but more so an all-female prison. Some are tossed-out courtesans . . . prostitutes."

"One hundred and thirty were prostitutes when I visited six months ago. Many had turned themselves in during the freezing cold of 1816, the year there was no summer. Bad weather impacts forgotten women and those abused the most by society."

"So you've visited your older cousin before, just to do social work?" Livingston makes a loud slurp at his wine. "Admirable,

Carew the Younger, but Madame Rosebud's not Bridewell. Madame Rosebud keeps her roses clean, and without thorns. They even have associates to keep the gentlemen in line."

I tilt my head to him and say, in the manliest voice I can, "So you like declawed kittens? That hardly seems right."

"A hundred or so is not that much," Lord Lange says. His cheeks are red like he has something to hide about the prison. "Young Carew, be careful. The young always try to push too much too fast for change. That only causes more problems."

"Let the young have opinions, Lord Lange," says Flanders. "But Bridewell is for prisoners. Declawed or not, Madame Rosebud's girls are not criminals."

"You are right." I nod and smile and refrain from scratching my sideburns. "They aren't. They are some of over two thousand prostitutes in London who have to find love and care as they age or realize how disposable they are. Bridewell is a prison, but offers more care than the streets."

Lord Lange grits his teeth. "That's three percent of the population of London. That's not that many."

"I suppose. That's at least one prostitute per twenty houses. Everyone can share. These women each would have a place to stay for the month."

The peers laugh. Carew doesn't.

"And, gentlemen, if you add that number to the poor, the permanently infirmed, or even the immigrants, that's a lot of people who need access to physicians." They are listening to me now, the way rich men do when they are annoyed that their coal delivery is too late, too big, or too dusty black. Like coal could be another color and be useful.

"They aren't our concern, young man. If they need assistance, they can pay a bone doctor." Lange says this and sneers at Carew.

It's a slight to my physician. I feel it, but my alleged cousin doesn't respond. He's blinking a lot, yawning, barely keeping his eyes open.

After tucking my drawings back into my satchel, I stand. "I think we'll have to agree to disagree. My cousin is ready for bed. I've kept him out long enough."

Carew, my family physician, tries to fist his hands. "Stop." His words are slurred.

Livingston snaps his finger under Carew's nose. "He's not moving. Gentlemen, I think we are going to need to help the physician to be on his way."

The other two men look at each other. Lord Lange steps forward. "He didn't even drink. Come on, Carew. Snap out of it. It's some type of palsy."

Flanders disappears, not that the old man can be helpful.

"This will be fun." The earl ducks under Carew's arm and guides him down the steps. Lange sort of follows but then disappears at the cloakroom.

I'm fearful of the type of medical attention the good physician needs. All I know is getting him out of White's and away from the prying eyes of hypocrites is the best prescription.

Chapter 11

SCARLETT—SOME KIND OF HELP

Out on St. James Street, we stand in the shadow of link boys as they wave fire. My heart pounds as Carew leans, half flopped over, on Livingston. The earl, despite his heavy drinking, is fit, but he struggles to keep the taller physician upright. I'm holding Livingston's hat, gloves, and my own. Boy, I'm a weakling.

"Out in the fresh air, that should rouse him, Lord Livingston?" My voice is a plea. I'm asking the earl as much as Carew.

This isn't right, and it is my fault.

Livingston's out of breath. "Let's—"

"Stop. Unhand him." A man runs at us. He's in a dark mantle, flopping like a cape. His gloved hands shield his face and keep on his hat. "Mr. Carew? Did they hurt yuh?"

Livingston bucks up. Surprisingly, he's ready to fight.

But the man, I've seen him before. Mr. Carew's driver? "Benny, over here."

He nods. "Did dey beat him inside? Did dey do that?"

"No, Mr. Benny," I say. "White's didn't do this. Cousin Carew just sort of lost all his energy."

"I knew it. It's happened before. He's been working nonstop, no sleep for two days. I don't think he ate."

"There was plenty in White's," I say, "but he refused."

"Stubborn." The driver grabs the bulk of Carew shifting the burden of supporting the physician from Livingston. He leads us across the street. "I knew he was working too hard. No rest for days, visit after visit. His aunties will kill me."

Stewing in guilt, I follow behind. "Let's take him to Anya House. The Duke of Torrance can summon help quickly."

Benny shakes his head. "I'll take him back to his home in Cheapside. He needs to lie flat and sleep."

Carew will definitely be more comfortable there, but that sounds like a long drive. I look back to White's, thinking there must be a physician inside, and see a man looking down from the extravagant window.

It's probably Lange or Flanders. One helped a little. The other not at all. Scotland, you haven't missed a thing at White's Gentlemen's Club.

Climbing into the carriage first, I guide the limp Carew to the seat.

"Cheapside is too far," Livingston says as he climbs inside. "I know a better place. Eighteen Half Moon Street off Piccadilly."

Benny tilts his head, but it's too dark to see the young man's expression. "But that's—"

"I know where it is, young man. I have friends there who will help." Livingston's tone seems dire. "Hurry. Time, we can waste no more time."

"Dis is too much." Benny gives me a mean glower, then he slams the door shut and gets the carriage moving.

My cosmetic seems smeared as Carew's head has bumped my jaw. He probably has some of my coal black dusted into his tight curls. The attached pieces of long sideburns are still intact on my face.

I'm not caught, but maybe I should be. Chasing after me has made Carew sick. He doesn't deserve this.

Why won't he wake up? "What is this, Lord Livingston? You seem to know."

"Well," he says rubbing his chin, "I don't think it's a permanent palsy. Not eating or drinking can cause weakness. This could be an infection. It could be many things."

"Maybe he has something in his medical bag that can help." I know he has one. He often brings it with him. Striking up the carriage lamp, I illuminate the hideaway compartments beneath the seat. Pulling open the door, I hide a gasp when I find a short gun, a blunderbuss. My nervous fingers knock a bottle and peppermint wafts. For a moment, I think about waving it under Carew's nose.

Finally, I reach his bag—smooth leather, brass clasp.

Tossing the hats aside, I drop to the floor. Stashing my treasured satchel inside, I exchange it for the bag. Quickly, I work the clasp, which makes a clicking noise when the brass lock opens.

"Is anything helpful in there, Carew the younger?" Livingston peers out the window.

My fingers dip inside again, I find tools and a bottle. I lift the glass to the light. "It's laudanum. That won't help. The last thing he needs is a drug to keep him sleeping."

The earl takes the bottle and for a moment it looks like he wants to take a sip. He catches me staring and hands it back. "Might have hurt my arm. Never mind. We are almost to our destination."

He looks out the window again. "Don't fret. Your cousin will be fine."

Fine? I want to put one hand on my hip and give the earl a talking-to about when simple situations or conditions go from bad to worse.

The carriage stops.

Carew rouses for a moment. "What? Time to work?"

"No, cousin." I need him well. I stare into the eyes and they close shut.

"Driver," Livingston says, "help me get Carew out."

They do and I follow, once I put the bag back into the compartment. "So we'll get food in him and sleep in here?"

Livingston slips under Carew's arm. "We'll get something for him."

I leave my hat with the carriage and bounce up the steps of the town house, following the men.

The door opens. I hear loud laughter. My heart pounds as I enter behind the men like a girl who lost a puppy.

The strong scent of rose water slaps my face. The entry and the front room are dimly lit. It looks like the walls are painted red and puce. Tiny, sparse candles show paintings that bear different types of roses.

Velvet-covered chaises are everywhere, as are scantily dressed women lying in repose.

I step back and knock into a gentleman. He jostles a wine goblet that looks like it holds a claret. Luckily, none spills. A woman in nothing but a thin muslin shift which exposes her bosom leads the fellow up the stairs.

Another woman with titian-red hair comes to us, and Livingston kisses her hand. "Madame Rosebud, how are you?"

He gives Carew to me and Benny. The physician flops onto my shoulder.

I'm too shocked to care that Carew dribbles on my coat. "This is a brothel." Oh, Papa, don't look at me now.

Benny has the biggest grin.

Oh, he knew the address. "Mr. Benjamin, Mr. trusted man-of-all-work. The joke is on me. Well, on me and Carew."

Livingston addresses the flamboyantly dressed woman in fiery crimson. "Madame Rosebud, my friend is ill. I think he needs tender care. Stretch him out with a girl who will help him wake up."

"Of course, my love," she says. "Whatever you're paying for."

My hand would be on my hip if I wasn't afraid of dropping Carew. "Benny, no. We need to take him—"

"Carew is always saying he's too reserved. He tells me he wants to do grand gestures for his next woman." Livingston chuckles, but it sounds so evil. This is Sodom and Gomorrah. "Nothing is grander than Madame's flowers."

"He means his novels. But he never does anything he dreams."

"Carew the Younger," he says to me, "one of the rosebuds will take care of that."

I clasp my physician's arm, trying to hold him back, but two big men dressed like eunuchs in priestly robes grab Carew and hoist him up the stairs. A big chesty woman follows and goes into the same bedchamber. Only the men come out.

The earl is laughing. "The man will wake up and thank me. My work is done."

From the bottom of the steps, I watch in horror and curious amazement. Beautiful, scantily clad women bounce about. They aren't modest. They aren't scared. They seem proud of their bodies. They refuse to be covered.

Carew's driver gawks. "I've dropped men off here before when I drove a hackney. Never been inside. These walls are red."

I grab him by his mantle and shake him hard. "Benny, come out of your lusty trance. We need to get Mr. Carew out of here. You know he doesn't wish to be here."

"Don't. From all his patients, all the hours of work, and fretting over yuh, maybe he deserves to be catered to."

"Benny, he's barely conscious. He can't make a decision. And what do you mean fretting over me?" I lower my rising voice as another prostitute seeking an old man dances past me. "Help me get him out of here."

"How yuh get him past de guards?" His head turns from side to side. "They mighty big."

I hope Benny's talking about the soldier like footmen, not the courtesans dancing around us and taking patrons upstairs. But these women are chesty, endowed with big *delights*.

"Maybe a good sleep in the arms of a beautiful woman is what he needs. The man been working too hard and being made crazy 'bout his odd-dressing cousin. Too much."

"Driver of Carew," Livingston calls to Benny. "We'll send for you."

Dismissed by the earl, the poor fellow looks away. "Sorry, Carew the Younger, but I can't get in trouble. Not like yuh."

The driver makes the sign of the cross and backs out the door. It slams. The noise rips through me.

I'm left on my own to rescue my physician.

Standing in Madame Rosebud's, I need to figure out a plan fast. The red wall makes the light look like flames. More men are coming into the brothel. I'm standing in the corner trying to figure out how to get upstairs past the eunuchs.

I begin to cough. The fragrance of roses has replaced all the fresh air. I'm drowning in rose water.

"Good, you're staying, Carew the younger. I thought you'd run off. I like a fellow built for adventure."

I salute him. "Yes. That's me, alright. They don't call me Carew the Younger for nothing."

Livingston claps at my ridiculous statement. If this is how men truly act, no wonder it's so easy to fool them.

The earl turns back to Madame Rosebud and whispers something in her ear.

She giggles and commands a young woman to come to me. "Younger Carew, this lady is for you."

My goodness, this brunette girl is my age or a little older. She takes my hand and leads me between the eunuchs up the stairs.

"Don't fret, Carew," Madame Rosebud says. "Chrysanthemum is particularly gentle. She'll make a gentleman's first time easy and memorable. She'll take care of you."

Livingston walks away with the buxom woman in charge. Before entering a room with her, he calls out to me. "You're bright. A great researcher, but books all the time can make you dull. You need to live, Carew the Younger. This is my gift, because you're very promising."

Long arms with sparkling jewels reach from inside the bedchamber and pull him. He laughs and willingly goes.

Livingston and the madam are on the opposite end of the hall.

"I'm Chrysanthemum," my assigned prostitute says. Her long

brown hair falls in curls about her face. She takes me to the room, a room next to the one I saw them carry Carew.

This bedchamber bears the same red color as below. It has a few tables with objects and bottles. And of course, there is a bed with white sheets. I wonder if they are truly white or if the candles are playing tricks.

"Sir, I see you looking next door. Gentlemen often prefer blondes, but I'll take care of you."

"No. I'm concerned about my friend. He fainted. I need to check on my cousin."

Chrysanthemum starts attacking the buttons of my waistcoat. "Daisy will take care of him."

I step away from her and knock a table by the door. A basin of rose water dumps on me. "Sorry. See, I'm nervous."

"Well, you smell better than most of the men here. That's why we use rose water all the time."

"Washing your clients may help keep the spread of disease away."

She releases me. "You're training to be a physician. I can tell. I know some." Chrysanthemum scrunches her pretty young face at me. The grimace I suppose is meant to be seductive. "Nothing to be afraid of, sir, it's—"

"Oh, there is much to fear. You need to get me into the room next door. I'm convinced my cousin is having a medical emergency. You don't want a dead man on your hands."

Chrysanthemum drags me closer to the bed. She's fiddling with my cravat and quickly has it off and begins on my buttons. Soon, she gets to my surprise—my bandaged bosom.

She steps back immediately and shakes her fingers at me. "You're not who you say you are."

While admiring the skill it took to quickly unbutton and defrock me, I refasten my shirt. "That's what I'm trying to say."

She shrugs and comes at me, kissing me along my brow. "You can imagine what comes through our doors. I can please you."

I back all the way up until the door latch jabs me in my back.

"I didn't come for affection, but I do need your help." I take coins from my pocket and put them into her wandering hands. "You're very lovely, but I need you to take me into the room next door, with Daisy."

"You do prefer blondes." She looks up. "Typical, they have all the fun."

"Ma'am, please. The man next door is ill. I need to make sure he doesn't die and . . . the Duke of Torrance will pay for your inconvenience."

"Torrance?" Chrysanthemum's voice rattles with fear. She covers up her chest like someone is watching. "I know him. We all know him."

Oh goodness. I don't want to think that Torrance is like Livingston. He's supposed to be lusting for my sister, not a flower.

Chrysanthemum must see the confusion on my face and begins confessing. "Torrance paid Matricaria Chamomilla, our Russian courtesan, to be nice to the Marquis of Prahmn. Any friend of the duke is a friend of ours."

She reaches out, lifting her hand to mine.

Tentatively, I take her hand, and she leads me next door.

Once inside, I'm . . . horrified. Then I'm mad and jealous.

Daisy is on top of my physician, trying to wake him, slapping kisses down his bared chest.

He's flat on his back, motionless on the mattress. Boots on. Jacket and shirt off. His breeches look in place, but she's probably as fast as my prostitute. "Is he dead?"

"Well, he's sure not moving." The naked woman looks to have at him again.

"Daisy," Chrysanthemum says in rash, hushed tones. "Plans have changed. This one needs a doctor to take care of the doctor."

Pouty, Daisy glances at me, then she huffs. "Fine. He's no fun for such a handsome man."

She picks her robe off the floor and slides it onto her naked body. The brazen thing stops at the door. "Pity, he's mighty handsome . . . and a handful."

That saucy look boils my jealous blood. She leaves, and I catch Chrysanthemum's arm. "Thank you. Can you go get his driver? Mr. Benjamin is outside. Torrance will pay more. Please get the guards to let us leave without being serviced."

"Serviced? Guards? The attendants keep us safe. They'll do what I ask." She puts her hand to my chin. "We get all kinds here. Take this cosmetic off. It will stain the sheets. That will cost the duke extra." She floats out the room.

I fall against the door and lock it. It's bright enough to see where I've trapped us. A basin and small candles sit on the bed table. Their smoke and the fishy tallow smell mixes with the scent of rose water. They highlight the ornate frame of the bed, the half-clothed physician lying flat.

The room feels small and again, red paint is everywhere. It feels like it's closing in. I, Scarlett Wilcox, will not panic—even though this is the textbook definition of compromise. A brothel. Two people unwed. One bed. One barely dressed man. Compromise.

I tremble but move close to the footboard where his tailcoat hangs. I tug his boot. "Mr. Carew. It's me. Scarlett. Don't be afraid."

Why would he be fearful? I duck my face into my hands. These most certainly are little-girl nerves. My cosmetic goes everywhere. I can't see. The paste from my sideburns has sealed a lash. I must wash. Searching with one eye, I see a basin on the bed table. As I head to it, the pine floors creak under my boots like the room is haunted.

This doesn't feel romantic or salacious or even sensual. It's odd, and I'm itchy.

I scrub my face. The basin is filled with more reeking rose water. Just as I get all the cosmetic and glue off my skin, Carew growls.

My nervous fingers hit the bowl. It jumps off the table, spilling everywhere before landing on the floor. My breeches, Carew's discarded shirt and tailcoat are stained black and soaked in sickly sweet rose scent. We're going to smell like a brothel forever.

Keep yuh head, cool-headed Scarlett. That's how yuh win.

Flinging wetness from my hands, I sit on the bed. Carew doesn't move. "Awaken, sir."

Is he breathing? Is that noise distress? Panicking more, I shift closer and wave under his nose. Rose water drips on him. Now I'm wiping stinky water from his face, his chest.

Skin to palm—his chest is hard. Little silky hairs coil at my fingertips.

"Sorry." He hasn't consented to my touch or to be here. If this is not a compromise, I do not know what one is. "So sorry, but please wake up."

I shake him until I hear, "Scarlett."

But is that God, Carew, or my conscience?

"Scarlett." My physician huffs.

Is he choking? Checking for an obstruction in his airway, I finger his lips. Smooth and unfortunately wet from my dripping, they open like I have some sort of power over him.

"Me more powerful than you." I forget myself. "Whoa." I clamp my mouth. I can't be thrilled that Mr. Stuffy is barely conscious and under my command. "You actually need me. I didn't think you needed anyone."

He works his jaw. I think he's trying to say something. I dip closer and he snores in my face. At least his breath is still minty. "Carew, we need to get out of here. This is a scandal."

Knocking him, making him shift, I examine him for injury, for beauty. *Well made* are the words that come to mine. Unlike me, he's very muscular. The ligaments and tendons are defined, curved and strung tightly like a good violin.

There's a scar along his ribs from some childhood accident he once told me that made him want to know more about medicine and healing. His stomach is flat, almost too lean, which surprises me, for he loves dessert and he's always talking of the aunties fattening him up for a nice girl. His belly button is cute. It's slightly raised, but mostly inward. His stomach must've been bound as a child, as my mama did to us, to make the button flatten.

He grumbles and half turns. A little taut backside becomes exposed, for the fall flap of his breeches is undone. That will need to be buttoned up before those thick limbs move.

Where's Daisy? She needs to redo what she undid.

Yet, the thought of another woman touching him is abominable. I want to be a physician, so I must be comfortable with all forms of undress. I take charge and make him lie flat again. Then I seize his breeches and take my time sliding velvet-covered disks into resisting buttonholes.

My cheeks are aflame. This is intimate, touching and fastening and aligning him to the cloth and the buttons while my knuckles skim his skin.

Done. I back away. I can't admire my handiwork. This is a compromise. I've compromised my physician. One word of this gets out, and my freedom and Carew's is over. The duke will make me marry him or him marry me—but we'll be done.

Focus, Scarlett. Carew's shirt and waistcoat remain wet. "Can we escape with just a tailcoat?" I grow warm, thinking of him as I stare at the sculpted sinews that squeeze and pump life into him. Daisy is right. He's a beautiful man. "Let's go with the jacket."

Groan.

"Carew?" I drop the coat and sit beside him, patting his forehead. "Don't be warm. Please don't have a fever. I've spilled all the water. I have nothing to break a fever."

An icy palm grasps my hand. The physician weaves his fingers to mine. "Scarlett?" He rears up and hugs me. "It's a dream, you've come back to me."

When a half-naked man embraces you and says he's dreamed of you, that must mean something. It takes a moment for his eyes to open again. His palm cups my cheek. "I fainted, didn't I? I hate when that happens. Been working too hard. The past few days, the past weeks have been terrible."

Carew's arms wrap about me. "What a nightmare. Then you

stopped talking to me." His embrace tightens. Then it slacks. "Oh Lord, Scarlett. Don't do that."

The look he gives me, glassy eyes open to a slit, rips at my heart. Just add tears, and it's the gaze he offered when he came out of Mama's bedchamber with Katherine's stillborn in his arms. That glassy-eyed frown appeared when trying to convince me my mother wasn't in pain anymore. The same wet countenance whispered Papa was gone.

I shake Carew. "Don't ever look at me like that. Ever."

"Okay, Scarlett." His eyes shift around, then slowly focus on me. "Won't. Just don't leave me. I'm not myself, but neither are you."

Carew chuckles and then puts his hands on me.

I stiffen, then relax as his fingers smooth my arms. They cascade and tickle my neck. He finds the ribbon in my hair and whips it away. "There you are, Scarlett."

My freed braid hangs down to my shoulders. I want to push my hair back.

"Much, much bettah. And I wager at midnight, your beautiful eyes become pure black."

Groaning, yawning, he flexes and scoots until we are next to each other, hip to hip. Gloriously muscled, he stretches an arm and hooks it about my neck. Then he slumps. I put my hands to his chest to hold him up.

He growls, "Did you kiss me, Scarlett? Did I kiss you?" His voice is weak. He sounds horrified. "My apologies."

He starts to fall. I grab him and shake, hard. "Mr. Carew. Wake up. We need to leave."

When his lids flicker open, the brownish-black lenses are clear, no cataracts. Not that he ever had them. In fact, they're perfect. I see the bed table, the fallen clothes, the red wall—everything but me.

Before I fall into that black pit of wanting him, I pound on my physician's chest. "Carew, get up. Our prostitutes will be back to rescue us."

"No prostitute. You should not consummate the joining of

flesh . . . You need to hold dat till yuh married. Not here, little girl. Not this. Not you."

Little? Not now, not his old way of teasing me returning. Not hating Stephen Adam Carew is impossible. I hate him.

And when he topples, I let him fall. I want him to spill onto the wet floor. But on the way down, he grabs me and bumps his lips into mine. And I want to kiss him. I want to kiss him hard to shut his stupid mouth. I want to kiss him big, like I'm bad and bold . . .

But he's not in his right mind.

I am. So I push him away. "Let's finish getting you dressed."

"W-a-i-t." His breath is pepperminty. Our hands tangle and I'm not sure if we're trying to escape or undo the good work I've done buttoning his breeches.

The knock on the door makes him release me, and I drop to the sopping floor. Now I'm wetter and more in love with this fool than ever. "Sir, our prostitutes have returned."

Yawning, groaning, Carew slaps the mattress. "I've ruined you."

Yes, you have, for others, for any other man, for a long time.

I hate him, but I hate me the most. Because of him, I'll continue putting my heart on a shelf out of everyone's reach. "Be quiet, Carew the elder, and we may get out of this."

His eyes are shut. His breaths ease, but his smile makes my insides mushy, like warm butter on toast. "Missed you too, Scarlett."

"Carew, Carew the Younger. Open the door."

I launch to my feet and pretend nothing has happened when I let Benny into the room. My physician has the nerve to snore.

Chapter 12

STEPHEN—ONE WEEK LATER, STILL IN TROUBLE

June 9, 1817
Fourteen Fournier Street
Cheapside District, London

It's very bright when I step out of the house onto my portico. I believe I had my housekeeper and Benny shutter every window and draw close all curtains at my town house on Fourteen Fournier Street. I needed darkness to recover from my foolishness, my shame. The way my eyes hurt and how I can't stop blinking suggests my penance is not enough. I have to pay more. And the exact amount I need to dole out, I'll find out sooner facing the world than hiding.

Yet, I'm surprised the Duke of Torrance has not darkened my door or my face.

"Good morning, Mr. Carew." Benny comes out of an entrance near the lowest level of Fourteen Fournier. He's dressed in his dark mantle and hat, ready to start our day. "Plenty of appointments fi catch up on, sir. But a week of rest is well earned."

I'm at the top of the steps at the first level. He's coming from his quarters, where a future wine cellar will go. This floor houses my study, parlor, and a small dining room. Upstairs holds bedrooms, perhaps space for a future nursery.

Of course it could be a current classroom for my young bride, bride-to-be. I can't believe I compromised my friend. I'm a fool.

Benny comes up my stone steps. Two away from the top, he stops. "Yuh ready to talk?"

Talk about me being a fool, no. Talk about how I need to go propose to Scarlett Wilcox for compromising the girl in my supervision . . . no.

I wave at him. "Benny, I promised my housekeeper a light schedule. After a few appointments, I believe I have to go see about a young woman."

Those eyes of his are full of skepticism. "Mr. Carew, meh not a physician but since dis is the first day that yuh up and about from fainting in a gentleman's club and sleeping in a brothel, meh think a light day would work best."

Guess Benny wants to talk about it. The more he does, the stronger his accent becomes.

I glance up at my eaves and then the pretty blue sky. "In that list of faults, I hear nothing about Miss Wilcox."

"What about her? She neva sleep in a brothel. Meh assume she gets plenty of rest."

I cup my hands to my eyes to hide my frustration. I deserve this torment. A glance about my peaceful neighborhood, I see that many properties have been restored as I've begun with mine.

Fournier Street is a testament to deliberate effort and planning. The people who decide to move here do so to be committed. "This section of town was once home to many leaders in textile. The Huguenots were chased away. We who move here are all building the future." I guess after losing Eveline, I got my assets in order. This house is ready for a bride.

My neighbor, Mr. Croome, rides by in his large dray. He's the head of a proud Blackamoor family and possesses a booming cloth business. He and his wife and their two daughters live at Nineteen Fournier. The shimmering new slate roof is the first undertaking they've done on the large corner lot.

"Sir. Yuh need to—"

"The work we've done here makes me proud, Benny. The fresh white paint and gorgeous tiles overhead look good. This is very different from my parents' pine board home in Port of Spain."

"Yeah, yuh finally put down roots and Eveline Gray flew away. Mr. Carew, yuh have a way of avoiding t'ings until too late."

"How can I avoid things, Benny? My house and finances state I'm ready to wed. That wasn't my circumstance with Eveline. I had a plan. She couldn't wait. Apparently, my behavior last week says I couldn't wait to ruin my friend." I cover my face. "Oh, Benny. I must be one of those predatory individuals who seek out brides fresh from their cribs. My mother married very young. It wasn't good. Sometimes, I think I was sent away, so I'd not see her troubles."

Benny reaches the landing, grips my shoulders, and shakes me. "Come out of dis foolishness. Yuh have no new bride, young or otherwise. Unless yuh proposed to your housekeeper, yuh safe."

I take a full breath. Then grab Benny's hands and shove them away. "Well, I need to propose. As a gentleman, it's the only right thing."

"Sir, dis about Scarlett Wilcox? That lady not telling anyone. When I got yuh out of Madame Rosebud's, she made me promise no talking. Or she sew meh mouth closed."

I want to laugh. Scarlett does have a temper, but I don't think she'll actually harm anyone. Well, I haven't known her to do so.

Yet fragments of Scarlett trying to throttle me or shake me awake dance in my head. Nothing is clear—not what she did or what I allowed to occur or even the liberties I took. "There are two things I know for certain—well, fairly certain. I passed out in White's, and I was with Scarlett Wilcox in a brothel. Both of these things are wrong."

Benny folds his arms. "Actually, di Duke of Torrance and di

Earl of Livingston are responsible. One let her dress as a man. Di other bought her a prostitute."

"But it was me in bed with Scarlett Wilcox. Me."

My man-of-all-work comes at me, his stance aggressive.

He slows when I put up my fists. "Benny?"

My man stops. "Hold on a minute. Miss Wilcox said yuh shirt and waistcoat were wet. Did yuh lose yuh clothes with Wilcox in bed?"

Everything is blurry. Did I kiss her or was that a dream? "Maybe?"

Benny starts to spin as he marches from side to side on my portico. "I saw yuh in bed with no one. Yuh and Miss Scarlett?"

So, Scarlett can keep a secret better than I. "I know . . . pretty sure nothing happened." I rub at my brow and start to laugh at myself. "You took the job of being my man-of-all-work for adventure. I've given you plenty this last week."

Benny stops. His back is to me. "May meh be frank, sir."

Isn't he always? "Yes. Speak."

"Yuh always talking about Scarlett Wilcox."

"No, Benny. Well maybe."

"Yuh do, and especially since Torrance's ball last year. And definitely after Eveline Gray. Even when yuh argue yuh praise Miss Wilcox. Do yuh love her?"

"No. No. I like her. She's brilliant. I promised her father to mentor her, not take advantage of her." I'm watching Benny shake his head at me. "Go on say it. Tell me how foolish I am for complaining about someone I've compromised."

"Don't worry, sir. Perhaps she can work at the hospital yuh wanted."

"Work with her? I'm not trying to die early, but last week's escapade shows it's possible Scarlett Wilcox will kill me."

He gets closer. "If she want yuh dead, why didn't she tell di duke?"

I open my mouth to say he's wrong, but Benny is right. "There's a reason I keep you around."

He releases a big sigh. "Hopefully, it's not to pull yuh out of brothels. But di brothel is my fault. Livingston said to go there. I didn't listen to the smart person in di carriage."

"Miss Wilcox." My tone sounds flat. I'm not asking a question. More so confirming that she's smart and I'm an idiot.

"Sorry for getting worked up," Benny says. "Have yuh eaten? If yuh haven't, yuh can go back in. No going anywhere."

I want to offer Benny a cutting remark about him not being responsible for me, but my judgment seems faulty. "Two eggs, toast, and a scone that tastes of cinnamon. And my housekeeper has plied me with lots of coffee. Do you accept this, Benjamin?"

"Very good, sir. Don't mean to be a stick in de mud, but I was advised to take yuh nowhere unless yuh had a proper meal and rest. The consequences dem did sound dire. Miss Wilcox can be a terror. She threaten fi mek di duke send me to freezing St. Petersburg if meh fail yuh again."

Scarlett's way with words and threats are chilling. "Benny, did I give Miss Wilcox flowers? That's part of what little I can remember. Daisies."

Benny looks at me as if I've lost my mind again. "Prostitutes, Daisy and Chrysanthemum, led me to the room where yuh lay half naked. Miss Wilcox stood fully dressed as a man. Do those flowers come back to yuh remembrance? Or dey bed part?"

"Oh, that. I'm dead."

"Wilcox and dey two flowers have more sense than the earl."

My head aches anew. This is not the conversation I wish to have.

"Sir, look pon dis way. Yuh here, alive, not inna jail, and no newspaperman talk 'bout, 'Trinidadian Immigrant Doctor's Fall from Grace.'"

"I'm a physician, but you're right. The newspapers won't give me the courtesy of getting my profession right."

Benny taps his foot. "Been checking dey papers every day. So far, no mention of any t'ing at Madame Rosebud's or White's."

If I sigh, I'm sure all the air, good and bad, will leave my chest and I'll be a deflated puddle on my steps. "In the future, do not listen to the Earl of Livingston. He lives for brothels. I on the other hand—"

"No one holds yuh interest for long, not since Eveline Gray, 'cept Miss Wilcox."

"You know the aunties. They haven't exactly liked anyone else. They continue to try to find another candidate but they compare them to Miss Gray, now Lady Derand, a baroness, not a physician's wife."

"Sir, when yuh lost Miss Gray, yuh change up yuh plans. Yuh did waan fi be more successful, and yuh overwork yuhself fi reach deh. Look pon Fourteen Fournier. Yuh a real gentleman, but yuh need fi relax. Consider dis escape a blessing in disguise."

Benny is usually a good man to noodle out problems with, but this logic has taken a left turn off the main thoroughfare. "I don't understand. How am I blessed if I did wrong?"

"Scarlett Wilcox comes with de dowry from the Duke of Torrance. Yuh know that will be a big bundle. Yuh can get back to building dat hospital. Marrying her comes with money. Yuh can have it all, de practice, de patients, de hospital, and de pretty wife."

"A practical marriage?" The last thing I'd ever do is use a friend for my gain. Still, there's much to consider and to be thankful for. "Well, it seems Miss Wilcox protected me from contracting a condition or adding to the fatherless count of children in London. I'm very fortunate to have friends like you and Miss Wilcox. Benjamin, I thank you."

Offering an understanding smile, he says, "At least yuh weren't nauseous when I got yuh. When I drove de hackney, I had tuh clean out meh carriage when drunkards became ill."

Being compared to the sick and sotted is not a comfort.

"Let's go, sir."

We head down and walk to the rear where the mews is. Benny, as always, has my horses and carriage ready. He flings open my

Berlin's door. "See, no refuse. But it do smell of roses. Couldn't get rid of di smell."

My laughter blends with Benny's, but then he sobers. "Should've listened to Miss Wilcox. Better sense and less to clean."

"But at least the experience scared her. She'll know better than to be dressing as a man pretending—"

"No, sir." Benny's head is moving up and down as if he is a marionette and someone is pulling strings. "Don't t'ink she t'inks dat at all. The young woman talked to meh man-to-man so to speak. She shamed me, sir. Pretty wise for a man . . . woman."

"Wait? What?"

"Miss Wilcox, she's a good one. Didn't seem to care for her own reputation, and she wasn't trying to trap yuh. A good one."

"She needs to take more care. Running around town in disguise is dangerous."

"You live a careful life, Mr. Carew. Maybe too careful."

"I'm not a saint, Benny, but I care about my reputation. Men like Livingston can live like fools but still be listened to." I grip the door handle hard. I want to rip it off. "I don't have that luxury. I hate to say lady's right."

"Lady?" Benny shakes his head. "Sir. Meh yuh lady."

Of course. Yes. A woman who risked her safety and reputation for me, should be mine. "Benny, I'm stupid."

"So, yuh propose to her, den let her meet de aunties so dey can't spook her."

The aunties are married women of our immigrant community. They are treasures. Only one, Telma Smith, my beloved Tantie Telma, is related. But the aunties adopt everyone, everyone who lives in Cheapside and has any percentage of the Caribbean in their blood.

"If the aunties get wind of meh taking yuh to Madame Rosebud's." Benny grimaces. "Meh in trouble."

I cross my arms, dragging creases across my indigo waistcoat. "I can handle the aunties. But I have bigger things to attend to. I owe it to Miss Wilcox to make sure her honor is preserved. Her father and the duke would expect it."

As I get into the carriage, Benny nods. "Des funny. Miss Wilcox knows a t'ing about honor. She bribed the two prostitutes to keep yuh reputation safe and get yuh out unseen."

He closes the door. "Meh a better opinion of Scarlett Wilcox. Not spoiled. She has principles. She fights for 'em, and yuh. Where to?"

"To Anya House. I need to thank her, then wring her and Torrance's necks, then claim his permission and Lady Hampton's to wed Scarlett Wilcox. It's the honorable thing to do."

Benny dips his head. "If yuh say so. Gonna wait over there long time."

"Why a long time?"

He pulled at the puffed cloth interior, the carpeting on the floor. "Could try to get rid of the rosewater smell at de duke's. De mews's well equipped. Then need time to dry." Benny looks like he's calculating figures. "Yes, four hours. That should be enough time for yuh to wait for Miss Wilcox to return."

"Return? Is she across the Thames? We can go there. And I can check on two patients along the way. That will give me more time to come up with a way to propose. It should be a grand gesture. How do I come up with one on such short notice?"

"Sir, we will still have to wait. Miss Wilcox, or shall I say Master Wilcox, will be at Somerset House again this week. She talked to herself. She finding de words to say to the earl when des both there. Something 'bout anatomy."

"No. Benny? She's at it again." I release a long breath. "I'm gonna need to calm down. Let meh go get a tonic for Master Wilcox and let my temper ease. Can't get my proposal wrong. It'll have to be big for her . . . and Torrance. There, dat's a plan." I take long breaths and roll my tongue and collect myself.

"Very good, sir."

I get out and head inside my house. Then, I'll be shortly on my way to catch my wayward manly bride. I hope when Scarlett marries me, she'll stop this ridiculous dressing like a man. Maybe the only way to protect her is to marry her.

Hmmm. Making her a physician's wife and impressing upon her the need to avoid our name being linked to scandal might safely clip her wings. A wife . . . my wife. Suddenly this solution doesn't sound so bad. Since the Duke of Torrance and Lady Hampton have been unable to keep the good-hearted Scarlett from ruin, maybe I'm up to the task.

Chapter 13

SCARLETT—SOMERSET HOUSE, ABOUT LAST WEEK

Another week of the Annual Exhibition—this time, I send a footman from Anya House to check that today's lecture would happen on time. The duke accompanies me. Mr. Thom is not up to driving, so I stay at Anya House. I must admit to liking it more and more than Ground Street.

"Your Grace, will you accompany me here every day? Or just for today's anatomy lesson?"

"I received a rather strange bill from a Madame Rosebud for two guineas."

There's humor in his face, but his pallor is dull.

"I had a little adventure. It's handled, but two flowers earned the money."

"Is that the same as an angel earning her wings? These British sayings sometimes are difficult for me to grasp."

"Something like that, Your Grace."

He doesn't ask for more, so I'll keep the details to myself.

Though he's spending time away from his project, and even Lydia, I enjoy these moments where he tries to explain art. These paintings are . . . well, some are lovely and colorful.

The duke's tastes, except in waistcoats, are different than mine. Many of the exhibits that he enjoys are not great to me.

Nonetheless, I appreciate how he's deliberate in spending time with me. I don't want that to ever change.

We move to a lower canvas. This one illustrates a school scene where teachers or administrators have come into a yard to stop a fight between boys. "Now this is interesting, Your Grace."

The duke glances at the tag. "By an artist called Mulready. The painting is named *Fight Interrupted*."

He steps back studying it. "The shading and color make it very lifelike. Impressive."

"And that's why this art is for you or Georgina. To me the colors are nice, but I want to know what happens to the boys' aggression."

"Hmm. How so, Scotland Wilcox?"

"Just because they aren't fighting doesn't mean the tension's gone."

"And that is why I love showing these to you." His gaze goes to the left and then right. "You always speak to the heart of any matter. You see past the obvious."

It's obvious that Katherine is not allowing Lydia to spend as much time at Anya House as she did last year. Her birthday is next month.

I want to tell the duke I'm sorry Katherine doesn't love him. That I know how it feels when you hope for something that's not true. I'd also tell him not to settle for anything less than what he deserves.

Funny, forward and bold Scarlett Wilcox, even dressed as Scotland, can't say or admit the obvious when it comes to feelings. I glance again at the painting. "It's rather charming. And still very true. Boys get to be ready to rumble. Everyone else waves fans."

"I thought we were working on a way for you to rumble. Or are you going to be like Lady Hampton and wiggle your way out of our bet?"

I turn to him. I see pain in his eyes and immediately wonder about his health. "If I ask how you are feeling, you won't tell the truth. So I'll ask if you are giving up."

"Nyet, but one must be wise enough to know when the game changes."

"Is this a chess analogy? I still haven't learned to play."

He moves us over a little and I notice he's leaning on his cane, sometimes almost using it to feel his way. Odd. The duke's too young to depend on it, but I know his condition deprives him of strength. From what I've studied, it's chronic, but not constant.

"We are back to Dirce," he says. "I feel it is less menacing on a second visit."

I catch his gaze. "Are you the bull today? Or are you one of the hapless others?"

"That's my Scarlett, direct and fatalistic."

I take the cane from him and turn the crystal head toward a lit sconce. It adds a sparkle and glow to it.

He stands erect, not needing the cane.

"Does this add to your confidence? Is it a weapon, or are you getting us ready for when you need it?"

He offers a soft chuckle before taking it back. "A little confidence now." The sparkle is smothered in his palm. "S. Wilcox. You are given to be frank. I'm patient up to a point. You've had a week to sulk. Are you ready talk about your returning to Anya House well after midnight last week?"

How do I say I compromised a man in a brothel and not have the duke demand a duel from Mr. Stuffy? "Your Grace, does an interest in a person work the same as an interest in art?"

The duke comes a little closer. "Art conveys emotion. You've been emotional all week. I would suspect that someone who masterfully pulled off a masquerade at White's should be pleased."

"Does everyone become a spy for you?"

"Yes, eventually, but I saw your face. I know an unhappy Wilcox when I see one."

The presence in the window—that was him?

He nods like he's spying on my private thoughts. Blast it. Maybe he has some Cossack way of doing so.

"Thank you, Your Grace, for not intervening."

"Well, I trust you. And I did check to see that Mr. Carew was still alive, not dead from what happened at White's. I'm your friend. I'll not judge. Tell me."

I shrug, then smooth my cranberry waistcoat. It goes well with my buff breeches. Again, I will admit the duke's tailors are amazing. But I don't want to admit much more. "Nothing out of the ordinary. You know how it is when men gather."

He peers down at me. If he wore spectacles, I'd swear he was a minister sent to condemn my soul. But this is Torrance—part brother, part father, part friend.

"Scotland Wilcox, I don't have to tell you of the dangers to your reputation, your friends, and family. It will be awful if you are exposed."

That's new, this tone of condescension. I can offer one right back. "Well, I'll admit that the three pals, Livingston, Carew, and I, went to a brothel after White's. I used your name at said brothel to make sure no one would speak of us being there or expose me as a woman in men's clothes with my new favorite courtesan, Chrysanthemum."

The duke stands there frozen as if all his joints have stiffened.

"Your Grace?"

"Sorry, I think I just witnessed my life pass before my eyes. It was too short, and without as much color as it should have." He releases a big sigh. "You like to stun people. Are you craving attention? Is that why you pick arguments? I don't think this act will win the man you love."

I glower and want to say no. I'm not that shallow.

"Wilcox, do you know how much more Lady Hampton will hate me if she learns that I let you act like this?"

"And her opinion matters, why?" I keep my chin lifted and try to act angry. It's hard when I see he's hurting in his soul.

"Oddly, her opinion matters greatly. That's the thing of loving someone who does not love you back."

Why is he so smart, and everyone else, including my heart, so stupid? "Carew is brilliant. As passionate as I am about research, he's the same about medicine."

The duke lifts my jaw. His light-colored fingers are now inked with the coal black cosmetic. "If he can't see your worth, then he's not the one."

"Does that mean Katherine is not the one for you?"

The duke almost turns, but then he catches my gaze. "Sometimes love doesn't last. Sometimes it doesn't win. Too much has happened between Katherine and me. No one is brave enough to admit that maybe we both have been betrayed. That we have pain that's shared."

I put my hand on his arm. "I'm sorry."

"Wilcox, you're playing a dangerous game. Can you assure me you will be smarter than any of these men and courtesans and remain without scandal?"

"Yes, Your Grace."

"Can you assure me that only Mr. Carew knows of your play-acting?"

"Mostly, Your Grace. I'm sure he told his driver, and Chrysanthemum probably told Daisy and Madame Rosebud. Will Madame Rosebud tell Livingston?"

His head tilts to the side. "I'll make sure the flowers stop talking."

He must believe me, if he's tidying up my loose ends. The duke hasn't ordered me to return to Anya House. "I still have your trust. That means something."

"Well, I pray you continue to fool everyone. Once Lady Hampton knows, she'll stop you and Lydia from visiting completely. That will ruin me."

"I'm of age. At twenty-one, I no longer need her consent. Why does everyone think of me as if I were Lydia's twin?"

He gets very close. "Did Lydia have a twin, too?"

"No. But she . . . I was thinking that if someone is born the same day, they could be a sort of twin."

The duke, for the first time since I've known him, looks shaken.

"Why does Katherine hate you? It can't be for anything that's happened since Tavis died. It has to be from before. What did you do to Tavis Palmer, the late Lord Hampton, that is unforgivable to my sister? Help me understand? Trust me."

He looks around like he's waiting for someone to interrupt us, but at this early hour of the exhibition, the visitor count is light. "Come with me."

We walk for a moment and come to the entrance where the marble River God of Thames sits in judgment.

"I knew your sister long ago. Tavis took advantage of me and her."

"Did he lie? Tavis was sweet, but he had a forked tongue."

The duke looks as if he'll take his cane and strike the marble. "Pitchfork tongue would be a more apt description. For Katherine to believe that I always loved her is to realize all the years of hating me are a waste of her life."

"How many years ago did you know Katherine?"

"Long enough."

"Do you still love her, from that time?"

He looks down at me, and I know he doesn't know anymore.

"One can wait too long to be loved." The duke adjusts the cane in his hand. "Scarlett, you gave me permission to find a man for you to marry. I've waited a year on purpose. Marriage for someone as gifted and as smart as you should be more than a name on a science report."

"And it gave Katherine another year to see how much we need you—"

"That *I* need *you*. And that I love my Lidochka like she's my daughter."

The way he says it sounds more than a wish. "When Katherine came back from St. Petersburg, she gave birth to a stillborn. Are you the baby's father?"

He winces. "I wish that was one of Tavis's lies. That the baby lived. My son was born the same day as Lydia."

He glances away. He surely sees the pity in my eyes. "Was Tavis good to Katherine, to help her heal?"

"Tavis wasn't there. They didn't see each other or marry until much later."

The duke frowns. "So she didn't marry him when she discovered she was with child, but after giving birth. Could she still have been waiting for me?"

He stands close to the River God and slaps the statue's shoulder. "You hear that? She might've been waiting for me."

The smooth marble god appears ready to rise and stir the waters . . . but has my admission given the duke false hope? "But she did marry Tavis. They seemed happy. Every day he made her laugh. They'd still be together if he were alive."

The duke clasps his hands onto his cane. "Look, here comes two of your marital candidates with important names to put on paper—the angry physician and the wayward scientist."

"Can the option be neither? They are both very disappointing."

"Unfortunately for you." His shaking fingers grasp mine for a moment, then he ducks them to his side. "I'll leave you to them. Try to be home . . . to Anya House at a reasonable time."

The duke begins to walk away.

"Your Grace, I understand, too, about falling out of love. Disappointment is an incredible poison. I hear it can be fatal."

"Many things are, Wilcox. That's why you have to live with no regrets."

My true friend disappears, going again into the long hall.

Livingston and Carew seem to be exchanging words as they get to Somerset's steps. And I wonder why two men who are able to partake in all aspects of science seem so miserable.

Chapter 14

STEPHEN—WHERE IS DAT GIRL?

The sky is overcast. Everything, even the grass I'm trampling, looks gray. I don't smell rain in the air, or blood. I want to see the latter. If I were a different man, Livingston would be carted away. He'd know the blade in my pocket. He could've gotten Scarlett ruined. I look at him, with his arrogant wasteful pedigreed nose lifted, and want to knock him flat in the courtyard of Somerset House.

"You seem angry, Carew. I heard you've been flat on your back for a week. You should thank me."

I gawk at the clueless fool and sigh. "Thank you for not abandoning me in White's. That could've been detrimental."

The fool bucks up and walks with more pep in his step. "You are welcome. And any time you want flowers, just let me know."

"Do you and Madame Rosebud have a special relationship, or are you fine with sharing?"

My words make the earl stumble. Hopefully, they make him realize the danger he puts himself in.

His stride returns. "Have you spoken with your cousin? It's my understanding that he had the best new flower."

I groan and grind out, "I'll be seeing him shortly. I'll let you know."

"Capital." The fool can't contain his smile. "No one goes to Madame Rosebud's and doesn't have a good time." His tone gets louder, as if I didn't hear him, but I'm trying not to curse. Then he stops. "What is it, Carew? I'm trying to befriend you and your cousin. Sebastian's new marriage and kinship with the Wilcoxes has opened my eyes. Will you not reciprocate my attempt at friendship?"

Well, at least he's trying. Then I see Scarlett Wilcox, again disguised as Scotland Wilcox. "Livingston, I appreciate the effort. I'm distracted, and I hate being distracted."

Livingston's troubled, needs-to-be-punched face clears. "Good. You and your cousin have been fun company."

I stop on the first step. "You give us this attention because you're bored?"

"When your best friend gets married to a woman he actually loves and likes spending time with, you'll see how empty your schedule becomes."

That puts everything in a slightly different light. "Sir, you don't have to go to extremes. I'll dine with you again. Now let's get my cousin, and we'll head somewhere for lunch. There's Scotland." I point to the top of the steps. "I'm sure he had as good a time as I."

"Not today, but soon, Carew." The earl hums a merry tune and becomes more animated as he takes the steps. Must be terrible to be brilliant, wifeless, and friendless in London.

I follow, and soon we are inside with the River God and Scarlett.

"Lord Livingston, Mr. Carew," she says in that fake low voice. "Are you as excited to observe anatomy?"

Livingston grips the lapel of his charcoal-gray tailcoat. "The young fellow doesn't have a problem with his memory. Today is indeed anatomy."

He looks back at me. "We have to show the young lad we are still in our prime."

"Then that is sad, sir." Her tone is low and deliciously sarcastic. "I hope for more vigor and purpose when I reach your elevated ages."

He crumples like his wrinkled jade waistcoat. Taking off his beaver hat, he stashes his gloves inside. "Mind your elders."

After the earl says this, he turns to me. "Is your cousin always so rude?"

I smile. "Yes. It is one of his most endearing qualities."

"Well, gentlemen," Scarlett says, "I'm going back to the exhibition before going to the Royal Society lecture."

I grab her shoulder. "Not so fast, cousin. Let's take in the exhibition together."

Livingston follows but fortunately gets involved in another conversation. I use this to put more distance between us and Livingston.

"Why, Scarlett? Why keep doing this? We got away with this last week. Why tempt fate?"

Scarlett glances at me like I'm the idiot. She looks ridiculous with those bushy sideburns and that black powdery makeup along her jaw. I absolutely hate how it mars her soft skin. She's in trouble. "Well, last week was our first time we lay . . . lied together." A smile blooms for a minute, then disappears. "We should keep walking. More people."

"You looked after me. Cousin, I wish to thank you. What if we get out of here and go for an ice?"

"Plying me with a treat for being a good little boy? No, thank you."

She isn't a good boy or girl. She's loyal. Not many others would've stayed, especially the way we tease . . . used to tease each other. "Then how about this for a proper treat? Marry me."

Livingston wanders toward us. "Carew? What did you tell your cousin? He's all red in the face."

"Should I tell the earl, Scotland, or will you?" I say this like a dare. It's thrilling to feel some power in this situation, for I have none. I compromised Scarlett Wilcox. The remedy is marriage. There's no other fix that would be honorable. "You will be leaving London shortly."

Her eyes widened, but then she and Livingston burst into

laughter. "What a kidder my cousin is. He means I am so busy with research I will have no time for another Madame Rosebud visit. Like I said in White's, my lord, my purpose is to learn about eye anatomy and the dissection process. I've no time for much else."

"Cousin Scotland," I say. "You shall make time for leisure. You need more than studies in your life. I insist we go with my plan."

Livingston shakes his head. "The only time I see Carew the elder this flustered is when he's goaded by the fetching Wilcox lass. The girl has blossomed into a beautiful, curvaceous goddess, and Carew the Elder pretends he doesn't notice, then he monopolizes her time."

I laugh but it's true. "I see it now. Scarlett Wilcox is wonderful to chat and tease."

Coughing, my cousin retreats, and goes deeper into the Great Room. We follow, and she dips her head.

"Carew the Elder, Lord Livingston, I apologize but I must go."

Clearly, she's exasperated. I clasp her arm. "Wait, Scotland."

"If you are fretting about me, sir, don't." She tweaks my cravat. Her fingers are long and graceful, even covered in white gloves. "Go fight with your friend, sir. You two are that, even if you don't wish to admit it."

"You two!" Livingston starts to clap. "You almost had me fooled, but Carew the Elder, you always give things away."

His eyes bore into mine. Then Livingston slugs me in the shoulder. "I knew it. Carew the Elder has a mistress. One who keeps you from the brothels. Probably from the drinking, too."

"Ah, a mistress?" I roll my eyes at the foolish man. "Yes. You got me, Livingston."

"Well, who is she?" The man of science begins his foolish investigation. "Where did you meet? Is she from Bath?"

Livingston might be brilliant on technical papers and conditions of the eye, but not jokes or popular literature.

"Explain. You can't be mooning over Eveline Gray. That was a year ago. Old news." The earl steps closer. "You sly Carew, come on. Confess!" His voice is loud. The man will cause a scene over lies.

"Lord Livingston, my cousin is being modest," Scarlett intervenes. Her hands fidget behind her back. "It's not a mistress, but my cousin is courting someone exquisite. Extremely fair and with expensive tastes."

The earl chortles. He's loud, and I know Scarlett has pushed things too far.

"Carew, you cad. Then you and a daisy from Rosebud's . . ."

I'm about to defend my honor and sort through Scarlett's lies, when I realize Livingston is complimenting me. "You've been saving all your money for her," he laughs.

That's a lie, but a brilliant one. I'll let him believe it. "I don't wish to brag."

Livingston rubs his hands together. "Then it's true. And the expensive ones have spies everywhere. They can tell when a man strays. Good work, Carew the Elder. We'll keep last week to ourselves."

"Well, you got me there."

He taps me on the shoulder. "I understand completely. Good behavior until you seal the deal. Big dowry, am I right?"

In for a pound . . . My intention is to wed Scarlett Wilcox. She does in fact have a dowry provided by Torrance. So I throw up my hand. "Yes. Sure. Big. You have me there. This woman has my complete devotion."

Somebody shrieks nearby.

Two women arrayed in colorful gowns, one blue and the other burgundy, rush toward me. My insides sicken.

The aunties have heard, and they're coming this way to congratulate me on my half lie.

Chapter 15

STEPHEN—ATTACK OF THE AUNTIES

The noisy women heading toward us cause Livingston to flee. "I'll see you two in the lecture room."

The earl dashes off, leaving me and Scarlett to greet my excitable aunties.

"Perhaps Lord Livingston thinks they've come for him." Scarlett's whisper reaches me before I can tell her what we should do about our situation.

But the aunties have come. The women surround me and offer big hugs and sloppy kisses.

"I heard," the tall one, Theodora Randolph, says. "Dear boy, you have a girl. You are courting. I have prayed to God for this moment."

Auntie Theodora grabs me in a headlock and shakes me like a sack. "You are finally over the broken heart Eveline Gray gave you."

This pronouncement stings, but I have no time to grouse. She slings me to Telma Smith, my Tantie Telma. "Let the boy go, Theodora. He needs to breathe."

Stroking my arm as if I'm a kitten, Tantie Telma says, "Oh, dear boy, this is an answer to prayer. We have prayed and fasted for someone to come along."

I can't say anything. This is humiliating. These two act as if I'm nothing without a wife. Taking my time to build my practice and improve myself to be better prepared for the next wifely candidate is a tragedy to them.

"Tantie Telma and Auntie Theodora." My hidden accent appears, loud and proud. "*Stan ex to me, dou dou darling.*"

Tantie Telma looks impressed since I mimic what she often says, wanting me to *stand next to her, sweet little darling.*

Auntie Theodora must be in a good mood. She hugs me again. "Funny man."

Her cohort, my actual aunt, Telma, pushes her out of the way and embraces me. "I'm so glad you have morals. I heard de man say mistress." She pounds her chest. "That stabbed meh right here. I didn't know how to save you from the evil of your ways."

"I guess mindin' your business is not a t'ing," says Auntie Theodora. "Men, but a proper girl to court." Tantie Telma smashes my head to her bosom. "Right, Stephen?"

"Of course not. I'd not dishonor—"

Scarlett's laughter is all I hear. She's trying to make it sound manly, but I can tell she's moments away from crying happy tears. "No, he's courting a proper woman, but she's very shy."

Auntie Theodora jerks me to her and leads me to Scarlett. "And who is this young man? We haven't seen him before."

Overwhelmed by the scent of my aunties' dueling perfumes, I can't answer before Scarlett. "Scotland," she says. "Mr. Carew has been showing me around. Treats me like family."

Tantie Telma grabs her hand and squeezes. "I his mama's sister, Telma Smith. That's my friend and an auntie to Stephen, Mrs. Theodora Randolph."

If they give Scarlett a bear hug, that coal-black cosmetic will go everywhere. I break free and intercept, drawing Scarlett's gloved hand forward, forcing them to shake.

"My distant cousin on my father's side has just arrived and is getting used to the climate—"

"And social graces." Auntie Theodora doesn't look impressed.

"Sorry, ma'am," Scarlett says. "But I introduced Mr. Carew to his future wife. That is, if he's ready to propose."

Oh, she has jokes. Scarlett doesn't even realize that it is we who have to marry, not some imagined woman. "I can't propose,"

I say, and give her the evilest of eyes. "Not until I bring the lady in question to meet my aunties and de community."

"You hear that, Telma? This boy has good manners." Theodora casts a skeptical squint at Scarlett. "You have to bring her around soon. How about Friday?"

Panic.

If they see Scarlett after seeing Scotland, they will know they've been deceived. Come on, Carew, under all de ole talk, I need to get to a serious topic. "Tantie Telma, I need to come by and check on Maryanne. How is she?"

"Less pain this morning. Deh baby will be here soon." My aunt does a little circle dance, her gown of bright blue floats about the hem. A matching scarf is woven in her tresses. "We can't wait. First ones are often difficult. Stephen, can you tell if it's going to be a boy?"

"One cannot." I shake my head. "That's superstition and an old wives' tales."

"Who you calling old?" Auntie Theodora points her finger at me.

Scarlett steps forward. "How is your daughter carrying the baby? High or low?"

"Maryanne is carrying low. That belly wanna touch the ground."

Scarlett lifts her hands. "Is her stomach wide?" She spreads her arms and mimics the shape of a wide pregnant abdomen. Then she does the same but rounding her hands vertically. "Or is her stomach high?"

Both the aunties say, "A high hill bump."

Tantie Telma squints at Scarlett. "What does that mean? Do you have an opinion of her health? Are you a physician, too?"

"Studying, ma'am. And according to medieval folklore, I suspect the young woman will have a boy. It's just an old wives' tale as Carew says, but I believe old wives have knowledge."

Scarlett, dressed as a man, talks about a woman giving birth and predicting the sex via the wisdom of old women. There's a joke in there. "Well, tell Maryanne I'll be around soon to check on her."

"Good, Stephen. My girl is strong, but there's nothing like having another set of eyes on her." The tension in Tantie Telma's face eases. Then she looks at me as if I'm hiding something.

"Stephen, tell us of your girl." Auntie Theodora glares at me as if she's daring me to interrupt her. Like I'd try. "Tell us more of this woman. Who is she?"

"He's caught the eye of a very beautiful, wealthy young woman." Scarlett's voice sounds deeper. She could pass for one of the braggarts we sat with at White's, Lord Lange or Lord Flanders. "I hear she's a true *diamond of the first water.*"

Yes, Scarlett Wilcox is loyal and brilliant. I think back to that fiery aurora-red gown she wore at Torrance's last ball. Goodness, so pretty. A diamond, even if its waters are the Thames.

Both women seem to settle and smile from ear to ear. I smile, too. Scarlett fits most of the criteria I have been looking for—not demure, not quiet, but born of pedigree, an impeccable dresser when she wants to be, and yes, beautiful. Above all, she is loyal. Madame Rosebud's proved her to be wonderfully loyal.

"Stephen, I knew you would not disappoint me." Tantie Telma puts her full attention on Scarlett. "Tell me, where is this girl from?"

The girl should stop digging that hole deeper, so I step in. "Jamaica," I say. "Her parents are from Jamaica. She was born here."

Scarlett nods. "Yes, Jamaican roots."

The aunties seem happy, but just before I bow and drag Scarlett away, Auntie Theodora says, "Praise be to God. We never thought you'd get over Miss Eveline."

"You mean the secretive Baroness Derand," Scarlett says. Her voice echoes the tone when she read me the elopement from the paper last year.

"Scotland, Auntie Theodora introduced me and the former Miss Gray five years ago. Our timing wasn't right. I hope the couple is very happy."

Tantie Telma starts fanning herself. "Well, yuh haven't heard the latest then. It's what she gets for breaking yuh heart and wedding de Scot. No offense, Scotland."

Scarlett dips her head. "None taken, ma'am."

"We shouldn't say a word." Auntie Theodora's cheeks darken. They highlight her burgundy carriage gown well. She looks at Tantie Telma. "Should we tell him? I don't want to ruin him; he has a new love."

This sounds cryptic, and like an excellent time to get Scarlett out of here. "I'm sure it can wait. Aunties—"

"He needs to know, Telma. God forbid we die tomorrow and we have dey secret." Auntie Theodora looks like she wants to talk now.

"We haven't met Stephen's new girl yet. She may not be good. We know Eveline." My aunt nods to Theodora, then stands a little straighter. "I'll tell him."

Scarlett's about to laugh, and I might, too. The aunties are everything wonderful that excitable women can be.

Tantie Telma puts her hand on mine. "Stephen, Eveline's husband has annulled her marriage in Scotland. She's back to London. De girl has come away with her fortune. She's single and wealthy."

That wasn't what I was expecting to hear. I feel terrible for Eveline. I take a breath, and under the scrutiny of these lovely ladies and Scarlett, I say, "I'm sorry to hear that. It's terrible when marriage ends."

These women look at me as if they expect me to dance for joy. They mean well. They've always been so supportive, but running back to Eveline now is ridiculous.

I'm actually happy that Scarlett's invented an excuse, so that the matchmakers can't try to draw me into their schemes.

Auntie Theodora frowns. "We want our young women married. And we hope it is within our community, people of Jamaica and Trinidad and Barbados who come to this land for freedom and education or to learn a trade or build a business. I hate when someone from the outside causes ruin."

"Hush," my aunt lightly scolds her. "We are in mixed company. And, Stephen, please don't be mad that we've told your new friend about the love of your life. Eveline is so lovely. Perhaps Scotland would like to meet her."

"No." My words sound rushed and harsh. "Scotland travels a great deal."

"What about the new lady, Stephen?" Auntie Theodora's voice is low. She's trying to be sweet. "Does she travel a lot, too?"

"Yes." I know when I say it that I've just ruined the ruse. Scarlett nudges me from behind.

"Travels?" My Tantie Telma now glances at me with the gaze she offers her husband when he disappears. "You ashamed of us? She a peer's daughter or something?"

Oh, this is not going well.

"She does travel," Scarlett says, "but she'll be back at week's end. I believe she has upcoming charity work to do at Bridewell. You're supposed to join her, Stephen, are you not?"

The little vixen for the win. I should celebrate her ability to tell falsehoods without blinking. That deserves an ice. The aunties gawk at one another.

"Sounds like a woman of substance, Telma." Auntie Theodora clicks her fingernails. "Still, you should bring her to church. We have a special service on Friday and then a picnic at Telma's house."

"Fine." I'll have a whole week to come up with an excuse. "I'll see if she can make it."

"You must come, Stephen," Auntie Theodora says, and pinches my cheek.

Tantie Telma hugs me. "Maryanne will want you to come, too. There will be so much excitement, I'll feel better if you are there."

"What about the fancy *accoucheur*? Last time I visited, didn't you say you hired one for Maryanne? I remember you saying he's a colleague of the famed Sir Richard Croft, the accoucheur to Princess Charlotte, the Princess of Wales. I'm sure he'd love to come."

My aunt looks sheepish. She doesn't trust him, but probably hired him because it sounds regal to have one. She wraps her palm about my folded arms. "I'll feel better if you are there. There will be cassava pone."

Tantie Telma makes that rich dessert like my mother. "Yes, ma'am."

Auntie Theodora glances again at Scarlett. "Scotland, you come, too. I want you to be a part of the community. And there are plenty of ladies your age. You might fancy Miss Eveline."

I rub my chin, noting how they ignore me and have moved on to harp on the next perceived bachelor in their midst. Having a fake mistress or a fake single man about might prove useful.

A moment later, I realize I spoke too soon. Dez eyes are back on me.

"Stephen, we can't wait to meet this new woman." Tantie Telma smiles so big. "We must meet your new love and her people."

"Of course." Oh, Lord, I've stepped into a trap set by cassava pone and Scarlett. "Let me get Friday arranged. Come, Scotland. We are late for the lecture."

The smile on Scarlett's face disappears. "We must go. We'll have seats in the back."

Scarlett and I bow and take leave of them. We are almost to the Royal Society meeting before I can no longer hear the aunties or persuade Scarlett to stop laughing.

"Wilcox," I say, "you laugh like a girl."

That makes the chuckles halt. Her nose wrinkles and red paints her light cheeks. Now I laugh. Then stop when I witness men and women staring. Scarlett's gloved hand is clasped about my arm like I'm escorting a princess.

"Sir, do you feel less faint?" I fan at her face. Judgmental people move away.

Scarlett draws her hand away and frowns. Disapproval ages her face. I feel the scold. It scalds my conscience.

"We did nothing wrong, Carew."

"I did." I hang my head. "I've been doing everything wrong. I have the kindest clients who've chosen to love differently. They are some of the best. People who have a reason to be wary of the ton or society have been the first to accept me as I am. I have no excuse for being a fool."

"I guess you're used to being a fool of one kind or another. But it's admirable what you do, Carew, helping everyone. You are a good man. Whenever you do build your hospital, it will be grand. It will help many."

That touches me, but I must focus. "Can I thank you for last week? Benny told me how you looked after me. You're a good man, too, Scotland. And I'm a bad one, an often hypocritical one. Forgive me. Oh, and marry me."

Something changes in her eyes. The jet lenses smoke a little. Then she breaks our gaze. "Anatomy awaits."

Scarlett walks faster.

She bumps into Livingston. "Sorry, sir. Is the lecture over?"

Livingston frowns. He looks cross. "Not exactly. They have male models today. One fellow was the model for the equestrian statue for Wellington." He folds his arms in a pouting stance. "Let's come back next week for the naked women."

Scarlett slips further away. "I came to learn. I shall learn something from the models."

She steps around the earl. I chase after her but can't stop Scarlett from going into the lecture hall. I follow and sit beside her. As a physician, there's nothing shocking about nudity.

As a man intending to marry the woman I compromised, I'm uneasy. Yet again, I have to sit unaffected and stew while the blushing, sketching Wilcox girl gains an education on the differences of men and women's anatomy, watching the exhibition of a naked man posing with all the endowments of a River God.

Chapter 16

SCARLETT—THE PHYSICIAN'S CARRIAGE

By the time I emerge from Somerset House, it's late in the day. My physician seems to be at a loss for words. We cross the street.

"My carriage is in the close mews." Mr. Carew seems well, but he hasn't said much. I suppose he's still shocked by everything.

"How are you feeling, cousin?"

The handsome man cuts his gaze at me. "We are almost to my Berlin. Once inside, we'll be able to talk freely."

That isn't his typical stern lecturing voice. Maybe he's still feeling ill.

I look at him walking closer to me, crowding me. This is punishment. And I'm an easy mark, because I care. Goodness, I hate being stupid, hate caring for someone who'll never see me as an equal.

We arrive at his carriage. He waves at Benny to stand away from the door. Carew rips it open. A wave of hot rosewater fragrance hits my nose.

"Rancid." Tapping my boot, I turn and look at him. "Have you been back there?"

"Scarlett. That's from last week. The smell won't die." He sighs hard. "Now, please get in. I've been thinking of us."

Thinking of us? As I start to climb in, he says, "The bottle of water and rag are for you. I need to see and talk to Scarlett, not Scotland."

Carew's tone is a mixture of anger and begging. Somehow that seems about right for us.

He gets in and sits with me on the same seat, then tosses his hat and mine to the other side. Without saying another word, he opens the bottle. Pouring some onto the cloth, I sniff lemon and rosemary. It's not just water.

"It will help get that stuff off your face and aid in any blemishes the cosmetics may have caused."

He stares at me with his beautiful eyes—more begging—until I begin to scrub my cheeks. When all the coal black comes off, the towel looks filthy.

"Better," he says. His countenance is close to me. "Is all this costuming necessary?"

My hands in these gloves are sweaty. I wrench them off and put them in my pocket. "Yes. Women aren't allowed to attend the Royal Society, remember?"

"So, the cosmetics and risking scandal is just to advocate for a woman's right to see a nude man. Surely there are easier ways."

His tone has become smug. I can match his—always could. "Well, if my prostitute Chrysanthemum had dallied a little longer, I'd have had a full view of *you* in such a condition. You can say you're welcome. I buttoned your breeches all by myself."

His whole face darkens, and he looks straight ahead. "So you are ready for more of an education? Or will any man's breeches do?"

Wait. What? "No lectures. You can leap to your own opinions without my participation."

He glances at me with a look I can't trace. He takes the damp cloth from my fingers and wipes gently along my jaw, then rips off my sideburns. His motion is quick and painless, but I guess he's used to adhesives and bandages.

"Why bother lecturing you, Scarlett? You see no risk to your own reputation. The Wilcox name is not exactly spotless, so muddying yours by viewing a man's posterior or physician's breeches has little to no consequences for you."

Well, it was more than the model's buttocks. A lot more. "I came for anatomy. I stayed for adventure."

The cloth tumbles in his fingers, then he sets it aside. "Scarlett, I care about your reputation. I care about you. And though you've been to Somerset and White's and—"

"A brothel. Don't forget about Madame Rosebud's. I did this all as Scotland Wilcox or Scotland Carew."

"What if you were Scarlett Carew?"

"No, Scotland is the name when I dress up to be in men's spaces. It was my brother's."

His mouth gapes open. No doubt preparing to say something witty or demeaning. He looks down at the floor. "I didn't know you had a brother."

"Most don't. He died at age six."

"How old were you?"

"Six."

He closed his eyes. "Fraternal twins. I'm sorry, Scarlett—"

I turn from the pity in his eyes and glance out the window. The route his man is taking us is familiar. I'm being dropped back to Anya House as a naughty child. "Since I now have so many names, I'm glad you chose Scarlett. You should use my first name, as if we are friends."

"We are, and have been forever." A sigh blasts from his nostrils. "And since we are now sort of related, and definitely entwined, you must call me Stephen." He folds his arms. "How did your twin—"

"A high fever."

Stephen slaps the seat. "That's why last year when Lydia had a fever, you had the idea for willow bark tea."

"I've studied everything I can. It's for Scotland. I stayed at his side that long horrible night. I held a compress on his head, trying to cool him down. Papa went to get a doctor. Then I fell asleep. My fault."

"No, Scarlett, you were just a child. These things happen."

Tears wet my face. I haven't thought about the exact moment of losing my brother in so long. "I woke up, and he was all red. The compress I had been using to cool him was on the floor. If I hadn't fallen asleep . . . If I'd worked a little harder . . ."

My eyes close.

I feel stupid for being so emotional in front of Stephen, of all people. Oh, Lord. I can't stop crying. "Sorry."

A hand grasps mine. Stephen tugs me to him. "Not your fault."

The peppermint on his breath feels clean, cleansing in a sense. Then his deep melodic voice whispers. "Not your fault. De longer yuh live de more yuh learn. I've seen everything done well. And death, he still comes."

I'm against his chest. His heart is strong.

"Now stop crying." He pulls a handkerchief from his pocket. "Dry dem eyes, Scarlett."

Stephen taps his roof.

His driver stops and then comes to the window. "Yes, Mr. Carew."

"Benny. Head to Gunter's. We will remain in my carriage while you order pineapple ices. Then we'll take our treats to Anya House."

"Yes, sir, Mr. Carew." Benny stares at me. "You're right. She's much prettier without all the paint."

He walks away.

Stephen still has his hand behind me. "Now tell me who has cataracts. You have been working hard to help someone."

No one can ever say Stephen Adam Carew isn't smart. "Let's get the ices first. You know I'm much easier to bribe with sweets."

"I remember when it didn't take a bribe to get you to talk to me, Scarlett. Even when we fought, I knew you cared. You've been easy with me. Then something changed."

The man is literally inches away from holding me in an embrace and kissing me. A real kiss, not just a bump in the night. And if he did, him doing so in his right mind, would mean something?

But he doesn't. His hand absently plays with my fingers along the seat. Stephen is clueless. I have to realize he'll never become wise when it comes to my heart. I shrug. "Things change."

"Fine. Sweets. Then talk." He shakes his head. "Deal. I guess you doh ketch fly with vinegar."

I'm not an insect, but at least this imagery gives me wings and agency. I can do what I please and buzz and annoy Stephen even if I'll always be a mosquito, a no-see-um, that he can't actually see.

Stephen's carriage parks in Berkeley Square across from Gunter's. Benny dodges traffic to retrieve two pineapple ices. I wonder what whimsical shape he'll retrieve.

My carriage mate now sits on the other side. The caring man who just held me tight has gone away. Why must I be weak for him to show me kindness?

"Why do you look at me like that, Scarlett?" His voice is low. "What have I done?"

Folding my arms, I lean forward a little. "What do you think you've done?"

"Other than compromise you in a brothel, can't think of a t'ing."

I laugh. "So that's why you look so pensive. That's a new look for you."

"Pensive," he repeats. "I have to figure out how not to disappoint the aunties. They will be expecting me to bring a beautiful woman with me to Wesley's Chapel on Friday."

"That's the church on City Road?"

"You know it? Of course the Wilcoxes would know it. It's one of the more liberal churches in London."

Liberal's a nice way of saying welcoming of all people, all races . . .

on Friday. On Sunday, I suspect the Wilcoxes, aunties, and de community are allowed in the last pews. "We went when Mama was well."

"Mrs. Wilcox was a beautiful, gentle soul. She could handle Mr. Wilcox."

"And he, her. My parents loved each other fiercely. They fought but always made up."

"My father was an honorable man but his marriage to my mother was more duty. Her father made the arrangement happen." Stephen softens his tone. "It never was loving. My mother was unhappy for years. She died while I was away at school. My father was killed in a rebellion two years ago."

"I'm sorry, Stephen. You know tragedy."

"I do. That's why I want to change the world, Scarlett."

Another honest moment between the two of us. I don't want it to end, but I have to poke. It is our way. "My parents stopped going to Wesley over the missionaries and other things."

Stephen stretches, then rubs his neck. "I'm conflicted. Missionaries bring food and medicine to hurting places, but Wesley's sends missionaries across the seas to teach the savages. I don't like to think of my homeland as savage."

"The hang it on their beastly papers put it. It mirrors their attitude."

He grimaces and again looks away.

Then I realize he's trying not to argue. That means he'll share less and less. We can't get along. "Well, I hadn't expected you'd agree with me and find fault with the missionaries. I suppose no one is safe from your judgment."

"Yes, Scarlett, I have strong opinions. I may not rail at everything like you or frolic in costume, but I have them. And it bothers me, the hate. That my church is a symbol of unity for my community but uses even harsher words for those in the West Indies. 'Devils' and 'heathens' are commonly said in sneers."

Stephen releases a bitter chuckle. "You go places feeling you have to defend your sex; I have to defend my nation. Patients think I will treat them with magic or bones of some sort. They should know I save my secrets for special people."

"Like I said, that's why the Wilcoxes stopped going. We come from proud Jamaican stock."

Stephen sighs. "At least at Wesley's, I'm not relegated to the last row like at St. George's."

He groans deeply, then again plasters a smile to his lips. They are smooth and not ashy today. "You said other reasons?"

"Yes, the sickness. They know it's in our blood. Wilcoxes can ostracize ourselves. No hypocrites required."

Stephen raises a hand then drops it to his knee. "It's scary. The suffering, no one wants that for their family."

"Why go, when we are as good as lepers to the nice Wesleyans?"

His dips and he nods, then says, "I can't fix that. It's terrible. But I need help now. Scarlett, will you dress properly and go with me on Friday? If I don't have someone with me, my aunties will again push for me to be with Eveline. I don't want that."

I'm supposed to go? I'm supposed to be the one he's courting? "Why? Why me?"

"Why not you? You came up with the ruse."

"Surely, you can make up an excuse, Stephen. Then you can be in love again with the woman you were going to marry last year, once you completed your three-part plan. Or was it four?"

"I do like the way your mouth sort of hisses as you say my first name, but I'm not interested in her or my aunties' games. I much prefer yours." He folds his arms. "You should know I have no intentions to marry her. How can I trust her, knowing she kept secrets?"

"Perhaps if you were honest with your intentions, she wouldn't have been so secretive."

He frowns at me. "I was honest with her. I was building my practice and exploring the idea of opening a hospital. I have priorities. My practice has now tripled in size. I can support a wife and household comfortably."

Why does it feel like he's made some sort of pronouncement for my benefit?

"Course you don't understand." Stephen sits back. "You keep secrets so you would take the side of a secretive woman."

"So my way of fighting for my beliefs makes me the same as an untrustworthy woman or missionaries for heathens? Good to know."

Stephen laughs in my face. "Playing dress-up is an odd form of rebellion."

Noting my frown, he puts his face in his hands. "Stop looking like that. Sorry. I'm trying not to get us into an argument. We have much to discuss. And, Scarlett, I know you're bright. I realize you're passionate, but you don't take reasoned risks. That's dangerous."

"Is that why you were so fretful about me seeing a man in the nude? It's too dangerous?"

"Scarlett, you should have the decency not to look."

"Decency? It was a science presentation. I was in a brothel with you and several men of science. They slobbered over scantily dressed women. You probably would've, too, if you hadn't fallen asleep."

Beating the back of his head against the seat, I hear him chanting. "I'm not going to let you make me angry and say something I don't mean. And the fault of the brothel visit was not yours or mine but Livingston's."

"Do you listen to yourself? Men can look all they want at a woman's body, whether for science or lust, but women are supposed to have decency and not look. Hypocrite."

His jaw tightens. The spark in his eyes blazes like fire. "It's not the same. A doctor has to be comfortable looking at all bodies."

I shrug and mouth h-y-p-o-c-r-i-t-e.

"Scarlett—"

"If you're not, then you simply understand that now I'll have an image for comparison. Today's lecture gave a very good comparison."

"Good comparison?" He mimics my voice but then adds, "Woman. Where deh get such ideas? Why, yuh crazy girly?"

Wow. His temper has loosened his tongue. His accent is so strong I smell salty sea air. I tap my brow. "Believe it or not, I think. I read. I've seen da Vinci sketches of the beauty and wonder of the human body, and I must say that Mr. Model was well muscled, very well strung. I believe an audience of females shall be well pleased. Is that why you don't wish us to know? You like limiting our pleasure?"

"Deh . . ." He sputters and goes silent. Stephen's rich complexion becomes pale.

I've stunned him into silence. I feel powerful. And it's wonderful to offer him these sentiments men voice all the time, while women are expected to stay silent and not look.

Several minutes and miles go by before he says a word. "You want to shock me, Scarlett. Fine. I'm shocked. Yuh wanna say shocking things, but yuh act like yuh have everything well in hand until things go wrong. With medicine you have to be open to learning, setting expectation, and failing. Clearly, you're not ready for that. Why keep playing? I thought you weren't a child."

Now I'm stunned silent.

"I've known you since you were nine. Scarlett, do you know how hard it is to see with the care-for-nothing attitude?"

"I'm twenty-one. Back then I let you into my chaotic house because Mama needed help. Physicians coming to Ground Street are rare, and I already live with the consequences of what happens when we can't get help."

He lifts his hands and then jerks them to the tufted seat. "Your mother was one of the best women I've ever known. Patient, always composed. Never frivolous, and forever trying to clean up disasters. I promised your father on his deathbed to be a mentor, to protect you and your family. I've not done a good job. I owe it to Mr. Wilcox, to fix this."

Tears threaten again, as I sit fighting the shame he wants me to feel. "My father was a good man, but he valued my mother's wisdom. As opinionated as he was, he sought my mother's advice. Mama was amazing, but I'm not her. I've learned to clean up my own problems."

His palms grip the seat as if to keep him in place. "You take it upon yourself to put yourself in jeopardy, Scarlett, while in my care. That creates problems which I need to clean up. You forget everything that can potentially harm you and embroil your family in scandal. How many fake courting schemes can the Wilcoxes endure?"

"I do not put anyone but myself in danger."

"Do so."

"Do not. And I kept you out of danger. How are you going to lecture me? I'm not working myself to exhaustion until I faint in a gentlemen's club or a brothel. Maybe if you'd opened that hospital, you wouldn't have to travel all over London."

"Don't change the subject, Scarlett. Can you not see how much I care?"

Of course I can. That small part of my heart that bears his name loves that he does. But those pieces need dissecting. Anything that makes me weak or wish for things I can never have, like the love and respect of a man who doesn't respect my dreams, must be cut away.

"I see you thinking. Let that brainbox work. The duke and I, we are respectable gentlemen. We live to protect. Livingston cares for nothing but his pleasures. He took you to a brothel."

"But he did offer to pay for my prostitute. That's a gentlemanly act."

I love how Stephen sighs at such a ludicrous statement. His nostrils flare. He struggles with the carefully controlled demeanor he wishes to portray.

I want him to burn.

I want him, Stephen Adam Carew, to burn with the fire of seven suns. *Burn away the fears that make you walk such a tight path. Burn it all down and be free.*

That's what I want, too, because I'm on fire. I see the care, the passion, the caution, and I smolder for him. I suck in a breath and fan my jacket to let out heat. "You might be respectable now, but when you were young and not an aged frump, you probably were wild. I know the duke was scandalous before. He and my sister—"

"Excuse me. Lady Hampton knew the duke before?"

"Uhm . . . yes." I bite my tongue. I can't tell Torrance's secrets. "It doesn't matter. You're just being a hypocrite, Stephen. You think you're wise, but you are stuck, stuck in mud that's as old as dirt."

He rubs at his face. "You're mixing metaphors. And I'm younger than . . . dirt. I'm not stuck. I'm a gentleman. There are many men who aren't. They'll use you. You deserve better."

"Do these users happen to model naked and have the attributes of well-hung gods? Then maybe I wouldn't mind the company."

"Scarlett, you don't know what you're saying. A deflowered woman—"

"Is looked at a little worse than one paid for her services? Hypocrites put women in horrible positions. I go to Bridewell. I provide aid to forgotten women, and I keep going back to provide aid."

His brow wrinkles. "You do that? It's not safe. What kind of aid?"

I smirk at him and say, "The best that a valiant woman can give. Definitely more than well wishes and prayers. More than missionaries who travel abroad but can't help the sick and poor at home. So many hypocrites. Most physicians are loath to go to my side of town."

"You know why, Scarlett? You know the stigma of the chronic disease. Many don't know what causes it or if it's catching."

Sinking in against my seat, I feel like weights press against my shoulders. "That's why I must help."

The door opens. Benny has returned. "Two cold bowls. Uhm. Is everyt'ing alright?"

"Fine." I take the cold dishes and marvel at Gunter's treats.

One's shaped like a banana, the other is a bunny. Stephen looks up at his driver. "That's all they had?"

"Yes, sir."

"Thank you, Benny. The molds are so innovative." I stab the banana-shaped one with my spoon and put the tip in my mouth. "Not a drop will be wasted."

"Put a whole ice in your mouth?" Stephen groans and wipes at his face. "Benny, get us to Anya House as quickly as possible."

This tone is different. Did he just growl like a bear? What? He doesn't like his bunny bowl?

"Yes . . . yes, sir." The driver runs away. The carriage jerks forward.

Stephen's frown grows. It may be permanent. He's not looking at me but the bowl and my spoon. Does he want to say something? Unless it's an apology, I want nothing more from him.

I'll eat my ice, knowing the good physician won't say a single word, not until I lick my bowl clean.

Chapter 17

STEPHEN—ANYA HOUSE—VIXEN OR BRAT?

My carriage rumbles forward, but I sit still with a freezing bowl of an ice that's shaped like a bunny.

My companion licks her spoon, and I shiver.

She slurps and curls her tongue about a banana-shaped ice, and I'm pained. Every mouthful, I count the seconds for the ice to melt on her lips. It's difficult to watch, knowing I want to yell at her, me . . . I want . . . wanna kiss her. Instead, I'm stuck envying a silver spoon, dying a little more each time it sweeps into her mouth.

"Anya House is a lovely estate in Mayfair."

I hear her words, but my mind is focused on the bit of ice drizzling down her plump bottom lip. I'm stunned at how beautiful that outrageous mouth is dripping with sweetness.

Oh, soursop. If the ice were my favorite fruit, I'd fight the spoon.

"Are you feeling well?" she says in a sugary voice as she bites down on a big piece of the banana-shaped ice.

I gulp for air and look down at the limp bunny melting in my bowl. Life's not fair.

"Stephen, this is so good. You must try it."

Another piece of ice goes in. Her lips form an O. She sighs in delight, and I'm heated. What has happened to me, to her . . . to us?

She leans over holding the spoon out to me. "Stephen, we'll fight later. Eat your ice before it melts."

It's been on her lips. It's wrestled with her tongue. I dip my head and slip her spoon between my lips. "Pineapple. It's sweet and tart. It's you."

She laughs and continues enjoying her treat.

I want to look away, but I can't. There's something in me that wants to watch her finish every dripping morsel.

With the cold bowl on my lap, I continue to grasp the seat edge. I want to punch Torrance for putting me in this situation. Then I want to punch myself for putting me in this situation.

Then I want to thank the stars, the universe, for letting me be in this position, no one else.

I keep my hands still, for I don't know what I would do with myself . . . if she offers me anything else.

It takes all of this for me to realize I don't just like Scarlett Wilcox . . . I *want* Scarlett Wilcox. And I think that's been my problem since last year's ball. It's why I kept delaying proposing to Eveline. I said it was my work or my schedules, bumbling fundraising, or becoming situated in my practice, but truthfully, no one has me this out of control. Nothing I do can harness the euphoria of matching wits with Scarlet. She's potent and addicting, pure laudanum. To withdraw from her is to feel panic, chaos, and hopelessness. I must have Scarlett Wilcox.

She licks the spoon again. "Something wrong? We have a truce. You're letting your ice melt. We'll pick back up arguing when we are done." She sighs. "Just like we used to."

"What changed, Scarlett? Until last week, I haven't seen you in months. Have you been avoiding me?"

"Yes."

That's a direct answer, and more succinct than I expect from my vixen.

I'm a fool. The duke made me her chaperone to make me see

what's been true this whole time. The Cossack is right to put me with Scarlett. He knew I'd wake up and want the rose with the thorns. I must have the pain and the pleasure of this forthright woman. "Marry me."

Slurp. "What?"

"Marry me, Scarlett."

"You're not making sense." She tilts her head. "Are you about to have a palsy again? Stephen, you don't sound well."

"What is well? Oh, I'm sick alright, sick about us."

She shrugs, scoops the last of her ice and sets her spoon down with a clang. "I guess we fight again."

"No. We don't. You will wear a dress Friday and be Scarlett for me. You'll do your best to impress the aunties."

"Excuse me?" Scarlett wipes her mouth on my handkerchief. It's one of the most alluring things I've ever seen—her patting the corners of her lips with her pinkie finger, then suckling the digit free of sweetness. "What dress?"

I have to blink a couple of times to hear the words she's saying. "Scarlett, you have dresses. I've seen you in them."

"You're going to eat your ice? Your bunny-shaped ice is half melted."

"Take it. Lick the bowl clean. You made haste with the banana." I slap myself hard in the face, for Scarlett does as she's told, and I'm tormented until she finishes off the creature.

Does she know how tempting she looks? Again, I thank myself for being in this position and not missing a moment.

How long has she been this beautiful, this sultry?

"Stephen, you're quiet. You're angry I ate your ice, but you did give it to me. I should have realized you didn't mean it."

"No. Not at all. I enjoyed watching you."

Her gaze darts from mine. It never does that. "Scarlett, I just have so much on my mind. I have a couple patients—"

"Patients?" She fidgets on the seat, and I notice how her tight breeches cling to her legs. "Do tell, Stephen. I'd love to help."

"Well. Ah. You can't. What a patient tells his doctor is confidential. How would it look if I went around town telling everyone my patients' ailments?"

The energy in her leaves. She withers on the seat like a sad puppy. "Physicians collaborate all the time. In the Royal Society, men of science and physicians offer details of conditions and then debate treatments. It leads to discoveries and new ways of doing things."

"That's physician to physician, not physician to physician's wife."

She clangs her spoon like it's a noisy toy. My bowl goes on the bench as Scarlett drops to the floor, kneeling in front of me. "No more talk about marriage."

Her mouth looks soft and full and luscious. She moves close to my knee and opens the hidden compartment under my bench pulling out her satchel. Her papers and that special notebook, they've been in my possession all this time.

"Lord Livingston talks to me," she says. "He respects me."

Who can be reasonable, when the vixen with the glorious mouth that probably tastes like pineapples is inches away?

I pinch myself to remind myself I've known her forever. That I owe her father. Then I hear my own father's voice. *Deh pickney grow up pretty fast.*

She's still kneeling and looking up at me, a beauty, a rose blossoming in plain sight, and I'm terrified.

I have to go about things right. But what is right when Scarlett kneels before me like a choice offering to the gods? This reaction must be part of the alleged heathen blood in me that an English lass makes boil.

"Please sit, Scarlett. I need you off your knees. If anyone is to be made humble, it's me."

Still oblivious to my struggles, she sits beside me.

"That isn't what I meant."

"Stephen, I was carried away when I spoke with your aunts. You go to church and explain that your new lady has left you. They'll believe that. Miss Gray did."

"Scarlett."

"And the auntie women will help you reunite with the former baroness. You must be ready to marry her now. As you said, your practice has grown."

I grasp her hand and draw her close. "What are you saying?"

"This time, Stephen, don't delay. Marry Miss Gray and be happy."

Her voice is low. She clutches the satchel to her chest like it's a rope keeping her tethered to her dream world. I'm finally letting my eyes see the beauty who's been my friend for nine years.

"You have planned this all out for me, Scarlett. What if I don't want Eveline? What if I've brought women to my aunties I knew they'd object to? What if I acted as if I mourned the loss of Eveline to keep from entertaining someone who'd slow down my practice. What if deep down I hesitated with Eveline because I knew she was not the one for me? What if I haven't been seriously interested in anyone because, deep down, I knew I'd already met the right girl?"

"Hesitation is what you do." Scarlett smiles and gazes at me with eyes that look like a lamb about to be slaughtered. Then I see a glint and a pout. "Go to Wesley's Chapel alone. This time, welcome the aunties' assistance in finding you the right wife."

Scarlett remains next to me. I've kept her hand. She can't be quite this innocent. She has to see . . . must realize . . . I can't think of any wife but her.

"After today, Stephen, I won't be a concern to you. Mr. Steele will be back. He's my usual minder. Then by month's end, I'll have a fiancé who will not care how I occupy my time. That's part of my criteria to be married. My husband must let me have science."

The overpowering rosewater scent has to be suffocating my brainbox. I couldn't have heard . . . what I heard. "You won't marry me, but you want a husband?"

"The duke will pick one for me."

"Scarlett, you know so little about marrying a stranger. A husband can be very possessive. No man worth anything will let his wife gallivant around."

"Well, I know enough to have figured out I can't be a good wife to you. You've said your wife must be demure, quiet, born of pedigree, an impeccable dresser, and beautiful. And above all of this, she must be loyal and wonderful."

"That's you, when you make an effort." I kiss her hand. It smells delicious and fruity. "You're letting one of our mere hundreds of arguments confuse you. Why are we talking about this when I need to chat with Torrance first?"

"He'll gather candidates in a week or two."

"Scarlett, you can't refuse me. I compromised you. I've thought of nothing else. I owe this to you, your father and the duke to make the situation right."

She puts a hand to my cheek. "You still don't get it. How can you be handsome and stupid?"

"You're not marrying anyone else. That's not possible. Marriage is something to be decided by a chaperone or guardian not—"

"Not a girl." She sighs, her eyes have tears.

I'm desperate to eat my words. It never occurred to me how much I cared about her until I became jealous of her looking at a naked man and licking a spoon.

The carriage stops, and she grasps me by the barrel knot of my cravat. "Stephen, goodbye."

She tugs my face to hers. Readying to fight with her and Torrance, I expect a kiss on the cheek.

That's not what my Scarlett offers. Her lips claim mine. My mouth opens, and I taste sweetness of pineapples. Her tongue curls under mine, and I become her happy spoon.

Her arm wraps about my neck. Part of me is conscious of where we are. I wave at the window to make sure Benny doesn't interrupt.

The kiss deepens. My pulse chases hers. I fight her tailcoat to feel her, not buttons.

She pulls away. Her face turns slightly. "We should get out. We've arrived."

Scarlett is close enough that I smell sandalwood on her throat. The awful rosewater fumes from the brothel lessen when she fills my nostrils.

Her eyes, wide and dark, glitter at me. "Goodbye, Stephen Adam—"

I can't let her finish. We can't be done, when I just figured out what I want. I tug her back to me and teach the woman of science the proper mathematics of a kiss.

A kiss—its volume is infinite. It should take time, time without limit to explore the depths of her, her sweet mouth. Easing to the floor with Scarlett in my arms, I find the circumference of her hips and hold on to her with one arm. Half propped up along the cabinets beneath the seats, I let my free hand do division—splitting open a waistcoat, a shirt placard, and untucking the hem of some sort of shift.

"Yes, Stephen."

This agreeable whimper alters my universe. Again she says my name, and I reach for the planets, the heavenly bodies of a bosom bound in bandages. I count the rotations of linen about her chest. These are the layers I must traverse to free her, to find us, to find our universe.

Scarlett straddles me and I understand that there's a hidden beauty to her wearing breeches. Undoing a fall flap would be more accessible than layers of petticoats in the confined space of a carriage.

I tug a button. I stroke a waist. Silky skin and strong abdominals wait for me. Yet, we are on an open street in front of Anya House. There was more privacy at Madame Rosebud's. The way we are dressed, a molly-house for gentlemen would do.

The humor of it all, how wrong all of this is, breaks my desire. "Scarlett, we need to stop. Scarlett—"

Her mouth covers mine. Her kisses grow more intense. I hear whispers for more, whimpers to love her, a list of wanton anatomy. Her textbook knowledge of parts and functions blisters my skin.

If she uses a Latin term, I'm done.

"Don't hesitate, Stephen," she says. "Give me something to remember of you. A comparison."

"Remember . . . what are you saying? Goodbye? No. This is a beginning."

She stops. "Why can't you be normal? Why must you think of tomorrow?"

"Because that's who I am. Temptress, tormentor, who are you?"

I pull my hands from her hips and fall to the smelly floor. The brothel's rosewater scent is like smelling salts. It brings me back to my senses. "The duke can get us a special license. Or we can do that Cossack marriage thing Lord Mark and Georgina speak of. I want you as my wife as soon as possible."

Her head tilts as she hovers above me. "I just like that you want me."

Her smile is wicked as her hands claw into my jacket. Her fingers slip against my waistcoat. Like a scalpel, her fingers find skin. With a firm hold, she dips close and kisses me.

I savor her and laugh inside at how quiet talkative Scarlett has become. She's studying me like I'm an exhibit. Yet, I just want to love her.

Her heart pounds against my chest. Again, I forget myself, all the promises I've made to the duke, her late father, and even my soul. I tow her to me and taste warm and sugary Scarlett until she moans my name. "Stephen Adam Carew, take me."

Nothing has ever sounded so good.

I savor her lips, draining all the honey this haven of beauty, this hive of wonderment, offers.

My hand finds her hips again, the breeches, the fall, her buttons. It takes everything to stop. I raise my hands high. "I'm begging, Scarlett. Let's do this right."

Frowning, the honeybee pulls away. But I'm already stung.

Her eyes are wide. She's staring at me.

"Listen." I say. "You will marry me. I've compromised you in a brothel, and now in my carriage."

"No one saw. The prostitutes won't speak of it."

I point to the glass behind me. In her mirror-black eyes, I see the reflection of Benny's hat, the back of his mantle. "He's always right there to open the door when my carriage stops."

Her gaze flicks up and she leaps away, backing onto the seat. "Command him not to tell."

"It's not that simple, Scarlett." Breathing heavily, I sit up. "Benny's loyal. He'll protect us, but that doesn't change what I know, what we almost did. Your trust in me deserves bettah."

"Better?"

"Yes. That's what I said. We're going to marry. And Friday, you'll go with me in a dress to the aunties. You'll be pretty and introduced as my wife."

She's silent. Yet, her gorgeous eyes are wet. "Thank you for the decent kiss. I like comparisons. These were better."

"What comparisons, Scarlett?"

"Immaterial. For I must decline your offer. The duke knows beautiful women. He'll arrange for you to have someone good to bring to the aunties. Good day, Stephen."

Scarlett opens the door, bounces off my seat and runs into Anya House.

I'm stunned. Why would she say yes to a moment of passion, but not a lifetime? We can plan and build a life.

My head is all over the place. What did I let happen? What did she do to me? Why do I know she just won whatever game we've been playing?

A knock on the carriage door startles me. "Great, Scarlett. We need—"

The door opens and disappointment hits my gut.

Benny leans inside. "Yuh going to get out and chase her? 'Bout time yuh realized yuh love her."

What?

"But since she's left yuh, guess she don't feel the same."

Looking up at a frowning Benny makes me feel more foolish. "You think you can get the rosewater smell out of here, so the next time I lose my mind, the stench won't cheapen the moment to a brothel?"

Benny's frown deepens. "Did yuh lose yuh mind, sir? Or did yuh find yuh heart."

I 've lost my mind and Scarlett's gone. Was I grander, more passionate, more of a hero when I was out of my mind? "She said I bettah now and not then?" I work my jaw and say, "Better."

"Yes, sir?"

I wave him away, but as I sit up, he says, "I'll get the smell out wit help from di duke's mews. That should give yuh plenty of time to go fix what yuh did wrong."

I check my buttons, tweak the position of my cravat. "I need to get this right."

Benny tries to help, but I force myself out of my carriage. Again, I wave away assistance. Straightening my wrinkled tailcoat, I start walking toward the front door of Anya House.

I must find the fleeing bride-to-be. I'm annoyed, hot and stiff. She's left my skin feeling like fire.

But I want her, want her back. I need her fighting with me, kissing me, sending me to crazy places, where every time we talk, touch, taste seems safer and more sensible and secure.

I don't understand why Scarlett is willing to be with me in a brothel, wanting to bed me in my carriage, but won't wed me. What has soured her to the idea of marriage. These unions can be respectful and lustful . . . and become loving.

I'm not my grandfather. I won't force a marriage by confessing to a compromise, but I'm not giving up on Scarlett. She needs to tell me why my hesitation to have at her in the carriage has chased my vixen away.

Chapter 18

STEPHEN—CHASING THE ONE THAT GOT AWAY

I hurry up the pavement to the doors of Anya House. Footmen are at the ready to take my hat and gloves, but they are with my pride in my reeking carriage.

Head lifted, acting like everything is normal, I enter and in a casual tone ask, "Do you know where Miss Wilcox has gone?"

"Gone, sir?" the lead man in silver liveries asks. "The miss is in the library. I've been told she's been there all day."

He glances at me directly after issuing such a full-throated falsehood. Scarlett just passed through these doors.

There's nothing else to ask the duke's henchmen, and I walk deeper into the hall. Should I head to the library upstairs and be caught in our seventy-fifth compromise? No. Catching her changing from menswear to Scarlett-wear would be disastrous.

Sidestepping a pile of lumber, I find construction dust on everything. The hall looks like a battle has been waged.

"Excuse me, sir." A man carrying a large crate passes me and heads into Torrance's study.

That's a sign. Go to the man who knows everything about the Wilcoxes and establishes alibis and lies. The duke will know why Scarlett doesn't want to marry.

Moving into the study, I notice the tapestries are gone. Chairs, too. Sheets cover the floors. I move from the path of two big blokes carrying wood. "What's going on? Where's Torrance?"

One of the workers points toward the bookcases which are emptied of his books, chessboards, and vials. Then the two leave me with lumber and more sheet-covered items that are too difficult to move, like His Grace's large desk.

I cough a little from the yellow haze in the air. I don't see the duke.

Going to the desk, I peer out the large window that sits behind it. The floral gardens and high maze are luscious and green and Scarlett-less. My gut tightens. Why do I feel like the longer I'm away from her, the less likely we'll be able to resolve the problem between us?

Noises rattle from behind the sheet-covered bookcase. A worker comes from the hall with tools. He lifts the sheet and disappears.

Knowing I'm well rested and have eaten, I can assume I'm not seeing things. I go to the sheet and uncover a large hole. It's the entry to a secret room.

"Torrance? What d'yavol is this?"

"A moment, Mr. Carew," he says. He's coughing, leaning on his cane, pointing out where he wishes sconces to be placed to a carpenter.

This is not good for my patient's health. I'll find Scarlett later, after she calms. I can't let Torrance do things to trigger another health crisis, so I grab his arm and hurry him outside into the sun and fresh air. "This construction is not good for you. And what have you done, Your Grace? Is the dining room still here?"

"Ah, Mr. Carew. A little less of the ballroom, a little less of the garden. But rest assured, the maze is fully intact. Scarlett still has her view of the gardens. She demands that." The duke waves at a gentleman who's entered his newly built lair to join us outdoors.

The fellow comes and has a satchel like Scarlett's. "Progress seems to be going well, Your Grace."

"Splendid," the duke says. "Mr. Carew, this is Mr. Samuel

Pepys Cockerell. He's a wonderful architect. He studied under Sir Robert Taylor."

I'm sure those credentials are impressive, but I'm more concerned with my patient. We don't know what triggers his bouts of suffering. I know the stress of construction and the dust can't be good. "What's going on, Torrance?"

"I'll leave you to the maze." Cockerell folds his papers. "I'll tell the carpenters to add the additional compartments. A rack for flintlocks is unusual but this is the stage to add nooks." He walks back into the chaos.

"Guns, Torrance?"

"One can never be too careful. A third member of the Court of Chancery has resigned. You probably missed it in the papers. It was a little-known earl."

"Not Lord Ashford?"

Torrance's brow furrows. "No. Ashford isn't on the court, but he often presents cases of titles and custody. A different peer has fallen." He looks around and then motions me forward. "There're too many people around. Let's go into the maze."

Resigned, I follow. The notion of him having weapons or needing them is very disconcerting.

"Well, you have seen the bones of my secret room. When it's complete, a hidden latch will open the bookcase and I can hide . . . my treasures."

"More rare chessboards or more guns?"

"Da and a few of my father's flintlocks. He was an expert marksman. Of course, my more delicate chessboards, the rarest finds, will be in there and out of reach of those who may not show them proper care."

The duke leads me deeper into the maze. "Chess," he says, "with its twists and turns brings me infinite pleasure." He stops after we've taken a few turns. The boxwood hedge is lovely, perfectly green and trimmed. A stone bench is nearby. "Carew, my friend, you look concerned. Are you well? I heard you haven't been feeling well."

"I'm well, but I'm hunting Miss Wilcox. She ran from my carriage."

"Tsk tsk." The duke chuckles. "Well, thank you for bringing her back from Somerset House. Meetings here ran long." He glances at me, like I do to examine a patient for illness. "You and poor Scarlett cannot help but argue. Such a shame."

"Oh, this time we got along too well. I asked her to marry me. And then she ran."

Torrance blinks a few times. "So you just figured out that you like her. And that she's a woman?"

"I've always liked her." I put my hands to my head like I can stuff my sanity back into my cranium. Goodness, every bit of me smells of that awful rose water. "But now I want to marry her."

The duke sits on the bench and takes deep breaths. "My, what a change."

"Torrance, I knew that dust would get to you." I reach and pick up his wrist, checking his pulse rate against my pocket watch. "Well, everything is still beating properly."

"I'm fine, Carew. You, on the other hand, do not look well at all. But you smell like roses. Can't be all bad."

Dropping his wrist, I nod. "Things can be bettah . . . better with your help."

"Avoiding brothels during the day with Miss Wilcox might help."

"We didn't go there again . . ." Oh. I'm dead. "Torrance, you know about that whole crazy night and haven't tried to duel with me with one of your father's guns? I guess I'm fortunate."

He glances up at me blinking. The sun is behind us, in my eyes. He must be calculating my usefulness. "So you've come to beg forgiveness?"

I wanna beg, alright, but not to him. "The night at the brothel was a combination of my stupidity, Livingston's zeal, my driver's deference to fools, and Miss Wilcox's iron disposition. I would never willingly take her there. And she was kind enough not to leave me there."

"Scarlett is one of the good ones—loyal, pretty, clever."

The sun beads sweat on my brow, while Torrance looks as cool as a Gunter's ice. "Why do you sanction her behavior?"

His laughter rumbles in his chest along with a thunderous cough. "You think I want her at a brothel?"

"Of course not, Torrance."

"You can either help a mule or stand back and let it kick you. I'll let Scarlett Wilcox do what she wishes, for you cannot stop someone so determined. I'd rather she be safe and confide in me, no matter what happens. Scandal is harshest on women. I don't want her trying to navigate this world by herself."

There is a twisted sort of logic to that. "Doesn't it drive you crazy that she could be disgraced any moment?"

"Perhaps a little. But it seems to bother you a great deal more. Why is that?"

The remote throbbing of a well-deserved headache starts to ramp. "I've known the family a long time. Mr. Wilcox was someone I greatly admired. He introduced me to so many people when I first began to practice. I owe him."

"Then helping keep Scarlett safe is not too big of a request." He taps his lips with his ring finger. One that I notice has a small gold band. "A bold woman," he says, "is something magical to behold."

"I . . . I just wish she was more cautious. Her mother was such a levelheaded woman."

"Mrs. Wilcox suffered the same condition I have."

His tone doesn't sound like a question, but I see no harm in answering. "Yes. And she was remarkable and dignified. Such a credit to her husband."

"Was she faithful to Mr. Wilcox?"

A snap sounds behind us. It echoes as if it has come from deeper in the maze.

"The construction," the duke says. "Pay no attention to it. Continue talking about Mrs. Wilcox."

"Of course she was faithful. Mrs. Wilcox was the kind of

woman who'd never bring scandal to her family. She stressed that to her daughters. Not quite sure if they listened—"

"Did it not strike you as odd that only Lydia Wilcox has this same condition? Unless the other Wilcox sisters still have a chance of coming down with this sickness later in life."

"No one knows how it happens. From the small amount of research I've seen, these are chronic issues. Sometimes the parents show no sign and the illness befalls their child. There's just not enough known."

The duke folds his arms and leans back along the bench. "My sister Anya, I'm convinced, died of this."

"Your father was British, Duke. I've seen this in people with color in their skin. It ravages Blackamoors the most."

"Well, perhaps the brown-eyed people of London have more explaining to do about their heritage. My mother sent a picture of Anya. When all the renovations are done, I'll find an important place to display it."

I hate bothering him when I can tell he isn't up to his best, but things can't wait. Matters of honor cannot. "Torrance, I want to marry Scarlett Wilcox. I can't keep pretending that she's my cousin, my male cousin, especially now that I want her to be my wife. She met the aunties of Cheapside as Scotland. They want to find 'my cousin' a nice girl."

"Well, cousins do marry here in Britain." The duke begins to laugh until he coughs. "Carew, how do you get in such predicaments?"

The duke sees the humor. I see the scandalous illustrations that will be the rage of London.

"Carew, it seems we both have problems getting Wilcox women to marry us."

Oh, he's humored, but let me bus' de mark. "Torrance, it seems this isn't the first time you've tried to marry one of them."

His face changes, saddens. Bus' de mark.

"Scarlett accidently admitted you knew her sister before. That would have to be after Inverness and in St. Petersburg."

"Da. I knew Katherine Wilcox 'the younger,' but I don't know the older, this woman who has become a viscountess." He struggles and sighs deeply. "I don't know her at all. I suppose as we get older, they do, too. Girls change. Women, too."

"Your Grace, do you need to be out here? Are you feeling well?"

He stares past me and looks to the house. "Scarlett loves looking at the maze in the mornings. She loves the bay window. Used to remind her of the one at White's, until your great adventure."

I look down at my dusty boots. Benny spent time polishing them. "Our outing didn't change her. She's been different since last year, since your ball."

"Carew, can disappointment make someone act out of character, or could you have been deceived all along?"

There is not a drop of mirth in his words, but I hear truth in his pain. "As Shakespeare writes of Othello and Desdemona, jealousy can quickly turn love into hatred. But Scarlett's not jealous, and Lady Hampton merely despises you."

"What a conventional attitude you have, physician." The duke shakes his head. "Lady Hampton is jealous that I have the means to show affection to whom I please. My current object is my Lidochka. She must ask herself, how can a man who doesn't love me love the child of my flesh, bone of my bone?"

The passion in his tone is unnerving. Shouldn't have quoted Shakespeare. It's armed him to push me off a poetic cliff . . . a deserved cliff. "Your Grace, we were talking about Miss Wilcox."

"Scarlett is jealous that you can have science. You can go to lectures, visit patients, while she must contend to matters of the home and art she doesn't wish to know or care for."

"Torrance, look at Anya House. You're building a secret room fit for a king because you feel like it. I was there last year; you brought an elephant to Miss Lydia Wilcox's birthday. That is hard to contend with."

"Why contend? Why not be content that this child, who may

not know tomorrow, gets the best of every day?" He taps his cane on the ground. The tip hides in the thick freshly cut grass. "I should not raise my voice."

"You are being wonderful to the Wilcoxes. More generous to them than I think anyone, but—" I raise my hands. "I surrender the point. Do as you please. My birthday is in December."

"Da, at the end of the year, Carew. I will remember."

"Actually, if you wish to give me an early gift, convince Scarlett to come with me to Wesley's Chapel. She promised the aunties that I'm courting a beautiful girl and that she'll accompany me to church on Friday, and then to a picnic-dinner thing. It's hard to describe, but I want them to meet Scarlett."

"You want me to convince Scarlett to dress in a gown and go with you. Not breeches. Done."

The man still chuckles, while the word *breeches* gives me the image of her straddling me on the floor of my carriage as we drown in passionate, rosewater hell. "I need you to do more, Torrance. I compromised her. I want to marry Scarlett. I need you to make that happen."

All the laughter stops. He's glancing up at me. "How am I to make that happen? I'm not a tsar. And my barrister says my powers as a duke are, apparently, limited."

Why would he check? I clear my head and get to the point. "You have a bet, Torrance. I know she said you'd pick who she'd marry. Tell her me."

The duke plays with his cane like he's considering lifting it and giving me a whack. "This is quite a change. I'm hearing intensity and passion. Not so much love."

Now I'm silent.

I care a great deal for her, but is this wild desperate feeling love? "I don't know. But I'm not waiting around to let someone else swoop in and sweep her off her feet. I want to be the man who carries her away."

Torrance looks like he's thinking. That's dangerous.

"Your Grace, do I need to go to Lady Hampton? If I mention

one of the ways I've . . . the way Scarlett has been scandalized, she'll give her permission."

"That's unnecessary and dangerous. Katherine could turn against you. She did after my son was stillborn, did she not?"

His son. The duke knows. I'll not lie to patients. I'll keep their lies. This is a rare truth. "She didn't want me near the house. For a long time, I was a reminder of that night."

"Where is my son buried?"

"St. Pancras. Torrance, I'm sorry. I didn't know he was yours. The Wilcoxes didn't volunteer information."

The wind blows. Yellow particles scatter in the air.

"Your Grace?"

He stares off into nothingness. "Are you ready to concede that your definition of the perfect woman is wrong?"

"Torrance, what are you talking about?"

He moves his hands like he's directing instruments. "I believe you said, 'The perfect woman is demure, quiet, born of pedigree, an impeccable dresser, and beautiful.'"

"Yes. Yes, Torrance. And Scarlett's all of these things. She's loyal and wonderful."

"Quiet and demure? My Scarlett?" He shakes his head. "And even if she were to become all of those things, or become less of herself to please you, what are you going to change to be the type of man that she wants?"

Comparisons . . . she said something about comparing. Oh Lord. Is there someone else? "Your Grace, I probably know. You remember how we studied at Inverness. The answer's up here." I tap my brow. "I just need to stop and find it. Give me a chance to find out. Just one."

"If the aunties are expecting the perfect woman to show up with you, I can arrange that. I can have a cultured, sophisticated woman prepared to meet them."

"But I want it to be Miss Wilcox. I don't want a substitute, un-less she can be so impressive that it keeps the aunties from plotting to reconnect me to Eveline Gray. My old love is now without a husband. I don't want Eveline, or anyone but Scarlett." Scarlett and time is what I want, more than . . .

I hear what sounds like a footfall. The duke doesn't move. Must be my conscience making noise, because I've bungled things so badly. "Can you convince Scarlett to marry me?"

He shrugs. "I think you need to figure out why she doesn't want you."

Oh, I know she wants me, she just doesn't want to keep me. "I'll ask her now. Where is she? Do you have her in a tower?"

"Nyet. But the bay window." He points to a large bay window above the protrusion of the duke's new secret lair. The lacy puce curtains are spread wide.

"That's Scarlett's room? Seems a bit feminine."

"Don't let the tailcoat fool you, Carew. Scarlett picked every decoration. A Vasilisa or Cinderella in training. Or for you, my Shakespeare-loving friend, she's a Kate after finding love." He shakes his head and waves his cane provocatively. "Now, let her be. Anya House is her sanctuary. I wish my estate as a refuge for as long as she wishes, regardless of any bet."

Why did the duke's voice rise so suddenly?

Guess this impasse will have to hold until I see her again. "Fine. Get her to come with me Friday. I will find out whatever she wants. I'll be whatever she wants. I'll not lose her."

The duke stands and hobbles closer. "You talk of grand gestures. Bring her elephants because you can. Scarlett Wilcox knows what she wants. Make it your mission to find out what it is. Don't plan. Do. I suspect her list is specific, and probably scientific."

That's Scarlett through and through—a satchel of curiosity and research notes. Yet, a set of lacy curtains gives me greater hope. Maybe I wouldn't always be her mentor. Maybe she could be my respite from the strain of seeing sickness and disease and heartache every day from my patients. "There must be something sweet and romantic about her, too. Torrance, my foolhardy list wasn't complete. It needs frivolity and laughter to balance all the sadness my medicine can't heal."

"And if she is none of those things? Will you still want Scarlett Wilcox?"

If the carriage floor is any indication of our life together, then we can both be highly illogical and lusty, too. "I'll do anything, Torrance. I'll be a good husband. I'll strive to be the man who can make her happy."

His brow rises. "If you are willing to change for her, that says a great deal about you."

"Scarlett Wilcox is the most loyal person I know. She's worth every sacrifice. Let me talk with her. I can figure it out, perhaps, before Friday."

He stands and shakes his head. "No seeing her until then."

"No visit? No supper? No walks in a maze?"

"Nothing. I'll work to convince her to go with you Friday. Or I'll have a substitute ready. You play by my rules. Come here Friday. Maybe the time apart will give you both clarity. And do leave off the rosewater soap. It might be what's driving her away."

His laughter follows me as I leave and head to the mews. Hopefully, Benny has the scent gone by now. I glance back at Anya House, at that bay window, wishing I could see Scarlett before I leave.

My prayer is that she's not too stubborn and will venture into my world of Cheapside. I want to show her that she belongs there with me. Nonetheless, my fears of failing begin to spin. Friday is not enough time to plan. And I can't believe my prospects are in the hands of the flintlock-hiding, grieving, mad duke.

Chapter 19

SCARLETT—ANYA HOUSE, MAZE OF TRUTH

The duke's lush maze hides me completely. The walls loom high enough and are thick enough to keep away prying eyes. The smell of gorse and heather, the maze's coconut and honey scents, attempt to smother the ghastly rosewater fragrance on my clothes and the fire raging in my chest.

Stephen Adam Carew. I can't believe you want me and wish to marry.

"Miss or Mr. Wilcox, you can come out now. The physician has gone."

I lift from my crouching position, straightening my waistcoat. I dust my boots and trudge the twists and turns of the maze.

The duke sits on a bench. Without looking at me, he waves a handkerchief. "I was going to ask you to remove the costume from your face, but you already have."

"Mr. Carew was kind enough to make a little elixir. It was gentle on my cheeks."

He nods. "Must everything that man makes smell of rose water?"

When I sit beside him, he squints and stares at me. "Good to see you as you. There's no lead in those cosmetics?"

"Of course not. I'm a woman of science. I'll not risk making my teeth fall out. I do like to eat. You think that's my frivolous side?"

The duke begins to chuckle, then sobers. "I suspected you were listening. Carew is brilliant. His care has improved the health of many. Lydia and I have him and you to thank. The two of you together could be an amazing team."

"What kind of team? Him telling his little wifey what to do? That's not a team."

The duke shrugs. "Georgina likes domesticity, baking, home-making, I don't think she would consider that being told what to do."

"You don't want me burning down the house baking." I tug at my waistcoat and carefully refasten buttons that Stephen has un-done. "Perhaps he should hire a staff for these needs. Leave me to charts and research books."

"Have some sympathy for him. It sounds as if you've had a stable home. Mr. Carew grew up very fast. His family experienced great turmoil in Trinidad. Then when he was at Inverness Royal Academy, his mother died. His father became a rebel, fighting for his island's independence from the country Carew now calls home."

"His father was killed by the British?"

"It's unclear, but it's a heavy weight to become something of substance in a foreign land. Carew feels he has a lot of traditions to uphold while building his success in Britain."

Thought I knew everything about him. Guess I didn't. "Where are his loyalties? Here, Trinidad?"

"Apparently, it is to you and the aunties."

This is true, but the situation is impossible. "Did you tell him that I can't marry him?"

The duke's face goes blank. "Let's chat man-to-man."

Easing my satchel of drawings to the ground, I prepare for a Russian story that's going to persuade to me marry my physician.

Everything stills. A blackbird flutters nearby. A peacock butter-fly flaps its spotted yellow wings and flits past us.

"It's very peaceful here, Scarlett. Sometimes peace is all you can claim. Mr. Carew lives in Cheapside. You'll find it very nice."

Slouching against the bench makes the top button in my burgundy waistcoat pop open. "I met the aunties. They seem a bit much."

"Oh, they are," he laughs. "Those ladies are the informal welcoming committee, especially on this side of the Thames, for immigrants. The old Huguenot area stands where once a great Jewish population lived. It's home to many immigrants. Many well-to-do and up-and-coming Blackamoors have made roots there."

He sniffles, and I offer the duke the cloth that holds my fake sideburns.

The duke declines my offer, waving his hand to dismiss me. It's a motion that drives Katherine crazy. I understand better why it does. I stuff the handkerchief into my pocket. "I want to hate Stephen Adam Carew."

The duke doesn't respond. At least two minutes pass of the blackbird singing before he says, "It would be easier to hate the ones we care for when we can't quite find the energy or the words to make peace."

Well, Stephen and I make peace when we're not talking. In his arms, everything finds mates—arms, lips . . . waistcoats. "I still want to hate him."

The duke pats my hand. "Truly? My dear Scarlett, he's exactly what we are looking for."

"What do you mean, *we?*"

"Carew has a brilliant mind. He's accepted in the rarefied spaces of the Royal Society. He's already doing research in the areas of medicine which are your concern."

"Wait a minute. What are you saying?"

"I choose Mr. Carew to be your husband." The duke flashes an innocent-looking smile, but his words strike like lightning.

"You have to be kidding. After this week, he's the last man to want me in science."

"But he wants you, Scarlett. And you've been in love with him a long time. Those are two important things."

"He *wants* me? I teased him with banana-shaped ice and kissed him in the carriage, that doesn't mean . . ."

The duke tilts his head to the side. "I'm going to pretend that's an innocent statement. And if it's not, that's more reason to marry."

"Maybe I'm too young. For I must surely have missed the part where Mr. Carew and I can stand to be around each other without arguing or kissing."

The duke raises praying hands. "I'm holding on to hope that these are all innocent statements. Or maybe keep kissing him. That will create understanding. But you have more. You protected him in White's and Madame Rosebud's, that means you care deeply and he can trust you deeply. That's enough."

Standing, my hands go to my hips. I let them since I'm not trying to pretend I'm not a woman or emotional. I'm signaling that it's not enough. "I want more. Stephen Adam Carew can't give more."

He lowers his hands to the bench. "Fine time for you to figure that out. But I've watched you two together. I think there is much more to be gained by both of you."

"You didn't see his reaction to the naked man. But you—Why is your face scrunching up?"

He blinks six times. "My life seems to be speeding up and spinning out of control the more I talk with you. Enough. I've decided. You gave me power. And please don't tell Lady Hampton anything about a naked man."

The duke begins to rise, but I ask, "Tell me why you are meeting with the Earl of Ashbrook."

Sitting back down, he twirls his cane. "He's a trained barrister. I needed some legal advice."

"Yes. He's very good with criminal trials for the Crown, but lately he's taken on a number of situations for custody at the

Court of Chancery." I'm frowning, showing him that I'm concerned. Custody would involve minor children. "If you wish to talk about the trouble you are in, I'm here for you, Your Grace."

"That's comforting. But I'm not in trouble. I needed to know a few things, like whether, if I locate where my son is buried, I can give him his proper name, give him his honor on the headstone. Mr. Carew just told me the location. Ashbrook's advisement says I have rights."

A gasp leaves my mouth. "So, I'm right. Katherine's stillborn was your son."

He nods. "That's why she hates me. I don't think I can blame her. I didn't know. I never intended to be gone from her for very long. Now she wishes me gone forever. My sickness will grant her wish."

"You are doing well, Your Grace. And we are pitiful. That's not your fault."

"Katherine believes it is. And on that, we can agree."

His tone is bittersweet.

And I'm crying again. "If my brother had lived, I would hope he'd be like you. Funny, dedicated. Obsessive, like me."

"And bothersome." He stands slowly, like a man weighed down with sandbags. "Don't forget that. I think everyone can agree that Torrance and the Wilcoxes are bothersome."

I'm not sure who moves first, but suddenly I'm in his embrace.

"My sister Anya was feisty like you, Scarlett. So inquisitive. Like a butterfly, I wouldn't hold back her wings, not when she was learning to fly. Just didn't know she'd soar and become an angel. My mother sent a painting of her. The last one painted of Anya. I didn't know how much I missed that face."

His breath whimpers. I think his face is wet. Hard to tell when mine is.

"I can't be everywhere, Scarlett. I need someone who can help you fly."

"Mr. Steele?"

"He's busy with my dealings, but Mr. Carew will do. His code of honor is exactly what I need. I'll negotiate a marriage between the two of you."

"What do you have on him that is going to make him agree?"

The duke pats my back and releases me. He wipes at his lapel. "Nothing. But he needs a favor. A beautiful woman to meet his aunties."

"Yes, Your Grace, choose for him a woman who's demure, quiet, born of pedigree, an impeccable dresser, and beautiful. And of course, she must be loyal and wonderful." I mock Stephen's tone when I say this. "Friday is four days away. Where are you going to find a demure prostitute on such short notice?"

The duke's palms are up, moving like they are an imaginary scale and he's weighing things. "No, a prostitute won't do."

He comes back to me and lifts my chin with his pinkie finger. "Why get a professional when I have a diamond of the first water here? I know you can pass any overprotective auntie's test."

"No. No. All Mr. Carew and I do is argue. I'll embarrass him."

The duke leans in. "Merely kiss and quiet him. No argument." He takes my satchel and my hand and walks me toward the house and his odd new construction. "You've played a man for two days under incredible scrutiny. You can play demure and elegant for a day as well."

"I don't know. If I blunder—"

"You are charming, Scarlett. My tailor did wonders for this outfit, but for this assignment I will bring the modistes of the spring season to you. They will create a perfect outfit for your Friday outing. I'll get you a book on social graces."

No. This is ludicrous. "Thank you for your graces, Your Grace, but Mr. Carew is expecting someone exceptional."

"Trust me, Scarlett. You will be his perfect woman. Now, you go change before Lady Hampton and Lydia arrive. You will be an angel on earth. Anya will be proud."

"Angel? Hardly. Carew's going to object."

"The physician will see you dressed as someone who can be presented to the queen. Trust me."

I want to protest, but I actually don't mind. "I want to make him dread every moment fearing for what I might say, but not how I look."

"Scarlett, how about a compromise? Let's try to be nice. Get him out of trouble with his aunts, and figure out if, with kindness, you can be a good match to Carew. I'm sure he'll reward you with some innocent thing that I don't need to hear about."

With a small curtsy, I take my satchel and go into the construction. Avoiding the lumber and dust, I turn and look at the duke. His movements are slow. The decorative cane, he's leaning on more. I'm frightened for him. We need my friend in our lives.

Glancing at the proud, handsome man, I wonder why Katherine cannot forgive a man who is obviously sorry. Why does it feel as if something more that my sister's wrath is torturing him? It's more than his illness or winning the silly bet. I doubt the troubles have anything to do with an angel.

Chapter 20

STEPHEN—THE BUSINESS OF DISCRETION

Light streams through the window of St. Margaret's Church in Westminster and falls upon me and the prostrate minister I've been called to attend. The cross of Golgotha, big and wide, from the brown-tinted window, places a mark on his brow.

"Don't make it hurt too badly, sir." The fellow is desperate. "You fixed the arm up pretty well last time. I hate being so clumsy."

Allegedly, tripping over a stack of hymnals has made the minister this way.

"Glad you could come so quickly," he says.

I nod and know it's not so quick. He's the third patient I've seen since sunrise, but I will keep his secrets as I do others.

Hands on my hips, I take another glance at my surroundings. I don't think it wise to move the patient from the church floor. Being in the shadow of the raised pulpit and baptismal font is sort of comforting.

"Can you fix me, Mr. Carew? I hear you're the best at this sort of thing."

Stooping low, I return his praise with a confident smile. "Of course, but we must do a reduction. That will require you to be held down while I twist your leg to get the bone realigned. You've snapped that femur in two."

Biting on his lip, he nods his consent.

I hold his hand. For a moment, my dark hand covers his light one. "I will give you laudanum to dull the pain, that is if you wish it. I recommend it. The pain will be worse before it's better."

"Laudanum?" He sort of cracks a little smile. "Sure. But there is brandy in my office, if that will help."

I nod to his assistant, a young page in flowing white robes and a dark collar, who runs off to get it. Then I look up at faithful Benny. "I'll need your help."

"Yes, sir, Mr. Carew. Anyt'ing." He takes my indigo tailcoat, laying it over the sidewall of a walnut pew over the choir loft, making sure my small copy of *Sense and Sensibility* doesn't fall out.

That would be something Scarlett knows about me. What have I gleaned from her over the many years that I've known her?

"Mr. Carew, weh need tools from the carriage?"

"Bring the braces." Responding to Benny, I try to push away my distracting thoughts. "I have laudanum in my bag. Though I have faith in the brandy, I think a little laudanum will be more helpful when I align the bones."

As the minister winces, Benny leaves. The page returns with an amber-colored bottle, and I motion to him to give some to the minister. The hurt man greedily gulps from the glass rim.

"There's no bleeding," I say, "and no bones protruding through the skin." When I tug on the femur, I can easily feel the separation. "You're sure that it was a stack of hymnals that did this? It's a significant break."

"Not going to lie to you, Mr. Carew, not in a house of God."

His words sear. As a man grounded in faith, I can truthfully say mine is at an all-time low—low in myself, my fellow man and precisely, a fella-woman.

Rooting through my leather bag, I look at what I can use—clamps, knives, bottles of medicine—but my mind is drowning in a sea of Scarlett. It's been a day, a mere twenty-four hours since our kiss and compromise, and I can't stop thinking of her.

What is she doing? Is the activity in menswear? Or in nothing at all?

I rub my troubled brow. I'm slow and deliberate, but my dreams are not. They race through my mind bringing memories of her—her smile, her laughter, her witty barbs. The woman is clever. Why haven't I noticed before? Why is my logical mind the last to know?

Was I out, dashing between patients, when this metamorphosis occurred?

When did those mirrored eyes that could cut a bloke turn to smoke, turn to fire? When did that harsh wit become desire? What miracle has made her the woman I want?

"Sir, di braces. Also brought di splints. Mr. Carew?"

"Oh, yes. Thanks, Benjamin."

Gawking at me, he shakes his head. "Oh, meh boss have it bad."

"What's bad?" The minister rises slightly from the floor. "You said—"

"He's not talking about you, Reverend. It's me." It's me, me, oh Lord. Standing in the need . . . Never mind.

The man strokes his silver hair and settles back onto the floor. "I'm not going anywhere, son. You can talk about her."

"I didn't say it was a her."

Benny and the minister look at me as if I've lost my mind, but truly, I have. "Let's get on with this." I take a small glass from my bag and fill it halfway with laudanum and top it with brandy. "This will burn a little."

The minister drinks my mixture. "Go on. Talk to us."

While my manservant and the minister wait for me to confess, I struggle with the sleepless nights this situation has caused. How can I rest when my mind keeps sending me to dangerous places, of her and me and that terrible, no-good carriage floor?

Oh goodness, she deserves so much more. She's not meant for a harried moment, but a lifetime.

"Mr. Carew." Benny nudges me.

"Thank you, Scarlett. I mean, Benny."

My man-of-all-work gives me that yuh-a-fool-but-my-boss look.

He hasn't mentioned catching an eyeful of me and Scarlett. "Don't ever bring her a banana ice again."

The minister, writhing on the floor, looks up. "A banana ice would be good right now. Cold and sweet."

"Was pineapple flavored, just shaped like de banana." Benny is trying hard to keep his accent low. But there's a rhythm to his scold. "Pineapple is de favorite of Miss Wilcox. But yuh know that, sir."

Did I? Of course, I did. "Let's get started, Benny. I need you to hold his shoulders." I turn to the young man. "You can help, too."

"A pineapple ice sounds good," the page says. "Tart and sweet."

Oh goodness, that description, sort of like sharp but soft, is Scarlett. I get down on my knees.

I grasp the distal, the lower part of the leg, and begin to apply pressure.

The minister cries out. Tears well in his eyes. "Say something. Distract me."

Benny and the page look at me with my driver saying, "Tell de man. He's close to God. Could help yuh."

"There's a friend. My poor attitude has made her hesitant to marry me."

I begin my pitiful story as I add traction to the minister's upper thigh, aligning the broken bone. When I'm done, I carefully splint the leg and bind it tightly with bandages, bandages similar to the ones Scarlett uses to hide.

After leaving a grateful minister at St. Margaret's Church, who, like Benny, believes me to be an idiot when it comes to my love life, I head to Cheapside. I try to read my novel to keep my hand from hitting the carriage ceiling and signaling to Benny to go to Anya House. I want to see Scarlett. I can't sleep for thinking of her. I barely eat. I'm sick missing her.

If I don't show myself and explain, I'll be driven insane by Friday.

Yet, two things keep me from going: the promise I made to the duke, and that small problem of not knowing what to say. Apologizing for being an idiot seems, well . . . reductive, at this point. I need to offer her something, something that shows I've grown up. Asking for marriage wasn't the answer. Or maybe, it wasn't the right question.

Heated at myself, I fling my hat to the other carriage bench. I'm fevered. Clearly, I'm ill. I'm definitely not thinking correctly. Something other than my pride is broken, destroyed.

Soon, we've turned onto Watling Street. The traffic has lessened, so we'll arrive at Three Watling, the home of my aunt, Telma Smith, in minutes. She lives in the heart of Cheapside, immigrant side. Her home sits grandly among the two-story houses along the spacious street. Blocks over are warehouses which provide numerous shopping opportunities. The wide street has a mix of wood and of limestone construction. It's very different from Port of Spain, but now that Trinidad is under British control, perhaps it will change to become this. My dada would hate that.

The notion that foreigners wish to come and transform the island's culture is odd. Coming to London, the immigrants want to add to the fabric of society, not change it. My stomach becomes queasy as I think of the constant friction that exists—the dueling pride of where I come from versus the city I now call home. If only everything could be as uncomplicated as straightening a broken limb or bolstering a diet. Funny. I didn't realize how uncomfortable I am with change, or the wanton disregard of how beautiful a house of wood and a thatched roof looks in the moonlight.

The carriage stops, and soon Benny opens my door. He takes one look at me and laughs. "Oh, yuh are not prepared for the aunties. Yuh already flustered."

I tug on my tailcoat and straighten my wilted cravat. "Funny man, tell me what to do. You be the boss. How do I win Scarlett Wilcox?"

Benny's face becomes serious. He takes a step or two. "What Shakespeare do? Yuh always reading. Miss Wilcox reads."

"Not sure Shakespeare is the right guide. His plays often end with death for the couples. Romeo and Juliet, dead from youthful indiscretions. Othello and Desdemona, dead, by indiscretions, lies, and war."

Mouth dropping open, Benny gawks at me. "'Bout the book now. The *Sense and Sensibility*. Do dey die?"

"No. Hmmm. I'm not Edward, and Scarlett is not a patient, long-suffering Elinor. Livingston is more Willoughby, wild and stupid. That leaves Colonel Brandon and Marianne. Reserved, handsome older man and a romantic girl given to whimsy."

Benny's giving me that look again, the mix of you're stupid but you're my boss. "Doh Brandon get rest and eat? Yuh know how yuh get."

"Benny, not now. I'm fine."

"Whimsy sounds like yuh need sleep. Otherwise, bad idea. Maybe your tantie—"

"Whimsy as in puce curtains. Benny, you might be right. Whimsy! I can't see Miss Wilcox until Friday, but you can deliver a note, a note with whimsy."

"Mr. Carew, not following. Don't matter. She smart. She get it."

She's brilliant. And too serious. "I almost won the ladies' challenge last time with the Shakespeare I quoted in Anya House. Perhaps if I offer Miss Wilcox a little *Sense and Sensibility* now, it will show her I understand. Maybe she'll welcome opening her life to a little of my sensibilities."

"And yuh get some sense. If you say so, Mr. Carew."

Benny is not convinced, but he isn't the audience I'm looking for. Scarlett Wilcox needs to see that I'm unpredictable and vibrant and can be an excellent partner for her. The Marianne in her will like this.

"Yuh smiling. Yuh have a plan?" He closes the door as I put on my hat. "Perhaps the two of yuh can be less serious."

"What do you mean?"

" 'Member when yuh had to go get Lord Palmer from a gaming hell?"

"Yes. Miss Scarlett Wilcox advised me." I'd forgotten that. She sent me after her brother-in-law. The fool was in a gaming hall. Even when she was younger, she was forthright, trying to save everyone. With Scotland's death and Lord Hampton's troubles, Scarlett has had to be serious, too serious. "More whimsy is what we both need."

Readying to see my aunt, I calm and smooth my cravat, making sure the loops of the barrel knot are in place.

Barrel knot. Scarlett used barrel knots on her cravat. Did she choose them because of me? Her father rarely wore cravats. The duke's fashionable knot is the smaller trone d'Amour. I shake my head. Scarlett might've selected it from something she read or heard about it from my talkative driver. "Benny, make sure you're not disclosing to anyone about the scandalous situations I find myself in. People must trust me."

My driver squirms. "I don't tell a lot of people."

"Benny!"

He waves his hands. "Sometimes, too good to keep quiet. Sorry."

I pull my hands together. "Please, Benny. Lives could be ruined if what I've rambled to you becomes known. Discretion, Benny."

"Yes, sir. Discreet. Sure, Mr. Carew."

His face seems fretful. I hope he doesn't tell anyone about the vicar's mysterious fall. St. Margaret's has a history of having difficulties with their rectors. In 1806, one died mysteriously caught in the bells. "Well, wish me luck. I'm going to check on my cousin Mrs. Halland. I know that she has an accoucheur for the pregnancy. But . . . I want to check on her. Childbirth is not easy on women."

I've seen the horrors and heartache when what looks like a perfect birth goes awry. Benny's frowning. He's read my thoughts. He's been with me when things have gone wrong. He's stayed close and has dragged me away when the grief feels all-consuming.

"Sorry, Benny. I don't mean to imply that anything is wrong with my cousin, but I want to do all I can to make sure all is well."

"Yes, sir." His voice is low, but confident. "Mrs. Halland, all our women, deserve de best care. Her husband ah big man, an important sailor. Don't he report to Miss Gray's . . . the former Miss Gray's . . . Well, the now—"

"Benny, it's Lady Derand, until further notice."

He nods. "Don't let them push yuh back to Miss Gray. Yuh got a girl . . . sort of. Very handsy with Miss Wilcox. One woman at a time for Friday."

I sigh, long and hard. "I'll be back as soon as I can. Then I will have a note for you to deliver this afternoon." With my leather bag in hand, I leave my man and head up the pavement toward my aunt's front door hoping this can be a quick, uneventful visit without gossip or something being said that I'll regret.

Chapter 21

STEPHEN—AUNTIES OF CHEAPSIDE

My aunt's home, framed with arches and limestone corner-stones, is the pride of the neighborhood. It takes a couple knocks on the door before her maid, Mrs. Ellis, welcomes me. "You are looking handsome but tired, Stephen Carew. Are you eating? Are you working too hard?"

"I'm doing my best, ma'am."

"Well, you will eat before you go." The old woman has a good spirit, she leans in close with her bronze apple cheeks glowing. "So proud of you."

She says this every time she sees me, like I will forget. But the sentiment makes me smile. Mrs. Ellis knew me when I was still fresh off the boat. She, like the aunties, watched my practice grow.

I feel a little sick, seeing that others can notice the maturity in me, while I haven't afforded the same to Scarlett. I wonder what she's doing. Is she still mad at me for wanting to marry her?

"You are frowning, dear." Mrs. Ellis takes my hat and coat. "Make sure you eat something. You know your aunt is fretting about everything. Eat something, that will make her happy."

"I'll see what I can do. How is my cousin, the mother-to-be?"

"Mrs. Halland is moving a little slow." The maid sets my hat on the table in the pink-painted hall. Then she rolls her hands up, tucking them inside a white starched apron. "She's not eating as much as she should. The poor girl is in some pain."

Discomfort is to be expected at the end of confinement. "Don't fret, Mrs. Ellis. I'll see what I can do to bring everyone cheer."

"Very good." Her warm smile returns, and she leads me the short distance to the parlor.

I come inside and my aunt puts down her needlepoint and rushes to me. "Dear boy," she says. Her expression of surprise makes it sound as if she hasn't seen me for some time, rather than two days ago. "So good of you to come, nephew."

"Of course, Tantie Telma."

She grabs me in a hug a bear would offer with pride. For a minute, I am swaddled in the burgundy-dyed silk of her gown and perfume that smells of rose water.

My nose wrinkles.

It's a common smell. I hope it will stop reminding me of brothels and Scarlett.

"Dear heart," my aunt says, catching my hand. "Your face is scrunched up like you're in pain. Do you have a headache? Or are you hungry?"

"No. I'm fine, I just—"

She mashes me against her bosom. More roses, more thoughts of Scarlett, the brothel, the carriage and how wrong all of this is.

I free myself from my aunt. "Tantie Telma, I am fine. And I ate before I . . ."

That look on her face is as if I told her I quit practicing medicine. "A small plate won't hurt."

Her lovely face explodes in a grin. "Come with me, dear boy. You look thin. You need a wife to cook and look after you." She leads me to the dining room, a room with papered red walls. "When is the last time you had a home-cooked meal?"

"Yesterday. At my home."

"It's late in the day. Poor dear is starved." She pushes me into a chair at the end of the oak table. "Now relax. Tantie Telma will take care of everything."

When she rings a tiny brass bell, Mrs. Ellis comes to the entrance of the room.

"Yes, ma'am," the maid says. "What would you like? A little ham? A little black cake?"

"Can you please bring a full plate for my Stephen?"

Before I can say anything, Mrs. Ellis has fled to fulfill this request. She soon returns with a white dish filled with cuts of pheasant, roasted ham, a big spoonful of thick callaloo, and spicy blood pudding. In her other hand is a bread plate with two types of rolls, cheese, and cold meats. "I'm glad you are eating," she says. "You look a little thin."

I don't consider myself thin or thick, but if I eat everything the aunties try to serve me, that will no longer be my situation. My uncle is a large, happy man, but suffers from gout aggravated by such rich foods.

"Too many sinful treats, ladies." I pull my hands together and pray for strength and room in my stomach. Dumping a few delicious forkfuls down my gullet, I tell myself to slow down. But I'm so sick about a certain miss I can't eat much more. "Gluttony is wrong."

Tantie Telma gives me the evil eye as if I've suggested to burn down her house.

"She only does this because she cares, cousin." My cousin, Maryanne, otherwise known as Mrs. Halland, waddles into the room. Dressed in bright blue, she comes to the table. Her caramel skin glows. The yellow-and-blue-striped head wrap anoints her brow like a crown.

I help her and her very large stomach sit into a chair. "I came to see you, cousin. Heard you had some pain."

"A little." She grabs my hand when I lean in and kiss her cheek. "Good to see you, too, Stephen." Maryanne offers me a saucy look as she takes my fork and devours a few bites of my barely eaten plate. "My mother-in-law says I'm having a girl. My mama says you have a new girl."

I'm reaching for the Laënnec stethoscope, a birthday present last year from Torrance that will help me hear the babe's heart-beat. "Well, I don't want to brag."

Honestly, I can't. If Scarlett is unwilling to come, I'll know nothing of the woman Torrance will have ready for me Friday. "Let's have a little listen."

I take out my stethoscope and put the round tube made of hol-lowed mahogany to her chest and then to her stomach. The tube amplifies the echoes of heartbeats, two strong hearts beating. "Everything sounds good. Nice and strong."

"So the baby is well?" Tantie Telma comes closer. "I see a wiggle."

My cousin winces. "She's active, Mama."

She? Well, the bump that carries the uterus is large, not wide, indicating a boy according to Scarlett. And Maryanne's carrying low; another indication of a boy, if I am to believe the woman who researches and observes everything. Well, she's probably right. "The babe sounds good. Will be here soon."

My cousin takes a nice long breath. "Whew. My husband will be so excited to come back and meet his daughter. Daughters are nice, but a firstborn son is special for a man."

"A healthy child is special. And a happy mother is especially important. Cousin, I need you to keep eating and finding ways to be calm."

"That's exactly what the accoucheur said." She looks down, as if she wasn't supposed to mention him to me.

"His advice is correct." I say this with no jealousy implied. My cousin's health is all that matters, no matter how things come in and out of vogue.

"But so many things can go wrong." Tantie Telma frowns. She turns and begins opening curtains, letting in the evening light. "I just want to know that everything has been looked at." She glares at me. "Where's your friend? He knew about babies."

"Looking to hire more help?" I offer a weak laugh. "He's gone away. We may not be seeing him again soon."

To keep everyone from dwelling on Scotland Carew, I call to

Mrs. Ellis, who I know is listening. "Ma'am, can you bring more gravy? I think my cousin may need more."

"More gravy coming up. And your favorite should be fresh from the hearth. Cassava pone."

What? Buttery, moist, cakey, chewy delight. It's my favorite thing. I want to clap, maybe dance a jig. It's the dessert that is first to go at any gathering. "An edge piece, please."

When Mrs. Ellis brings the whole cake on a platter, steam wafts. The caramel and nutmeg smell takes me to Mama and Port of Spain.

I cut a slice, right on the browned edge. No raisins in this, or pumpkin. But it smells dense and delicious. Before it's on my plate, Maryanne says, "Tell us more about your girl, Stephen."

If I had a mouthful of pone, I wouldn't have to answer questions. But my cousin is too quick.

"You'll meet her Friday. I don't want to bias you with a wrong word."

"How would knowing her name bias me?" My aunt gives me her offended stare. "I think you're stalling. You know a certain woman is now free. You don't have to make up someone if you don't want us to know you are lonely."

Holding her stomach, Maryanne starts to laugh. "Oh, Stephen has a girl, Mama. Look at him. I mean, he didn't buckle when Eveline flew away." She winks and leans forward. "With a name, he knows you and your friends will work up a complete report on her and her people before the sun goes down. Stephen wants you surprised."

I stuff a big forkful of the pone into my mouth, then I nod. It's true. The aunties' connections are wide and deep, just like those baby bumps. I clear my mouth and say, "I want you to meet her first, then investigate."

"Will Eveline Gray, the Baroness or former Baroness Derand, be there, Mama?" my cousin asks. "Mama thinks she is good for you, I don't."

My aunt stops pacing. "She shouldn't have married outside of our community. If she'd waited for you, she'd be happy."

"Would she?" I glanced at Tantie Telma. "Tell me why."

"Of course she would. You are respected, Stephen. Your practice is flourishing. She wouldn't be wretched."

I don't respond. I honestly don't know if the former Miss Gray would be happy or less wretched. The baroness had a secret life that didn't involve me.

"Tell him the rest, Mama. That the auntie network has determined that you should forgive her and redeem her."

"Tantie Telma, I'm not a priestly Hosea. And she's not the prostitute Gomer. Miss Gray loved someone. It didn't work. There's nothing wrong with trying to find happiness."

"Well, Stephen, before I knew you had a girl, I invited her to my picnic on Friday. She will be at the church service. If I knew you had someone new in your life to love, I would let her be. How does one send someone away from attending church?" My aunt loses her train of thought and puts her hand onto her face like Scarlett. "It's likely she will come to both."

This is terrible; the aunties still wish for me to marry Eveline. If Scarlett does come, how will she take the attention people will give to Eveline?

"Tantie Telma, gossip about a newly annulled woman can't be good. Perhaps you should advise the baroness to stay away. Let the ink dry a little more on her Scottish paperwork."

"I hate how people can be." My aunt turns away. "I've already told her that I'd try to get you to walk in with her. That would make her comfortable."

What? I'm to be made a sacrifice to make Eveline comfortable? What about me? "I will be with my friend." My tone's heated and I add, "You should truly try to dissuade her mother. Mrs. Gray is sensible. Let her know the aunties' matchmaking has failed."

My cousin chuckles, then winces in pain.

I go to her side. "This little one has a good kick."

My aunt turns pale. "You slow down on your eating."

"Eat. Slow down. Don't eat." My cousin shakes her head. "All the advice is contradictory."

"Maryanne," I say. "You take it easy. If you want to eat, then do so. But I think your baby will be early."

My cousin smiles. She pushes the dinner plate away for a spoonful of cassava pone. She's an edge piece girl, too. "The accoucheur tells me not to have worries. He says we have plenty of time because the baby hasn't turned. He's a colleague of Princess Charlotte's accoucheur."

"Wow, Princess Charlotte." My tone is sarcastic and causes Tantie Telma to spin around.

Her eyebrow is arched. "It's fashionable to have one, but Stephen knows things."

It is good to hear her faith in me. Though I'm busy, I'll always have time for them.

"And we know a thing or two, Stephen," Tantie continues. "If this new woman isn't up to our standards, at least we know Eveline."

"Even though she is virtually a divorced woman? Annulled. Pretend it didn't happen." Maryanne says this aloud. I thought it, but I wasn't going to say anything. The aunties, all of them, love to gossip about people's mistakes.

"Maryanne, our girls with education and dowries are targets for peers and other men looking for good women with money."

"Money does trump race." My cousin smirks. Being married with her own household has emboldened her tongue. Must be more of that growing and changing.

My aunt gawks at her for a moment, then says, "Eveline's mother has been ambitious, but I don't think they talk much anymore. She's probably against the anullment. We'll see on Friday if attitudes change."

I don't recall Mrs. Gray being such, but all things can be true. Ambitious mamas trying to make good starts for their daughters will overlook the potential problems that can happen between families coming from Cheapside and Mayfair.

I've seen the results of marriages not built on love and a set of common beliefs. I think of Scarlett's sister. Lady Hampton seemed to have misjudged the peer she married. Maybe that's why she's hesitant to entertain the duke's offer. But what of their past? They were in love or lust once to conceive life, lost life.

"All is still well. Right, Stephen?"

"Yes, Maryanne, except you cannot have my pone. Mrs. Ellis, I know you are lurking. May I have a container to take some cake with me?"

"I'll bring you something." Mrs. Ellis's voice is filled with humor. She'll come back with something, even Wedgwood if I promise to return it.

I sit down again, eating this delicious treat with the intention of taking more. But I make a mental note to add forceps of various sizes to my cabinet at the bottom of my carriage. They come in handy in helping pull a new life into this topsy-turvy world.

Chapter 22

SCARLETT—MODISTE DIVINE

Standing in the threshold of the room assigned me at Anya House, I appreciate the elements of practicality and whimsy. The dark stained wood of bookshelves surrounding the bay window would make a fairy proud. I picture her as Mama with a crown, sitting there casting wishes or rocks at the heroes or stubborn physicians passing by.

That's silly for a woman of science. Yet, as I look at all the scraps of silver, crimson, and blue fabric, I want magic. I want the joy.

I step further inside, carefully navigating the thick ivory rya edged with majestic gold threads. Fallen dressmaker pins are scattered everywhere. The battling modistes, as I like to call the ladies the duke hired to create the perfect walking gown, have left my tidy space cluttered.

"You deserve this, you know."

I turn to see the duke propped against the doorframe. He's in a white, flowing robe, like a priest.

Bending, I pick up a silver pin. "I think it's a lot of fuss, which could poke out an eye, if I'm not careful."

"You will be careful, Scarlett. You always are. But you don't have to be."

His tone sounds sarcastic to my ears. "I think I've taken enough risks."

"In disguises, yes, but never as Scarlett Wilcox. You exist. You can stretch your wings, take as much space as possible. It's not wrong to do so."

Pointing to the fabric scraps everywhere, on my table, over the cream-colored blankets and bedsheets, all over the floor. "Seems like the modistes are doing that, not much room for anything else."

He stoops and picks up another pin. The sharpness gleams. "I find it fascinating that this tiny bit of metal can enter silk, bunch it into gathers, and never leave a mark. No evidence remains of the help it gave to bring something into existence." The duke looks at me. "Leave your mark, Scarlett. Don't be afraid to try."

Katherine comes inside. She slips to his right. For a moment, they are close enough to dance. Their gazes fight or twirl about a past neither speak of.

"Excuse me," she says.

He moves quickly, like Katherine has commanded him to fetch something. When she's fully inside, he dips his head back in. "I'll go get a maid to tidy up this creative process. Oh, and the special tools you wanted, they arrive tomorrow."

After offering a bow, he disappears.

My sister and I stare at his retreating form.

"That's odd," she says, still looking into the corridor.

"What do you want him to do, Katherine? Sweep you off your feet? Make some sort of compliment so that you can retort willfully, hurling something sharp and hurtful."

"I'm sorry." She looks up at the smooth ceiling and folds her arms over her modest light green gown. Its high collar and neckline scream hide, ignore. Hard to do, with someone so pretty. "The duke knows how to upset me."

"Apparently, he does that by just breathing." I find a pincushion on the bookcase. I pick it up on behalf of the absent fairy and start collecting the pins. "Katherine, when are you going to forgive him?"

"When he lets me out of this silly bet." She moves to the book wall, adjusts the gauzy muslin curtains and fans herself.

Katherine looks at the door. Is she hoping the duke will come back to fight with her?

Isn't that why I look out the bay window, to see if a physician's carriage is heading to the mews? It's silly; I can't truly see it from here.

"What tools, Scarlett?"

"Special scalpels." She squints at me, but I am mum. I know she wants to know what they're for. She has her secrets. I have mine.

"This is a very pretty room. We could do something like this at Ground Street. Then, Scarlett, maybe you'll like it better."

"No. It must stay the same. It's not my room. Well, it wasn't supposed to be."

Her eyes grow wide. "It's your room, Scarlett. It's been yours—"

"Since Scotland died."

She comes to me and cups my cheek. "He'd want you to make it your own. It's good you've memorialized everything he was, but you have to keep moving forward."

Katherine hugs me. I want to believe her.

"I didn't know you were still mourning."

"How do you stop?"

There are tears in Katherine's eyes. "I lost a stillborn. I think of how gray his skin was."

"I remember how you cried, how we all did. But is that the same as losing your twin? Scotland and I played and fought and told stories at dusk. We wished on stars at midnight. And my brother was the only one to tell me I wasn't crazy for having dreams."

My sister turns away. "The duke's modistes have exquisite taste."

That moment of vulnerability is gone. Katherine picks up scraps that match the yellow-striped walls.

"This is very untidy." She schools her voice to show none of the emotions from before.

I give up. I release myself from trying to be more attached to her. "The modistes are good."

She moves to the bed and flips through the sketches. "Do you know which gown will be made?"

"Not sure. The duke will probably choose a few. He's nice taste."

Katherine keeps looking at the pages, adding comments about buttons and hems. It reminds me of Mama fussing about the outfits my sister would take with her on her trip to St. Petersburg.

My sister was to represent Papa's efforts to expand. Her governess taught her culture. She was the perfect ambassador for Wilcox Coal. So beautiful. She's still absolutely lovely. Her existence is large. She exists to take up space. People notice her when she lifts her head and smiles. "Katherine—"

"Yes, Scarlett." The frown on her face silences me. "You were going to tell me who the duke has picked for you."

"What?"

"He has to have picked someone because of the ridiculous bet I made. Why else would he have new gowns made? He doesn't need to work this hard to buy your affections. He won you with the library, and now these special tools."

I put down the cushion full of pins. "Unlike you, he listens, and he answers questions. He treats all of us, especially Lydia, like we're precious."

"You are precious."

"Never felt like that. But I didn't deserve to, I let Scotland down."

"No. No, you didn't." She runs to me and, for a moment, it feels like we're wrestling. But it's just us trying to figure out where our hands go. We embrace as friends who haven't seen each other in a while. And maybe I haven't seen this side of Katherine in years.

There's no control. She's frenzied, trying to convince me I'm not to blame.

"Fevers are dangerous. That's why I'm so scared when Lydia has one."

"Scarlett, it's not your fault."

Again, I want to believe her, but I'll live with the image of Scotland's red face forever. "We need more physicians. There needs to be learned men and women who can care for people, *our* people. The duke's science meetings let everyone come. That definitely will help."

"Well, don't count on him to continue to be helpful."

I jerk away. "What has he done? Help me understand why you are so bothered by the nice things the Duke of Torrance does for our family, and now London."

She spins on her low heels walking away from me. The action is fast. Her hem swishes from the motion. "Sooner or later, he will grow tired of making me look bad and move on to the next situation to exploit."

"It's been three years. If he didn't want the best for us, I think we would know by now."

Her lip quivers. "I know I don't seem rational, but Torrance is a strategist. This is merely another chess game."

I want to ignore this circular logic, but Katherine seldom opens up. "You tell me to forgive myself. That Scotland's gone, and it was years ago. Yet in the same breath, you want to pretend the duke is the same. That nothing has or will ever change. Which is it? Haven't we all grown and changed?"

She doesn't answer. Instead, she picks up a piece of bobbin lace. I actually like this one: not too puffy, not too old, not something I'd expect on women sent to the nunnery. She holds it up to my face. "Time passes whether we like it or not."

"Now that sounds like something the duke would say."

Katherine groans and balls up the lace. "It's part of some plan. I knew him before. He does nothing by chance."

"You can't see he's changed. Have you ever looked into his eyes and seen the hurt in his soul?"

"Can't. If I stare, I'll fall for his charm. And if he's good, then I'm the villain. I can't be made wrong for protecting my heart. I'm not wrong, just a woman who's learned to survive." Covering her mouth, she turns toward the window and squints as if she's trying to read something off a bookshelf. "The print on these leather spines is tiny."

My sister is wrong and scared. I need her to be Katherine the Brave. "If you want to know something, you have to go and seek it out."

She closes her eyes. "I'm out of time, aren't I, Scarlett? Has he chosen someone for you? Will you be meeting candidates to see if he's found a man to marry you?"

Maids enter. "Ma'am, and Lady Hampton, we'll have this tidied in a moment. Please step outside."

The ladies have brooms and baskets. Another has dust rags. My room shall be orderly in no time.

We move into the corridor; the duke and Lydia sit at the top of the stairs.

"Baba Yaga sounds terrible." Lydia's in her nightgown and pink lacy robe, a match to mine. "How could your mama tell you of a story about a mean ole woman who lives in a house with chicken legs?"

"Well, there was usually a moral attached to it." The duke sounds humored and unguarded. "Maybe it doesn't translate well into English."

Lydia stands up and puts her arms about his neck. "Then you teach me Russian. I want to know everything."

He hugs her. "I will, my love."

Katherine coughs.

The duke sighs and releases his hold on Lydia. "Of course, that will have to be alright with Lady Hampton."

"No. Then she won't let me." Lydia leaps like she is about to throw a fit and starts to fall.

The duke grabs her—and they fall back on the landing.

My pulse pops in my veins. The thudding is monstrous, hiding our steps as we run to them. My heart doesn't slow until we reach them.

Our little girl, so fragile and sweet, is wrapped tightly in his arms. My new tools, the tiny scalpels, would be required to separate the child from his embrace.

"You both alright?" My voice is small, like I'm caught in wind.

He nods but his eyes remain closed.

A murmur, a whisper that feels like praise, is said in Russian. Nonetheless, this is another Wilcox disaster diverted by the duke, another thing for Katherine to twist and claim as his fault.

Another lesson for me that love isn't enough.

Chapter 23

SCARLETT—WHAT WOULD A LADY DO?

It's Wednesday. Two more days before I see Stephen again. I stand in front of the long mirror, wondering about the winning gown and the note he sent. His fancy parchment is in my hand. I don't exactly know what to make of it.

I've thought about it all night. I'm at a loss for what to do.

"There is no need to fidget, Scarlett. You'll look beautiful." The duke stands at the threshold. The maid has left the door open as she goes to get the matching cape pressed. "You were made to wear crimson."

The color is bold. Maybe too bright. "I settled on this because Katherine objected."

"You're a Wilcox."

"Is that your way of saying that we sisters are contrary?"

"Pretty much, but you'll look lovely in it. The physician will not be able to take his eyes from you."

Through my enchanted bay window, the warm morning sunshine reflects onto my table where the other dresses lie on tissue paper—safe blue, a white one with shiny silver. "This will make me stand out."

"What's wrong with that?" His voice is strong, almost bubbly, like he's inspecting his creation. The duke seems chipper with a longer stride, but he's always happier when everyone spends the night. Katherine, Lydia, and I stay in Anya House in the rooms he's made permanently available for us.

"Most of the time, I wish to hide."

"Ah, your love of disguises. Well, instead of a waistcoat, you will have a lovely fichu and cape."

"Your Grace, it's a very bright choice."

He nods in that funny way he does. "Do you know that a candle will still burn if hidden under a basket?"

"It can also set the straw on fire. And burn down the whole house." I shake my head and hold back my unexplainable, unwanted fears. "Not sure I want to be responsible for setting London ablaze."

"A light needs to be seen. Not hidden. You're flame, Scarlett. You wish to merely show a spark of your brilliance? Nyet. You must be willing to burn to get what you want."

I turn to where he remains at the door. "Is that what you are doing? Burning up your enemies?"

He squints at me, and I point him to the *London Morning Post* on the bed. "Seems another member of the Court of Chancery has resigned. More mysterious circumstances. Lord Flanders seemed like a nice man."

The duke doesn't blink. "*Seems* is right."

I go to him, crossing the self-imposed distance. "Have you taken your revenge on everyone who's your enemy? When is enough, enough?"

The duke chuckles. "I think you've listened to Katherine too much. She assumes I have special powers."

"I'm not her. For I see you, all of you." I retreat and he follows. "Did you do it? Have you made these men resign?"

He shrugs. "I believe they've decided that their old-world views are no longer needed. Each has voluntarily resigned."

"Because something damning has been discovered. To avoid scandal, they've relented their power. Is that how you work?"

He shrugs again. "Let's consider what you say is true. I may have obtained some information that newspapermen might enjoy printing. These alleged paragons who sit in judgment, hypothetically, have done some very terrible things. One could say it is a way to save their valor, to resign without bringing scandal to their families."

"How honorable, Your Grace. Again, when do you stop?"

He sinks into the seat in the bay window. "When all the guilty are punished, or I die. The guilty must be punished, Scarlett. I'm hanging in there."

"Did you target Tavis? He wronged you."

His smile flattens to a harsh line. "Yes, he wronged me by lying so completely to Katherine that she refuses to see the truth."

The duke hasn't answered my question. Did he target Tavis? Did the duke put into motion all the actions that would make a desperate man take his last bet? "Are the slights against you enough to make Tavis pay with his life?"

The duke doesn't answer at first, but then he says. "*Lózh' kozaku ne k litsu*, which is to say, lies do not suit a Cossack. I'd never do anything to hurt Katherine. Knowing the pain our separation caused—everything that it cost—I could not. But Tavis was a fool. He had magic and didn't know it. He's gone. I wish him well in hell."

That is the strongest thing the duke has said about my brother-in-law. Cold as a Gunter's ice. Heaven help us, the day he no longer has feelings for Katherine. I need to help him see that she's still hurting from Wilcox secrets.

"Scarlett, I do not mean to make you fretful. But I am running out of time. One doesn't have forever to fix everything. You and Lydia need to be protected."

I stoop and take his hand. "Then you keep fighting. Your light can't be hidden, either. You're too good."

"Am I? Katherine thinks I'm the d'yavol. Maybe she's right."

My heart hurts for him. He has power but nothing to help him heal. Like my father, the duke has money and the strength to fight for others, but maybe not for himself. "You need to battle for your health. No one else can manage the wars you've started."

His smile at me is brief. "Scarlett, you may be right. Mr. Thom had an incident today. He ran the coal wagon into a ditch."

Incident? Or accident? My heart pounds. "No. Is he . . ." I want to ask if he's blind or dead, but I can't get the words out.

"Scarlett, he's well, just a little shaken up. He didn't want to come here, so I had him sent to Ground Street. While his sons are away trying to build trade routes, he needs to be watched. The wagon is in my mews being repaired . . . Scarlett? You look unwell."

"I'm not ready. I can't do the surgery yet."

"Scarlett? Tell me what's going on. I got you tools without asking questions. You're risking your reputation to do eye research. What have you discovered? Enlighten me."

"You were at White's. You saw how the scientists listened to me. I've discovered the procedure to restore some sight."

The duke offers me a thoughtful look. "Is that all? Why the urgency? Who needs help?"

He's glancing at me, waiting for a confession. I trust him enough to give him one.

"Mr. Thom is losing his sight."

His head tilts. The duke looks away toward the floor. "Continue."

"You know? Of course you know. The lenses of his eyes have darkened with what I can only describe as a hardened white mucus. The cataract has taken sight from one eye. It may take it from the other."

"Will this work on any clouded lens, not just cataracts, this couching method?"

"You were listening. I think it should. The tools are what is needed for the delicate surgery."

"Risking everything for a friend." The duke kisses my hand and then releases my fingers. "You are the most like me. I'll put my resources at your disposal for Thom. Develop the skills."

"It's not that simple. Knowing the parts of the eye is not the same as taking tools to fix the eye. The lens must be dislodged without hurting the eye. As you can imagine, it's a delicate procedure."

He nods. "There's someone with the skills of a surgeon who might be able to help."

My lungs deflate, and we say it together. "Mr. Carew."

Chuckling, the duke wears the smile like this has been his plan all along. "Yes, the man whom you have tender feelings for, who now wishes to marry you, began his medical career as a surgeon. He's the best of both worlds. He has the erudite thought of a learned man, but doesn't mind getting his hands dirty. Surgery is work gentlemen won't do."

"You forgot to add that he reads frivolous novels, too. Most gentlemen don't do that."

The duke leans back a little on the window seat. "I never considered Shakespeare frivolous. And I do remember you being moved by his words, when Carew said them to your sister."

"Well, now he's sent them to me." I go to the table and pull Stephen's note from under the crinkling tissue paper. "Here. The verse is from the author, A. Lady."

"How clever, for you are a lady even in disguise." He reads the page aloud. " 'Her skin was very brown, but, from its transparency, her complexion was uncommonly brilliant.' "

The duke's cheeks brighten. He seems to scan the paper for something unladylike for my delicate ears. "Nothing untoward," he says, then he continues. " 'Her features were all good; her smile was sweet and attractive; and in her eyes, which were very dark, there was a life, a spirit, an eagerness, which could hardly be seen without delight. I am delighted by you, Scarlett Wilcox. Your Humbled Servant. S. A. Carew.' "

"Romantic d'yavol." The duke looks up at me. "This passage is from *Sense and Sensibility*. I believe the Prince Regent is an admirer of this author. Scarlett, can you not see what Carew is saying?"

Blinking to ensure my eyes haven't glazed over, I shrug.

"It is a compliment. May I ask why you can't see that the good physician thinks you're beautiful, transparent, and with such life it's hard for him to take his eyes off of you?"

Said like that, my traitorous heart races. After all these years, he sees me. "But how do I respond? What do I say? Georgina is the one who loves these novels. Perhaps I should ask her?"

"Send him a note entirely from you, S. Wilcox. No guises. No pretense. Let it be you."

I take the note back and hide it in my palm. "If Mr. Carew were the earl, it would be easier to write to him. Drench the foolscap in rose water and offer to pay his passage to a brothel, the man of science would listen."

The confusion on the duke's face is priceless. "Well, Lord Livingston—"

"No, Jahleel. I know Scarlett will listen to you to her detriment. So please do not convince her that that drunk, marriage-hating man, is the one she should marry." Katherine storms into the room. She's pointing and raising her tone. "Scarlett's convinced a marriage of convenience is what she wants. And love is a foolish emotion. On that I agree, but please spare my sister from someone who will make her miserable. Save her from my mistakes."

"Katherine, which of your mistakes are we discussing? Tavis or Tavis." He smothers a laugh.

Katherine hisses at him. "You're impossible."

Before the duke says something that will make my sister leave and take Lydia, too, I move between them and catch her pointing finger. "The duke would never choose a fool for me. He's chosen Stephen Adam Carew. And I think His Grace is right."

Now Katherine laughs. "Mr. Carew. Our family's physician? The man you constantly annoy?"

"He's also a trained surgeon." I say with a sense of pride. "That can come in handy with the proper tools."

"A surgeon? You mean when he was a bone doctor in Trinidad." Katherine's tone is haughty. "What good is that to you? You need to wait."

I can't believe the slight is coming from my sister's mouth. "Now I see why you married Tavis. You two are alike. You are both silly about titles, when more substantial things should matter."

She looks away, toying with the cuff of her gown. "He was my husband. Of course we should be alike."

"Yes, you and Tavis bonded. And you accepted his prejudice against any expertise that doesn't come from Mayfair. Did you enjoy the physician his family sent? The gentleman hated every moment he stood in our house."

"That's not what I meant, Scarlett. This ridiculous bet makes me say things that are insensitive."

"No, Katherine, it's what you believe. Is that why when Mama passed, you were reluctant to call upon Mr. Carew when Lydia was sick?"

With her gaze flickering between me and the duke, she backs up. "No. He's a busy man."

The duke's grin fades. "You'd let Lydia suffer because of your foolishness?"

"No. That's not it. He was there to deliver my . . . Lydia. It was a troubled birth and for a long time, every time I saw him it reminded me of loss and pain." Katherine weeps. "There was so much blood, then not enough."

The duke doesn't make a joke. He moves swiftly and holds my sister, first by the shoulders, then fully letting her fall into his arms.

Her sobbing is wild and loud.

Yet, I know why. She won't tell anyone that she and Mama were both pregnant. That Mama gave birth to lively Lydia, while Katherine had to hold a stillborn in her arms. I was fourteen, but I remember how Mama's pregnancy kept her in her room, bedridden. We hardly saw her for months. Katherine's pregnancy kept her sad and big and full of shame.

All of their pain, it's still in that house. It's here in this room. Pain needs to be expressed to be expelled from the heart. "Sister. Did you ever give the child you lost a name? I know I hurt less when I say Scotland's name."

Katherine trembles. Through her tears, I hear her. "You shouldn't have said—"

"I'm tired of not saying. Of pretending Scotland or your still-born child didn't exist."

She pries away from Torrance a few inches. I watch their eyes lock.

They weep together, and he says, "Andrew Charles would be a good name for our son. Of course, his middle name would be a patronymic of Jahleel."

Confirmation of their past relationship, and why she hates him: his abandonment.

Very gently, the duke folds her fully into his embrace. "Tavis, on his deathbed, told me. I know why you hate me. It's deserved. I hate me, too. If I had known, I would've made another choice. I would have given up—"

"Please." Her mouth quivers. "Don't say something you don't mean. Something we both know is a lie."

She weeps harder. And I see the duke's soul withering in his red, red eyes.

The duke whispers Russian words in her ear. It must be a prayer, a wish for forgiveness, a hope of peace.

And I ache for Katherine. She gave her love to a man who left her. He disappointed her when she needed him.

Tears roll down the duke's cheeks, and he supports strong Katherine like she's a fragile crystal chess piece from one of his rarest sets.

Gathering my research notes and Stephen's letter, I flee the room. Those two need privacy to finally share what was lost. Time should stand still for them. Perhaps everyone at Anya House will now gain peace.

I'll go to the duke's study and write a response to Stephen. I plan on sending him something that says, I see you, and I trust you enough to share my thoughts and perhaps more. If he's the one for me, he'll sweep through every guise and recognize my heart.

Chapter 24

STEPHEN—MEET THE GUARDIANS

Friday has arrived. A mile or two from Anya House, I eagerly await being alone with Scarlett. Sitting in my carriage listening to the clip-clop of horses' hooves, I hope she's brave enough to accompany me to Wesley's Chapel and the picnic today. Her response to my note arrived late last night but made no mention of either. Her response to my whimsy didn't give me encouragement at all.

Nonetheless, if she dresses as Scotland and comes with me, I'll take the opportunity to introduce my *cousin* to the community and hope the aunties don't consume all our time introducing *him* to eligible young ladies.

Chuckling at the foolhardy notion, I pray I can make Scarlett feel comfortable with me, to accept me and to want me as badly as I want her. If my dreams of her are any indication of the level of my desire, then I'll take her any way I can have her.

Her response thanked me for sending my overture, but she sent no poem or romantic words of her own. The vixen sent pages of research notes, a request to review her sketches of the eye, and a formal solicitation to return her source material.

Not what I wanted.

Though the work is intriguing and brilliant, there's nothing to convince me that she's changed her mind and will marry me. If anything, it's a plea to be her science colleague. I'm not Livingston. I have nothing to add or a judgment to offer. Yet, I'm sure there's much I can teach her, but I don't want to be research. I don't wish to be a resource on medicine. I need her to be an escape for me. I want her to be my joy . . . not more work.

But if research is what wins her heart, isn't it worth it to try?

Knowing us, a few moments alone, and we'll fall into compromise number five thousand. Oddly, that does brighten my spirits. I shall *work* to make her want me again.

The carriage stops and Benny holds my door. I bound out, but my feet feel icy in my slippers. I adjust my cravat, plucking at the barrel knot. Then I clutch Scarlett's parcel to me.

"Sir, is there de problem?"

A big one. "I'm not saying I'm nervous, but what if I am?"

Benny grabs my hat and dusts the brim. "She responded to your note? You didn't seem unhappy."

"Yes. She sent something." I clutch her answer, the pages. "Her sketches."

My driver smiles. "Da woman trusts yuh. She's protective of de sketches. Why yuh fretting, sir?"

Benny's brown eyes don't detect the many problems awaiting me behind the duke's doors. Out here, and in my community, I'm a big deal. I own land and my own home. I have clients throughout the city, even the ton. I can win a fair divorcée with my credentials, but maybe not a Wilcox daughter who's protected by a duke and a feisty viscountess.

Benny gives me a quick nod. "Yuh want to come up with a signal? In case yuh need to run for it?"

"No. I don't . . ." Maybe that isn't a bad idea. "What do you have in mind?"

Benny struts in front of me. "Well, yuh don't have a flower to cast off." He taps his hands together. "I come up with something."

The harder he's thinking, the more foolish I feel. "Never mind, Benny. Thanks, but no thanks."

"Mr. Carew, de lady very smart. If she's changed her mind, yuh know quickly."

This is true. Scarlett Wilcox is not Miss Eveline Gray, now Baroness Derand . . . maybe.

"If di lady don't want yuh, yuh know straight away. She don't play."

It was that directness about Scarlett that I both admired and fretted. Yet, if she's changed her mind about liking me, would she allow me a little room to change it back?

Delaying, I rub my neck, then readjust my cravat. "Maybe you're right, Benny. We need a signal."

He squints at me. "Fine. What if I say there's an emergency?"

"What emergency, Benny?"

"I don't know. Something good. Like last night. You had to go to that shop on Bond Street."

"Last evening was terrible. Those burns on the watchmaker's daughter were horrible."

The salve I made of lard, turpentine, honey, and chamomile will make the burns to her lower extremities heal faster. An island remedy. "People need to realize how dangerous a hearth can be. The poor child's apron caught fire. My salve might prevent bad scarring. But Benny, I don't want to frighten Miss Wilcox or myself."

Benny has that look, sort of dazed, eyes narrowing. "Okay, Mr. Carew, not sure what yuh said, but if I see yuh in distress, I'm gonna come up with something."

Wishing I hadn't brought up an escape plan to Benny, I leave my driver and head to the doors. If I make a bigger fool of myself, so be it. A dependable fool is who I am. Clutching Scarlett's parcel, I step into her world.

Walking into Anya House, everything looks normal—polished marble, servants going about their duties. Yet, there's a feel of magic in the air. Suddenly, I'm more hopeful. Something special is about to happen.

I give my hat to the eager set of hands of Torrance's silver-clad footman. I glance at the steps that lead to the upper level and turn to the closest servant. "Can you let His Grace know Mr. Carew is here?"

Before this young man can leave, I hear commotion and a winded whinny. Around the corner comes the Duke of Torrance on all fours. Lydia is on his back and the two are playing. The child has his cane, whipping it in the air.

"Again. Horsey!" She's laughing, tossing her head back. The child's the picture of health. And the duke doesn't look too shabby. His pallor is normal, not yellow or a weak-looking gray.

"Whoa," I say. "You two are making quite a ruckus."

"At last, someone with common sense has arrived." Lady Hampton looks radiant and frustrated. She comes down the stairs, but her face is happy, only her tone sounds cross. "They've been at this for over an hour."

The lady before me seems transformed. Her luminous face is trying hard to suppress a smile. Lady Hampton is a beautiful woman. Though we are close in age, she could easily be mistaken for her early twenties . . . Scarlett's age.

Nonetheless, where is my science inclined, always serious friend? My heart sounds loud. I bow my head to the viscountess. "Lady Hampton, I think both my patients can have a little fun."

"Both? Jahleel. Have you been ill again?"

The duke takes his time getting up. "Nothing to fret about. The dust from little fixes about Anya House has made me unwell." He glances at her like he's just seen this woman. Then his lips curl up. "Thank you for being concerned."

What has happened here?

Is this the right Anya House?

Oh, my goodness. Torrance has worn her down. They are civil. The rascal might win her after all.

"Katherine, it's fun." Lydia catches his hand like he was getting away from her. "And Duke don't hurt that much, not today."

"And how was I to know that old Mr. Wilcox never did this for our Lydia?" The duke dusts his hands on his dark trousers. "A man must be willing to be a fool for such a precious child."

"Well, you have the fool part right." Lady Hampton covers her mouth. "I mean you're effortless with Lydia."

"No mean to Duke, Katherine." The little girl hugs him about the leg. "He's my bestus friend."

If Torrance is about to launch a sarcastic barb, it melts on his tongue when he looks down at the child. "It is time for your nap."

Lydia says, "No nap. I want to play."

He stoops again and glances at her eye to eye. "I heard you've been very good now that we are back to our regular visits. Isn't there a birthday coming—"

Lydia's eyes grow big. She runs to Lady Hampton. "Nap time. I don't want anything to spoil my birthday."

Something whips across the viscountess's face, but she takes the child up the stairs. "You will take a restful nap. Then I will come downstairs and talk with the duke about future plans."

Her tone again is tight and harsh . . . a return to normal.

At the top of the stairs, Lydia yells down. "Be nice to Scarlett today, Mr. Carew. She doesn't need a pony, just some nice words."

The child runs to Lady Hampton, and they continue to Lydia's room.

I pat the duke on his shoulder. "So close. But keep working, old man. You may get things right and have a more permanent truce with Lady Hampton."

His countenance changes. "You think so?" He shrugs. "Sometimes it's truly too late."

He sees me staring at this rare slip in the mask he wears. The cheery hopeful expressions—are they merely disguises for Lydia?

"Now, Carew, don't reprimand me. Whenever I'm up to it, Lydia and I will play. She will have all my time for as long as that is." The duke glances at me. The unanswered question of how long I think he'll live is in set in his blank countenance.

I don't know what to say. I wish I was more medicine man than physician. Then I'd have a cure or restorative to give him, to offer the duke continuous strength and all the time he wishes.

Wouldn't mind a little bit of that potion myself.

"Well, Torrance, is Lydia correct? Is Miss Wilcox going to join me today for church and the picnic?"

"Perhaps you should ask her companion." He points to the stairs.

Craning my neck so I can view the upstairs, I expect to see Lydia doing some sort of skit to gain a little more time before taking her nap, but it's the elderly woman who serves as the child's nurse.

Mrs. Cantor carries a deep reticule with knitting needles sticking out. When she comes down, she says, "Miss Wilcox will be ready in a moment. The modiste and maids are almost finished."

The duke nods to her. "Mrs. Cantor will be coming with you and Miss Wilcox, in case you remember that my Scarlett is of age and feel the need to visit flowers."

The insinuations are heavy and . . . accurate. I come with the best intentions, but rolling about on my carriage floor is never far from my mind. I fold my arms. "I'm a gentleman. I know Scarlett Wilcox is no longer a child and needs no nurse. We've a scheduled day of entertainments. I wager we'll be out past midnight, if not longer. The aunties' celebrations go long, like a party in Mayfair that can end as late as four the next morning."

Nonetheless, since the woman in question didn't respond to my romantic gesture with an equally whimsical gesture, I'm now quite certain that tussle in my carriage was induced by too much sugary ice and not the romantic feelings I seek.

Sigh. I've read too many novels. "Your Grace, I'm the family physician. I'll keep her safe."

"Remember that, for she's nervous and eager to please."

Eager? Scarlett? I squint at him, not understanding.

"You sly d'yavol. I told you not to see her, and you send her a note that has her giddy."

Scarlett? Giddy? "But she responded by sending me sketches of an eye? How is that . . ." It hits me like lightning. How many times has she told me I'm stupid? "She only shares her research, her meticulously labeled sketches, with people she trusts and admires."

Torrance shakes his head. "I think that's quite romantic for our woman of science to do. I believe she's taken with you. If you can convince her to marry you, you will meet no objections."

My pulse quickens. "Your Grace, I never thought—"

"It's probably for the best, Mr. Carew. It might lead to difficulties." The lilting voice draws my attention to the top of the stairs.

My heart stops. Scarlett?

Full cardiac arrest seizes my chest. I can't breathe, but in the very best way. My gaze has been captured by a goddess. The most beautiful creature in the world wears crimson. The gown designed by angels heightens the red in her light olive complexion. She shines with the brilliance of diamonds.

An ivory fichu covers her bosom and sweeps into the square neckline of her dress. What she's wearing is respectable for church, a little much for the picnic, but this nymph is more suited for dancing under the stars.

Silk swathes her hips. The fabric skims noticeable thighs as she descends from the upper landing. Ruby pins gather her long tresses into a delectable bun. The woman glides in satin slippers.

I'm beside myself. She's an angel.

"Scarlett?" I can't believe my mouth still works. "Is that you? Of course it is. I'm amazed."

My throat begins to close up as she floats to Torrance. My heart starts again, pounding, fearing that this is a dream and I'll awaken alone and hungry, starved of this beauty.

The duke leans closer to me. "Close your mouth, Carew. Flies and pollen can come from nowhere."

This vision wanders away to stand in front of the mirror. "I hope I'm acceptable . . . to meet the aunties. I trust that they'll not recognize me from Somerset."

Scarlett's voice is always cultured, but there's a slight tremble. I've never seen the lithe thing without confidence. I take comfort that she's as nervous as I.

"You are beautiful. No one will, can . . . We are on this road to discovery together."

I pinch myself, and it hurts. I'm not dreaming. This is true. I'm well, well rested and have eaten. This feeling of euphoria is no delusion or figment of exhaustion.

Her eyes, glittering black mirrors, shine as she asks, "You received my note? Will we have time to discuss it along the way?"

"Of course. We'll make time." I'll command it to stand still. "Anything you wish, Miss Wilcox." I step to her and offer a deep bow, for such beauty demands it. "It would be my honor to take you today . . . to church and the aunties."

"Mr. Carew," the duke says, "your current enthusiasm is why, even as a trusted family friend, there must be a chaperone. Mrs. Cantor will make sure there are no incidents."

"Torrance, you can't think I'm going to take her to a brothel. And there will be no ice, unless—"

"Unless I'm very good." In her eyes, there's laughter and joy.

I'm drawn to those lips, and goodness—everything else. "I'm sure you'll manage."

"Manage what?" Lady Hampton comes down the steps. "And what's this about a brothel, Mr. Carew?"

"Poor joke, sister." Scarlett's voice is smooth. It's like she's singing a hymn of respect and love. "Stephen Adam Carew would never do anything untoward, unless I'm very good."

The affection in her voice, that's what I wanted in her letter. But hearing it, viewing it in her countenance is more wonderful. I shall become learned on Scarlett Wilcox.

I take her hand, and everything slows. "I've been kicked in the head, Lady Hampton, Miss Wilcox. But I've survived. I can attest to the truth, a mule can learn. A mule has learned."

Scarlett smiles. "Then there's hope for us."

"Jahleel, do something." Lady Hampton's harping sounds a little hysterical. "He's practically seducing my young sister here in Anya House."

"Lady Hampton, calm yourself. Mr. Carew is respectful. Miss Wilcox is sensible. They both understand what is at stake. *Our family* just escaped scandal a year ago."

I retreat when Mrs. Cantor puts Scarlett's matching crimson cape upon her shoulders. Lady Hampton's pitch gets higher.

"You are doing this to win a bet. Jahleel, this is my sister's happiness. Do something."

Scarlett flutters past them like they are nothing but noise. She gets closer, her gaze pinned on me. Those jet mirrors billow with smoke and fire. "I'm ready, Mr. Carew."

I claim her, her palm, and kiss her fingers. It would be too bold to kiss her mouth. "Me too."

I hear a shriek. Lady Hampton's pointing and waving. "He's mauling my sister."

I wasn't . . . was I?

The shadow of the crystal cane clouds my vision.

The next thing I know, the duke hauls me away, dragging me toward his study. Guess I should expect Torrance to find the strength of giants to protect one of his Wilcoxes.

Chapter 25

STEPHEN—SECRETS IN THE HIDING ROOM

With head shaking and cane snapping along the floor, the duke ushers me into his office. "Oh, Carew. You are smitten."

I stare at him, trying to pretend I know not what he talks about. "The office is back to being clean and tidy. You must've given up on the expansion."

"You think so, sir. I think you're stalking a confession."

I tap the bookcase where the opening was. The dull echo sounds hollow. I pull out a few leather spines. Nothing falls or opens. No special room. I guess he will face his mother when she arrives.

"Mr. Carew, I see you are happy with my choice to meet the aunties."

"Yes. Wait, choice as in candidates? This isn't like before, when you tried to match me with Georgina Wilcox?"

"Why would I match you to Georgina when she's married to someone else? I don't think a woman should marry a second husband while still having a first." He sets his cane aside and sits on his desk. The largest marble chess set is beside him. He palms what I believe is a jade-colored pawn and moves it a square forward. "You've allowed yourself to see Miss Wilcox's beauty and maturity. What of her intellect? She's not a baker. I don't think she knits."

"I know Scarlett is smart. We all do."

"Do you know that she wants nothing more than a marriage of convenience? She needs a husband who is tolerable and who will publish her scientific work."

"Nothing more? Not love and affection?"

"It appears you and I are the romantic ones. We want the beauty, the brainbox, the body. A good woman is a temple where I will forever worship."

No lies are detected in his flowery speech. "Scarlett Wilcox is the smartest woman I know, probably the smartest person, but she's a woman. Torrance, there's an order to things. I expect a wife to want me, to want my children, to want to build a home."

"I think Scarlett capable of all that if she is motivated, properly incentivized."

"Torrance, this is not a business decision."

He laughs at me, a hearty bitter chuckle. "Marriage is a business. The objective is to build and expand one's territory. A union maintains legacy and prepares rewards for your children's children."

I cross my arms and lean against the bookcase. "I saw a marriage as a business, it was abysmal. If you ever marry, I don't think you'd say such."

"Who said I never married?"

His tone is harsh, as if I've offended him. Then he begins to laugh and moves a corresponding piece from the pearl-colored side of the large chessboard.

"My experiences do not matter. Only Scarlett's happiness. She's the most truthful person I know. Always direct, no pretense. She is the only person other than Lydia who's truly innocent."

Our conversation is odd. It makes me nervous. "I need things to be direct, Torrance. What is it the rest of us are guilty of?"

He stops looking down at the chessboard. "Scarlett made Lady Hampton to tell me of our stillborn child."

Scarlett, bearer of the truth. "Torrance, that's good. You've talked."

"A little. I didn't mention the new grave marker for him, or how stunned I was that the date, the third of July, is the same as Lydia's birthday. How odd?"

I don't blink. "I wish I could've spoken of this earlier, but I must keep my patients' confidences. And I only recently learned from Scarlett of your history with Lady Hampton."

"Excuses." He tilts his head but seems satisfied. "The grave is being redone. Something fitting for the son I lost. I'm not like others who wish to forget."

"Never forget the person, but the pain has to be forgotten or it's consuming." I wrench my cravat, tightening the barrel knot. "For Miss Wilcox to make you both come together must mean you and Lady Hampton have matured, and she believes you'll not retaliate over this news."

"Retaliate? Carew, the young lady and I are very close. Her lost twin, Scotland, and my Andrew bond us. Scarlett and I know what it's like for the world to tell us to forget what we've lost."

I want to say that if I'd known the babe was his, I'd have told him, but that would be a lie. My sacred duty was to Mrs. Wilcox. Mrs. Patsy Wilcox wanted everything kept quiet. "Scandal, Torrance, can be dire. The Wilcoxes had to do what was best to protect their daughters. One scandal affects each girl's prospects. Blackamoor women in this world, whether in the rarefied air of Mayfair or the sulfur stench of the Thames, have to be beyond reproach to marry and make legacies for their families."

The patter of slippers and arguing voices sound outside the door. Faster than lightning, the duke comes toward me, pulls a chess piece, and the bookcase opens. He motions me inside.

I follow.

The duke hits something along the wall and the tomb closes. We are still in the dark, until curtains are opened. Torrance lights a torch and gives it to me, pointing at the sconces lining the room. When I have one lit, he closes the curtain. As I light the rest, I notice the beautifully appointed room is brighter than a thousand suns. I step back and douse two. That lowers the light enough to keep me from blinking.

Lady Hampton's voice vibrates the fake wall. "Where are you two? Out the window to avoid reason."

She sounds mad, but I'm here with a madman.

"Torrance, I keep secrets. The ton and the upper class have the most. No one knows about your condition or what you suffer."

"Scarlett knows."

"We've already agreed that she's the smartest person we know. Unlike everyone else, she would pick up the signs of illness, the carelessly placed pain vials, and the increased use of the cane. And if she sees how bright this room is, she'll suspect you're having problems with your vision."

Scarlett's eye research in my hands is the greatest overture, an overture of the best kind, her trust. "Her notes on the couching procedures say that you ordered her special tools. These are not just for the friend with cataracts, are they, Your Grace?"

"Mr. Thom has very bad cataracts in both eyes. She's done research to help him, and perhaps me if necessary."

I'm pained for my friend. "Torrance, why didn't you say something?"

"Secrets, my friend. We all have them." He moves to one of the shelves along the wall that displays some of the most intricate chess sets I've ever seen. He picks up a queen piece that shines like crystal. "I would hate to never see my treasures."

The duke carefully puts it back. "During my last health crisis, the lens, as Scarlett calls it, in my right eye dulled for weeks. It's clearer but could close again with another crisis. Her research on the eye can help both Thom and me. And for me, there's only one man I'd trust to do surgery. That's a physician who's been trained first as a surgeon. Stephen Adam Carew."

"You don't say it like Scarlett. Don't try." I hear footfalls again in the study, but this time near the hidden room's entrance. "Lady Hampton's still in there?"

"What is she doing? Looking for me in a desk drawer?"

This is foolish. Ignoring their games, I begin flipping through paintings that are stacked in the corner. One is of a landscape somewhere in the countryside. The artist is Cecilia Lance. The scene is so lifelike, it is as if you can walk right in. "Torrance, this should've been at Somerset's Annual Exhibition."

He waves his hand at me to quiet, and it's obvious who's immature in Anya House.

I look at another painting, this one is of the duke's mother and father, Princess Elizaveta Abramovna Gannibal and Andrew Charles, the Duke of Torrance. "Your mother is lovely."

"Thank you. She painted those. I'm still trying to determine where to hang them."

The last picture is of Lydia. She's wearing a dress similar to the princess. "She will love this gift for her upcoming birthday."

The duke ignores me, and I return to studying his secret lair. "Do we get to go free if we promise to have good behavior?"

"That's you and Scarlett's joke." He glares at me straight in my eyes. "Scarlett has a gift. Will you encourage her, or will you stifle her to soothe your ego?"

"I'd never . . . How do you know what she wants? And how do we know it's not me?"

"Well, you are a handsome d'yavol, d'yavol with an ego. I told Scarlett that I would choose someone who would let her continue to do research. Is that you?"

"You mean I have to let her continue to court disgrace?"

"Women have found ways to hide their quest for knowledge. Scarlett is not the first to dress as a man to get what she wants. Agnodice of the fourth century disguised herself to learn medicine to keep the women of Rome from dying in childbirth."

"Childbirth is dangerous, Tor—"

"Almas Begum did the same, hiding to practice medicine in the Mughal royal courts. I'm sure there are others whose names we'll learn when these brave women are exposed or when the truth outs after their deaths."

"Scarlett is brave, but I cannot stand by while she takes such risks. Her reputation and that of her family, my family, will be ruined. Unlike you, I don't have unlimited wealth to buy a fresh start, gain influence, or rid myself of detractors."

"If Scarlett were to accept you, then she is your family and then you are part of mine. Family is what matters."

I move to his right and watch his pupils follow. He does see me. The duke needs to when I confess. "I want Scarlett, but I want none of the games or wars you're playing."

He holds out his hand to me. "Shall you protect her? Encourage her mind? The brilliance you quoted and sent from A. Lady's pen, it can't only be meant for Scarlett's complexion. If you will help her in all ways including science, then you'll have my blessing. If not, you can leave."

Leave? Am I supposed to kneel or something, since these are things I can do? Torrance is sort of a prince. I take his hand and power it into a shake. "I will bring her caution, but never deter her. If Scarlett will marry me, I'll make her happy. We can shop together at Bond Street for waistcoats. I'll be so obliging."

"Or perhaps you can build that hospital and let her help. Sick people don't care who funded the creation, Carew. Even your community must see the value of women healers. And they must get rid of the prejudice or envy they might have at you bringing so much good."

I've been stalling on that. "I want a hospital. I see the need daily, but how can I prioritize a project, think of building with brick or stone, or slate without the woman I want to build a life?"

My knee goes down, for I know what I desire. I know what I feel. I'll show Scarlett. "I'll be a smarter chaperone this time, Torrance. I will win her hand, her mind, and her heart."

With a small half smile, he commands me to get up. The duke opens the hidden door. We exit and he closes it.

"What about the sconces?"

"They'll be doused later. Those paintings must be hung." He moves to the desk. "Katherine touched the board. She touched a knight."

The calm, cool duke looks flustered.

"What piece?" I ask. "If I put it back, will you calm?"

Ignoring my suggestion, the duke paces. "She did this. She moved the alabaster knight to G4."

Is this a world tragedy? "Torrance, why is this bad?"

He's grasping his chin. "My bishop is in check. That woman. Why?"

"You're upset because she put that green, stone-looking piece in check."

He sighs like I am a heathen. "It is jade, Carew. And the viscountess's move does put my side in check." He raises his voice. "That's too easy of a move, Lady Hampton. You know I can simply slide my bishop and take your knight. That would be checkmate. The game would be over."

His head swivels as if he's looking for a clue. "Why does she wish to lose? Why give up so easily, and after so many years and months?"

"Maybe she knows that Scarlett has chosen me. She knows she'll lose your silly bet."

The duke sinks against his desk. "Sometimes, it's too late. When things are in motion, they cannot be stopped."

Torrance slouches. He looks defeated.

And I'm fearful of what he's done that he can't undo.

The door opens. Lady Hampton and Scarlett come inside.

"They are both here, Katherine. Perhaps you should take a nap like Lydia."

"Scarlett, I checked. They weren't in here. Well, it doesn't matter. I want to know what has been agreed to."

"Lady Hampton." I step forward. "Torrance and I have agreed. I will escort Miss Wilcox with her other chaperone. However, because of the schedule of events, I'll have her returned by two in the morning, maybe later. Thank you for being generous and understanding."

"No. Back before midnight." The viscountess reddens as if she's about to explode. "There is no way—"

"No way for what, Katherine?" Scarlett glowers at her. "Balls normally end at four. I'm not the coal Vasilisa. I won't turn into a pumpkin at midnight. I assure neither my slippers nor Carew's carriage is glass."

"Coal Vasilisa?" Lady Hampton's tone becomes stern. "You're not a Cossack Cinderella, but you need to be returned by midnight."

"Don't impose upon me, a woman beyond the age of majority, some odd standard, one you didn't uphold."

Lady Hampton frowns and rounds to the smiling duke. "Jahleel, don't push her into marriage. They don't love each other. Last year, Scarlett claimed Mr. Carew loved what's-her-name."

"Eveline Gray. Or now, or maybe, former Baroness Derand." Scarlett seems exasperated and minutes away from pointing a finger in her sister's face. "Does it matter, Katherine? Or is forgetting the past a rule for merely you?"

"Does he love you, Scarlett? Do you love him?"

I was going to complain that I'm right here, that I can answer, but nawww. Meh gonna wait. Meh gonna listen.

Turning her wrath to me, like she knows how cautious I am with my words, my heart, Lady Hampton glares at me. "Scarlett won't be happy not having everything. She deserves to be loved."

The silence from me, the duke, from Scarlett, feels heavy, like Lady Hampton tossed one of those furry rya carpets on top of us. Then Scarlett hugs her sister, almost lifting her from the ground, then embraces the duke. "I shall have a good time. We will return when everything is done. Not a moment sooner."

With tears in her eyes, Lady Hampton looks up to the decorated ceiling. "Have a good time, sister. Mr. Carew, take care of her."

Scarlett curtsies, then takes my free arm. "Let's go."

Even if I had wanted to stay, a command from a determined woman cannot be denied. I offer a dip of my chin to her guardians.

Outside Anya House, a sad smile forms upon Scarlett's lips. "Make this worth the trouble, Mr. Carew."

Even with a Mrs. Cantor hovering, I'm happiest for this command. I'm taking an angel to church. I sense I'll have a devil of a time convincing the woman on my arm we can be happy. Though Scarlett often calls me stupid, deservedly, I have clarity. I know what I want. As I help her into my carriage, I'm more determined to prove to my logical lady I can sweep her off her feet.

Chapter 26

SCARLETT—A CARRIAGE, A MARRIAGE

Sitting next to Mrs. Cantor in Stephen's carriage, I try to relax. It takes him a few minutes to give Benny some sort of signal or directions. Now that we are underway, Stephen stares at me, and then my notes. Will he quiz me?

His long fingers flip through my sketches. The silence is unnerving. But I do look at him. It's been a week of not seeing or speaking, just letters. Over the past year, he's visited Anya House at least a couple of times a week. A woman can get used to his handsome face. At least his lips have a shine.

Be bold, Scarlett. "Sorry for our tense leaving."

Yawning and nodding, Mrs. Cantor looks at me. She pulls out her knitting—a scarf in progress.

His gaze captures mine. "No need to fret, Miss Wilcox. I have a surprise for us. Just be patient with me. It's my first time."

"You ignoring me, reading . . . criticizing my work. If this is your way of showing a lady a good time, I'm highly disappointed."

"Girly, just sit there, while I go through the *Georgie bundle* dat yuh sent."

He makes me smile, but I give him a little pout. "When did I become my sister? We Wilcoxes are not interchangeable."

"No, the Georgie bundle is an expression from home for big

package. You're a big package to me." He studies my papers, but he says, "Her features were all good; her smile was sweet and attractive; and in her eyes, which were very dark, there was a life, a spirit, an eagerness, which could hardly be seen without delight."

Stephen catches my gaze. "I'm delighted by you, Scarlett Wilcox. Your Humbled Servant. S. A. Carew."

He quotes himself quoting A. Lady. A nervous giggle slips and I cover my mouth. He takes down my hand. My satin gloves slide against his palm, but he strengthens his hold. "Tell me your thoughts on your patient."

Heated hands. Skin on fire. How am I supposed to have thoughts? "Stephen Adam Carew, thank you for the compliment and for you treating my research with care."

"Why blush? You know I've always respected your opinion. And you read my note."

"It's different said aloud. The words hold new meaning. I go to lectures and often read the speakers' past works. Makes more sense said aloud."

His head dips. I think he will kiss my fingers. Feeling the warmth and wet hot air along the tips of my thin gloves could be a torture. "Sometimes actions mean more."

Before I do something reckless like jump into his arms, I sit back, careful not to mash my chignon against the seat. "If I close my eyes, I can imagine you speaking of tests and scientific observations on gout. It was a splendid lecture at the Royal Society."

"That was over two years ago. You showed up as a man at Somerset House that long ago?"

"Yes. Mr. Thom, dear Mr. Thom, has been taking me. Now the duke makes sure I have a proper escort."

"Proper." He rolls his eyes, then his gaze falls again on me. "Can't believe someone as beautiful as you can hide in plain sight."

My cheeks warm, but I refuse to be easy prey for his flattery. "Like you and the duke today?"

His brow rises. "You know about his little hideaway?"

"Yes. I saw when he had it built. It's being kept hidden until the duke does a big reveal. Seems like a lot of work just to hide from Katherine."

"Never do that."

"Hide from Katherine? Oh, that's the pastime of my literal past."

"I meant hide from me. I want you to be able to say or do anything you want with me."

Silence comes to us again. Stephen shifts from reading my confused thoughts trapped in my head to my notes.

"There's no quiz, sir. Don't feel bad if you've had no time to review them. I know you are busy."

A smile crosses his lips. "This will be my fourth read."

I suppose that means I've passed some sort of test. When he finishes the last page, his eyes lock upon mine. I feel his fire.

"Uhm." I clear my throat. "So how will you introduce me to the aunties?"

"As Miss Wilcox, I suppose. They should know the family name. They'll also mention that the Wilcoxes have stayed across the Thames and not frequented Cheapside." He sets my notes to the side and stretches. "It's somewhat a shame that your family has not socialized more."

"As Mama always said, three daughters of marital age with a plaguing illness makes things difficult."

"Patsy Wilcox was no Mrs. Bennet. Your mother was a very levelheaded, practical woman."

Referencing more of his novels. That's fine, I'll watch his lips move. Always liked that, and I must say, he always looks good, but this emerald coat with shiny brass buttons is new. His face is nicely shaven. No bumps along his chin which sometime torment him. The natural wave to his hair is brushed to the side.

"Scarlett, is there some other way to address you?"

Oops. Forgot to pay attention to his words. "What do you suggest?"

"Perhaps something a little dearer? But you did reject marrying me." He rubs his jaw. "Pity. Fiancée is a nice title for you."

"You can joke, but this is an important detail to get right. At the exhibition, I was both Scotland Wilcox and Scotland Carew."

"How about a compromise. I can introduce you as Scarlett Carew?" He shakes his head vigorously. "That can't work since you were so against marrying me. Has that changed?"

"Such a tease. Do you think I actually believed you when you asked? I remember your talk of planning and grand gestures. Blurting a proposal out on a carriage floor doesn't seem serious."

"But I was serious. I am serious."

He's teasing. I release a nervous chuckle. "I've already failed your standards. I'm not demure or quiet. The Wilcoxes are proud, but I'm not sure if you count coal people as pedigreed."

His fingertips rub together. "You like to torture me. You want me to compliment you again? Fine. You're absolutely stunning, Scarlett. I've never seen someone so beautiful. You've obliterated my idea of the perfect woman." He sighs like a teapot releasing steam. "I said it. Happy?"

"Happy." I mimic the way his proud shoulders fall. "And you should know I let myself be pinned with these tortuous rubies just to be tolerable for you today." I roll my eyes. "And I sort of like obliterating things, but the duke told me a man's ego can be a fragile thing. Or was that my sister?"

"I'm not fragile." Stephen looks me dead in my eyes. Then he looks away. "Well, maybe a little fragile. Please don't turn that sharp wit on me today."

He scoots forward, closing the distance between our legs. "Scarlett, I love the aunties. They support the immigrants of London. But they can be a bit . . ."

"Domineering. Demanding. Demented."

"Pushy. Pushy is the word I was looking for." He sits back rubbing at his knees. His buff breeches look very good on him. The hue highlights his bronze skin. "The ladies mean well. And I know they want me to be happy. But they don't know how my tastes have changed."

The cogs in his mind, I see them turning. His brow has damp-ened. Is he perspiring? Is he thinking about what to say next? Why is he being so careful around me? "What has changed?"

"Well, they know I have an eye for women who are demure and pretty. You fit the part today."

"You mean I'm pretending to be pretty."

"No. That's not what . . ." He puts his hands to his dampening forehead. "Why am I tongue-tied?"

Taking off my long off-white gloves, I stretch to his side of the carriage to test his forehead for fever, but we end up holding hands.

Mrs. Cantor coughs. She shakes a finger at me, and I let go of Stephen. Pity, I like the way my palm feels surrounded by his.

He huffs and shakes his head toward my chaperone. "We have to look comfortable about each other if we must pretend to be courting."

Without saying another word, Mrs. Cantor closes her eyes. Tentatively, Stephen reaches for me until he clasps my hand.

"Scarlett, I owe you an apology. I've been unbearable treating you as a child when you've grown up."

"Well, I do do things that can be aggravating."

We laugh and it feels like forever since we've done that to-gether. He keeps rubbing along my knuckles, then he thumbs my wrist. We stretch until his lips meet a spot that causes me to shiver, a good shiver along my spine.

Mrs. Cantor's snores sound like trumpets. The noise imitates the racket the duke's men made sawing lumber for his secret room. I chuckle again.

Stephen's gaze bears down on me. It's hot, fiery. "What's so funny, Scarlett? Have I done something—"

"No. Not you. It's the duke and Katherine. They're unpre-dictable. I thought they'd reached a truce, but he's starting to hide from her. My sister looked so confused returning from the study."

Stephen pushes at his low-cut hair. The wavy curls bounce about his fingers.

The nurse's snores ramp again. He gives her a quick look, then pivots to me. "Lady Hampton stung him pretty well. She moved his chess pieces."

"Katherine touched his game?"

"Yes. Torrance seemed disturbed by it." Stephen chuckles again. "I guess she knows him well. Two people perfectly suited can learn to trust again. A woman should be able to give all of her with no regrets. All," he says again, "all of her wits, all her secrets."

Stephen isn't talking about my sister. His words are for me. Can I trust a man who wants to be my husband, who suddenly sees me?

"What are you thinking, Scarlett? Tell me."

"I'm envious of men. You get science and adventure. Men can have everything physical that comes with marriage and intimacy. And yet be able to walk away and go on with their life. Perhaps that's what Katherine can't forgive."

"Scarlett, I'm not walking away. I'm here. I want to marry—"

"With your love of novels, Mr. Carew, do you read aloud? I should like to know your sensibilities on the subject."

"Sensing you want to change the topic." He folds his hands across a waistcoat that isn't black or indigo but brown with hints of green that match his coat. That's new, too. "I have great sense and sensibilities on the topic. But I rarely read aloud. Many merely want a physician to talk of nothing but medicines and ailments. That's not what I want to do right now. I'm sitting with a pretty woman. I'd rather entertain her."

"Talking of medicines would be entertaining. I guess I have a singular fascination with it."

"I have a singular fascination as well. It's called Scarlett Wilcox." He shifts his hat, making space on the bench beside him. He wriggles his finger at me. "Come here."

The tone is low, spicy.

I guess Stephen is being playful. I can play, too. Peeking at him through lowered lashes, I toss him a look over my shoulder. "You want me at your beck and call, and yet you will not talk about medicine." I shrug. "Not sure this will work. You're cute and all but, sir, I'll be bored."

His head rears back. "Ma'am, I take that as a personal offense . . . and challenge." Stephen glances at Mrs. Cantor and waves a hand in front of her. The nurse doesn't move.

His smile deepens and he places those skillful hands on my knees and tugs me forward. This satin dress makes his motion easy to slide me closer.

"If I wore breeches, things would be more difficult, sir."

"Scarlett, if you wore breeches, I'd know exactly how to get to you. Not sure your chaperone would sleep through our . . . your racket. I believe you will be noisy when passionate."

My curiosity at what he will do gets the better of me, so I fall into our language, taunting. "Such bold talk from the man who bores me."

One quick tug sends me flying off the seat. Before I drop onto the floor, Stephen scoops me into his arms and plops me onto his lap. "Boring, Scarlett? Let's see if you can keep up."

Heated palms to my face, he tastes my lips. "You're salty, Scarlett. How do I sweeten you up?"

The notion to offer a fake yawn flees with his hands tightening about me. Then in the most delicious manner possible, he whispers, "I have copies of the *Medical Repository of Original Essays and Intelligence.* The reports were edited by a Mr. Mitchell. The pages have detailed observations about disease."

His breath floods my ear. I smell and taste sweet peppermint in his kiss. "One essay, my dear, was on cholera."

"Cholera? That's a digestive disorder."

"Uhmmm." Stephen's palms slip beneath my cape. His fingers lazily stroke the tender skin of my chest hidden by the lace fichu. "Yes, typically, it's not fatal."

"Not fatal, good." These words barely fall from my mouth before he's claimed it. This tenderness could be fatal, fatal to all my dreams. Stephen holds me firmly upon his muscular thighs. I dare not squirm or I'll miss the way his hands sweep along my back. When he strokes that spot between my shoulders where the tension builds when I spend an evening poring over science papers, I squeal a little.

His chest rumbles with smothered laughter. "Noisy. Just like I thought."

When his caress works free a knot along my neck, I squeak, then slam my lips together.

"You will awaken Mrs. Cantor. Would that be our eighteen hundredth compromising situation?"

"Lost count." I put my arms about his neck, and listen to him list the symptoms of cholera, then I kiss him. I love the feel of him, the strength of his caress, the gentleness of his hands.

His fingers settle mercifully on the small of my back. "There's more I wish to teach, to experience with you. Never a moment will be boring. I promise."

Trust him? Trust myself? If I were modest, I'd hop away, steal myself from the pleasure, the closeness and torture of wanting Stephen Adam Carew.

I've settled for pieces of him—his attention, his time.

I'm used to that, for I've always loved him and always hated myself for being so weak for a man who couldn't see me.

When his hand surgically slips to my thigh, and a bare palm strokes my knee, I know we've gone too far. I'm not ready for womanly consequences. "We must stop."

"Are you sure? I thought you liked my compromise. I whisper to you about medicine, whilst I find every spot along your skin that makes you noisy. See, good compromise."

"There's nothing more to search for. I'm not wearing disguises."

"Must be sure." He kisses me again, and I savor everything.

The peppermint, the heat, the feel of his heart pounding against mine.

"No more. I concede. You're not boring. And it's just me in the dress. It's just me."

"That's exactly what I want, Scarlett. Just you. Now let me tell you more signs of cholera."

With my palms to his cheeks, I angle his face to seek his deepest kiss. I can't resist anymore. I give up my power and tell Stephen Adam Carew, "I love you."

Chapter 27

STEPHEN—CHECKING ON HER PATIENT

The carriage begins to slow, and I slip Scarlett from my lap to the seat next to me.

I want to make a joke about us pretending we haven't been wrapped in each other's arms kissing like maddening fools. But I can't make a light or humorous statement, not when she's given me her heart.

Yet I can't say anything back. I want to blame the moment, the chaperone awakening. None of that is true. It's fear. I don't want to *jinx* this. I'd declared my feelings to Eveline. She was part of the community. She had the aunties' approval. Banns were to be read in a week or two.

Then she eloped.

The way things ended, I wrestle with it. I hold Scarlett's hand and there's some irrational fear that once I tell her everything in my head and heart, her feelings for me will go away.

I see it in her eyes. Those mirrors show fear. And I've put it there by not telling her I love her, too.

Mrs. Cantor yawns and is fully awake. She stares at us and offers a little cough, but I refuse to move my hand from Scarlett's. I need to get Scarlett completely alone. Then I will break my oath and tell her everything.

"This is not Wesley's Chapel. We are at my house on Ground Street. Are you done with me so soon?"

"No. We are beginning. Look at me, Scarlett. Trust me. I need you to trust me. My fear of losing you is deeply felt." I put my hand to her chin. "And I will if you can't see that I've changed."

She almost pulls away, especially when I see tears in those jet mirrors. Can't she see . . . Do words matter more?

Scarlett lifts her chin, then bursts out of the carriage.

I pick up the papers she sent. "We still have time to get to the church, but I thought you'd like me to look in on your patient." I clasp her hand. "Let's go see Mr. Thom together."

Her face, her beautiful face is shocked. She leaps into my arms. "I'll trust you. No one knows me as well as you."

Grasping her about her waist, I feel as if she understands me, too. Turning to the carriage, I say, "Mrs. Cantor, we will be back."

"Fine, dears. I'll knit while I wait. Don't be too long or be alone."

The sweet woman pulls out more yarn from her bag and begins making more of whatever she's knitting.

Lord Mark and his wife come out of the house. "Sister, Mr. Carew. What brings you here?"

I shake his hand. "We're on an outing, but I knew it would rest Miss Wilcox's mind if we checked on Mr. Thom and I offer my opinion on treatment."

Georgina grabs Scarlett and makes her twirl. "Simply lovely. And here I thought you only loved Papa's boots."

"Boots are inappropriate for church and an evening picnic." Scarlett looks at me. "I want to be appropriate. Demure, impeccable . . ."

Her voice sounds sad and makes my soul ache. I turn from her and grab my leather bag from the carriage, and then signal to Benny to take the carriage around.

My man winks at me. He approves of Scarlett, but who wouldn't? The carriage heads to the rear.

"You think our chaperone will finish whatever she's making, Miss Wilcox, before we are done here today?"

She shrugs. My attempt at small talk falters. Maybe I need to speak more on cholera.

"A chaperone," Georgina says. "This sounds serious."

"It is serious." I take my chance at redemption, clasp and kiss Scarlett's hand. "I'm serious about my fiancée. Scarlett Wilcox is the woman I will marry."

Scarlett's countenance blanks.

Georgina jumps up and down. "My goodness. You two!"

The sister hugs me and says again, "Scarlett. Mr. Carew. I'm so happy for you both. I never thought it possible for the two of you."

Squinting at her, I ask, "Why? Is it so improbable?"

"Well, you two always argue. And Scarlett never seemed interested in anything but Papa's boots and science."

"I have other interests, Georgie. And in spite of everything, I do like him." She glances at me with renewed coldness. "I can say I love him, just like I can admit that the sun is the moon if you wish. Both are bright, *Petruchio*. Petruchio, that's my pet name for Carew. Better than Mr. Stuffy."

Oh, she's big mad at me. The lady that doth quote Shakespeare's *Taming of the Shrew* is learned and angry. I'm in trouble again.

"Scarlett is glowing." Lord Mark is kind and still clueless to our dynamics. "It sort of makes sense that you two are always bickering. It gives me hope for Torrance and our sister Katherine."

Lord Mark shakes my hand again. "Getting another physician in the family is wonderful."

Scarlett wears a smile, but her eyes are not happy.

Georgina pulls her aside. They're discussing me and Torrance. I stop trying to overhear when Scarlett's tone becomes blunt. "Did you know that Katherine's stillborn was the duke's son?"

When I hear Georgina whisper yes, I flee with Mark to the

house. The second oldest Wilcox sister, the one closest to Lady Hampton, must be aware of the whole truth.

My hands are ice. The worst Wilcox lie is yet to come. I have a feeling it will be exposed, and all involved will pay a price.

Following Lord Mark into the house evokes so many memories. The matriarch Patsy would play the pianoforte for me when she was well. She suffered greatly from the sickness that the duke and Lydia have.

When gossip spread about the Wilcoxes and their suffering, I don't think they were as welcomed. People understood the sickness followed bloodlines. No one would wish this illness on their children's children. It's an unwanted legacy that hurt too many.

"Sir, are you well?" At the base of the stairs, Lord Mark stops. "Do you need a moment? A new engagement can be very exciting and taxing."

A clock moans. It's solemn, almost pained. I think I recognize it. "Is that Mr. Wilcox's longcase from his office?"

It chimes again and I am reminded of the patriarch's proud face when it sounded. How he tried to use his frustration of it losing time or odd chirps to hide the man's tears when sorrows came. "I thought Lord Hampton sold it off."

"No. Scarlett has it in her room." Lord Mark glances at me, and I trot up the stairs like a weight is on my shoulders.

"You sure you're well, Carew? Georgie has baked biscuits. Eating will refresh you. I'll send some up before I take the afternoon's deliveries."

He points at a bedchamber down the hall. "Thom is in Lydia's bedchamber. He's comfortable, but I believe his days of driving for Wilcox Coal are done. Not sure what Katherine will do now. I'll take on more, but no one works as hard as Mr. Thom."

More voices echo in the house below. One is Georgina's. The other is Scarlett's. I feel better knowing she's here and that she's entrusted me with her research. I want to be able to support her in it, but blindness is difficult to fix, and surgeries are dangerous.

My gaze cuts again to the matriarch's old bedchamber, or what became the chambers of Lord and Lady Hampton. The day the two wed at St. George's, I remember Mrs. Wilcox leaving her sickbed to witness their union. I, and a few members of the community, came. Georgina held the three-month-old Lydia. The babe was remarkably quiet during the service, but her pallor was yellow because of the sickness. Scarlett, skinny and boyish, seemed unmoved. She sat in the rear with Mr. Wilcox. The man didn't look impressed either. Even then, Scarlett could tell the difference between the sun and moon, truth and lies, between love and convenience.

She has to be able to see what I feel. A t'ing is a t'ing even if yuh don't name it. No jinx-jinx on wud I feel.

The longcase makes another noise. It's the oddest sound, sort of like it is running out of air or time. As I walk to the bedroom door, it definitely feels like the latter.

Pushing into Lydia's bedroom, I feel a warm breeze coming into the small room. Whitewashed walls hold pink decorations. The curtains on the window are light and airy. A tiny bed made for two, or maybe one, is in the rear with a thick rya leading toward it.

"Mr. Thom, it's me, Mr. Carew."

The man moans but doesn't open his eyes. "They sent for you. Am I done for?"

"Of course not. You make it sound as if Mr. Carew is a bearer of bad news." Georgina enters with a platter of her famous ginger biscuits. "He's our physician and soon to be part of the family."

Scarlett comes inside the room. She stands away from Georgina and closer to me. The move is obvious and feels cold toward her sister.

"Well, Mr. Carew," she says, "how is our patient doing, the treasured Mr. Thom?"

"Not much of a treasure," their man-of-all-work says as he tries to sit up from the pile of bedsheets.

"Steady, sir." Scarlett rushes to Mr. Thom and puts her hand on his shoulder. "So glad you're not much hurt."

"Nothing but my pride. Our duke is a good man. He's had someone watching since you told him I was having trouble with my vision."

Georgina lowers her tray of sweet-smelling goodies. "You told the duke, but not us, Scarlett?"

"You're busy being married. Lady Hampton's busy trying to best the duke and save the coal company. You don't have time and don't need new worries. Miss Scarlett is my friend."

"So you get to be selective with secrets?" Georgina bites into one of her ginger biscuits like she is ravenous or wild and stares at her sister. "A need-to-know basis?"

"Maybe he knows who to trust." Scarlett's tone is tart. "It's hard to be certain."

I try to calm them. "Ladies, please. This is about the patient."

Scarlett sits on the bed, her hand covering Mr. Thom's withered dark-brown digits.

He chuckles. "So you brought Mr. Stuffy to see me. Must be pretty bad off."

"Mr. Stuffy?" I glance at her, and she sort of shrugs. "I insisted upon coming, sir. I had to, once I reviewed Scarlett's notes. How do you feel?"

"Poorly," he says. "But I'm going to be fine. Mrs. Georgina and Lord Mark have been so kind." He squints toward Scarlett. "So, is stiff fella giving you a hard time today? And is you dressed as you or your brother? Boy, that Scotland was something."

"Our brother was," Georgina says. She's come closer, bringing along the scent of ginger and butter. "He'd be glad that Scarlett is gathering resources to help you."

"Even brought Mr. Stuffy. Oh boy." Mr. Thom lies back. "I guess that means I'm causing more of a fuss."

"Mr. Thom, be at ease," Scarlett says. "Me and Mr. Carew are friendly today."

Woman, friendly! With my hands all over her in the carriage and my thoughts imagining everywhere else, what does she mean friends? Livingston's my friend, sort of, but I'd never be in a carriage with him like that.

I'd never risk her reputation or mine . . . for friendliness.

I keep my thoughts to myself and become the professional I am. "Mr. Thom. It's my honor to look after you. You're a Wilcox by extension. I've looked after them all. I, Stephen Carew—"

"You mean Stephen Adam Carew. You have to say it like Miss Scarlett, with awe and respect."

That notion makes me smile, makes me think back to each time she's called my whole name, that perhaps it was with love . . . and aggravation. I lean closer to the patient. "Mr. Thom. I need to examine your eyes."

Putting my bag on the side of the bed, I dig inside and pull out a magnifying lens, a candle, and a small holder.

Scarlett's arms are folded. She looks fragile, like I'll find fault. I've seen this tension in some of our teasing. Must fix this now. "Scarlett, I need you—"

Her jet eyes open wider. I'm lost and then found in her pupils.

"What will you have me do?"

There's so much I want . . . need of her. For now, I light the candle, put it in the stand and hand it to her. "Hold this, then do exactly as I say."

"Yes, of course." Before she takes the items from me, she slips off her cape. It flutters and falls to the bed. As if I'm watching her descend the stairs at Anya House once more, I'm dazzled. The curve of her bosom, the flair of hips that shape her dress better than any petticoat—all are inches away. Her lips part. "What do I do?"

"Hold me . . . *it* close. The candle. Be careful of falling wax. Beeswax is hottest when molten. I don't want anything to hurt you or Mr. Thom."

A deep blush falls on her cheeks. My blathering has affected her. My God, she's beautiful. And she loves me.

Scarlett unpins her straw bonnet with the red-dyed feather

and hands it to her sister, who's nervously eating another treasured biscuit. The scent of ginger is replaced by jasmine. Scarlett
is absolutely breathtaking.

Her arm is outstretched. With her gloves remaining in my carriage, her arms are bare to her shoulders like a sculpted piece of
sleek bronzed statue. "Do I hold it like this, Mr. Carew?"

I'm speechless. I'm absorbed by the lines of her, the elegance
of her profile in a gown fit for a princess. How did she ever pass
for a man?

With a shake of my head, I clear my thoughts. "Relax, Mr. Thom.
And here, Miss Wilcox, stand here."

Drawing her from the bed, I have her in front of me again.
This time, I link our hands together and guide the candle to
within inches of Mr. Thom's right eye.

"The light's focused on the zygomatic bone." Scarlett's tone is
low but authoritative. "Should I move up?"

"Oh, Lord," Mr. Thom whimpers. "Zygo-might. That
sounds bad."

"Just say the cheekbone, Scarlett. The formality may frighten
the patient. And there's no need to impress me. I already am.
And yes, go up a little. Put the focus on my magnifier."

"Give it to me straight, Mr. Carew." Mr. Thom thrashes about
in the light. He calms when I have Scarlett move the candle.
"How long do I have?"

"To live?" I say, "A long time. To see, I'm not sure."

"What next, Mr. Carew?" Her voice sounds distant and formal.

I slow my nervous heart. I'm not returning her until after midnight. I have hours to fix us, to heal our newborn relationship.

"Let's look at the other eye again. I need to estimate the size."
Releasing my hold on the candle, I give her full control, but I
guide her placing my palm to her abdomen. I feel her tremble
against me. With more pressure, we move as one.

"Perfect," I say, and draw in a breath of her sweet jasmine and
the honey smoke. "Mr. Thom, keep holding still. Scarlett, a little
closer."

She backs into me and again my mind is gone. It takes a moment of concentration to stop thinking of her hips. "I meant to bring the light closer to Mr. Thom's face."

Scarlett responds and our movements again are fluid. She's an extension of me, or I am of her. "The left lens is completely occluded. It has a solid lenticular cataract blocking light into the eye."

"Mr. Thom." Scarlett's voice sounds full of tears. "That means the left eye is fully darkened. You see nothing. How long, Mr. Thom?"

"Nothing." The man grunts. "Not for two days. It went. Then I crashed the cart."

She leans against me again and steals my breath. "I've been fussing with the modiste and gowns. I should've been here."

"Scarlett, your being here wouldn't stop this." My hand lightly cups her hip, drawing her again to me, so near that her lovely neck is in kissable range, and I relax my hold, flattening my palm to keep from tracing what feels like the lace of a chemise, the edges of a shift or some undergarment that adorns her rich skin. I'm spun up again.

"Uhmmm." Dusting crumbs from her mouth, Georgie coughs, looking straight at me. "Too friendly, Mr. Stuffy."

My fingers give me away. They wish to paw into this silky gown and seek the pleasures and surprises of this woman. "Let's look at the right eye once more."

Scarlett nods.

"See it, my dear, the occlusion?"

"Like a flawed diamond," she says. Her voice is low. I hunger for it to again be in my ear. "The right side, the growth is slower."

I'm trying to focus on the patient who might go blind, instead of how blind I've been not noticing a diamond in my midst, a brilliant fiery gem who loves me even though I'm deeply flawed.

"The right eye has some cataracts but still has vision. It's not a candidate for the procedure. However, the left is definitely a candidate for couching. Very good work researching."

"Stephen, you agree with me?"

"Your analysis is right. I'm honored that you entrusted me with your notes."

Her cheeks turn red, Georgina interrupts. "Wait a moment. Are you saying the research my sister did, all these sketches she's created will help restore Mr. Thom's eyesight?"

"Yes, Georgina. Scarlett's diagrams have been used by the duke to commission the special tools needed for this couching technique. It should work, but how well is the question."

"Slouching," Georgina says, "Sis. You are wonderful."

"It's called couching. Don't celebrate. It requires a very sharp instrument to push back the cataract-covered lens completely into the eye. Light will then be able to reach the inside of the eye again. Mr. Thom will regain the ability to see shapes and colors," Scarlett says. "That has to be better than blindness."

I put my hand on her shoulder. "Before we get too excited, Mr. Thom must consider the risks. There are a lot of risks. And it can't be done here. It needs to be a hospital . . ."

My voice sort of dies. A year ago, I was working in a hospital that could do just that. But I stopped and built my profession for my aunties' approval. Begging for sponsors, when my own coffers are light, is hard for a proud man. Now I'm a lauded gentleman with no hospital to serve the community I love.

"Stephen?"

I rub at my face. "I suspect that Scarlett and the duke have a place that's suitable. I spent time there earlier." Now for the hard part. "Mr. Thom, there can be a lot of complications. Couching may only regain color perception. There can be infection. I'm not sure it's worth the risk."

Scarlett pulls away from me. We're separated for the first time. I witness her shiver. Like me, she must miss our bodies' heat.

"Like a fever? Infections cause fever."

She sounds small and scared and unlike confident Scarlett.

"Yes, a fever. Mr. Thom may also lose the ability to open and close the eye. The procedure will be painful. Anything involving the eye is. Mr. Thom, you must consider all these factors."

"None of the research accounting said anything about fevers."

"Scarlett, fevers arise whenever an operation happens. It's common, so it's not often mentioned. It's a reality of any surgical procedure."

"But fevers can kill," she says. Scarlett's eyes are big and fearful. She runs from the room.

I look at Georgina. She whispers, "Scotland."

She and her tray of biscuits head out after her sister.

"Mr. Stuffy, what do you think?"

I take his hand, as I've done thousands. "You heard the risks. I need you to decide."

"Would you do it?"

"Mr. Thom, if it meant a chance at seeing one of the things I treasure, then yes. It's worth the risk." Picking up my bag, and Scarlett's sketches, I head to the door. "I'll check with you next week. When you are strong enough, in July, we can do the procedure at Anya House. Scarlett Wilcox was right on this practice."

"Glad you now see how special that girl is, Mr. Stuffy."

On that I can agree. Except for the girl part. Scarlett Wilcox is all woman, and now all scared.

Chapter 28

SCARLETT—RACING FEET, RACING HEARTS

Georgina bangs on the door to my bedchamber. "Come out, Scarlett. It's not your fault. Scotland—"

"I need a minute." My heart races. I feel stupid. I've wasted so much time on this. I gave Mr. Thom hope. That procedure is supposed to help, and it can cost him his life.

"Please, Scarlett, let me in. We need to talk. We should talk about everything. I'm sorry that we didn't tell you the truth about Katherine's baby."

That's what she thinks I'm upset about? My sisters don't know me. That's the greatest tragedy of all. "Let me be. Tell Mr. Carew to go to the aunties without me."

"Scarlett, it's Stephen, we need to leave." The knock on the door is no longer gentle. "Scarlett, we need to go now to be on time. You know me. You know I hate to be late."

"How can I go? I'm a failure." I blow my nose on one of Mama's lacy handkerchiefs. "Go without me."

"Dearest Scarlett," he says. "I just sent your sister back to Mr. Thom for your cape. You will need it, and I need to see you."

"I'm terrible." I plop on the bed. The crimson satin contrasts my white bed coverings. Honestly, I want to be back at Anya House where I can be a recluse, but in style.

"Scarlett, please."

Stephen is sweet, but I can't be around him. I don't want to hear that I was good enough for a woman. Or that this is a minor mistake. "A fever can kill. It killed Scotland. That's my fault."

"Scarlett, are you near the door? I need this unlocked."

"What was I thinking? A woman doctor. You, and even Livingston, tried to tell me. I can sneak into every lecture and still learn nothing."

"Sweetheart, back away from the door."

"What? I am. Why?"

Wham. Stephen Adam Carew crashes into my door flinging it open wide. He tumbles and lands beside me on the bed. "I think I hurt myself."

Georgie's in the threshold. Her mouth is open. She has the tray of biscuits in one hand and my cape in the other.

Stephen points at her. "Stay, Georgina, outside. Give us a moment."

She leaves and closes the door.

Stephen lies beside me, catching his breath. "Miss Wilcox, I need you to come with me."

His tone sounds harsh. When he sits up, the way he rotates his shoulder with jerking motions, I know he's injured himself.

My tears flow. "I don't want anyone in pain or blind or hurt. I think you—"

"No. No thinking, Scarlett. That's when we both get into trouble."

He stands up and massages his arm. As I sit on the bed, he towers over me. "This is your room? It's bland. No fancy curtains? I saw you have some at Anya House."

"You broke into my room there, too?"

He waves his hands. "No. No. I saw from the outside." He slaps his forehead. "Now I sound as if I'm a stalking horse, watching from afar to learn about you."

"That's not you, Stephen. You aren't aware enough for that."

He starts to laugh, then lifts me up. "I had this vision of breaking the door down and tossing you over my shoulder. But my arm really hurts, and your dress is too lovely to wrinkle. So much for this grand gesture." His thumbs wipe tears from my eyes. His neck swivels. "This room doesn't seem like you."

"It's Scotland's. It will always be his."

The longcase sounds. Stephen's gaze remains on me. "That's loud and odd. Was it your brother's favorite, too?"

"Not as much as Papa's, but Scotland was supposed to get it and the coal business, if he'd succeeded our father."

"The odd clock says we need to go, but I have a spot in my parlor just for it. And when you decorate my blank and very boring house, you decorate for us, but particularly you. I need you comfortable. I need you."

"Is this a new proposal?"

He doesn't answer with words, but a kiss—slow and gentle. I lean into him as he tilts me toward heaven.

And I sob.

Suddenly, I'm off my feet. They dangle as he carries me into the hall. "Lady, get your cape from your sister."

I do as he commands, but tell Georgie, "Put Mr. Thom in my room. I guess I won't be back for a while. Knowing Katherine, she'll be away from Anya House as quickly as she can."

Stephen stops at the front door. He yells for Benny, and I look at this old house while hanging down Petruchio Stuffy's back.

Clip-clop. The clock chimes. I almost hear Mama on the pianoforte. I whisper goodbye. I don't want to be here with the lies.

The carriage stops in front of the house. I let Stephen put me inside as he dashes back for his bag. When he climbs in, he signals Benny to make haste.

There's no more pretense between Stephen and me about being respectable in front of our chaperone. He pulls me onto his lap, in his arms, wrinkling my gown as he cradles a teary me.

"You don't need to coddle me."

"Yes, I do, Scarlett. It's best to think of something else." Stephen leans over and places my sketches in the cabinet under the opposite seat, then pulls out a copy of *Sense and Sensibility*. "And since I can only think of you, we shall both find out what the beautiful brown Marianne is doing. Or perhaps Elinor has become wiser and found her friendship with the regal Colonel Brandon should be more."

"Stephen please."

"I'm done with medical discussions today. I find novels helpful. They help me relax and have happy thoughts when I hurt for my patients. Scarlett, I want our home life to be an escape. I need you to wrap me up in your love so tightly that I gain distance from the pain of not being enough. Working with the sick gives rise to the caregiver needing care."

He begins to read, but I repeat to myself the best line Stephen quotes. "I will be calm; I will be mistress of myself."

I keep listening and urging Stephen to whisper words to me until the hopelessness subsides.

It feels like mere minutes basking in the warmth of Mr. Stuffy-Petruchio's voice, but I know at least an hour has passed. One more turn, and the carriage stops on City Road in front of Wesley's Chapel.

Mrs. Cantor's asleep again. I do not want to wake her, but her assisting me while Stephen escorts me is the height of fashion.

I crawl off Stephen's lap and gently shake the nurse.

"Oh, we are here." She stretches and climbs out. "I do like this chapel."

The wrinkles in my skirt seem endless. "I don't think this is the effect the modiste and the duke wished for this outing. Being emotional has its costs. I'll not impress the aunties."

Stephen pulls my face close to his. "I must have you . . . free. You've taken a lot upon these delicate shoulders."

It would be wrong to start kissing him and miss church. "I'm fine. Wrinkled, but resolved."

"Know that I want you . . . to walk in the chapel with me. It means a great deal, but you mean more. Let's show our faces, then I'll make excuses and take you back to Anya House."

Demure, quiet, born of island pedigree, an impeccable dresser, and beautiful—that is the man holding me by my shoulders, giving me an excuse to hide.

"No," I say, and kiss his hands before pushing them away. "The aunties must see how you've wrinkled my gown."

Stephen smirks. "I've created havoc caressing you fully dressed. I'll have to remember to fix my approach. This will require research. You will help?"

The mirth in his warm eyes lessens the nerves I feel. "Seeing Mr. Thom was important to me, but so is this outing for you, but I'm all wrinkled."

"You, my dear, all will love."

What of you? I sigh and pack my hopes back into my heart. "The aunties will reject me. I can hear them now. The ragamuffin Wilcox woman has taken Cheapside's finest. Are you prepared for the arm-twisting they will do to send you back to Eveline Gray?"

Stephen's grin becomes a full toothy smile. "You're jealous. I like this turn of things. What can I do to keep this irrational side of logical Scarlett Wilcox at the forefront?"

There was one thing, but I knew he'd not say it.

It shouldn't matter. He's attentive. He's passionate. He broke a door to get to me. That should speak to his feelings. What does him actually loving me have to do with anything?

He tugs on his hat. "If you're seriously concerned about me straying, remember you are my fiancée. And I've claimed you before seeking the aunties' permission. I am a d'yavol."

I straighten his cravat, tweaking the barrel knot. "You didn't quite ask for mine either. I believe your aged memory is faulty."

He pulls me close again. His dark eyes dance with laughter and more. His hand of fine dark caramel snuggles my cheek. "You gave permission in the best possible way, darling. You love me, and you can't take that back. Remember, I'm an only child. I don't give things back. I don't share well."

"Those sound like areas in which you should seek personal growth."

"Scarlett, you're stuck with me." He steps out of the carriage. "We can run in front of the crowd now and be married in the Cossack style. Right now."

He's serious, I think. And his mood is light and frothy. Guess reading his novel has done so. Maybe they aren't so frivolous.

Helping me out of the carriage, he whirls me around and around until my slippers tap the ground. "Just so we are clear, I'm never letting go."

The man has always been arrogant and confident. I'm thrilled at the possessive turn. Is it enough, or is Katherine right?

My smart brainbox says words don't matter, not when you're mistress of yourself and Stephen Adam Carew will break down doors to get to you. My nurse pulls and straightens my gown. I smooth my cape to hide some wrinkles, but the crimson color screams *look at me*.

"Well," I sigh. "My hair? The pins. Is that perhaps presentable?"

Stephen spins me around again. "You're beautiful, Scarlett. Just as you are."

Mrs. Cantor hands me my satin gloves. "It's true, ma'am."

As Stephen tugs on his, he leans over to me and whispers, "You don't have to pretend or be someone else today. You're going forward, straight ahead in life. That will honor Scotland."

I wish to believe Stephen, and maybe I will tomorrow. Looking at the parishioners heading into church, the women following behind husbands, chasing after children while fathers stand at the side, I'm still stuck in a world where women can't do many things without the benefit of a man.

That doesn't change because I have one.

Holding his arm out for me, Stephen escorts me across the

street to Wesley's Chapel. We follow behind Mrs. Cantor to the large brown brick–framed rectangular building. I remember attending with Mama long ago.

People enter under a small portico. When we get through the facade, I see a poster. Stephen groans as he reads, "The Missionary Society has stationed over a hundred missionaries in Brussels, Ceylon, Bombay, Sierra Leone, Nova Scotia, and in the West Indies, Antigua, Nevis, Jamaica, and Trinidad."

He leans down to my ear. "At least this poster doesn't call these missions necessary to 'tame the savages,' as other church posters have. Perhaps the aunties' complaints have made changes."

Power from women? I must know more. Yet, that persona of confident Scarlett, of not being self-conscious, is again teetering on the ledge as I see women in colorful bonnets follow their husbands inside.

Stephen leads me into the sanctuary.

People point. Fans flutter. I assume the talk is about Stephen's mysterious woman.

The physician doesn't seem bothered. Instead, he lingers, waving here, talking to men there, making eyes at folks on the opposite side of the choir loft.

He takes me and my chaperone to the front. With a clear view of a baptismal font and platformed pulpit, he seats us on the second row, for God and everyone to see that Stephen has brought guests to the chapel.

Carefully, he takes my hand. Palm to palm, the union he lifts high pointing at the architecture of the old church. "Those columns, my dear Miss Wilcox, the ones that hold up the gallery above, are sturdy jasper wood. King George the Third, himself, had masts from some of his retiring ships dispatched for John Wesley to use to build this church."

He seems very proud of this. I suppose he has many interests other than showing us holding hands to the congregation.

"An Anglican king supporting a Methodist church is fascinating." Mrs. Cantor yawns. "And to use ships that have sailed around the world as part of the construction seems fitting for our king. He rules many colonies."

Stephen acknowledges her with a short smile. New tension comes from her statement, that I think a man from Trinidad particularly feels.

Then he begins to shift his gaze to the crowd. He's trying to be discreet but he's searching for someone.

I see one of the ladies from Somerset House barreling up the aisle toward us. With a large ivory bonnet sprigged with purple and pink flowers, this auntie is colorful and dressed in a fashionable gown of light yellow.

"There's my Stephen," she says.

He stands and this woman gives him a big hug. "Tantie Telma. I'm here, and I have brought that someone special. Miss Scarlett Wilcox, this is my aunt Telma Smith."

"Wilcox." She whacks him on the arm, like I want to do sometimes, but harder. "You were not kidding. You truly do have a young woman in your life."

I wait for him to say more, to use the F word, like he did with Lord Mark and Georgie.

"Scarlett Wilcox is a special young woman. I'm pleased for her to meet you."

I keep a smile. I don't want to react. I've given him and this day too much of my power. I want mine back. I'm mistress of myself, after all.

Can I relearn how not to love Stephen Adam Carew in the span of a sermon?

Another woman comes up to us. More hugs are exchanged.

"Miss Wilcox, this is Mrs. Theodora Randolph. Mrs. Randolph and Mrs. Smith are affectionately known as the aunties. They influence everything on this side of town."

Mrs. Randolph wears a wide-brimmed blue hat. Her carriage gown, the same shade of sky blue, matches. "Oh, she is lovely,

Stephen. I knew after you lost Miss Eveline last year, you'd stop with these fairy tales and become more serious."

"What fairy tales, ma'am?" I'm curious.

"Some sort of hospital. Wesley's Chapel has plenty of missions for the sick. A young man must build his practice and fortunes before he can turn to philanthropy."

Oh goodness. It wasn't just losing Eveline that stopped Stephen's dream. It was the aunties.

He offers a nervous chuckle. "Miss Wilcox, the aunties are about protocol and establishing—"

"Establishing their own ton, just like Mayfair. How sad."

These words slip out before I can stop them, not that I want to.

"Miss Wilcox is such a kidder. Such a wonderful sense of humor." Stephen tries to clean up my directness. The way Mrs. Randolph is now looking me over, I don't think it possible.

"Miss Eveline, the Baroness of Derand, is here somewhere, Stephen." Mrs. Smith glances at me and then does another fast look.

Oh dear. She's recognized my disguise. "You're . . ."

Ready to explain, I brace, cut my eyes to slits. "Yes, ma'am."

Mrs. Smith nods. "You're one of Cesar Wilcox's daughters. Good on you, Stephen. Peers like to descend and steal our eligible girls. You've taken one back."

"You know me," he says with a little bit of breeze, accented relief releasing in his word. "I'm de ole tief when it comes . . . to this one."

The begging in his eyes to be easy cools my anger a little. These women actually make him nervous.

Mrs. Randolph waves to a young woman entering the chapel. "Here comes Eveline. Perhaps she will tell us the name she has chosen, now that she's free."

Mrs. Smith grins and claps my hand. "It won't be Carew thanks to dis one."

Stephen's old love, the newly divorced baroness, walks down

the aisle with her head up. Her motions are light, like a bird or ballerina. "Good to see you, Mrs. Randolph. Mrs. Smith."

Even dis one's voice is airy . . . and effective. I see Stephen stiffen.

It's the scent of rose water radiating from her extended hand that affects me the most, and I know exactly the name this woman wishes to be called. Well, at least the name she went by at night. Chrysanthemum.

Eveline Gray—the young woman Stephen wanted to marry last year, the one with the surprise public elopement to a baron, who has returned from Scotland with an annulment—is earning her keep at Madame Rosebud's on 18 Half Moon Street off Piccadilly as one of the prized courtesans.

Chapter 29

SCARLETT—TELMA'S PICNIC-BALL

The evening sun lowers, making the blue sky appear orange. Standing on the stone patio of Stephen's aunt's Cheapside home, I overlook a grand picnic. The chapel service took hours, but I wasn't that hungry. Rose water will now forever steal my appetite.

Stephen didn't recognize Chrysanthemum. I'm not sure she recognized me. Guess we all clean up well.

"Dear, you eat like a bird." Mrs. Smith, whom Stephen calls his Tantie Telma, has a large green lawn full of people feeding themselves on exquisite food and sipping fine beverages.

"I'm not that hungry, ma'am."

"You seemed very moved by the service. I'm glad Stephen has a girl with a faithful calling."

Well . . . okay. I have a calling and faith, but I'm not sure what that means among this community since a few have noted we stay across the Thames. The more ill Mama became, the more it became known we have the chronic sickness in our blood. One can feel when we're not welcome.

"Can I get you something to eat? Stephen usually runs around the whole time not eating. I'd hate for you to feel you can't partake. You're not ill, are you?"

The fear in her voice is real. "Ma'am, I'm fine. You have hundreds supping with you. Your lawn is filled with people on picnic blankets listening to sweet music. You needn't fret about me."

"Good. You are well." She smiles. "But you must eat, but later. Enjoy the violinists. They are easy to hire. The banya players, or what they call the banjo here, are more difficult. We must stick to our culture. We have it, you know, even if we dress like the rest of London, we still have our own."

Mrs. Smith sips from something made with hibiscus and honey. She abandoned her hat for a brightly colored turban. "I hope you're not upset Stephen's spending so much of his time doing errands for me, visiting with everyone. He's a friendly boy. I think these celebrations help him relax."

"No, ma'am. He's been a wonderful guide, almost too wonderful, making sure I'm comfortable."

"He's my late sister's only son, though he acts like my son and one to all the aunties." She claps and he hears it from the other side of the yard. I watch his ears crane up. "That boy's very attentive. He'll make a good husband."

She points to him and then me. "Get her a coupe of sorrel."

"Please, ma'am. I am fine. I'm not thirsty."

"Nonsense, you must drink. It's the least you can do to let me know you will try and participate."

The woman is not subtle. But who can blame her? She wants to know if I will force Stephen to leave his community. The way he loves it, it's a part of him, part of the deal; like concessions in a wedding contract. I nod. "Sorrel is fine. I'd love some."

Tantie Telma smiles and offers more signals to Stephen. He dashes off. His coat is somewhere. His cravat has loosened but is still hanging on for dear life. I'm not sure what happened to Mrs. Cantor.

While I'm not the most overdressed, I give that distinction to a couple in silver. She's in her bridal gown, I'm sure. And her fellow has large silver buttons on his tailcoat and waistcoat.

A young pregnant woman waddles over to us. It's Stephen's cousin, Maryanne Teresa Halland, Mrs. Smith's daughter. "Miss Wilcox, are you enjoying yourself?"

"Yes. This is lovely."

"That's why she hasn't moved from the patio, she's here holding up the wall," Mrs. Randolph says to Eveline as they enter the area. Eveline looks at me with a sympathetic gaze. Mrs. Randolph sneers a little and makes it clear I'm an outsider. They keep going into the house. "Oh, Stephen. Great sorrel. Thank you."

That's Mrs. Randolph's loud voice, greeting him as she takes the sorrel Stephen meant for me.

"Overwhelming." Mrs. Halland rubs her belly. "It can take a little getting used to. And Mama loves parties. You should've seen the t'ing Mama threw ten years ago. I was just ten when she gave a ball to celebrate the passage of the first slave trade–banning bill. The patio where we stand had white linen–covered tables with all kinds of food. She hired footmen."

Mrs. Smith comes and puts an arm about her daughter. "Since then, I like these long picnics. It's a little fussy, but still happy and free flowing."

Stephen saunters over as he has every twenty minutes, this time with a coupe. "Hey, pretty lady, I have sorrel and a bowl of pepper pot."

I take the beverage and sip. Then put it on the patio ledge. "Delicious."

He's about to put a spoon in my hand when he slowly drags off one of my satin gloves and then the other, stuffing them into his waistcoat pocket. "Be careful, this is not ice. It's spicy."

"Does she not like spicy?" Mrs. Smith lurches a little. "We love spice."

"Ma'am, I love spice and flavor. Your nephew likes to tease. You see, we came to a new understanding over a bowl of sweet pineapple ice."

His aunt smiles and seems more at ease. "Come, Maryanne. Let's get you seated comfortably in the parlor before that baby falls out of you."

"My daughter needs to leap out," she says, and waddles into the house. Mrs. Smith look back at us, then follows.

Stephen's smile disappears. "That baby does need to come. It's been days of early contractions, and he hasn't turned. The accoucheur should've tried to induce."

I lift his chin. "All will be well." It's very quick, but I see his true feelings dissolve, hiding behind lips that have a caramel and coconut smell. I want to draw the light Stephen back. "Perhaps you need to go get that novel and read a bit."

"Guess you understand why I like to escape into books. I love a little whimsy." He sighs. "My fault though. I can't go a whole day, or even a half of one, without thinking of people and their conditions."

"I guess you really do understand the lengths that I go to to help."

"That, my darling Scarlett, I do." He dips into the bowl and then brings the spoon to my mouth. "A little okra, flavorful peppers, and delicious cinnamon, thyme, and cloves. My aunt makes it the best, though she has to substitute wiri wiri for Jamaican Scotch bonnets. Hot, fruity, tangy peppers."

I take the spoon and the small bowl from his fingers. "It does smell good, but have you eaten, Stephen? I seem to recall that you often forget to take care of yourself doing for others and passed out on me. It was most embarrassing."

"Meh t'ink you can find a way to keep me awake. I'm sure you did not try hard enough, last time. Perhaps you need another opportunity to try."

The gaze he offers makes me hot, but he shifts around acknowledging this one or that one. Stephen acts all innocent as he slips his free hand under my cape about my waist. "The spice makes you swoon, Scarlett. Let me hold you up."

Wanting to laugh and forget that people are watching, I feed him and then take the same spoon to my mouth. The heat of the remnants of the pepper pot burns going down. "Wow. That's good. Very warming."

"See," he says. "Much bettah." His accent is on full display. I love it. I love the freedom he has here.

"Oh, it's better. But do make sure, sir, you can deliver on the promises your brown eyes offer." I feed him again. "Then I'm sure I'll be very satisfied."

"Dah standards are low if mere satisfaction is what yuh want."

His aunt tugs on his shoulder before he kisses me. "Stephen, I see you're making Miss Wilcox too comfortable on the patio. I need your assistance. I want meh daughter to rest."

"Yes, Tantie Telma. I live to serve." He pulls away from the lean he's had over me. I remain still, supporting the Grecian column at my back.

"Duty calls, my dove." Stephen backs away and goes with his aunt. She swats him as the two go merrily inside.

It's picturesque here.

I'd love for my sisters to be here. We've missed being part of a community. We have customers in Cheapside and a few family friends who visit from time to time, but nothing like this. I wonder what our lives would have looked like if this had been our world and not the other side of the Thames.

It will be dark in another hour, but couples are still coming. A few get up and dance to the violinist's song. Some sing what sounds like a hymn.

People with filled plates, cooked meats that smell of garlic, flit past my solemn stance. Black cake and coconut bread is being served. It all smells wonderful.

Yet, I stay at my post next to the Grecian-styled column.

One lady says hello. Another says that they were once a customer of Wilcox Coal. Many conversations are animated, louder at times than the musicians.

A man passes with a plate full of johnnycakes. Those were my mother's favorites. I'm sure that someone has salted cod or herring to go with the fried dumplings. A lady squeals when he presents her the tasty offering, and I hear my mother's dropped consonants in this lady's pronunciation of her Jamaican "betta."

Stephen dances near. "Your chaperone is asleep in the parlor, but not before hinting to my cousin that we are very affectionate creatures."

"An indiscreet nurse who may feign sleeping. Stephen, I'm shocked."

"Two glasses of the claret have made her quite the chatterbox." He leans in and kisses my cheek. He smells of rich sweet blackberries. He might've had a bit too.

"I don't have to return you to Anya House until two. Unfortunately, people will still be here. No one likes to leave Tantie Telma's party early. Usually, I stay and help tidy her lawn. Put away things, and of course take as much cassava pone as I can."

He dips his head close again, like he wishes to whisper in my ear, but I think he wants to kiss. "In case you were wondering, Benny is now full of roast pork."

"Save it, lover boy, until we are alone, and I've forgiven you."

"What have I done wrong, Scarlett?"

I put a hand on my hip. "What do you think, friend? Or is there another F word for me?"

Tantie Telma comes to us. "You two make a beautiful couple. When will you be married? Do it soon, so you're young enough to play with your children, Stephen."

I smile at the bundle of energy and nod like I agree.

"Get her to mingle, Stephen. People have questions."

He smiles at me and then goes into the house with his aunt. The music is good. I think I hear Handel's *Messiah* on the banya.

Then my ear picks up Stephen's lengthy *bettah*. My Trinidadian expatriate comes again from the house. This time he has another punch goblet. "For you, sorrel." He looks at the half-drunken one on the ledge. "Oh, I didn't forget. You just haven't . . . Sorry."

His head dips to mine. "Make an effort, Scarlett. I need you to be a part of this world."

"What do you want me to do? Ask them why they put so much

effort in gathering and socializing and yet condemn the same thing in the ton?"

"Scarlett."

"I've heard three talk of my sisters' marriages and wondering why I don't want one of *them* Mayfair types. Should I saunter about with you and be on display? So I can hear more whispers of the illness that plagues the Wilcoxes?"

He bites his lip.

I shut my eyes. "I need to be *bettah* at being demure."

"Scarlett."

"See, I haven't forgotten your list. You should've added lustful, hard of hearing and stupid. That would be the perfect woman here."

"While I want the former, you will never be the latter two."

"This. From the same person who said when we arrived, 'I must have you . . . free.' Why? You're not."

Putting the goblet on the ledge, he puts his hands on my shoulders and removes my cape. Tossing it to the ledge as well, he bows. "Dance with me."

He takes me into his arms and swirls me to the music. Relaxing against him, I smell caramel and peppers in his clothes. "They need to meet you, Scarlett. If they talk with you, they'll see how wonderful you are."

"Why don't they see how good you are? They say a prophet is without honor amongst his kin and country. Is that why all your good work, your dreams are ignored?"

Stephen steps away. He pours sorrel from the first goblet into the other. "You don't understand my community, Scarlett."

"What's not to understand? I've been standing here doing research. I've listened to dozens of conversations, especially from Auntie Theodora. Your Tantie Thelma hired an accoucheur to deliver her first grandchild. You deliver babies every week. I know that it pains you when something goes wrong, but you're the best. I see how dedicated you are. But they chose someone else, some stupid man with a membership to White's."

He knows what I am saying. Some of our Blackamoor communities will always want the ton's peers, those with the whitest of skins, to be missionaries and healers to the browns everywhere. They trust their medicine, their physicians, not one of their own.

"You are good," I say to him. "You have nothing to prove. Your life doesn't need to be ordered by what the aunties think."

Stephen drinks from a goblet, draining it. "You're right. It's bettah yuh stand here looking uncomfortable. The woman of my dreams, that's who I think you are. Yet, I must be wrong, for you'll not take a simple risk for me and be social. Why is there no resistance to taking an insane risk but you become a pile of bricks for an easy one? You've built a wall or tower and refuse to come down and participate in this gathering?"

"Risk? You mean like the ones you're unwilling to take because it will upset someone? Does being a part of this community mean giving away your power? How can you be a master of yourself and fearful of being snubbed?"

"It's a blessed picnic. You should be eating and dancing and enjoying yourself. Can't you live a little?"

"What is living? Am I to be more like the aunties—snubbing women and making them not be honest in their skin? Why wear a gown if they think I'm rubbish."

"Do breeches make you powerful, Scarlett? No, I think you'd still be here on the wall acting like a little girl waiting for everything to be perfect or for someone to come enable your thoughtless behaviors."

"Thoughtless? They are called dreams. Shouldn't someone help mine come true?"

Clamping his lips, he turns from me. "There's my aunt's maid. Let me go help Mrs. Ellis. She might need me."

"Go, Stephen. Leave knowing I see you. I always have. I'll only stop seeing the true you, brave, selfless, stupid . . . stupidly loyal you, when you turn away."

His footfalls stop for a moment. Then he presses forward.

Wishing to leave, I hold the third glass up and empty it swallowing all the sweet sorrel. Then I remain on the patio watching time and people go by.

Mrs. Randolph is arm and arm with Chrysanthemum. The older woman is looking at me again, waving her arms. I think the auntie wants her to confront me.

I have no fear about what they can be saying. Chrysanthemum or Eveline is a decent woman. That shouldn't change because we're outside a brothel, wearing different disguises in Cheapside.

"There you are." Mrs. Cantor has awakened. "Mrs. Halland, Mr. Carew's cousin, wanted you to visit with her. She's in her mother's parlor."

"I'll do so. Thank you. If you want to hold my spot . . . Never mind."

Mrs. Ellis, the aunt's maid, is arranging more platters on the table. I want to tip my hat to her. No one will be hungry here. "Ma'am, which way is the parlor?"

She stops what she's doing and takes me into a yellow-painted room. It's sunny and happy, filled with sofas, but not that many people.

"Mrs. Halland, Mrs. Cantor said you wished to see me."

The lady is lying back with pillows. "I heard you weren't moving about. I can't. Perhaps we cannot move about together."

I sit, and from the open window, I see Mrs. Randolph chatting with Stephen, drawing Chrysanthemum into the conversation. The three of them look happy.

And I feel like I'm on the other side of the Thames.

Chapter 30

SCARLETT—PARLOR PANIC

Mrs. Halland, who insists I call her Maryanne, tells me story after story in her mother's home. I'm laughing so hard at the humor of her childhood. Then she tells me of her older brother. He serves with her husband in the navy. They were all children together: Maryanne, her husband William, and Stephen.

I stop chuckling at a picture of the three jumping off drays, apple picking in the countryside. She's rubbing her big belly a lot. "Do you want me to go find some apple tarts?"

She giggles. "No. Being almost buried alive in a barrel of tart crab apples is enough for me." The small clock on the mantel chimes. It's eleven o'clock. Time has sped past us. We must've been in here for hours chatting.

My new friend winces and pats her abdomen. "I don't think the little bunny wants anything sour."

"I know a little about medicine. The movement is good." I grip her hand, or she grabs mine. "You both are going to be all right."

Maryanne stares at me. There's strain and tears in her golden-brown eyes. "I'm scared. I don't say it to my mother. To anyone. But I'm fearful. And every day that this babe isn't born, I think we won't make it."

"Hey, you're going to be fine. And this baby will be healthy."

I know not if anything I'm saying is true, but I must comfort her. I have faith that all will work for our good. Maryanne and her baby will be well.

Stephen and Mrs. Randolph come into the room. "There you are," he says. His expression shows relief. "See, Auntie, she hasn't run off."

"She's lovely, Stephen," the woman says as she takes a close seat in the parlor. "The Wilcox girls are well known. Two have successfully married into the ton."

No rolling my eyes. No being demure. I keep my face light, for I know she's not giving my family a compliment. "Yes, they have."

Mrs. Randolph plays with her perfectly pressed lace on her blue gown. "I don't mean to sound trite, but it was expected that you'd follow suit."

"Oh my, I didn't think you thought about me at all." When I see Stephen looking up, I try to soften my tone. "I mean, we Wilcoxes keep to ourselves."

"Love knows its own success," Maryanne says. "If I had to marry a man with a title, I would hope he'd have a kind heart and that I'd be brave enough to follow mine."

I clasp her hand. "One has to be brave to love. There's no other way."

Stephen smiles at me. I feel he wants to say something but then closes his mouth and sits on the edge of the sofa.

Mrs. Randolph moves away from us, then sits on a lavender-striped couch by the window. A mantel, more chairs, and a table separate us. She stares at me. Do the wrinkles in my satin offend at this distance?

I remove the fichu and show off my shoulders. Not sure it helps that Stephen's drooling, wetting those oft-ashy lips as he looks at me. Must admit, that since we've been kissing, he's kept them moisturized well.

Mrs. Randolph stands and moves like she's a barrister presenting a case to jurymen. "I like being direct. I suspect you're just a friend that Stephen has brought along because Eveline, the woman he loved and lost, was also to come."

"Auntie, can you please not do this? Scarlett is the woman I'm courting." His eyes are on me. I'm not sure if he's begging for me to ignore her barbs or dig in. "Please stop."

"Yes, Auntie," Maryanne says. "Scarlett is lovely, and she's as vexed at Stephen as she is in love with him. I think that's a good combination."

My cheeks warm. I hate that my heart shows so easily. "We were talking about drays and apples. How did you come up with that?"

Maryanne sits up a little. "And who was tense about a certain young man falling and busting his britches?"

"Now, Maryanne." Stephen wipes at his face. "You told her about the apple picking gone awry? I thought we were never to discuss that, or that you'd only focus on my heroic part."

"Yes," Maryanne and I say together, and laugh anew.

Twisting from Maryanne's wincing face, I say. "Stephen Adam Carew knows how I like doing as much research as possible."

"What's his favorite novel?" We all whip our heads toward Mrs. Randolph. "Do I need to repeat myself? The way our Stephen loves novels, he would have said it."

"I don't know."

My statement makes Mrs. Randolph grin like a tiger. "See, I thought—"

"Because he likes so many. From *Sense and Sensibility* to that one story with Darcy and Mrs. Bennet. And he's always talking about Shakespeare." I lean toward Maryanne. "I'll have to tell you how he almost became engaged last year by making people swoon by reciting Shakespeare's lines from *Taming of the Shrew*." I frown at him. "But you don't like when I quote from the play, do you?"

"You choose the wrong lines, Scarlett." He offers a half smile. "But I say if you deny to wed, I'll crave the day when we shall ask the banns and be married."

"Shakespeare." Mrs. Randolph wrinkles her nose. "Stephen does have many interests. But how would you've learned of them?"

"I've known him for over seven years. And for most of that time, we couldn't stand each other. In fact, I hate him a little right now."

Stephen frowns, then looks down at me. "Well, it's hard to take to a woman who knows so much and is often right. Then you, Scarlett, have the nerve to leave your leading strings and change to corsets. Before I knew it, you were grown, opinionated, beautiful, and for some unknown reason . . . you believe in me, even when I doubt myself."

"That's a deadly combination for you." Maryanne chortles and winces. "Oh, Scarlett is great, Auntie. She has spunk. She'll keep Mr. Know-it-all sharp."

"My man-of-all-work calls him Mr. Stuffy. Sometimes Petruchio."

"Oh, I like that bettah." Maryanne lies back and sucks in a huge breath of air.

My eyes are on her and then Stephen. He takes out a pocket watch. I believe he's timing how frequent her pain comes. That baby's coming soon.

"Distractions are a good thing." Stephen glances at me, then his watch. That's a signal. "But, Mrs. Randolph, you don't need to quiz Miss Wilcox. This is your first time meeting us as a couple, but you should know that I think we are more than a couple." He's not looking up from his watch. "You see we are perfectly suited. And I want her to be my wife. Part of me stupidly wanted the aunties' approval, because I respect you for what you mean to the community, but you can be wrong. I've grown up enough myself to know it. I want Miss Wilcox, and if she'll have me, I think I'll settle for well-wishes once our banns are read and we've wed. What say you, Miss Wilcox? Will you accept this proposal?"

"That's exactly my point," Mrs. Randolph says. "Outsiders take the best of our community and then they turn their hearts to making money. You want to assimilate more and emulate the ton?"

"I thought that was what you did, Mrs. Randolph, when you dissuaded Mr. Carew from pursuing a hospital."

"She has you there, Auntie." Stephen glances at me, then sets his gaze to his watch.

"I need more answers from her before I will entertain any appeal for a marriage." Mrs. Randolph flutters closer to the sofa. "When is Stephen's birth—"

"December fifteenth." I shake my fingers at her. "Oh, please ask something more difficult."

"Favorite dessert."

"He likes sweets, but I will say cassava pone. His aunt makes it perfectly. Yours, Mrs. Randolph"—I lower my voice—"is crumbly and often dry or was it burnt."

She gasps. "That is not true. My desserts are delicious."

"Sometime delicious, more often dry." His cousin snickers, then winces.

"It was only dry that one time." Stephen, ever the diplomat, tries to smooth things over. "Auntie Theodora, I think you've asked enough of Miss Wilcox."

"I know you, Stephen, to be a very busy man. I find it odd for you to come today with such a beautiful young lady that no one has seen you with and expect us to believe you found time to actively court her. This is some cruel joke."

Straightening her blue hem, she turns her gaze back to wrinkled me. "What's his favorite color?"

"Dark blue. It brings out his eyes. But the new emerald-green jacket is my favorite. You look good smashing into doors for me."

"If he weren't a doctor, what would he do?"

I look at Stephen and begin to chuckle. "Oh, that must be a trick question. If he were in Trinidad, he'd be an herbalist, a true medicine man. Here in London, I don't know."

"Ah haw, see."

"I don't know because Stephen has so many interests, maybe

a Shakespearean actor . . . but he likes the details of the law . . . and he was first trained as a doctor pulling teeth." I flash an adoring smile at Stephen, one that implies, *Darling, I know you like the back of my hand.* "Oh, give us a hint."

The man beams.

He's eating up the attention until Chrysanthemum comes. Stephen dips his head to her and excuses himself.

"Eveline," Maryanne says, "sit with us and help calm down Auntie. I think she's doubting Stephen's commitment to our new friend Scarlett."

The beautiful girl, whose skin is almost light enough to pass into any world, sits. She looks better without the wig. Her natural dark brown hair is braided into a refined chignon. "I can tell you, Auntie, that Stephen never stopped talking about Miss Wilcox when we courted. She always managed to get under his skin. His mentions of her became unbearable after the Duke of Torrance's ball. He attended and didn't invite me. It was crystal clear where I stood with him then, and when what I believed was a better situation came along, I took it. Scarlett Wilcox was in his heart way before me. I knew someday he'd figure it out. Seems like I was right."

Mrs. Randolph frowns. She sits back in her chair like she wishes it would rock. "She's an outsider. You chose one, and now you've left him. You should come back, be one of us."

"I gained an annulment in Scotland, but the baron has my dowry. At least I have my freedom. I'll figure things out. Be at ease, Auntie. Miss Scarlett Wilcox will go to any length to save Stephen. That kind of love is hard to find."

I smile at Chrysanthemum. I guess she recognized Stephen and me both at the brothel. She's a good person, even if her life isn't what she wants right now. I hope she can make the life she wants. "I do charity work at Bridewell, there may be positions there to help—"

"The baroness does not work."

"This one does, Mrs. Randolph. I have to work until everything is resolved or I no longer care that I was cheated. Bride-well? A friend of mine had to go there recently." Chrysanthe-mum looks sad but resilient. "Daisy is doing better."

Mrs. Randolph leaps up. "Wait. Do you two know each other? Who's Daisy?"

Maryanne screams. Her pink gown is wet. There are spots on the lace that look like blood.

I hold her hand. "Go get Stephen, Chr . . . Eveline. He'll know what to do."

Both women run out of the room. It's just me and Maryanne and a baby ready to come.

"You promised all would go well, Scarlett. Be a woman of your word."

"I am." Most of the time. I strengthen my grip and hope the medicine man, the physician previously trained as a doctor, is as good as I know he is. Then I pray for the blessing that Maryanne will be one of the lucky mothers who live and have a baby born alive.

Stephen makes everyone in the parlor leave but me and Mrs. Smith, before he heads to the kitchen.

I'm still holding Maryanne's hand when Benny comes. He has Stephen's bag, towels and iron forceps. They look scary, but the jaws might be needed to pull the infant from the womb.

Mrs. Smith paces. "The accoucheur said she still has weeks."

"Sometimes they are wrong." I try to calm her. "Babies have their own timing."

"Mama, the pain." Maryanne pushes on her stomach. "He's too high up. My baby is going to die, and so am I."

"No. We have a chance. Tantie," Stephen says, "go get sheets. Lots of clean sheets."

The mother takes off running.

Heaving, Maryanne asks, "What will the sheets do?"

"Nothing. I just know she needs a distraction. Doing some-thing will get her not to focus on . . ."

"The dangers." Maryanne closes her eyes. "Glad you and Scarlett stayed. I hope we all have a long friendship."

Stephen's sleeves have been rolled up. His hands have been scrubbed. "Maryanne, my assistant here is going to take off your gown. She's going to get you unclothed to your chemise. Your baby needs freedom. I'm going to get you both free. Get to it, Scarlett."

"Yes, sir," I say, and I begin to undo buttons, pulling the fabric-covered disks through holes that seem to have shrunk to half their size.

"Take your time, Scarlett. I need you calm."

Stephen's tone is flat. There's no emotion or anxiety in his voice. I can't read him at all. I don't know if he truly believes that all will go well.

He lifts his cousin, and I get the dress and layers off her. Maryanne is sweaty, and her chemise is soaked.

I gaze at Stephen, and again I sense nothing. I'm filled with dread as I recognize the noises I heard in Mama's room when both she and my sister were in there. Katherine kept screaming, just as Maryanne does.

Her mother returns with a pile of sheets.

"Lay them on the ground about the sofa." He looks at me. "Scarlett, when I lift her up again, pull the sheets underneath her."

Nodding, I wait. When he has her hovering an inch above the cushion, Mrs. Smith and I work fast to cover the sofa in linens.

He sets her back down and goes to her legs and peeks below the chemise. "You've not opened. A woman's body is a miraculous thing. The baby will not come out that way."

I go and pick up the clamps. "We pull . . ."

I set them back down. I know that won't work.

The despair. I feel it smothering me. That day. The day Katherine bore her babe. I hear screams like she's in the next room.

Mrs. Smith is weeping.

Mrs. Ellis comes in with buckets of water and more cloths. I wet one and hand it to Mrs. Smith. "Mop her forehead. Keep her cool."

"With your permission, Maryanne, Tantie Telma, I will do a dissection of the abdomen. I will get the baby out and then I will close the incision. It's the only way."

My eyes are too blurred with tears, but I hear them agreeing.

The next thing I know, I'm being dragged from the room. "Scarlett." Stephen is shaking my shoulders. "I need you. I need you to help me. But I can't take you back in the room unless you are the brave woman I know."

"The brave one who's seen too much death."

"And that's medicine. Scarlett, I see life and I know death. There's a chance that all will be well. A small chance. But I know death wins if we do nothing." He releases my shoulders. "If you can't, I understand. It takes a lot to step into that room knowing you might not be of any help, that what you do can hasten death. But I've made my peace with it. I'll be brave for them."

I don't know what to say. Have I been playing all this time? Have I been too naive thinking I can change the world?

"Scarlett, you're brave. I need you. I was going to give you a choice, but I see that if I leave you, you'll never be able to get over your dread. All the things a mind like yours can do won't happen, not if you're always captive to fear." He kisses my forehead. "I won't force this. I'll let you know—"

I clasp his hand and hold on tight. "Tell me what to do. I should wash my hands."

"Yes. I'll show you how."

I follow him to the kitchen. Hot steaming water is on the stove.

Mrs. Ellis is there making as many pots as she can. "Any word?"

"Mr. Carew is about to perform a caesarean. I read about it in bunny dissection."

Stephen scrubs my hands and then his once more. "Well, the medicine men often talked of this practice from Africa. Cleanliness, they say, makes the gods happy. Keeps the incident of fevers away."

"Yes, no fever."

Mimicking how his arms are raised, I run with him back to the parlor.

Benny has come back with more bottles.

Stephen takes the one marked laudanum. "Cousin, this will help with the pain. Don't push."

She nods, and he gives her three tablespoons.

Then he takes a bowl and pours foul vinegar and laudanum in it. "Scarlett, expose her abdomen, pull away the chemise.

It's wet anyway. I do as he says.

"Please," Maryanne whimpers. "Save my baby. My husband needs to see his daughter."

"That's right, Scarlett. My friend and I have a wager. He says if you're carrying low, that's supposed to be a boy."

"I think your friend made that bet based on observations that Maryanne was carrying low and narrow, not what was actually seen. Upon seeing your cousin, I would say low is an exaggeration."

His aunt is pacing and praying. She stops and looks at Stephen. "Boy, are you crazy? Makin' sinful wagers when we need His favor for a healthy baby."

"It's not sinful." He looks at the clock on the mantel and then at me. "It's just a wager at midnight. I say if it's a boy, you marry me as soon as a license is possible."

"And if it's a girl," I ask, as I mop Maryanne's brow.

"If it's a girl . . . You leave with me and journey to Gretna Green and we marry as soon as we get there."

Maryanne cries out. "You two are silly. Just agree to marry. Be happy any way you can."

"I like any of these options. Decide, Scarlett." Stephen's voice holds power. "The baby's coming."

I'm scattered and scared. Every scream Maryanne roars mirrors Katherine's. My ears echo. They fill with yesterday's sorrow.

I hear sobs—Maryanne's, Katherine's.

I remember Mama praying then whispering, "Be strong. Be strong."

That awful day, Stephen was in the bedroom. I was told to stay downstairs, but I heard his broken voice saying, "So sorry. So sorry."

And again Mama, strong, resolute Mama, whispering, "Be strong."

Lifting prayers to the heavens, he sinks his hand onto Maryanne's abdomen. "Scarlett, Tantie, hold my cousin's arms. Keep her still."

Stephen has the scalpel in his right hand. "Maryanne, trust me. I dug you out of the crab apples. I'll gather you and this new life and bring you to safety."

"I start now." Stephen makes an incision through the skin. From the dissection classes and anatomy sketches, I know the fancy name of subcutaneous tissue. Red bubbles and gushes. Stephen takes towels and stanches the flow, but he doesn't stop. He cuts again.

Maryanne twitches, she screams, but Stephen has made a smooth stroke through the uterine wall. I want to close my eyes, but I can't.

I don't want the dreams that rage in the dark. I must watch life drawn out of her flesh.

Everything grows still and quiet.

The baby cries and cries. The child lives.

Stephen raises the babe. "Scarlett, come hold him."

I do, scooping the little one into a towel.

"He's breathing, Maryanne." Tears roll down Stephen's cheek. "Scarlett. He's breathing."

"Let me see." His cousin lifts her head. She's sobbing but it's different than before. This is joy. "My son. We all win."

Stephen ties off the umbilical cord and uses scissors to snip the cord. The babe is free. He's in our world, and I move him closer to his mother's face.

Maryanne looks at peace, happy. "He's beautiful."

But this procedure is not done.

Stephen draws out the burgundy placenta and then uses silk to suture the uterus and the skin. He wipes more of the vinegar-laudanum mixture along the stitches. Using clean bandages, he wraps his cousin's abdomen.

Mrs. Smith takes the baby. "You rest, Maryanne. He's so good. You did so good."

I cover the new mom in a fresh sheet.

Then I join Stephen sitting on the couch near the window. I bring with me a tub of fresh water and clean away the evidence of surgery from his hands.

When I think it's all gone, I wrap a towel about his arms.

"Stephen. You're wonderful. But I remember."

"Woman, remember everything in the morning. We can talk about everything then."

He yawns and I know he's tired. I can't destroy his peace.

"Scarlett. Let's rest. You know how I get without my rest. Then we'll talk wedding details. No getting out of this. We won the wager."

I want to agree, but what I know will destroy everything. I have to tell him, tell everyone what I know.

"Oh, Stephen. Forgive and forget an old fool." His aunt is rocking her grandson. "You should've been caring for Maryanne all along."

His cousin opens her eyes. "Thank you, Stephen. Thank you, Scarlett."

"Yes, thank you, Miss Wilcox. Oh, call me Tantie Telma, too."

"Then it's Scarlett," I say.

"Soon to be Scarlett Carew, but once we rest." Stephen waves to me like the duke. "Come, Scarlett."

I think of now, not tomorrow. That makes it easier to simply fall into his arms. "Rest, Maryanne," he says. "In the early morning, I want you to try to suckle. Your son will need his mother's milk."

Stephen sounds so encouraging, but the real wager is not

when or how we marry. It's if the horrible birthing fever will arise and claim Maryanne before dawn. A fever can take this good moment and make it tragic.

All I know is that I'll stay in Stephen's arms and be alert all night. I'll not sleep until Maryanne gets up to start her life again as a mom.

When I know she's out of danger, I have to leave. I have to go from this man, this community, and return to my world and tell a father about the twin that lived.

Chapter 31

STEPHEN—TANTIE'S HOUSE

Sunlight warms my lids. I reach for Scarlett and miss. Stretching, I open one eye and then the other. I confirm the worst. I'm lying on my tantie's lavender sofa alone. I guess she tired of sleeping beside me on the sofa. My aunt is old-fashioned, but I would love nothing better than to sneak into a guest room and snuggle with my future wife.

Scarlett handled the situation so well. There was only one time I became fretful for her, but the strength of that woman continues to amaze me.

The smell of bacon and toast scents the air. That means Mrs. Ellis is up and cooking. She's fabulous and her cassava pone— the one Tantie claims as her own—is always moist.

I'm so thankful that I don't smell rose water. Seeing Eveline again, I didn't realize she liked that fragrance.

My cousin sits across from me in a nearby chair. "Oh, you are finally up. You're a heavy sleeper."

Maryanne sips tea.

I flop back down, wondering if everything was a dream. Did I end up coming to Cheapside by myself? Did I fall into a deep trance from too much cassava pone?

"Benny brought you some fresh clothes a day ago. And some peppermint liquid."

Good ole Benny is always looking out for me. "But where's my woman? Scarlett Wilcox. Where is she?"

"Stephen, she left Saturday about noon. She drew me a diagram to help me latch on. I folded it and will save it for my husband. I think he'll like such a picture."

Friday, we arrived here. What day is it? And is my woman going places as Scarlett or Scotland? Both surnames bettah be Carew. "Maryanne, do yuh . . . do you have a paper? Do you know if the Royal Society or the Annual Exhibition is open?"

She shakes her head. "No paper, but since it's Sunday, I doubt anything is open. Stephen, are you well? Do I need to hire a physician for you? The accoucheur might be good for something, something that's not babies."

Gotta kinda agree with her. Missing signs of distress for any woman, particularly Blackamoor women, is common because of some misguided belief in higher pain tolerance. I'm not sure what the accoucheur's problem is, but the attitude has hurt our women. My hospital will be different. My wife and I will make it different.

"Cousin, would it be silly of me to ask you two very important questions?"

Wincing, she leans over to take up her cup. Her movements are stiff. She touches her stomach, then gets the cup. "Ask anything, you dear man."

"A baby boy, that is what you had?"

Holding my breath, I wait, hoping for a yes or a live child. Anything else would be a tragedy. From the couch, I see her formerly round abdomen is flat.

"What is with you, Stephen?"

"Please, just answer—"

"Yes. Little Stephen Scotland Halland is good. He's better than good. He's perfect. You and your Scarlett are an amazing team." Her face frowns. "You should marry her, no matter what she's done."

That tone—part sympathetic, part *you're stupid*—gnaws at my gut. I sit up fully and rub my jaw. There's at least a day's worth of shadow. "I've been asleep for a while."

"Well, you didn't sleep for a long time. You and Scarlett both stayed up checking on the baby, checking on me. You two saved our lives. But like I said, it's Sunday."

I stand up to get my blood pumping. "Did Scarlett go upstairs to sleep?"

"No, Stephen. She's gone. I don't think she wants to see you again."

I'm pacing before I can stop myself. "No, she surely went to refresh herself. And Scarlett and I argue all the time. This is no different, except we didn't argue. We saved lives together."

Maryanne shakes her head. "She didn't want you obligated to marry her."

"What Auntie Theodora says is irrelevant. It's what we want that matters."

She sighs. "Does she know how you feel? I asked her if you'd ever told her you loved her. She said you told her you had to marry."

I open my mouth to defend myself, but I have nothing to say. Walking the length of the room; I do it so many times, I'm dizzy. "She knows me. She knows she drives me crazy. And I know how to drive her crazy. She knows how I feel."

"Apparently, she doesn't. A woman can't go on a hunch."

I shake my head. "No, there has to be another reason."

Maryanne sips her tea. Then she looks up at me with sad eyes.

"Come on, girly. Yuh know. What did I do? Or what she's doing? Does it involve wearing breeches?"

Maryanne squints at me like I've lost what little sense I had. "Stephen, she said she knows the truth and she has to make things right. If it meant losing you, she didn't want you obligated. Her doubts about how you truly feel were enough for her to walk away."

I sink back on the couch. "Make things right" . . . There's only one thing that could mean. She must've figured out that Lydia is

Katherine's child, which means Lydia is the Duke of Torrance's daughter.

Scarlett has left me to correct the lie of a situation which I helped perpetuate. She has gone to share the truth.

"So, that's it?" Maryanne squints at me. "You're not going to go fight for Scarlett?"

I rub my hand over my face. "I did something for my patients. I helped them carry out a falsehood. I thought it would harm no one. Scarlett is correct to set things right."

But she will pay.

Her sisters may never forgive her. And the duke. He's been punishing all who've wronged him. "I must own my part." I rise. "I need to face consequences and go win back my woman. Maybe stop a war."

Maryanne salutes. "Go to it. She's good for you. Make sure she knows this time that you love her. No jinx in that, not with the right woman."

I will. "Benny." I call to my driver and prepare to fix the situation.

Upstairs, the little baby boy starts crying. I hear my aunt's movements upstairs. "Pickney, don't cry." Tantie's voice sounds so hopeful. "Grandma's coming."

She brings down the little boy. I peek into the swaddled bundle and see an olive-colored baby reaching for the sky. And then he's passed to Maryanne for lunch.

The babe's suckle is strong.

"That's the best sound, cousin. You and the baby, whole and well."

She covers the hungry boy beneath her robe. "I have a job, Stephen. You do, too."

I scoop up the pile of clothes and go up the stairs to bathe and plan. Then Benny and I will go track down Scarlett, the woman who deserves my whole truth.

Chapter 32

SCARLETT—HUMMING THE BLUES

I walk with the duke into the churchyard at St. Pancras Old Church. The sun is high above the cemetery. The renewed warmth in the damp air might be enough to burn away the early morning fog. The duke is quiet. He's been that way since I told him that Lydia is his daughter.

"If you did not want me to come, I understand. A man needs privacy . . ."

"To grieve? Scarlett, some things are beyond grief."

He stops and opens his greatcoat, probably to release the steam of his anger. "You're a faithful friend. I do not mean to raise my voice. Come."

We start walking again. Clippings stick to my boots. Papa's boots were meant to roam all over, why not a cemetery?

A tree waves from the corner of the property. It shades an edge of the old church. Hymns soak through the limestone walls. Sunday service is occurring. I wonder if the duke wants to go inside. What does a man pray for when everyone he has helped has lied?

He stops and takes a big whiff of the air. The smell of freshly trimmed heather is in the breeze. "I have given this situation almost three years of time. That could very well be a lifetime, my lifetime."

"I told you because you deserve to know. I've betrayed my

family and the man I love to tell the truth. How you handle things is a reflection on you. That's your legacy."

"What do you want? Allow the guilty to make amends? Do you suggest I sit around between pain medicines and listen to their worries? Am I unreasonable, knowing they'd let me die without the truth?"

My breath leaves me. I struggle like my chest has caved.

Katherine, Mama, and Stephen knew.

Georgie must know. She and Katherine are close.

I shove my hands into my sky-blue walking dress. "I was kept in the dark. I only remembered that my mother didn't scream from the birthing pains that day. Only Katherine screamed. Patsy Wilcox was strong, but not that strong. Helping Mr. Carew deliver Mrs. Halland's baby helped put all the pieces together."

"Remind me to have Mr. Steele send her a present."

"Your Grace, if you'd told me that you knew Katherine from before, I would've known that her son was your son right away. I just thought you wanted Katherine. She's pretty. She annoys you like I annoy Carew. I didn't know that there was more."

"I loved Katherine more than life. I left her to fight for our future. I thought I could have everything, my father's legacy which was owed to me, and love. By choosing to gain what's lawfully mine, I lost her. I lost my son. I could die tomorrow, and Lydia would never have known her true father."

He shivers, probably from the cool wet day and the regret and sense of unfairness surrounding us. But we're in a cemetery. When has the grave played fair?

He holds his crystal cane in front of him. I'm sure he wants to appear emotionless, but I see tears. When Benny took me yesterday to Anya House, I went to the duke and told him immediately. Katherine and Lydia had already gone. They were meant to be there until tomorrow. My sister is getting out of her agreement. No wonder the duke is so discouraged.

He sent me away, upstairs to refresh myself, but that was to allow him to sob alone in his study.

When I wipe away my own tears, I notice the duke has moved to the plots where our loved ones are buried.

Boots shuffling through the cut grass, I catch up.

He points to four stones laid close together. The top two read—*Patsy Wilcox, Cesar Wilcox*—my beloved parents. Just below is Scotland's stone, a brand-new slab of marble with fresh etching. It proudly bears his name. The marker next to it is also new. Gone is the marker that read *Infant Wilcox*. This one reads: *Andrew Jahleelovich Charles, the Viscount Audben.*

"Such a strong name and title. Katherine said you liked your father's name."

A bitter chuckle falls from his lips. "She'll be angry I didn't ask her permission to set a new gravestone. My son should have the honor he's due."

I put a hand to his arm. "I guess Lydia will start calling me Tantie Scarlett."

"The world will change. I shall claim my daughter. No more lies."

He kneels, groans and rubs his knee. Whispered words asking for forgiveness rise. More tears fall down his pale cheeks. Mine are tumbling out as fast.

The sun shifts overhead. The music, the beautiful pipe organ from the church, dies.

The duke is slow to stand. He's in pain. He should be in Anya House being comforted. I put a palm to his brow. "You're warm. You have a fever. This could have waited."

"Scarlett, you're the most like me. Do we truly understand what the word *wait* means? Does it ever apply to us?"

The man has a point.

Never ever will I tolerate injustice. "I can't stand delays or being told 'when you are older,' or, 'it's just for men.' I'm older, I've been a man, and still nothing makes sense."

A worker in a dark cloak comes over. "Your Grace, good to see you. We've been doing the extra maintenance as you requested. Thank you very much for the grant. It's deeply appreciated."

"A bench, sir, would be a nice addition. Somewhere here."
The duke half turns, waves his hand and points a few feet away.
"Right there. I think that would be lovely. Send the bill to Anya
House when it's complete."

"Yes, Your Grace." The man bows and backs away.

"A grant for the cemetery? Then you've known for a long
time."

"About my son? Yes. Tavis, on his deathbed, told me of the
stillborn. I wonder what the d'yavol would have done with
knowledge of Lydia. Sold it to me? I would've paid for such information."

"Please don't destroy the Wilcoxes or Mr. Carew." My plea is
raw, but I'll beg for them. As wrong as they are, they are my family and the fellow I love.

"I'd come to suspect about Lydia. My mother sent a portrait of
my sister to dedicate Anya House. It's the mirror image of my
daughter."

The breeze picks up. It scatters more bits of cut grass. Heather
and clover scent the air. The duke's shoulders hunch. He seems
very tired. My fears for him, for his health, increase.

"A bench would be nice here," he says. "I intend to come
often and tell my son about life. Provide him the lessons a good
father should offer. Tell him about his sister. No twin can be forgotten."

I don't know how to give back to him what we've stolen. Time
can never be returned.

"Scarlett, you look fretful. Marry Carew if you want him spared.
You and Lydia are blameless. Nothing bad will come to the innocent."

"I'm fearful for the others. Please, Your Grace. Be magnani-
mous. You've made your detractors pay."

"Oh. You know another member of the Court of Chancery has
resigned. Seems Lord Lange likes Dover pills. He ended up in
Bedlam for disorderly conduct. Reporters happened to be in the

area when he was released. The details of his fall from grace will be in Monday's paper."

I wish harm to no one, but I didn't like the scientist that much. "I know you are angry. Stephen Adam Carew keeps his patients' secrets. He keeps yours."

The duke shrugs.

"You're angry at everyone, but my sister and my mother did the best they could to survive. You know how cruel scandal is."

I appeal to his humanity. I know there's some. There's a great deal.

My eyes sting. I drop down and touch Scotland's stone. "Everyone will be in pain. And I've done it. I betrayed everyone because you needed the truth."

"Scarlett, you're my friend. I love you like the sister I lost." He puts his hand under my chin. "Rise, please."

"Scotland's stone is pretty. The pink and white marble, the deep etching. Thank you."

The duke embraces me, and I him. "Like I said. Scarlett, you're the most like me. You and I shall never forget those gone. Now, come. Let's go back to Anya House and have some hot tea. There we can plot our revenge against the world over chess. It will be your first lesson."

I laugh at the duke's foolishness. I have no expectations that he'll refrain from doing something. I will be protective of him, my Scotland. I will be his humanizing Anya. My hope is my betrayal of my family and Stephen, the ending of the lies, will someday be understood as the way to gain everlasting peace.

Nonetheless, when we enter his carriage, I make sure to mention the troubles of Eveline Gray and the baron who's taken Chrysanthemum's money away.

The duke takes to his bed as soon as we return. I'm not sure he's going to be in crisis, but my stomach is tight. Worries start.

I leave the lovely library with a copy of Fuseli's anatomy pictures in my arms. I'll stay the night in my pretty room. Though I want to see Mr. Thom, I don't wish to see Katherine or Georgie. How do I tell them I betrayed them? How will I comfort Lydia from the lies?

Once in my room, I see the spot where my sketches usually sit on my table. I forgot to get them back. Fleeing from the man you love makes one forgetful.

Sitting on my bed, curling into the pink bedsheets, I relax and then ready to remove my boots.

Plink. Plink.

A pebble hits my window.

Plink.

I rise and go to my bay window and draw the curtains wide. Looking out, I see—

"Scarlett!"

Stephen? Stephen is down there with Benny. They have a ladder.

It's been a damp summer day, and he has no jacket. What's he doing? Doesn't matter. "Go away."

Slam. The top rung of the oak contraption slaps against the edge of my window.

With Benny steadying the ladder, Stephen climbs. "Scarlett!" he yells. "What light through yonder window breaks? It is the east, and Scarlett is the sun."

"What are you doing, Stephen? It's dusk. The sun is setting."

Benny starts looking around like someone is coming. "Dis bad idea. Mr. Carew says he needs to give yuh a grand gesture to prove how much he cares."

"Care? I care about all humans. Go home, sirs. Get some rest. This fever will pass."

"No. No. Miss Wilcox." Stephen rears back like he's forgotten he's dangling precariously on a ladder. "I more than care, Scarlett. I love you."

"You are desperate and delusional. You need sleep and a meal."

"If I need sleep, it shall be in your arms. Your body needs to be tucked close to mine. We need to share warmth and breath. My heart needs to beat with your pulse."

My mouth goes dry then slack. What do you say when the man you love tells you he wants you? He must not know I betrayed him. "I need you to wise up. Stephen, we were a season. The moment for us has passed."

"Scarlett, you're smarter and braver than everyone. If I were half as brave, I would've told you how I felt long ago." His voice is closer. "I didn't want to jinx you loving me." He's halfway up. "Arise, fair sun, and kill the envious moon, who is already sick and pale with grief, That thou her maid art far more fair than she."

"You are insane, and not listening, Stephen. And you could fall and hurt yourself."

"Dats what I told him, Miss Wilcox." Benny is straining to hold the shaking ladder. "Yuh got him touched in the head."

"Bullocks to both of you. Good night." I start to close the window.

"Wait." Stephen climbs faster. "With love's light wings did I o'er-perch these walls; For stony limits cannot hold love out, And what love can do that dares love attempt; Therefore thy kinsmen are no stop to me."

I duck my head against my palm. "My kinsmen are not here. They're across the Thames, hiding from the aunties. But there's the Duke of Torrance and he's mad. Big mad about all the lies."

"See, how she leans her cheek upon her hand! O, that I were a glove upon that hand, That I might touch that cheek!"

"Stephen, goodbye. Take him home, Benny. Make sure he sleeps. I'm closing the window now."

Having reached the glass, Stephen knocks. "Scarlett. I do love nothing in the world so well as you."

"That's strange."

"That's not quite the response line from *Much Ado About Nothing*."

I open the window. "I'm not the one climbing up a wall going on about love that you refuse to admit until I leave. Can't you see I don't want to fight to be loved? I'm the third of three. Count them . . . three sisters, not four. I know the truth. Truth has set you free. Go home."

"Scarlett, I can't betray my patients' trust."

He's eye level. Stephen has climbed all the way with a white billowing shirt that's open and showing a touch of smooth chest and little dark curls. The indigo-blue waistcoat dangles. Dang his eyes shine.

"I'm an idiot, Scarlet but I see you. I know you are a warrior for truth. I love that about you."

"Why? I'm a misfit who likes research and books and my papa's boots. You shouldn't love me. I can't be trusted." I'm heaving, breathless. "Go home. Or go to the aunties. Tell them they were right. Deh find yuh a nice girl in your community."

"I don't want a nice girl, Scarlett. I want you."

Hissing, I try to close the window on him, but the frame gets caught on the thick tube of his Laënnec stethoscope. "You dunderhead. You could break that."

He knocks the window open. As I scramble to get the expensive scope, Stephen pulls himself inside. "Ready to talk?"

"This is improper. You shouldn't be here." I hand him his tool, point to the window. "Go, now."

Stephen puts the stethoscope to my chest. "I hear a heart beating. I want it to beat for me."

His actions are quick. The scope goes onto my table, and I am in his arms. Our buttons, the brass buttons of his waistcoat plink against the silver ones of my carriage dress as he kisses me. He tastes of peppermint and sweet pone. Then his lips trail my cheek, the curve of my neck.

Stephen puts my hand to his chest. "Touch me. I'm here. You can't make me leave, not without knowing my love."

"I know you do. Now go."

"You know I love you, but you want me to go? Scarlett, please."

"I be-tra-yed you. Stephen, I learned the truth. I didn't consult you. I went to make things right. So, go. I can't obligate you."

"But you love me?"

My lips tremble but stay shut. I'm breathing hard to keep my tears at bay. "Go."

He nods, backs to the window and pushes the ladder away. "No, girly. I can't go. I need my woman."

A crash sounds as the ladder falls away. Benny makes a small scream. Stephen looks down. "He's alright." He motions for Benny to get up.

I look to the window and his man is up dragging the ladder away.

"Scarlett," Stephen says, "I won our bet. I'm not leaving, not without you."

My Romeo sits on the bay window's pink cushion. "And I have half a pan of cassava pone in my carriage. You never leave the aunties' party without taking a snack, Scarlett. That's rude."

"I had no pockets in my gown. I needed to leave quickly. When you decide to destroy the man you love, you have to be quick about escaping."

"I'm destroyed without you." He curls his fingers. "Come to me, Scarlett. Please, be mine."

"Didn't you hear me. I told the duke. I remembered the night Lydia was born. Only Katherine had birth pains. She screamed like Maryanne. Only Katherine was pregnant. Lydia was a twin. Everyone has lied to her."

Stephen stands and walks to me. "Yes. And everyone is wrong. When I figured out that the father of the stillborn was the duke, not a random fling or worse, I didn't know what to do. The stillborn was a twin. Jahleel Charles has to be Lydia's father, too. I looked at Lady Hampton and hoped she's doing the right thing. I make no excuse, other than that a patient's privacy is something a physician lives by. You'll have to learn that if you wish to be a physician working at my hospital."

"What?"

He shrugs. "Fine, our hospital."

"Don't taunt me, Stephen. Women can't—"

"A woman can do what her husband allows. Why would I stop

someone as gifted as you from healing people? And with the initial S as in S. Carew, I don't think anyone will notice which brilliant Carew is the author to your future research papers."

I glance up into his eyes. Handsome, with his brown eyes slightly black, slightly red beaming at me. "You don't care that I broke your trust. That I have not been proper?"

"I'm in your bedchamber, Scarlett. We've compromised each other too many times to count. Heaven help us, we been to a brothel together."

"Yes. We did share a prostitute. Couples bonding?"

"Scarlett, if I had far less scruples, I'd have been in your breeches. What is proper about us? Not a t'ing."

His smooth lips are close. Can I trust them? I run my thumb along the bottom.

He makes a sharp intake. "Do I have cassava pone on me?"

"No. Well, not anymore."

"Kiss me and make sure."

I do, because I love him. With his arms surrounding me, I'm swept away. Our lips collide like shooting stars. I love him, with every breath, every taste.

"I love you, Scarlett. I've been afraid to say it. Every time I have, I lose. I never want to lose you."

"I'm here, unless I vanish while you're unconscious because I need to do something."

"My work is tiring. Loving you is tiring. But it's a good tired."

In his arms, we dance to some song of praise that we whirled to on his tantie's patio. Our button music clinks again. "We sort of make music together."

His hand cups my chin. "O, that I were a glove upon that hand, That I might touch that cheek!"

He dips close and kisses my nose. He whispers, "I love you," and puts his mouth upon each eye. His breath is yummy.

"Have you been eating my dessert?"

"Needed to keep up my strength until I found you." Stephen scoops me up into his arms and kisses me.

It's magical . . . for three seconds, before a crystal cane shatters on Stephen's head.

My love falls to the floor. I flop on top of him in a heap.

On the thick rya on the floor of my bedchamber at Anya House, I roll to Stephen's side and finger his scalp for a cut or a lump.

The duke smirks. "You hurt there, Scarlett? Didn't mean for you to fall. I'm liberal, but we must talk about having men in your room. Which is to say, no men in your room."

I rub Stephen's cheeks to rouse him. "He's unconscious. Was that necessary?"

"Yes. Yes, it was." The duke shakes his head. He leans over to try to help Stephen up and almost loses his balance. "The cane is crooked," he says. "I'll need to get it fixed."

The duke takes his time walking to the door. "Have your gentleman caller go to another room. A special license will be here in the morning. When Romeo awakens, take him to the maze. Both of you can shout your love, your intentions to be man and wife. Then you are wed the Cossack way. That will clean up this final compromise."

I'm shaking Stephen. He's not budging to agree or complain. "Your Grace, I thought you have to do that in front of a crowd."

"There's no size requirement for the audience. Mr. Steele is back. Princess Elizaveta is here, and I'm sure Mr. Carew's man-of-all-work is out there, too. Talkative little fellow. We will be witnesses. Get it done. Steele will have a proper license in the morn. I need . . . need to go rest."

The duke stops at the door. "Tell your husband that all debts between us are paid. I harbor no ill will. What he did or participated in was to protect his patients. I understand. Now, I must protect my family."

The duke stumbles a little but leaves and closes the door.

"Did you get that, Stephen? You can stop feigning sleep. He's told us what we need to do. Congratulations. We must wed."

Stephen sits up. "Yes, my sweet." He bits his bottom lip. "And I'm sure you won't mind postponing our wedding trip. Torrance is struggling. I think the sickness is rearing. We need to stay and be of service."

I drag this man of mine to his feet. "That's the life of physicians."

"Physician plus one. You're a physician's assistant. You need plenty of training, my dear. The Stephen Carew school is now open."

"And what must I do for admission, sir?"

He takes me in his arms, smiling the way he does, and whispers, "Love me, love me forever."

"That's something I can do." Seems I have. Now he loves me, too. I grab his arm and drag him to the door. "Let's go be Cossacks, get the cassava pone from the carriage, then you can feed me in the marital bed."

"That's all you want?" He kisses me and makes me breathless. "Definitely have to put you through an intense physical program, madame."

"Well, my future husband, present-day physician, is smart enough to prescribe the right type of medicine for a lifetime of love."

"Scarlett, that I do."

"I do, too."

Epilogue

KATHERINE PALMERS, LADY HAMPTON—THE BET AND CONSEQUENCES

June 30, 1817
22 Ground Street, London

I still can't believe the news. Mr. Benjamin, who came to retrieve the longcase clock from my sister's room, delivered the *London Morning Post* with the announcement. SCARLETT WILCOX HAS ELOPED WITH MR. STEPHEN CAREW.

I take a breath and read it aloud to Georgie. The soft sweet smell of chamomile greets me as she sips her tea. "Good for them."

"Does the paper say if he gave her a pony?" Lydia comes into the parlor. She's spinning in her blue butterfly dress. It's one the modiste made while designing Scarlett's. She spins, the muslin floats about her ankles. "I think Mr. Carew should get Scarlett two ponies, 'cause they love each other and they married."

A loud noise, multiple horses trotting, pounds close to the house.

Georgie looks out the window. "Unless Mark has magically turned the coal dray into a barouche with six horses, looks like we shall have company."

"It's obviously the duke. Coming to show off his new carriage.

Probably wanting to take you, Lydia, for a ride in it." I smile at how her little face brightens. "You are dressed for an elegant day."

The little girl dances. "Oh, I love how he thinks of me. Bestus friend. Katherine, can you come with us, too? You said you would be nicer to my bestus friend."

I keep my frown at this new spectacle to a minimum. I need to do better. Jahleel didn't badger me with questions or accusations when Scarlett told him about our son. He was gentle and kind.

That was so unexpected, for I would rail. I would blame me. I would make me feel as low and as dirty as possible. A woman has one job, to protect the baby growing inside. I failed our son. Jahleel. Me.

Georgie looks up and catches my glance. "Perhaps you should go. Maybe make a list of what the Duke of Torrance likes and dislikes. You did promise to be his special friend if he found matches for your sisters before you could."

She's smirking. And I am a little giddy. I shouldn't've let Jahleel hold me. The way his hands have always found ways to remove my angst should be studied. Can one hate a man and be desiring of his touch?

"Katherine!" Lydia is getting more excited. "Please come. I want us all to be the bestus friends."

"Very well, if he asks, I'll go. But don't you have a bed to go make up? I don't know if you can go if you have—"

The child runs with the speed of the wind. The bouncing of her feet echoes.

"Check on Mr. Thom. He's now in Scarlett's old room. I believe that his eye surgery will be next week, when the lovebirds are back from their wedding trip." Georgie smiles. "Yeah, my little sister's going to be happy. And my older one will be a mistress. How exciting."

I sink onto the bench of the pianoforte and plunk keys. "This is not how I wanted things to go. I hope Scarlett is happy. I wish we could've seen them off."

"Boy, your smile is gone. You know she's liked Mr. Carew a long time. You just hate losing." Georgie sips her tea, then she looks up with doe-like eyes. "Perhaps with Scarlett having to manage her own household, maybe she will have more sympathy for the difficulties you've had to endure, managing our household and a business."

I want my relationship with Scarlett repaired. I want us close again. I don't want to be the stern one anymore. Frustrated, I sigh and pour myself a cup of Georgie's tea. The pot feels warm to the touch. "Mr. Carew. He was here when everything started. I feel sad and guilty when he's around."

"Not at the beginning of everything. You and the duke started in St. Petersburg."

Georgie has jokes for my plight. I know she means well.

Then my sister gazes at me with a sweet, sad expression. "Mark has sold a set of songs for an upcoming opera. We now have money to buy a house. Though he and I love this side of the Thames, we will be looking for our own."

"No." I put my cup down onto the saucer. "This great big house just for me and Lydia? That doesn't seem right." Less stern, more hopeful—I caution myself and ease my tone. "But I understand."

Relief sweeps across her face and she sags against the sofa like a weight has fallen from her shoulders. "I'm glad you're taking this well."

"Am I such an ogre?" I dash to the mirror in the hall. "Am I?"

Pushing at my lean cheeks, I don't see youthful ignorance. The beauty of resolve and strength stares back at me. I've aged, become wiser, but I've yet to dream my biggest dreams.

Georgie comes to me and takes my hand. "You're beautiful, Katherine. And you've spent too long mourning."

I reach for her hand and draw her close. "I want you happy, you and Scarlett. You both deserve that."

"Someone else deserves happiness and the truth. It's time to tell him. He and Lydia need to know. That little girl is healthy now, but that can change. How will you feel if we lose her and we still have all these secrets? Scarlett hates how we don't talk about Scotland. It would be very sad if we do the same with Lydia."

Pulling both her hands about my neck, I need her to throttle me so I will act. "The duke vexes me. Even now he's sitting outside in that grand carriage to make the biggest entrance. He will forever rub my nose in all my failings."

"He doesn't actually do that." Georgie turns to look to the window by the door, but all I see are those monster-sized horses.

"Look at how he's arrived in a big carriage. That is to taunt me. He's won the bet. I hate him. I hate that I hate him, especially when he's so good to Lydia. Then I hate myself, that I have to be the strict one. Then I loathe me for not telling him the truth."

I swipe at my eye. "I keep fearing that Jahleel will get bored and leave . . . but he doesn't. How do I console Lydia if I relent, and the man becomes bored and leaves?"

"You hate that perhaps you've been wrong about him, Katherine. Why can't you enjoy the man who should love Lydia? You must tell him. He needs to know."

"He's stubborn."

Georgie taps her foot. "Pot. Kettle. Katherine, he's been here three years. He's loved her every minute. Can't you see this? Why are you so afraid of letting the duke be a permanent part of her life?"

Tears begin to clog my throat. I'm back in St. Petersburg, thinking I've found my other half, but he wants more than that. He wants it all. "I loved him desperately. I lost every bit of me. Then he left and I continued to lose. I can't be made desperate again. I need him gone. I can't love him again."

"Sister." Georgie grips my shoulders, her fingers slipping on my plain gray gown. "What do you mean again? That would mean you stopped."

A knock sounds on the door. I'm actually thankful for it. "Coming."

I dry my eyes. "Well, let's get this done." I open the door and bow. "Let the bragging commence."

"Lady Hampton, I'm Lord Ashbrook . . ."

Popping up, I school my face. "Excuse me, my lord, but tell His Grace that though his presence is everywhere, he's not allowed to invite strangers to my house."

Lord Ashbrook looks confused. "Lady Hampton, this is not a social call."

"Make way for the princess." A footman in a silver mantle and a tall hat with feathers bellows outside our house. "Make haste for the princess."

"Princess?" I bow and retreat deeper into my house.

"Yes, Lady Hampton," the old woman says. "Do you remember me?"

My knees knock, then I bow again. "Yes, Princess Elizaveta. Do come in."

The regal woman enters, and I pull back almost into the parlor.

Georgie comes to my side and holds my hand. "What is the meaning of this? I mean, to what do we owe this honor, Your Highness?"

One of the princess's servants carries in a framed portrait. I look at it, the innocent face, the silver dress. The tears I've suppressed return. It's a trickle, then a full flood.

"Then you recognize her, Lady Hampton." Though her English is pristine, her Russian accent is strong. "This is my Anya, Jahleel's sister, painted the year she died."

Lord Ashbrook steps forward. "We do not wish to take up your time, but I'm here on behalf of the Duke of Torrance. You have been protecting his minor child. He's now in a position to make her paternity known and afford her all the benefits and renown she's due. The child, the daughter of a duke, shall now be called Lady Lydia Jahleelovna Charles."

The famous earl, one of the few Blackamoors distinguished as a barrister in the king's courts, I recognize. The sketches in the paper, even the favorable ones, do not do him justice.

He hands me documents which I know will change everything. Ashbrook's record is legendary.

He convicts wrongdoers.

He's here to convict me.

"Torrance would be here to do this himself, but he's fallen deathly ill. Please read them, ma'am." The earl's expression is sullen. "The nature is sensitive. Time is of the essence."

Ill? Always dramatic, Jahleel. Nonetheless, my hands tremble as I break the seal. Unfolding the fancy parchment reveals lines and lines of text. Legal words that must be Latin scatter the pages. But in very large, very clear print, are the words stating Jahleel and I were married at the time of Lydia and Andrew's birth.

The ink is bold and black, blacker than the darkest indigo.

An ounce of pride comes to my soul knowing Jahleel actually named our son after his father, a man I know he loved. That's an honor, especially for a woman who hasn't been to Jahleel.

I break a little more inside, thinking of the emotion, the loss that swept between us over our son. He offered no blame to me. For my sorrows surely killed the babe.

My tears fall on the papers that Jahleel has made come to pass. He's protecting Lydia. She's legitimate, not born out of wedlock. She's a Charles. There will be no shame or ostracization that comes from the snide ton or the gossipy aspects of the Blackamoor community. "Jahleel's done this, even though I've . . ." I can't say aloud how I've deprived him of our beautiful girl. I've been too fearful of him taking her away. No one can undo my lies. "How sick is he? I must see—"

"Bring my grandchild . . . to me." My wicked, shameful heart begins to throb. I'm more frightened. There's ownership in her voice. The princess has come to take my daughter.

Georgina moves to the stairs. "Lydia." Her voice warbles like a baby bird's. "Lydia, please come."

The child bounds down the treads. "I stopped in Scarlett's room. Mr. Thom says he's sleeping. And . . ."

Her beautiful eyes of black and bits of gold grow wide. She runs to the frame and claps. "Duke. Duke. He's had me painted as a princess. Look, Katherine. Look, Georgina, I'm a princess for my birthday."

I'm breathless.

Princess Elizaveta, the severe woman who stonily disapproved of me years ago, looks as if she's about to crack like a dropped porcelain doll. Dignified and stiff and shaking, she steps closer to Lydia. "The likeness is uncanny. Your hair's a little darker. Anya's was a lighter brown. My daughter's eyes were hazel like Jahleel's."

"Why does everyone look scared?" Lydia's little lip pokes out. "Where's the duke? Who took my duke?"

"Lidochka, my dorogaya. My Jasha's letters, his tales of you have made me so happy, so hopeful to meet you."

"Jasha?" Georgie looks confused. "Who's Jasha? Who's Lidochka?"

"Those are diminutives," I say. "Lidochka is Lydia. Jasha for Jahleel."

"Dorogaya is 'darling,' but only the duke calls me that." Lydia frowns at the princess. "Did he tell you you could say that? My duke?"

"He's mine, too. I am the duke's mother. Jasha would come to explain things himself but he's very, very sick."

"You keep saying that to scare me." I fold my arms, knowing he's done this on purpose. "I am already a thousand times sorry. He is in the right. He does not need to pretend to be ill. He doesn't have to go missing to announce this. Oh, please don't let him go to the papers."

Lord Ashbrook's neck, his chin jerks. "Torrance has no intentions of making the scandal more public. We just left him. He wants this discreet. He doesn't want his last actions on this earth to bring pain to the Wilcoxes, but he must protect Lady Lydia. She's his legacy."

This is too fast. "Lord Ashbrook, you're acting like Jahleel is dying."

"Ma'am, we just left him. He may not live through the night. He suffers the blood sickness. The duke has had a painful, chronically ill journey. I pray he survives."

"Nooo," Lydia begins to whimper. "Did he not wear his stockings? He tells me to wear mine to stay healthy. I haven't been sick in months."

The princess looks at me. Her rich skin pales to ash. "She suffers, too?" Her face blanks, the expression changes to one of rawness and pain. "This is the reason I wanted no marriage. The sickness is in my bloodline, his father's, and yours. When you told me what your mother suffered, I knew this was possible. More generations dying from the ancient curse."

Lydia begins shaking her head. "No. No more dying. The duke can't die. He loves me."

I go to comfort her, but the princess holds her hand out to stop me. She kneels to Lydia and wipes the child's tears on her white gloves. "The duke is your father. I've come to bring you to him. Your father wants to see you."

"I don't want to go to the cemetery. Papa's in the cemetery. Mama's there, too. I don't want to go."

The princess looks horrified. "My son still lives. We must pray and hold on to the hope he recovers."

"But my papa is gone. He's not the duke. Katherine. Georgina, tell her. I mean, I'd love for the duke to be my papa. 'Cause he actually loves me. Georgie? Katherine?"

My sister looks at me. She doesn't have the *I-told-you-so* look but something much worse. Her countenance reads we shall now lose Lydia because of all the lies.

I go to them and kneel. "Lydia, the duke is your true father.

My papa was your grandfather. My mother was your grand-mother."

"Katherine." Her chubby little fingers swipe at a tear. "You are just trying to make me laugh. You know I'm scared for my duke."

Hugging her like this might be the last time I am ever able to, I tell my daughter, "The duke is your father, Lydia. That is no lie."

Shaking her head, making herself dizzy, she backs up to the portrait. "Truth?"

She plops down on the floor beside the painting. Her legs are tucked under her light blue dress.

"I have a daughter whose voice melts my heart," Lord Ash-brook says, glancing down at Lydia with a sorrowful smile. "I'm sure Torrance's melts as well." He clears his throat. "I have a duty of service to my client. Jahleel Andrewovich Charles, the Duke of Torrance. The Court of Chancery, or what's left of it, has voted this morning to confirm unanimously the marriage of my client and Katherine Charles and upholds its validity to the time of the birth of their twins."

"Katherine, why is the man saying my mother is another woman named Katherine? And I'm not a twin. Scarlett's the twin. But you don't talk about him."

Georgie starts to cry. She runs into the parlor. From there she says, "We thought we were doing what was right."

I stand up straight. "I am . . . was Katherine Charles. Jahleel, the duke, is your father. You are my daughter. We've been lying to you. I've been lying."

Ashbrook steps forward. "It was to protect you, little one. The duke instructed me to make sure that's clear. I'm also to hand you this, Lady Hampton."

Fearful to take the papers, I draw my arms to my back. "State what these are."

"As payment for taking care of Lydia and keeping her hidden from gossip and harm until the duke was in a position to protect her." Ashbrook removes his spectacles for a moment. "I want to get the language right. As payment for the care and lodgings of

Lady Lydia, all debts are considered paid in full. These documents show that all of the late Lord Hampton's debts and liens against the property and business have been cleared. Everything is again in the Wilcoxes' possession."

"If he's buying our daughter, she's not for sale."

Ashbrook folds the papers again and slides them in the crook of my arm. "There's some odd language about a bet. He was very clear that he won, and that he expects nothing from you."

The earl shakes his head. "That must be the pain medicine speaking for him."

Then Ashbrook holds out a final paper. "This is a divorce decree. I suspect it should be dated to your marriage to Lord Hampton. I didn't know what date you wanted. Please return it to me when you've ascribed a date."

"We shall leave." The princess says, "Come along, Lady Lydia. Your father must see you. I think it will make him better."

"Duke . . . Papa? Better. He needs to be better."

I step in front of them and block the door. "No, I shall bring her."

"No, you won't," Lydia starts to cry. "You'll make excuses as to why we can't see him. You don't like my papa. He's my true papa."

Lydia turns and hides in the old woman's skirts. She's sobbing.

The princess bends down to her. "You come from a line of greatness. I know you are small and hurting, but you'll overcome. Lift your head, Lady Lydia. Come with me to be with your father."

My child, my Lydia, glances back at me, then up to the princess. "You don't lie. I want to go see Papa Duke. I want to be with my father."

They walk out of my house.

Dropping all the papers, I clutch Lord Ashbrook's coat. "No, don't take my child. We . . . I had the best intentions. I—"

"Ma'am, I work with my aunt to restore children wrongfully withheld from their mothers. While I feel for your circumstances, you've defrauded a man of his relationship with his child. He may succumb and never hear his daughter call him Papa. That would destroy me."

"This is destroying me. We thought we were doing our best."

He sighs and stops at the door. "If the duke recovers, find a way to make amends. Torrance is reasonable, and I know he will do all for his daughter."

"And if he does not recover?"

"Princess Elizaveta Abramovna Gannibal is Torrance's guardian, and now Lady Lydia's. She has full authority over how his child will grow up and where she will live."

The Earl of Ashbrook leaves.

Georgie comes to my side. "This is a nightmare. Do something, Katherine."

What can be done? Nothing if Jahleel dies. How can I fight the courts when we've lied so much? And who takes precedence over his mother? No one but a wife.

With assistance from a footman, the princess steps into her large carriage. Lydia looks back at me, the house.

I see tears falling down her baby cheeks.

I want to run and scoop her up and beg, beg, beg forgiveness.

But I'm just the mean lady who kept her from her duke, not away from the hatred his position bears, not the broken promises he left me with, or fickleness I assumed was Jahleel's character. Well, what I wanted to believe was his character. For he's good, more than I wanted to accept.

Jasha may die. I'm the villain. I am the villain.

Every second, I hope my child will run back to me. I sob, stand frozen in time, watching her turn away. Lydia climbs into the barouche. The stiff old princess, who I thought hated me, has my child on her lap.

Both hold onto each other as the carriage drives off.

I drop to my knees, weeping at my handiwork, all the harm my lies have done.

AUTHOR'S NOTE

I hope you enjoyed *A Wager at Midnight*, the second book in the new series The Duke's Gambit. Stephen and Scarlett's story is special. There's a *Gigi* riff going on, because I loved watching that old movie as a child with Mama. The 1958 *Gigi* film focuses on Gaston, a bored playboy who moves from mistress to mistress, while also spending time with Gigi, a precocious younger friend learning about haute society.

I get to dabble in a little of my Trinidadian roots and show another piece of history, the risk of pregnancy, healthcare for Black Women and Immigrant Communities, and the limitations placed on women in science. I also get to pay homage to the cross-dressing female doctors who disguised themselves as men to learn and practice medicine. While the first caesarean section was performed in Roman times and Africa, and in the UK in 1791 (that saved the woman's life), a cross-dressing woman pretending to be a man performed Britain's first successful C-section (see caesarean) sometime after 1816, saving mother and child. I also get to allude to Jane Austen (A. Lady) and how popular her work had become during this time. I also get to illustrate the diversity of *Sense and Sensibility*, the classic novel. I recently served as a historical film consultant to Hallmark. Catch the film.

The art mentioned as part of the Annual Exhibition is the actual art displayed in Somerset House in 1816 and 1817, as written in the newspapers, particularly the *Windsor* and *Eton Express*. Henry Fuseli painted and sketched many nudes during this time, so I borrowed his models for the Royal Society's lectures.

Again, this story centers around the history of the Black prince of Russia. Gannibal's lineage can be traced to many peerages in England. Gannibal and his second wife had ten children, one was Elizaveta Abramovna Gannibal.

While these stories are meant to be heartfelt and funny, they touch on serious issues of maternal health and the need for access to healthcare for the poor, Black people, and immigrant communities.

The disease affecting Lydia and the duke is an ancient disease that began in Africa, that still needs a cure. Sickle cell anemia has personally affected my family and friends. I have cousins who were ravaged by this horrible, unfair disorder. Discovering how the disease is passed through the generations, I felt compelled to weave it into this story. The blindness that can be caused by sickled cells blocking the lens like cataracts is a complication that some with the disease suffer. I felt compelled to put that in this novel too.

This series entwines the Wilcox sisters and the duke in a story of hope, politics, and undying love. The next one, *A Deal at Dawn*, will be explosive.

If you are a longtime reader, I hope you love the reintroduction of Lord Ashbrook (*An Earl, the Girl, and a Toddler*) and the artwork of Cecilia Lance (*A Duke, the Spy, an Artist, and a Lie*). The mysterious happenings in St. Margaret's can be explored in *Murder in Westminster, the Lady Worthing Series*.

As always, enjoy the diversity of the Regency and the inclusion of differently abled people. The time period had it all.

It is my hope that in Scarlett and Stephen's journey, you find that compromise in the right areas neither snuffs nor diminishes your light. In fact, it can burn brighter. *Let your light shine in the darkness, for darkness cannot overcome it* (John 1:5, paraphrased).

Visit my website, VanessaRiley.com, to gain more insight.

For more information on sickle cell anemia, contact:

The American Sickle Cell Anemia Association: https://ascaa.org/

The Sickle Cell Disease Association of America: https://www.sicklecelldisease.org/

St. Jude Children's Research Hospital—Sickle Cell program: https://www.stjude.org/treatment/disease/sickle-cell-disease.html

Mulattoes and Blackamoors During the Regency

Mulattoes and Blackamoors numbered between 10,000 and 20,000 in London and throughout England during the time of Jane Austen. Wealthy British with children born to native West Indies women brought them to London for schooling. Jane Austen, a contemporary writer of her times, in her novel *Sanditon*, writes of Miss Lambe, a mulatto, the wealthiest woman in the book. Her wealth made her desirable to the ton.

Mulatto and Blackamoor children were often told to "pass" to achieve elevated positions within society. Wealthy plantation owners with mixed-race children, or wealthy mulattoes like Dorothea Thomas from the colony of Demerara, often sent their children abroad for education and marriage opportunities in England.

Wesley's Chapel

John Wesley built Wesley's Chapel in 1778 and used architect George Dance the Younger, the surveyor of the City of London, to design it. Wesley's Chapel is Georgian architecture. John Wesley is the founder of Methodism. Please note, some of the harsher language of the posters from newspapers of the time were omitted.

Caesarean

Caesarean or caesarean section or C-section or caesarean delivery is a surgical procedure that allows a baby to be delivered through an incision in the mother's abdomen. It is often performed because vaginal delivery risks putting the mother or the baby's life in jeopardy. As in our story, loss of amniotic fluid in the womb (the sudden wetness when her water broke on the sofa) can lead to the death of the baby, the mother, or both if the baby isn't delivered quickly. The caesarean procedure dates back to 715 BC.

Moreover, nineteenth-century travelers in Africa reported instances of Ugandans performing caesareans. A healer or medicine man used banana wine to semi-intoxicate the mother and to cleanse his hands and her abdomen prior to the surgery. The patient recovered well.

The first recorded successful caesarean in the British Empire, however, was conducted by a woman. Sometime after 1815, James Miranda Stuart Barry performed the operation while masquerading as a man and serving as a physician to the British army in South Africa.

St. Pancras Old Church churchyard

St. Pancras Old Church churchyard is one of the oldest cemeteries in England. Saint Pancras is the saint of children. Many infant and stillborn children have been buried in unmarked graves or with headstones denoting the infant's surname of the family in the cemetery. The cemetery also has a number of foreign dignitaries buried in the seventeenth and eighteenth century. For all these reasons, this is the perfect cemetery for our fictional families to have lost loved ones and minor children buried here.

Jane Austen

Austin's first novel, *Sense and Sensibility*, was published in 1811, under the pseudonym A. Lady. Her next work, *Pride and Prejudice*, is attributed to the author of *Sense and Sensibility*. Austin does not become known as the author of these works until after her death when her brother posthumously publishes *Northanger Abbey* and *Persuasion* in 1817.

White's Club

White's is a famous gentlemen's club. Women were not allowed to be members or to visit as guests. The club is located in

St. James's, London. Gentlemen were known to come to read, drink, play cards and make outlandish bets. Today, membership is rumored to cost £85,000 annually.

Bridewell

Bridewell Palace, once the residence of King Henry VIII, was converted into a house of correction and prison in 1553. Subsequently, such institutions became known as Bridewells. Below is a list of some of the offenses that could result in imprisonment:

- Prostitution, with women often described as nightwalkers or accused of strolling the streets and picking up men
- Pilfering and other petty thefts
- Fraud
- Being runaway or disorderly apprentices and servants
- Begging
- Being peddlers and selling goods without a license
- Wandering or sleeping in the streets
- Having no visible means of earning a living
- Abusing the poor relief system (insulting officers, pawning the clothes provided, making fraudulent claims, carrying counterfeit passes)
- Committing various types of disorderly conduct, including swearing and drunkenness

Samuel Pepys Cockerell

Cockerell was a famous English architect who studied under Robert Taylor and who worked on projects during the Regency as a surveyor of St. George's Hanover Square, the Foundling Hospital, St. Paul's Cathedral, and Pulteney estates. He also designed Sussex Gardens.

Blood Research

Examining blood under a microscope can be traced back to 1656, when Pierre Borel, physician-in-ordinary who worked for King Louis XIV, looked at a sample under the microscope. In 1657, Athanasius Kircher, a Jesuit priest and man of science, looked at blood from plague victims and saw disease and described it as "worms" of the plague. In 1678, red blood corpuscles were described by Dutch naturalist and physician Jan Swammerdam.

Bloodletting or phlebotomy is the extraction of blood from a patient to prevent or cure illness and can be traced back as far as 400 BC. Physicians have used leeches and incisions of the flesh to perform the bloodletting to balance the humors, the bodily fluids, which can maintain health or eliminate disease.

Sickle cell treatments have investigated reducing viscosity to make blood flow better. Bloodletting can do this. This could've been an accidental cure that may have alleviated symptoms. Bloodletting was a normal treatment for all manner of conditions.

Black Russian Princes and Princesses

The Black Russian princes and princesses can be traced back to Gannibal.

Sold into slavery as a child, Abram Petrovich Gannibal was bought to be a servant to Tsar Peter I, also known as Peter the Great. As one of the tsar's favorites, he was elevated to a general-in-chief. He became the tsar's godson and one of the most educated men in Russia. Though not technically princes or princesses, his descendants were referred to by the press and laypeople as Black princes and princesses.

Author and poet Alexander Pushkin is a direct descendant. Many British aristocrats descend from Gannibal, including Natalia Grosvenor, Duchess of Westminster, and her sister, Alexandra Hamilton, Duchess of Abercorn. A more recent royal, George

Mountbatten, 4th Marquess of Milford Haven, a cousin of Queen Elizabeth II, is also a direct descendant. The 7th Duke of Westminster, Hugh Grosvenor, is also related.

Cesar Picton, Black Coal Millionaire

The Wilcox family is my homage to Cesar Picton (1755–1836), a very wealthy coal businessman. Originally enslaved from Senegal, he became a protégé of the wealthy Sir John Philipps, and by the end of his life was a successful coal merchant, having lived in Kingston, Thames Ditton, and elsewhere in Britain. Picton is often described as a "gentleman," which suggests his rise up the social ranks.

Benjamin Banneker

One of the first documented African American scientists is Benjamin Banneker (1731–1806). In addition to his research on the mating habits of locusts (cicadas), he is known for building a precision time clock entirely out of wood. In 1789, he made astronomical calculations that enabled him to successfully forecast a solar eclipse. He was a wizard in mathematics and astronomy and kept detailed journals.

Onesimus

An enslaved man given the name Onesimus offered detailed descriptions of an inoculation process that he undertook in Africa that exposed him to smallpox, which made him immune. Local Boston doctors listened to his enslaver and put Onesimus's procedure in place, saving hundreds of lives in Boston. This was decades before Edward Jenner discovered the smallpox vaccine in 1796.

Cossack and Early Russian Culture

There are several references to cultural touchstones from eighteenth- and nineteenth-century Russian culture. My approach is to try and define the word or phrase in context. Patronymics are names derived from the given name of a child's father. Historically these have been used to identify people in relation to their father. These names go after the given name and before the surname, similar to the English middle name, and are formed by taking the father's name and adding a suffix to the end, depending on the child's gender and the ending sound of the father's name. The masculine suffixes are -ovich, -evich, or -yevich, while the feminine suffixes are -ovna, -evna, or -yevna. For example, if a man named Sergei has a son and a daughter, their patronymics will be Sergeyevich and Sergeyevna respectively.

Normalization of Foreign Words

In the past, writers would italicize all non-English words within a text. This was meant to ensure a reader not stumble over the words. However, a reader knows if a word is unfamiliar to them whether it is called out in formatting or not. For me, the point of view of the speaker, as well as the point of view of the person from which the scene is written, dictates whether a word should be italicized or not. For example, Jahleel naturally speaks English and Russian. In his point of view, neither set of words are foreign. However, if he's been speaking English and switches to use a Russian phrase, it might be italicized to show emphasis on the words. Moreover, Georgina, having heard "dorogaya" before, will not be shocked or puzzled if it is used again.

RECIPE

Mrs. Ellis's Beloved Cassava Pone

This delightful treat is reminiscent of dense, caramelized blondies.

Ingredients:
- 2 cups finely grated cassava
- 1 cup finely grated coconut (fresh or defrosted frozen)
- 1 cup grated pumpkin
- ⅔ cup brown sugar
- 1 tsp. ground cinnamon
- ½ tsp. nutmeg
- ¼ tsp. ground pepper
- 2 tbsp. melted butter (plus extra for greasing the pan)
- 1 cup condensed milk
- 1 cup coconut milk
- ½ tsp. baking powder
- 1 tsp. vanilla extract
- 1 tsp. grated ginger
- ½ cup raisins (soaked in rum or water for a traditional Trini version)
- ¼ tsp. salt

Preheat the oven to 350°F (175°C).

Combine the grated cassava and coconut in a large bowl. Mix well.

Add the grated pumpkin and ginger to the cassava mixture and set aside.

In a separate bowl, combine the brown sugar, cinnamon, nutmeg, ground pepper, salt, and baking powder.

In another bowl, combine the condensed milk, coconut milk, vanilla extract, and melted butter.

Gradually add the sugar mixture to the cassava mixture, mixing well after each addition.

Gradually add the milk mixture to the cassava mixture, mixing well after each addition, until everything is fully incorporated. If looks dry add up to ¼ cup of water or evaporated milk. You need it to be a wet mix so the cassava cooks.

Cut parchment paper to fit the bottom of an 8x8-inch baking dish. Grease the parchment paper and the sides of the baking dish with butter.

Pour the cassava mixture into the prepared baking dish and spread evenly.

Bake for 50 minutes to 1 hour and 20 minutes, or until a toothpick inserted into the center comes out clean.

Let the cassava pone cool completely in the baking dish.

Once cooled, slice into squares and serve.

Enjoy your cassava pone, and watch the edges disappear first!

Don't miss Katherine and Jahleel's story, *A Deal at Dawn*:

When the shocking truth of Lydia's true parentage is revealed, doubt is cast onto Katherine Wilcox's devotion to her family from all sides. And what's worse, there may not be time to make things right: not when the Duke of Torrance's blood illness threatens to take him from the Wilcox sisters for good. She's spent years trying to remove Jahleel from her and her sisters' lives, and now she can only pray he finds a way to stay.

When everything she thought she knew is uprooted, seven-year-old Lydia struggles to believe anything unless it comes from Jahleel. She's also frightened that he might die, which may in turn cause a health crisis for her, as Lydia suffers from the same blood disease.

Jahleel has clung to the deal he struck with Katherine for a long time, hoping his love may one day be returned . . . yet, just as he is not who Katherine thought he was, he begins to wonder if Katherine isn't the woman he's dreamed of, either. But for Lydia's sake, he's willing to fulfill his end of the bargain—even if it means rebelling against the royalty authority from which he descends or letting go of a future with Katherine forever.

Visit our website at
KensingtonBooks.com
to sign up for our newsletters, read
more from your favorite authors, see
books by series, view reading group
guides, and more!

Become a Part of Our
Between the Chapters Book Club
Community and Join the Conversation